Vena Cork is from Lancashire, but has lived in London all her adult life. She attended Homerton College, Cambridge, where she was a member of Cambridge Footlights. She is married to the art critic Richard Cork and lives in North West London. She is also the author of *Thorn* and *The Art of Dying*.

Praise for Vena Cork:

'A high-octane drama seething with sexual tension and intrigue. A compelling story' *Sunday Telegraph*

'There's more to this methodical psychological thriller than meets the eye. Look no further for a real sense of menace' *Daily Mirror*

'The writing is superb' Bernard Knight, author of the Crowner John series

'Outstanding' *Time Out*

'You'll be gripped as this persuasive thriller races to its grisly conclusion' *Marie Claire*

'Profound and disturbingly good' *Nottingham Evening Post*

'The reader is compelled to turn to the next page and then the next in a frantic attempt to discover who is perpetrating the chilling acts of evil' *Oxford Times*

'A gripping murder mystery with a seductive edge' *Wigan Evening Post*

'An ideal read for winter nights' *Bella*

Also by Vena Cork and available from Headline

Thorn
The Art of Dying

GREEN EYE

Vena Cork

headline

First published in 2006 by
HEADLINE PUBLISHING GROUP

First published in paperback in 2007 by
HEADLINE PUBLISHING GROUP

1

Cataloguing in Publication Data is available from the British Library

ISBN 978 0 7553 2408 8

Typeset in Electra LH by Palimpsest Book Production Limited,
Grangemouth, Stirlingshire

Printed and bound in Great Britain by
Mackays of Chatham plc, Chatham, Kent

Headline's policy is to use papers that are natural, renewable and
recyclable products and made from wood grown in sustainable forests.
The logging and manufacturing processes are expected to conform to the
environmental regulations of the country of origin.

HEADLINE PUBLISHING GROUP
A division of Hachette Livre UK Ltd
338 Euston Road
London NW1 3BH

www.headline.co.uk
www.hodderheadline.com

For my dearest father-in-law, Hugh, with my love.

ACKNOWLEDGEMENTS

Thank you to Richard, Joe, Katy, Polly, Adam, Nalini and Evelyn, my ever-constant support system. Thank you to Lisa Moylett and Nathalie Sfakianos, my lovely agents. Thank you to Martin Fletcher and the wonderful team at Headline. And finally, thank you to Lara Murphy for a lovely day in Cambridge, which helped fix the site of Billings College, and a lot more besides.

Cambridge asleep in the curve of the River Cam, an antique necklace on the throat of an ancient beauty, its colleges polished gemstones set in a glowing circlet of green: Christ's Pieces; Parker's Piece; Coe Fen; Sheep's Green; The Backs; Jesus Green; Midsummer Common.

Midsummer Common on a midsummer morning. Early. Very early. But Annabel Ashe has not yet been to bed. The scarcely risen sun is already warming her bare and beautiful shoulders as she sways solitary across the tufted grass, drunk with life, love and excessive quantities of cocaine and champagne. Finals are over, a flash job in the City beckons, and the two fittest and smartest men in college are fighting over which of them should take her to the May Ball.

The world is a wonderful place.

If only it would stop spinning for a moment.

Her digs aren't far – just over the other side of the Common, but she badly needs to rest. She needs to sleep. Right now.

Eyes closed, she sinks down, kicking off her shoes and stretches, star-shaped on the ground, relishing the solid earth beneath her and the soft morning air on her skin.

I am a wheel. A spinning wheel in a spinning universe. The wheel of fortune. My fortune. What will it be? What will I be?

And then everything changes.

A darkness comes between her and the pale morning sun. She notices it first as a ripple in the atmosphere.

And a pressure.

Unbearable pressure.

She hears herself gasp as the air is forced from her body. She can't breathe. Someone is on top of her. Someone is groping under her tiny skirt and ripping off her pants. There is grunting and mumbling. Something hard, hot and meaty is rammed into her. Again and again. This is a bad dream. A champagne charlie dream. She opens her eyes and tries to focus. No dream. His face is next to hers, too close for her to see, and anyway there's something over his head. She tries to scream but his hand clamps tight over her mouth and now she really can't breathe. And all the time he's moaning and muttering. Incomprehensible words. Mad jabbering.

After a dozen lifetimes, there's an inarticulate cry and it's over. He sprawls motionless, lolling limply across her while sticky liquid trickles down her thighs. She heaves. Her mouth fills with vomit. Gagging, choking, she forces herself to swallow it back. He removes his hand and is silent, inert. Then, once more, he's writhing and wriggling, his sharp hipbone digging into her belly.

Please God not again.

He's stuffing something into her mouth: her own pants. There's a glint of metal, then her left wrist is twisted and excruciating pain explodes across the back of her hand. So bad that for a second she doesn't realise that the pressure on her body has eased. He's on his knees straddling her, and she can see him. Dark jeans, dark jumper, dark gloves, and beneath the balaclava, dark glasses. A giant insect. A black spider waiting to gobble her up.

Rage kicks in. She rears up and jabs her knee into his groin. He bellows with pain, and clutches his genitals. She crawls out from under him and tries to stand. But he's too quick.

The first blow dislocates her jaw and the second ruptures her spleen.

She doesn't feel the third because she's unconscious.

FRIDAY 24 JUNE

He lay on the bare bunk in the police cell and stared unblinkingly at the ceiling. If he looked hard enough, maybe, by sheer willpower, he'd be able to dissolve the solid space and see through to the stars.

But the stars were gone.

It was morning. Cold, dead morning.

He wondered how long it would be before they formally charged him.

The taking of a life: the worst crime of all. So final. Impossible to change, or reverse. When someone was dead, that was it. They were finished. No deciding that a mistake had been made. No thinking, I did the wrong thing there, let's try again and do it differently. No saying, 'I messed up, but give me time and I'll sort it out.'

Too late to say, 'Sorry.' Too late to say, 'I didn't mean it.' Too late for everything.

From now on it would always be too late.

He'd wanted to punish. Wanted to hurt – badly wanted to hurt. But not like this. Never like this.

The questioning had been interminable. In the window-less interview room it was hard to tell whether minutes or hours had passed. Time was suspended in a no-man's land of horror, where words and images spattered across his mind in an endless barrage, their deadly potency increasing with repetition. He wanted to sleep, to escape their remorseless truth, but the two detectives wouldn't let him. Every time they saw him drifting away, their questioning became more insistent.

He'd felt sorry for them as he witnessed their growing frustration. He wanted to help, he really did. But it was too hard. The awful knowledge of what he'd done had rendered him dumb and stupid, and their words glanced off the surface of his consciousness without making any sense at all. So he just sat, mute and passive as the wordstorm raged around him.

And by the time the sounds had separated themselves into coherent sentences, he'd become attached to his wall of silence, unwilling to conjure further pain by adding his own voice to the proceedings.

At one point the officers had disappeared and another man had slipped into the room. He was made to understand that this was his solicitor. The man wore black, and had a shaved head. He looked like a priest and invited confidences. It would have been so good to relinquish his burden, to tell all.

But words were an irrelevancy. His guilt was indisputable. Nothing he could say would change that, so why speak?

When the officers returned they resumed their questioning, but eventually, faced by his continuing silence they'd led him away to the cell.

GREEN EYE

'Sooner or later you'll tell us what we need to know,' the tall one said, before shutting him in.

This year, next year, sometime, never – it didn't make any difference.

It didn't change anything.

SUNDAY 19 JUNE

ONE

kissed thee ere I killed thee, no way but this, Killing
myself to die upon a kiss.'

She sprawled motionless across the bed, her face death-
pale, the hypnotic green eyes finally hidden behind alabaster
lids. Her thin arms, protruding from the flimsy muslin shift,
lay outstretched on the pillow in supplication.

He clutched the knife close to his chest. Her face swam
in front of him, and for a moment he thought he'd collapse,
all his weight landing on her tiny body.

'For fuck's sake, Dan, *Othello*'s yer high tragedy – not
an episode of *The* fucking *Archers*. You've just disembowel-
ed yourself. These are your last words. Make 'em count.'

'Sorry, Lee.'

'And why the fuck are you still standing? It says, *He falls
over Desdemona and dies.*'

'Sorry, Lee.'

'Stop saying sorry and fucking do it right. We go up in
two days' time, or have you forgotten?'

Danny let the invective float over his head. He deserved

the bollocking. Lee was right: he was crap, and it woul
be a miracle if the play were anywhere near ready b
Tuesday. But he had stuff on his mind. Too much stuff.

'Are you OK, Danny?'

It was Flora. Not Stella.

Stella hadn't even opened her eyes. She just lay on th
bed, her beautiful face, sculpted cheekbones accentuated b
choppy blonde hair, its customary serene self as Lee continue
his effing and blinding.

Flora's face, on the other hand was creased with concer
as she lumbered to her feet, fresh from her usual stilte
rendition of Emilia's death throes. It was a mystery to Dann
why Lee, with his obsessive perfectionism, had cast th
talentless Flora when Cambridge was heaving with red-hc
babes desperate for thespian opportunity to knock. Was
because she was Stella's best friend? *I'll come if my mat
comes too.* They certainly seemed to be a package – arrivin
and leaving rehearsals together, even if it meant Flor
hanging around for hours waiting for Stella to finish.

Not for the first time, Danny wondered if Stella had
boyfriend. And if there was someone, how on earth di
such a person manage to cop even a quick snog from Stell
without Flora muscling in on the act? Lee had indulge
in some lubricious speculation that they were a couple o
dykes, but Danny didn't think so.

His mobile rang.

'For fuck's sake!' Lee was showing signs of imminer
apoplexy.

'Sorry,' mumbled Danny yet again. He jumped off th
stage, and wandered to the other end of the Fellows' Garder
ignoring Lee's scowls.

'Jules, I can't talk.'

'You mean you won't talk.' Her voice was a beat away from tears.

'What do you want me to say?'

'Did you get the DVD? I put it in your pigeonhole yesterday.'

'Yeah.'

'Only you said you didn't know how to play the part, so I thought if I got you a DVD of someone else doing it, it might help. The guy in the shop said this one's quite famous. Lord Somebody—'

'Look, Jules—'

'I just—'

'You mustn't keep doing this.'

'You said we could still be mates. I just wanted to help you. As a mate.'

'It's been three weeks now, and every day you're calling and texting, and every time I turn round I just happen to bump into you. I can't take it, Jules.'

'It's so hard . . . It's been a long time, babe.'

'I've been thinking about the Ball. I know I said we could still go together, but maybe it's not such a good—'

The wailing in his ear nearly deafened him. 'You promised!'

'Yeah, but you'll just get upset and—'

'You promised . . .' She broke off.

As he listened to her pitiful sobbing, he felt the tears welling up in his own eyes. 'It's OK,' he said. 'Of course we'll still go together. It's OK, Jules. Don't cry.'

'Dan, are you coming, or do I have to give your part to young Sharon here?'

'I've got to go, babes.'

'I need to see you. We have to talk.'

'I'm rehearsing.'

'What about later?'

'I'm going to Perry's for supper. It's a godfather thing. Remember – my mum's coming up to do that filming. She's staying with him.'

'Do they know we've broken up?'

'Perry does.'

'I bet he's well-chuffed. He never thought I was good enough for you. He thinks I'm a cheap little townie on the make.'

'Not true,' lied Danny, knowing that was exactly what the Grimshaws felt about Julie.

'Have you told your mum?'

'I thought I'd wait till she came up. Better than doing it over the phone.'

'She'll be breaking open the bubbly, too.'

'Don't be stupid. She's very fond of you.'

'Yeah, right. So when can I see you?'

'Julie—'

'There's things I have to say.'

'We said everything.'

'*You* said everything. I just listened while you told me you'd always love me, but not in that way any more.'

'There's no point—'

'You owe me that much at least.'

'Danny!' Lee was gesturing wildly.

'Laters, Jules.' He switched off his phone and then ambled back to show that he wasn't going to let Lee push him around.

He tried to focus on Othello's murderous jealousy, but it was a bit too close for comfort. Jealousy was one of the things that had driven him and Julie apart – her stupid insecurity if he so much as glanced at another girl.

'That chick's gonna beat your balls and have 'em boiled for breakfast,' said Lee as Danny rejoined the group. Then he was nearly knocked down as Shareef cannonaded into him. 'Let's do Five, One – "*I am no strumpet etc etc.*" I still don't get it.'

Lee ruffled Shareef's hair. 'OK. Five, One it is, Sharon.'

'Perhaps Julie could pick up a few pointers on ball-bashing from your boyfriend,' muttered Danny.

What was Stella thinking? Best friends were supposed to share their innermost thoughts, weren't they? But Stella was as mysteriously opaque to Flora as the day they met.

It was the first day of their first term. Flora was in Hall, queuing for dinner when she heard a gasp. Behind her stood an elf girl, whose cropped white-blonde hair stood up in fluffy spikes, and whose enormous sea-green eyes were brimming with dismay.

'I've forgotten my card.'

Billings College had a system of paying for meals which involved swiping a student card through the till. No card, no food.

'I'm starving. I haven't eaten all day. Too nervous.'

'Me too,' Flora had said. 'I'll put your stuff on my card, if you like.'

The eyes grew so large they threatened to take over the whole face. 'Are you sure?'

'Take what you want.'

'You're an angel.' The girl piled her tray with so much food that Flora couldn't believe it would all fit into her small frame. 'I'm Stella,' she said, before demolishing the mountain of food with the commitment and speed of a twenty-stone trucker.

That's how it began: the closest friendship Flora had ever known. They were both reading English, and both, as it turned out, had a room on the same staircase. They became inseparable.

Flora stared at Stella. She'd made a daisy chain and was arranging it on Cassio's head. He was looking bashfully radiant, as if he'd just won the lottery. If Stella asked him to jump from the top of King's Chapel, he probably would. She had that sort of effect on people. Her sweet, self-contained serenity made them desperate to please. As one arty wag had written in the college magazine, she was *La Gioconda* of Billings, to whom all hearts were drawn, only to be tantalisingly kept at bay by the invisible force-field surrounding her.

Everyone thought that the only person to penetrate that force-field was Flora. She did nothing to dispel this belief. She'd never admit that she still hadn't the faintest idea what made her friend tick. Not really. Of course, they'd swapped life stories – Flora admitting to Stella how irrelevant her socialite parents had made her feel during the course of a youth spent largely with nannies or at boarding-school, and Stella once letting slip that as an adopted child she felt like an alien cuckoo in the nest of her driving-instructor father and nurse mother. At the time, this reciprocal confidence had seemed like a precious pact, but now, months later, Flora was sadly aware that real intimacy had proceeded no further.

Stella was smiling at her. That all-embracing smile that made you think you were the only person in the whole world who mattered. Flora was suffused with guilt. How could she rubbish her best friend in such a way? Particularly as Stella had now granted her dearest wish and finally come to one of Rest and Relaxation's Bible study groups to meet Dom and the others.

It was after their supervision on *Paradise Lost* with Dr Grimshaw. He'd said Stella's essay was ill thought out, badly argued, and showed an astonishing lack of background reading, principally of the Bible, the book on which the epic poem was based. Flora had felt awful. What with exams, plus helping Shareef do the costumes for the play, she hadn't lent Stella her essay notes as she usually did. Stella, sweet as ever, allowed her to buy lunch, and didn't blame her one bit, but later she'd said, 'Since *Paradise Lost*'s going to come up in the Tripos next year, maybe I will check out R&R – get a handle on this Bible shit. I can check out your boyfriend, too.'

Even now, two weeks later, Flora felt herself go hot all over.

'Boyfriend?' She'd tried to sound puzzled.

'This Lucas guy you're always on about. I'm beginning to think you're ashamed of him. Has he got three eyes and a hump or something?'

Flora had attempted a laugh. 'I've told you, he's not my boyfriend. He's just another volunteer at the refuge.'

'What do people wear to Bible study groups?'

Flora had been thankful for her friend's fanatical pre-occupation with sartorial matters. She didn't want to talk about Lucas. If Stella had her secrets, then so did she, and she wasn't ready to share them with anyone.

Not even Stella.

* * *

19

Joan Watkins cleaned the handset with an antiseptic wipe before carefully replacing it. Seconds later she heard Julie leave, and watched as she crossed the Green in the direction of Billings College.

She stood up, ungluing her legs from the plastic covering that kept the three-piece suite in good condition and ready for the company that might one day unexpectedly arrive. Julie had gone, and James and Christopher were also out. She took her keys from the sideboard and set off up the stairs. She made a cursory inspection of the students' rooms and through force of habit went into Danny's. After three weeks it was still a shock to find it bare and empty.

She moved swiftly on to Julie's bedroom, an extravaganza of mauve muslins, and felt under the mattress of the canopied bed for her daughter's diary, a confessional tome that was extremely useful at keeping her informed of the girl's every move. But a quick scan revealed nothing new. Since the entry three weeks ago, which read *My life is over*, scrawled across the page in purple Biro, Julie had abandoned her diary.

So Joan had no idea what was going on in Julie's mind, and she didn't like it.

She knew one person who'd be pleased about the break-up, though: Rosa Thorn, Danny's mother. Rosa Thorn didn't like Julie. She'd never actually said so. On the contrary, on the one occasion they'd met, she'd been as nice as pie to her. To both of them.

But Joan knew.

Rosa Thorn was too nice. Nice in the way middle-class people are to those whom they consider their social inferiors. Falling over themselves not to appear superior.

Joan hadn't been deceived. She recognised in Rosa Thorn a similar maternal vigilance to her own.

Rosa Thorn did not think Julie was good enough for her darling son.

What gave the woman the right to be so stuck-up? A lot of people would think the boot was on the other foot: that Joan had been extremely kind, taking a coloured boy into the bosom of her family. It was a pity Rosa Thorn couldn't hear Scott on the subject. It was only to be expected that he should feel protective over his baby sister, but his reaction to the news that she had a black boyfriend had been, even to Joan's ears, somewhat extreme. It was only because Danny's mother was as white as he was, that Scott had tolerated the idea at all. That, and the fact that Julie had had a bout of hysterics and threatened to do something stupid if Scott spoiled things for her. But even after eighteen months, Joan had kept him out of Danny's way when he came home on leave.

He'd kill Danny Thorn when he heard how the little rat had dumped Julie.

She replaced the diary and smoothed down the bed. She felt distinctly queasy, imagining Julie and Danny in it together, but in this day and age one had to appear tolerant. Allowing them to sleep together under her roof had caused her much soul-searching, but it was a means to an end. And it wasn't as though they'd even known that's what she'd been doing. They'd thought she had no idea that every night, Danny crept into Julie's room, and every morning at six on the dot he'd crept back to his own. She'd thought the closer Danny was bound to Julie, the more difficult it would be for him to extricate himself. How wrong could a person be? All her sacrifice had been for nothing. No more Cambridge graduate husband for Julie.

Joan made a plate of cream crackers and cheese and a nice pot of tea. Since it was Sunday, she used the Royal Albert china. But her usual delight in the intricate border of gilt and the red roses galloping across the cup was spoiled as she contemplated Julie's misery. She nibbled delicately on her crackers and stared out over the Sunday sunbathers on Jesus Green. The sight of so much bare flesh made her heave. She saw Preacher Man, wearing a heavy overcoat and woollen hat in spite of the heat, picking his way over the recumbent bodies. He was shouting, 'Repent ye children of the fleshpots before the Lord smites thee!' Although he was a nutter, she was inclined to agree with him. No good could come of such blatant cavorting. Today, his cardboard placard said *'Vengeance is mine,' saith the Lord.* Joan smiled grimly. She was with the Lord on that one. There were things she'd very much like to avenge, given half the chance.

She picked up Friday's *Evening News.* ZORRO STRIKES AGAIN. The headline screamed out at her. Joan shuddered. Men and their nasty little urges. That's what it always came down to in the end. The rapist had been dubbed Zorro by the paper, because his face was masked and also because of his habit of executing a zigzag knife-cut on the back of his victims' hands. In Joan's view this was an inexcusably lightweight response to such a serious crime – typical of the way today's tabloids dumbed everything down. This man had been terrorising the town for months. Calling him after Antonio Banderas in comic-romantic mode was hardly appropriate, particularly since the police seemed incapable of catching him. Mind you, his victims were all silly trollops who should have known better. Girls parading themselves on the streets of Cambridge dressed in little more than prostitutes' clothes. The latest victim, according to the paper, had been off her face on various substances, having spent half the night clubbing.

In Joan's view, she got what she deserved.

Unlike Julie, who'd been left with nothing. To all intents and purposes it was breach of promise.

Maybe a phone call to Scott was needed . . .

Joan's indignation swelled to such giant proportions that she didn't even notice when her neatly-shod foot ground half a cream cracker into the carpet.

The screaming was endless. Occasionally it stopped, only to restart a second or two later with renewed vigour. It was like an animal caught in a trap, or a particularly unspeakable car alarm, or the high-pitched clamour of a Tornado bomber crossing and re-crossing the sky above Chesterton Road.

April calculated that Cassandra would crack first. Her screams were less than convincing. She had her back to Hector and was wolfing down the last gingerbread man.

But Hector was no slouch. Although fully occupied, guarding the cache of felt-tip pens he'd recently snatched from his sister, he spotted the change in her voice immediately. In a flash he was on her, seizing the headless gingerbread man from her hand and cramming it into his own mouth. Cassandra's wails modulated into outraged squealing.

'Mummy, Hector's stolen my little man. My precious.'

She seized her brother's straw-coloured mane and yanked it hard.

Hector roared, 'Witch bitch! Witch bitch! Witch bitch!'

'That's it. Upstairs, both of you. Or else.'

'Or else what, Mummy?'

On the strength of what the kids saw in April's face, they fled.

'Don't come back down until you've decided to be nice normal polite children.'

'But, Mum—'

'Any more nonsense and you won't be able to stay up and say hello to Danny and Aunty Rosa.'

A dramatic hush descended. And continued for several minutes.

April resented the efficacy of her threat. She personally would have loved nothing better than to go to *her* room and chill for a bit. But no such luck. Thanks to the kids, she had very little time left in which to produce a particularly special meal.

Perry, as usual, was hidden away in his study, supposedly at work on The Book. Hidden away from the screams of his children and from the hours of preparation required in cooking for a dinner-party – even though it was in honour of Rosa Thorn, his much-loved foster sister. April loved him dearly, but sometimes the absent-minded professor thing went a step too far.

'Perry!'

No response.

'Perry!'

No response.

'Perry! Are you deaf or dead?'

'Did you call?'

Finally.

'I need a hand.'

'Five minutes.'

'*Now*, Perry.'

He emerged from his study in injured-saint persona. 'No need to shout, my darling.' He planted a smacking kiss on her lips. 'God, you're gorgeous. Even with flour on your nose.'

'Where's all this fabled help you promised? They're your bloody guests, after all.'

Perry's face was suffused with puzzled virtue. 'All you had to do was ask,' he said, following her into the kitchen.

'I shouldn't *have* to ask!' she snapped.

'Anyway, Rosa's very easygoing. She'd be perfectly happy with beans on toast. She'd hate you to go to any trouble.'

'One day I swear I'll kill you.'

Perry surveyed the room. The children's attempts at finger-painting covered the table, and most of the floor and every other available surface was piled high with dinner preparations.

'What a mess,' he said amiably.

'Don't be surprised, Perry Grimshaw, if I turn into a husband-beater. You're enough to try the patience of ten saints. I know how important Rosa is to you and I want everything to be perfect. So pull your finger out and let's get the show on the road.'

'Here I stand. Do with me as you will, wench.'

'Don't tempt me. Why don't you make a green salad?'

'Certainly. Where's the olive oil?'

'I do hope that's a joke.'

'I did mention that I'm meeting Rosa in college first and bringing her back here later, didn't I?'

'Yes, although I don't see why.'

'To keep her out of your hair while you're finishing of dinner.'

'How jolly thoughtful of you.'

Perry pinched her bottom. 'Where do we keep the pepper?'

April chased him round the kitchen with her rolling pin.

And there appeared a great wonder in heaven; a woman clothed with the sun, and the moon under her feet, and upon her head a crown of twelve stars.

TWO

Cambridge floats above the fens in its very own crystal bubble, untouched by the rest of the world – barely aware, even, that the rest of the world exists. At least, that's what I've concluded on my various flying visits to Billings College to see Danny.

Maybe this time it'll be different. Maybe this time Cambridge will clasp me to its learned bosom. Because this time I'm staying for a while.

The BBC have asked me to reprise my role as the estranged wife of an undercover policeman who also, somewhat unbelievably, is a peer of the realm, in their award-winning series *Law Lord*. I couldn't believe it when they said that the episode for which I was needed was set in Cambridge. And not only that, but they were filming in May Week.

I'm ecstatic. Especially since, following ancient tradition, May Week is happening, as always, in June, and the weather is midsummer perfect.

There's even a scene at a May Ball. Watching various

dramas set in the dream city of the fens over the years has given me a longstanding ambition to go to a May Ball, just once, and dance through the night in a diaphanous ball-gown, with a genius in a dinner-jacket.

Doing it on film is the closest I'm likely to get. Genius escorts in dinner-jackets are a bit thin on the ground in my life. My son, devoted though he is to his poor widowed mother, would rather eat radioactive dirt than escort me to the Billings College Ball. I don't suppose Julie, his girl-friend, would be too keen on the idea, either. As for Dr Peregrine Grimshaw, who has kindly offered me bed and board for the duration, Antipodean April is his partner of choice. Fair enough, I suppose. She is his wife.

It's still hard for me to see Perry as a husband, even though he's now been married for over five years. He used to have a reputation as the horniest young academic in town – never seen twice with the same girl. But Australia and April have changed all that. I'll never forget the night he phoned to tell me that he'd met the love of his life, his soulmate, the most beautiful girl in the world. I wanted to rush out to Sydney straight away and meet this paragon who'd brought such joy to my precious Perry. But for one reason or another I've had to wait all this time, and even though they've been back in Cambridge for a couple of months, because of work commitments it's taken until now for me to see them. I wonder if she'll like me. I wonder if I'll like her. We start off with the advantage of having one major thing in common: our love for Perry. And I can't wait to meet Cassandra and Hector, four years old and only ten months between them. Perry making up for lost time, I suppose.

So all in all, I'm really looking forward to hanging my

at in their house on Chesterton Road and seeing the new domesticated Perry at first hand.

I'm early. I know why – it's because I want to have Danny to myself for a bit before our evening chez Grimshaw. I know I'm here for a few days, and that Danny's coming down for the Long Vac next week, but I can't wait to see him. He hasn't been home at all this term, and I'm feeling very out of touch.

I wonder if Julie will be there when I arrive at his digs. I hadn't thought of that. She probably will.

Shit.

Not that I don't like Julie.

She's a very nice girl.

Although I still think it was a mistake for Danny to choose her mother's house for his second-year lodgings. It will have made it very difficult for him to move away from the relationship.

If that's what he's wanted to do at any point. Which he probably hasn't. But still . . .

First stop, Danny's digs in Park Parade. The house shines out in comparison to its companions on either side. Snowy net curtains shield the interior from the prying gaze of the people disporting themselves on Jesus Green, and a brass knocker gleams enticingly. When I rap on it, the curtain twitches. After a moment the door opens and I find myself looking into the baleful eyes of Joan Watkins.

'Hi, Joan.'

She glares at me. We've only met once before. Perhaps she doesn't remember me.

'I'm Rosa, Danny's mum. We met briefly last year. How are you?'

'Fine.'

'Is Danny in?'

'No.'

'Oh . . . Do you know when he'll be back?'

'Danny doesn't live here any more.'

'What?'

'Hasn't he told you? Strange – I thought you were such a close family.'

'What's happened?'

'You'd better ask him.'

'So where is he living now?'

'I don't know.' The door is firmly shut in my face.

Charming.

Unless Joan's kicked him out for some dark reason of her own, it's clear that Danny and Julie have had a major upset. I walk down to the river and sit on a bench. How do I play this? It depends whether it's a permanent or temporary estrangement. It sounds pretty serious if he's moved out. I watch a college rowing eight speeding up the river, oars flashing, perfectly in unison. I thought Danny might take up rowing when he came to Cambridge. Fat chance. My streetwise metropolitan son would rather be crucified than participate in such an uncool sport.

I phone home. After a very long time Anna answers.

'Is everything OK?' I ask.

'You've only been gone three hours.'

'Are you working?'

'Yes, Mum, I'm working. No, Mum, I'm not throwing a wild party. And yes, Mum, I'm eating properly.'

'I can't believe I have to be up here when you're about to sit your English A level. Talk about bad timing.'

'Mum, chill. Uncle Joshie's fussing over me like a demented old granny. It's difficult to revise at all with him on my case.'

Even after two years it warms my heart to think of Josh so devotedly looking after Anna. When he turned up out of the blue, the half-brother my dead husband never knew he had, it was like retrieving a tiny bit of Rob. He's lived with us ever since, while establishing himself as an artist. But this is the first time he's been left in sole charge. Anna can twist him round her little finger and since he's nearer her age than mine, I hope he can hack it.

'You will call if there are any problems?'

'Mum, you're only away for a couple of days.'

'A couple of days in which you have an extremely important exam . . . And Josh isn't used to being responsible for anybody except himself. Plus he's a bloke. They don't always compute in the way they should.'

'He says he's going to draw up yet another study-plan for me tonight. Since he's such a perfectionist it'll take all evening and I won't get anything else done.'

'But once the parenting novelty's worn off he'll get absorbed in his own work—'

'Mum, you're doing my head in. How's Dan?'

'Haven't caught up with him yet. I'm about to go up to Billings and find him.'

'Give him my love and say I'm making big plans for when he gets back.'

'Oh yes? Such as?'

'Let's just say me and Joshie are working on the birthday.'

'Why does that fill me with foreboding?'

'Go find your son, Mother, and let me do some work.'

'Any probs, I'm only a couple of hours away.'

'My point precisely, m'lud. Bye. Love you.'

As I walk over the footbridge towards Billings College I order myself to cancel the guilt trip. Anna is fine. In fact, she's probably better off without me communicating my empathetic exam nerves back to her. As her mother, I know I should be there for her. But as a single parent with a living to earn in a notoriously unstable profession, there's no way I could have refused this job.

My ponderings have led me to the Gatehouse of Billings College with its massive crenellations and elaborations. The world-famous Billings Archangels – Michael, Gabriel and Raphael – are poised on the parapet, great wings outstretched, exhorting the faint-hearted student to abide by the College motto inscribed above their heads: *Aut Disce Aut Discede – Learn or Get Out*. I know which I'd rather do. To me, the beings hovering above appear less like angels than predatory birds poised to swoop down on unwary inno-cents and drag them into the crepuscular shades of those grey stone courtyards, with their gargoyles and weird stone beasts leaping from buttresses, which make me shudder every time I see them.

Billings is a college built on a tantrum.

Nearly one hundred and fifty years ago, an American millionaire, Horace Billings, was so outraged when his son was refused admission to King's College, Cambridge, that he decided to build his own college, one that would outclass all the other more august edifices in the ancient seat of learning. It would be too late to benefit his child, but would show the luminaries of the university that he was not a man to be spurned. He found a site behind Chesterton Road and employed as his architect one Ralph Saxby, a friend and disciple of William Burges, creator of Cardiff Castle. With this, his only major commission, Saxby out-Burgesed Burges. He designed not only the buildings but also all the furnishings, hard and soft. The result is a crazy, nightmare version of the High Victorian Gothic dream.

When I enter the Porter's Lodge, the Head Porter, Mr Gordon, is polishing a pair of black boots. With the elaborately patterned waistcoat, based on Ralph Saxby's version of a William Morris design, and the shiny maroon bowler hat, Billings College porters are some of the last to wear a formal uniform on an everyday basis. But that's Billings for you — more dyed-in-the-wool traditionalist than any other Cambridge college. They didn't even admit women until 1997.

'I'm Danny Thorn's mother,' I tell him. 'I gather he's moved out of his digs. Do you know where he's living now?'

'He's back in college, madam. Locke Court, G staircase.'

'Thanks.'

'But you won't find him there now. He's rehearsing the Billings Amateur Dramatic Society May Week production in the Fellows' Garden.'

Danny's told me about Stanley Gordon. Nothing gets past him. He knows everything that's going on in the college, and a lot more beside. Including, it seems, the present whereabouts of my son. I'm impressed.

'Which way do I go?'

'Through Bacon, into Thomas More, past the chapel, into Locke and it's through the gated archway in the corner.'

'Thanks.' I make for the door.

'A word, madam—'

'Yes?'

'Visitors aren't permitted in the Fellows' Garden.'

I swallow hard, smile sweetly and leave him to his polishing.

I find the walled garden without any difficulty. It's bounded on all sides by the most stunning herbaceous borders, at their midsummer best. There's a rickety stage at the far end, and on it a group of students. I see Danny. He's not difficult to spot, being the only black face. I chide myself for even noticing such a thing, but I'm very aware how few African-Caribbean or mixed-race students there seem to be in Cambridge, and ever since he came up, I've worried that Danny might feel different. An outsider. He says not, but on matters likely to worry his mother, he's not always entirely forthcoming.

I want to hurtle down the garden and hug him. I can't help swelling with pride at the sight of my lovely boy. I know I'm biased, but I think he's a real dish, even better-looking than his father – tall and handsome, with Rob's high cheekbones and huge dark eyes. With a shock, I see that he's chopped off his braids. His hair is shaved close to his head, giving his features a nobility of line that hadn't previously been apparent. It suits him. I'm about to rush forward when I realise that I can't barge in. He'd never forgive me. His mother crashing rehearsals – how uncool is that?

I lurk behind the gateway, unable to resist seeing how my son is when I'm not there.

Not on top form. He repeatedly bungles his lines, to the fury of the director, whose working methods consist of cursing and waving his arms around a lot. Danny is struggling with

a speech about wooing Desdemona. It's long and complicated, and he keeps drying. As the director harangues
him, all the other actors shuffle about looking bored and
uncomfortable.

All but one. Leaning against the front of the stage sits a
girl so beautiful she takes my breath away. Her eyes are
closed and she lifts her face to the sun, oblivious of the
ranting onstage. She has to be Desdemona. It's great casting.
Brabantio has just remarked that Desdemona is 'A maiden
never bold; Of spirit so still and quiet, that her motion blushed
at herself.' This girl fits the description to a T. Stillness radi-
ates off her in a great wave. I find myself wondering what
Danny thinks of her; whether he fancies her. Then I pull
myself up. Until he tells me differently, Danny has a girl-
friend.

Julie.

Who's nice.

Very nice.

Since Danny's not at his sparkling best, there's even less
reason for me to interrupt. He'd be mortified. I'll just have
to hang around college until it's time to meet Perry.

I wander back through the cloisters of Locke Court,
gloomy even on this bright June day, and check out Danny's
staircase, half-expecting a headless monk to pop out of an
alcove. Nobody's around, except the bronze statue of
Horace Billings, posing pompously in the middle of the
court, but peering through a ground-floor window I see
Danny's guitar. I try not to feel hurt that he hasn't told me
about the rift between him and Julie. But then, as far as I
know, he hasn't told Anna either, and she usually hears
things before me. Do I bring up the subject or do I leave

it to him? Trouble is, I don't trust myself to say the right thing. His attachment to Julie happened, as far as I can tell, about a nano-second after he arrived in Cambridge. I've been very worried about the way he's been sucked into her life so comprehensively. So if things *have* gone pear-shaped, as far as I'm concerned, it's a good thing. But I mustn't show it or he'll freak.

As I reach the college chapel I find I'm smiling. Its theme is The Creation. Inside, carved flowers, fruit and foliage rampage up marble columns leading to a small dome, across which the beasts of the field, birds of the air and creatures of the sea run riot in brilliant colours as part of an intricately-fashioned mosaic. I've only been inside a couple of times; now's my chance to have a really good look. I open the door and go in.

I'm not alone. Two men stand by the altar.

'You shouldn't be spending your free time here,' the older one is saying. 'You should be out enjoying yourself.'

'Unc, I'm worried about you. This business with Mortimer is really taking its toll. I thought if I could set things up for your evening service it would give you a bit of a break.'

'Bless you, my boy.'

'Hey, it's no biggie. I'm off now. I thought I might collect Flora from her rehearsal and bring her back here for Evensong.'

As he passes me on his way out, the boy smiles. If only I were twenty years younger. With his corn-blond hair worn long and floppy, his deep blue eyes and tanned skin he looks absurdly glamorous.

That's twice in the space of five minutes that I've been

dazzled by beauty. Cambridge is, it seems, as they claim, *the* place for gilded youth.

The older man approaches. He, in contrast, looks like an El Greco monk, with his close-cropped hair, angular face and dark eyes. He's dressed in a shabby black suit, and there's a dog collar round his neck.

'Please feel free to pray,' he says. 'Evensong is at six.'

Then he, too, slips away and I'm left to my own devices.

And another angel came out of the temple crying with a loud voice to him that sat upon the cloud, 'Thrust in thy sickle and reap: for the time is come for thee to reap: for the harvest of the earth is ripe.'

THREE

'So that, dear lords, if I be left behind, A moth of peace, and
he go to the war, The rites for which I love him are bereft
me, And I a heavy interim shall support By his dear absence.
Let me go with him.'

The low melodious voice cast a spell over the late-
afternoon garden, completely contradicting with its
languorous tone the urgency of Desdemona's plea.

Flora looked around. She wasn't the only one in thrall.
Only Shareef seemed unaffected, as he sat under a tree
sorting costumes. Lee, Danny, the spotty law student playing
Brabantio whose name she could never remember, and the
couple of attendant lords were all mesmerised.

A fair number of the men in the college had at some point
thrown themselves at Stella's feet. In Flora's opinion her friend
was always far too kind to them all. Whoever they were, how
clearly out of her league, she never rubbished them, or made
them feel small. She'd always listen to their puppy-eyed
approaches, let them take her out a few times, smile her
ethereal smile, and only then give them the brush-off.

Beautifully.

Part of Flora felt sorry for these boys as they trudged away, shoulders bent with disappointment, but most of her was pleased. It meant all the more Stella for her. Some of her best times this year had been when Stella, having given some poor guy the elbow, would say something like, 'Do you know what I really want, Flo? A mug of cocoa and a plate of crumpets, and for you to tell me why exactly Grumpy Grimshaw thinks that John Donne-Un-done is the best thing since sliced bread. Have you still got some of that jam from Fortnum's?'

The absence of guys beating a path to her own door, however, was a relief to Flora. She was saving herself until she was married, so the fewer complications the better.

Or so she'd thought until Lucas.

He'd appeared at the R&R Bible study group just before Christmas. He was completely gorgeous, with his shoulder-length streaky blond hair and azure eyes, like one of the Billings angels brought to glorious life. The male students who worked at R&R were, by and large, a weedy bunch. As if, she sometimes thought, doing God's work had sucked out all their vitality and left behind only a pale facsimile. But Lucas was something else. After the discussion, Dom had introduced him. Flora was tall and skinny, with large hands and feet. She usually felt awkward with new people. But Lucas towered above her, giving her the novel sensation of being a fragile little woman in need of protection.

'This is my nephew, Lucas. He's come to help me run R&R. Lucas, meet Flora. Whatever you need to know about this place, she'll tell you. She knows more than anyone, including me. Now, if you'll excuse me, I must check our latest consignment of provisions from the supermarket. They're very kind, giving us all this free food, but some of it is occasionally a tad strange. This time I noticed forty boxes of hundreds and thousands lurking in there somewhere. They won't exactly fill Billy Whizz's beer belly, will they? Then I must talk to those four nice young people over in the corner. They're waiting for me to interview them about becoming volunteers, and I also need to have a word with Simon Smith before he disappears. I spotted him drinking Carlsberg Special Brew outside college at nine in the morning yesterday and I suspect there may be something troubling him. I must see if there's anything I can do to help.' He darted away in hot pursuit of the unfortunate Simon.

'Go, Unc,' said Lucas, giving Flora a ravishing smile. 'I don't know how he finds the energy.'

'No,' Flora had said. 'And yet he always has time to listen. He never turns away anyone who needs him, you know. I think he's a saint. I worry about him, though. One day he'll burn himself out if he isn't careful.'

'Well, stop worrying right now. I'm taking over the day-to-day running of this place. Give Unc a chance to focus on himself for a change. There's a book of devotional essays he's apparently been trying to write for years. If I can ease the burden here, maybe he'll be able to do it.'

'That's fantastic,' said Flora. There was a short pause and she began to panic. Maybe she was boring him. What could she say to keep him talking? 'What were you doing before you came here to help your uncle?'

'I've been travelling.' He'd given her another megawatt smile. 'Doing God's will across the globe.'

'Missionary work?'

'Yeah. Mainly Africa and South-East Asia.'

'How wonderful. It must have been very fulfilling, bringing God to people who've never known Him.'

Lucas's blue eyes suddenly burned. 'Yeah. But there's still so much to do,' he said passionately. 'So many lives to change.' Then he grimaced. 'Sorry. I get a bit carried away sometimes.'

'You sound as if you wish you were still out there.'

'No. My place is with my uncle now.' He'd grinned, glancing towards a group of their regular clientèle. The old men were surreptitiously passing a can of extra-strong lager between them in the vain hope that Dom wouldn't notice. 'There are plenty of souls for me to save here, don't you think?' Then he'd looked at her and said, 'If you like, we could go for a coffee and you could bring me up to speed on all the R&R gossip.'

Flora wondered if she'd died and gone to heaven.

And that had been the start of it. Next morning, Lucas was there for the early breakfast shift. He'd been really pleased to see her, and over subsequent weeks they'd become good friends. They shared the same views about how to bring Christianity into their everyday lives, and she loved his attitude towards the men in the refuge – respectful kindness mixed with a wickedly mischievous humour. She also admired the unselfconscious way he talked to everyone about God, as a trusted friend who was part of their everyday lives, and not some distant deity in the sky. And not just to the volunteers in R&R, who were all Christians anyway. No, Lucas would chat to people on buses, and in the supermarket, or just in the street, and within seconds bring God into the conversation in the most natural way possible. She thought he was magnificent, and felt inordinately proud to be with him when, as happened surprisingly often, he'd charmed some unsuspecting passer-by into listening and accepting one of the little pamphlets that he carried with him at all times. She'd persuaded Dom to roster them together at R&R whenever possible. It wasn't difficult. She suspected he approved of their growing friendship.

Lucas hadn't yet asked her out on a date. Not as such. But sooner or later he would. There was something very special growing between them. Flora knew in the deepest part of her being that they were meant for each other. Normally she wouldn't ever have expected anyone as fabulous as him to be interested in someone like her. She wasn't remotely in his league, either in looks or personality. But Lucas was different from most men: he saw her inner beauty. He'd told her as much. He said that she was one of the most truly good women that he'd ever met, and that he could see her beautiful soul as clearly as God could. They agreed about so many things to do with living a Christian life, including a mutual belief that the body was God's holy vessel and how it was good to keep that holy vessel pure and untouched until God revealed The One.

Of course, these conversations about ways of living had been supposedly a general exchange of views. But Flora had become more and more certain of the unspoken agenda between them. Lucas was telling her in his own way that she was The One for him. At some point, probably quite soon, he'd come out and say it directly. He'd ask her to marry him. They'd live above the refuge and run R&R for Dom. Lucas was there already. It was only a matter of time before they both made it their home. How great it would be, she and Lucas living a Christian life in fellowship and joy, looking after the poor and dispossessed of Cambridge.

But recently she'd started to feel guilty. About Stella.

She knew that her growing closeness to Lucas had led her to neglect her friend. She'd been so preoccupied with him in one way or another, that she hadn't been around on several occasions when Stella had really needed her. She felt very bad about it. Then Lee Watson asked Stella to be Desdemona in the Billings Amateur Dramatic Society May Week production, and Stella had said she'd only do it if Flora was involved.

'But I can't act,' Flora had protested.

'Please, Flo. I've wanted to do some acting ever since we arrived, you know I have. It's a great part – a fantastic opportunity. And if Grumpy sees me being a brilliant Desdemona, maybe he'll stop trashing my essays and be nice to me. But I'm scared shitless. I need you to hold my hand, help me learn my lines, comfort me when I fuck up. Flo, I really, really want to do this, but I can't face it on my own.'

What could Flora say? She'd agreed to help Shareef with the costumes and also to be the female understudy.

What she hadn't foreseen was that the girl playing Emilia would drop out at the last minute. Stepping into her role had been more difficult than Flora had ever imagined. She recognised immediately that what she'd told her friend was the truth: her acting talent was non-existent. However, the humiliation was worth it if it made up to Stella for her recent neglect.

All in all, she was glad to be involved with *Othello*. Even though it meant temporarily cutting down on her R&R commitments and Lucas, it was a sacrifice she was prepared to make. After all, she and Lucas would be spending the rest of their lives together.

'She's amazingly good, isn't she? Perfect.'

She jumped. It was Lucas himself, staring up at Stella as she begged so beautifully to go to Cyprus with her husband.

'What are you doing here?'

He turned away from Desdemona's outpouring and grinned at her. 'Came to help Uncle Dom set up for Evensong. Remembered you were rehearsing and thought I'd surprise you.'

Flora's belly did a backflip. Lucas hardly ever came up to college. Helping Dom set up for chapel was just an excuse. He'd really come especially to see her rehearse.

He's interested in every corner of my life. Just like I am in his.

When Shareef called her, she ignored him, intent on prolonging the moment. But Shareef couldn't cope with being ignored, and he continued to pester. Finally, she capitulated and went over to where he was sitting under the tree.

'Can you check which ones need mending?' he said, indicating a pile of trousers.

'I'll do it later.'

'You'll forget, like you did with Desdemona's dress. It was pure chance that nice woman in the Oxfam shop held it back for us . . .'

Shareef's voice was rising. Flora knew the signs: a tantrum was imminent. She hated the thought of him shouting at her in front of Lucas.

'I'll do it, all right?'

When she looked round, Lucas was talking to Stella. They were laughing. Her skin became suddenly clammy. A trickle of sweat ran down her face.

Two weeks ago at R&R, Flora had finally introduced them.

Stella was at her sweetest. 'Flo's told me all about your work here. I think it's fantastic, what you do for these poor people.'

Lucas had squeezed Flora's shoulders in a wonderfully intimate way. 'Flo's the fantastic one. She should be declared one of our national treasures. God's very lucky to have her on His side.'

Flora knew that Stella believed God ranked first equal with Father Christmas and the tooth fairy – a comforting fantasy parent figure when times were hard. She'd spent hours praying for Stella's immortal soul, unable to bear the image of that beautiful face contorted in agony as it burned in the everlasting flames.

But that evening, at R&R, her friend had kept her views to herself, and Flora had watched as the dazzling arcs of two angelic smiles interfaced.

Thinking about it, she shifted uncomfortably on the grass. Usually she was one of the last to leave the refuge. But that night she and Stella had been first out of the door.

So? It was Stella's first visit. She hadn't wanted to expose her to religion overload.

Now she watched as Lucas plucked some grass from Stella's blonde spikes and fluffed the hair back into shape.

A cloud obscured the sun and all the colour drained

from the bright borders. She walked unsteadily over to her friends.

'I'm finished, Lucas,' she said. 'Do you fancy a coffee in my room?'

'Not now. It's almost time for Evensong. Aren't you coming?' He turned to Stella. 'You too, Stella?'

Stella wrinkled her perfect nose. 'Not my scene.'

'Why not?'

'I'm a godlesss heathen. Ask Flora.'

'We'll have to do something about that,' he said.

Stella's smile was a challenge. 'Like what?'

'We'll have to find a way to open your heart to God.'

'Flora's been trying to do that all year. She's failed dismally.'

'Maybe she doesn't have my powers of persuasion.'

Stella smiled again. 'Maybe she doesn't.'

The afternoon heat intensified, sucking all the air from the garden. Flora couldn't breathe. She felt dizzy and clutched at something to steady herself: Lucas's arm. She dimly registered the concern in his eyes.

'Are you all right?'

'Bit of a headache,' she said. 'I think I'll skip chapel tonight. I'll see you at R&R tomorrow morning.'

'OK. A good night's sleep is the best thing for headaches. You take care now, Flo. Bye, Stella. You might not believe in God, but He believes in you.' He winked and sauntered off.

'What were you laughing about?' asked Flora.

'Nothing,' said Stella, staring at Lucas's retreating back.

'You were both looking at me and laughing.'

Stella smiled. 'Actually,' she said, 'he was telling me a joke.

'What joke?'

Stella shrugged. 'I don't remember,' she said.

Danny told himself that wanting to do something wasn't the same as actually doing it, and that as yet, he'd done nothing.

It didn't help.

When he'd dumped Julie, he'd sworn there was no one else. He'd said he wanted to be free. No relationships for a long while. He'd meant it. Yet here he was a mere three weeks later.

Lusting after Stella.

He'd finally acknowledged his feelings. This afternoon. It had happened just as he was about to smother her at the end of Act Five. He'd seen her lying in the bed, her perfect face upturned towards him, and he'd nearly collapsed, so strong was the emotion that engulfed him. And he knew beyond a shadow of a doubt that if she'd said, 'Kiss me,' he'd have thrown himself on her without thinking twice.

Hardly had he left Julie's bed before he was gagging for someone else. How about that for a Shallow Hal?

He'd met Julie during Freshers' Week. He'd gone to the college office to deliver an RSVP to the Master's sherry-party for freshers, and in the doorway he'd collided with someone: a small girl in a big temper.

'Watch it,' she'd snarled, and pushed past him.

'Charming,' he'd muttered.

The middle-aged woman typing at one of Ralph Saxby's more ornate pieces of office furniture didn't acknowledge his presence by so much as a blink.

'Can I leave this?' Danny put his envelope on the desk.

Without even looking at him, she indicated a row of pigeonholes.

Danny tried not to take it personally. He'd been in Cambridge for only a couple of days. He mustn't be paranoid. Things were bound to feel strange.

Things did feel strange. He felt completely at sea, tempest-tossed in a tumult of strangers with no guiding star. It was all so different from life as he knew it. For a start, there seemed to be virtually no adults around. Or even second- and third-year students. Supervisions and lectures didn't start till the following week and Cambridge was a mish-mash of freshers, eddying and swirling round the narrow streets of the town, drifting from place to place, pub to pub, party to party, rudderless – anchorless – on free fall. His room was shabby and cold, and the other students on his staircase were all public-school types who dashed up and down braying to each other in such a strangulated parody of the English tongue that Danny couldn't understand more than two words in every sentence.

To his astonishment, Danny discovered he was experiencing a severe bout of homesickness. He'd been so up for university – living his own life away from the restrictions of home. But now he ached to return to his cosy house in Consort Park and be back in his old life with his mother, sister and Josh, playing in the band with Dwaine and Delroy, going to the pub with his mates from school. Back in London. Great rambling London, with its edgy potential and endless possibilities. Not this grey, claustrophobic little city of odd corners and dead ends. It felt to Danny, as he roamed the historic streets, like being a hamster on a wheel, frantically going round and round the same circle. His first night he'd bawled into his pillow like a big baby. What a wuss. The Three Musketeers charging up and down the staircase like a herd of rhino at all hours didn't seem in the least affected. They'd undoubtedly dealt with homesickness at prep school when they were infants. But for him it was a lead weight, pulling him down, making him intensely miserable.

He couldn't imagine ever feeling comfortable in Cambridge.

And so, when he did meet an ordinary adult, it would have been nice, he'd thought wistfully, if she'd been a little less frigid and uncommunicative and a little more like a normal human being.

He'd wandered out of the office, and come face to face with the ball of temper he'd encountered a moment earlier. She was hopping up and down on the gravel path, cursing.

'Shit! Shit! Shit!'

When she saw Danny, the scowl on her face deepened. 'What are *you* gawping at?'

She was very pretty. Danny hadn't taken it in the first time. She had dark brown curly hair that bounced on her head as she moved, periwinkle-blue eyes, and a stunning figure.

'Is something wrong?'

She waved a shoe at him. 'The heel's come off. How am I supposed to get home?'

Danny suspected the question was rhetorical. He came up with an answer anyway. 'Borrow my flip-flops.'

'Wear your stinky old flip-flops? You're havin' a laugh, incha?' But she'd stopped scowling.

'My feet don't sweat,' he said. 'Have a niff.' He took off one of his sandals and thrust it in her face. She shrieked, but not in a nasty way. I'm in, he thought. 'Or you can take my arm and I'll hop you home,' he said.

She looked him up and down. Danny felt like a prime cut of beef in a butcher's shop. 'What you waiting for then?' she said. 'I'm Julie.'

'Danny,' he said, executing an elaborate bow. 'Lead me to your staircase, M'lady.'

'I'm not a student,' she said. 'My mum works here.' She jerked her head towards the office.

'Your mum's the Master's secretary?'

Julie laughed. 'She wishes. She comes on like the Master's bleeding secretary but actually she just does typing and filing and stuff. I came to cadge some cash, but she wouldn't stump up. Tight-arsed old mare.'

Danny laughed, but took care not to agree. Life with a mother and sister had taught him that females didn't always mean what they said. He liked Julie already. He didn't want her at some future date throwing it back in his face that he'd once agreed that her mother was a tight-arsed old mare.

She said she lived by Jesus Green. They set off, Julie clinging on to his arm far more, Danny suspected, than was strictly necessary. For the first time since he arrived, he felt happy. He and Julie slipped straight into conversation as if they'd known each other forever. Danny was glad she wasn't some stuck-up undergraduate who was cleverer than he was. He liked her directness and her gobby stream of consciousness – the vividly expressive words and phrases gushed from her mouth like steam from a geyser. True, most of it was rubbish, but he found it strangely touching. It made him, even at that stage, want to protect her and keep her safe.

When they arrived at her house she invited him in. It was super-clean, and super-crowded – full of knick-knacks and lace curtains and highly polished furniture, and a three-piece suite, covered in see-through plastic. Not remotely like his home. But it was, nevertheless, a home. And Danny, fresh from his lonely college room, was drawn to it like an iron filing to a magnet. This was normality. This house and this girl.

That's how it started. Her uptight mother, Joan, had accepted the romance once she saw that Danny wasn't messing Julie around, and Danny had found a home from home. In his second year, Billings College students had to live out of college, and since Joan Watkins took in undergraduates as lodgers it was an easy matter for Danny to put down her house as his digs.

But now, he and Julie were finished. And this thing with Stella – what did it all mean?

It had crept up on him over the course of rehearsals. He'd thought at first that maybe he was over-identifying with Othello. But in reality, he knew it was nothing to do with the Moor. It was those green eyes that seemed to see right inside him, stripping away all the shit to expose his weak and vulnerable core.

Yet, paradoxically, and in spite of her wonderful sweetness, Stella herself remained so separate. Impossible to know. How unlike Julie, who had no boundaries at all, and claimed the right to march through his mind at all times and ferret into every far-flung corner. Julie had wanted everything from him, but knew nothing. Stella wanted nothing, but seemed to know everything.

He watched her chatting to Flora and some blond himbo

who'd just appeared out of nowhere, and had an over-whelming compulsion to crash into their conversation. Break it up.

He jumped down from the stage, only to see the guy walk away. *Good riddance.*

'Who's your boyfriend, Flora?' He couldn't think of anything else to say.

'He's not my boyfriend. Stel, is there any chance you could help me with the costumes? I'm never going to have them ready in time.'

Stella's face was a picture of concern. 'I'd love to, babes, but I'm really panicking about my lines. I simply can't seem to get them into my stupid head. I thought I'd just go back to my room and brainstorm. Anyway, what about your headache? You need to go to bed and sleep it off.'

'I wish,' said Flora. 'There's just too much to get through . . .' She looked completely overwhelmed.

Stella squeezed her arm. 'I'll help if you really want me to, obviously, but I wouldn't be much use. I'm shit at sewing – you know that.'

'There's loads of ironing as well.'

'Remember how badly I burned that denim skirt you lent me? I'd hate to ruin some irreplaceable costume at this late stage.'

Danny found himself saying, 'I'll run lines with you, if you like, Stella.'

Flora cut in. 'No need. I can test her as I'm sewing.'

A small voice in Danny's head said that this was a good plan, that being alone with Stella wasn't a good idea. But then a large insistent voice – his own – was saying out loud, 'Actually, Stella and I need to do it together.'

Stella giggled and he went hot all over at the implied innuendo.

'OK. I'll test both of you.'

Bloody Flora. Why wouldn't she just piss off?

'We need to be alone. To concentrate.' He heard the aggression in his voice and felt ashamed.

Then he remembered Perry's dinner invitation. 'Shit, I can't. I'm due at my godfather's soon.'

Stella gazed at him. 'Your godfather lives in Cambridge? How nice for you.'

Was she poking fun? 'Yeah. Perry Grimshaw.'

'Dr Grimshaw's your godfather?'

'Yeah.'

'How cool is that!'

'Is it?'

'He's a wicked teacher.'

'I wouldn't know; he doesn't supervise me. Wanted to keep things in separate compartments, I think.'

'Hey – I owe him an essay. Maybe you could give it to him?'

'Sure.'

'Danny, if you're going to be out, is it OK to use your room to work on the costumes this evening?' Flora's earnest face interposed itself between them.

Danny had agreed to let his room be used for wardrobe since it was nearest to the Fellows' Garden.

'Yeah, cool,' he said, desperate to be alone with Stella.

'Is it all right if I make coffee? Say if it isn't – I don't mind.'

For the second time in minutes he behaved badly. 'For fuck's sake, Flora, of course you can make yourself a coffee.

Make twenty coffees if you like. I don't give a shit.' Immediately the words were out, he felt awful. 'Sorry,' he said. 'I'm in a hurry, that's all. If I don't go now I'll be late.'

'Bye, Flo,' said Stella. 'Are you sure you'll be all right?'

'Of course I will.'

'If not, I will stay and help. My lines'll get learned somehow, even if I have to stay up all night.'

Danny was touched by Stella's unselfish offer. What a really special person she was.

'I'll manage,' said Flora. 'Learning your part's much more important than sorting costumes.'

Stella gave her a hug. 'Cheers, babe. You'll get there in the end. Don't work too hard though.' She grabbed Danny's arm and dragged him away. 'Are you coming to get that essay then?'

Within seconds he'd forgotten Flora's hurt face.

Stella's room was at the top of her staircase. She ushered him in and Danny's heart began a painful thumping as he tried to ignore the rise and fall of her breasts under the thin top.

'Nice room,' he said.

'Are you sure you don't have time to go through some lines?'

Danny glanced at his watch and tried for cool. 'I could probably spare a few minutes.'

'Let's try the death scene,' said Stella. 'On the bed.'

'I can't do all the costumes *and* play Emilia. You said it would be a joint effort.' Flora tried to make Shareef listen, but he flounced towards the gate of the Fellows' Garden and refused to look at her.

She did think Stella might have helped. It wasn't asking much. On the other hand, it was undeniably true that her friend was no good with a needle. Flora always sewed on any loose buttons and mended split seams and hems for her.

And it was good that she was flirting with Danny.

Why?

Because it meant she'd be focusing on him. She wouldn't have any time left over.

For anything else.

Shareef had screeched to a petulant halt by the gate. 'I design the best production this college has ever seen, and what thanks do I get?' His tantrum was reaching a climax. 'Nothing. *Nada. Niente.* Lee's an ungrateful old queen. And now you're being difficult, Flora. You know I've got my work cut out finishing the set. The costumes are your bag. I simply can't do everything.'

'Neither can I.'

They glared at each other.

A dark-haired girl suddenly materialised from behind the gateway. 'I'll help,' she said.

Flora recognised her. It was Danny Thorn's ex-girlfriend. The one, according to college gossip, that he'd recently dumped.

The girl waited expectantly. Flora wondered how long she'd been standing there. Danny and Stella must have passed her, but she gave no sign that she'd seen or spoken to them. She must have hidden behind a tree.

'You're Mrs Watkins's daughter, right?' asked Flora.

'Yeah. I'm Julie.'

Shareef interrupted. 'Can you sew?'

'Got an A starred for GCSE.'

'*Fabuloso!* Just what we need! But I still can't see how we'll possibly finish.' His voice rose. 'The whole thing's a disaster!'

'I could take a couple of days off work.'

'Really? Do you have a nice boss who wouldn't mind?'

'My boss is a cow, but she owes me three weeks' holiday.'

'Where do you work?' Flora felt she ought to ask out of politeness.

'*Belle et Beau.* It's a dress shop in King Street.'

'Wow. They sell really cool stuff. Do you get free clothes?' 'I wish.'

Shareef cut through the girlie chat. 'Would you really take time off to help us?'

'Yeah.'

'Julie, you're a gem,' he trilled. 'Sorted, then. I'll leave you to it, ladies.' And off he went.

Flora was gutted. So much for Stella and Danny becoming an item. Having his ex-girlfriend hanging around would really cramp Danny's style, but there was nothing she could do about it. It looked like she was stuck with the girl.

Or maybe not. Maybe when Julie was in possession of all the facts . . .

'I heard about you and Danny,' she said, 'and I'm really sorry . . . but in view of that, there's something you ought to know before you commit yourself. The costumes are kept in his room because it's nearest to the Fellows' Garden. That's where we'd be working on them. I'm only telling you because you might find it a bit awkward.'

Julie looked her square in the eye. 'Danny and I are cool,' she said. 'It won't be a problem.'

GREEN EYE

'Great,' said Flora.

Cool? She didn't believe a word of it. Julie was a pressure cooker ready to blow. With a bit of encouragement she'd be gone so fast you wouldn't see her for dust.

Thou hast stolen my heart, my sister, my spouse; thou hast ravished my heart with one of thine eyes, with one chain of thy neck.

FOUR

One minute I'm admiring the stained-glass windows in Saxby's chapel, the next I'm looking into the face of an angel who's shaking my shoulder.

'Sorry to disturb you. Evensong's about to start and I thought maybe you'd want to be woken.'

It's the beautiful youth again. His eyes register compassion and concern for the elderly. I hope I wasn't slack-jawed and snoring when he found me.

I jump to my feet, attempting to sparkle. 'Must have dropped off for a second. Thanks for the wake-up call.'

'Don't let me chase you away. You're very welcome to stay and worship with us.'

'Actually, I'm late for an appointment.' I stride out of the chapel in what I hope is a suitably vigorous manner. I'm not lying. I promised to meet Perry at six. It's now quarter past.

His room is in Berkeley Court, one of Saxby's strangest creations, with its collection of grotesque stone animals – wolves, dogs, monkeys, griffins, even a hideously large bear

- which leap out snarling in menace from a frieze up at gutter-level around the court. And even more spectacular is the fountain against the fourth wall, with its three mythological sea serpents rearing up in wild spirals to spew gallons of water into the bowl below.

As I approach Perry's staircase, the door opens and the El Greco monk appears. His dark eyes burn. His voice, the trained instrument of the professional preacher, reverberates around the courtyard, drowning out the fountain.

'I'm telling you, Perry, if we don't all stick together it will be the end of everything this college has ever stood for.'

And there he is, my Perry, standing in the doorway. The Australian sun and the intervening years have etched a few more lines on his handsome face, and his hair is a tad thinner on top, but otherwise he's the same as he ever was. Forty-four and fabulous. 'You're too pessimistic, Dom. Whatever his faults, the Master wants the best for the college.'

'Depends what your definition of best is,' the man growled. 'Don't be taken in by him.' He stops abruptly when he sees me.

'Rosaleen!' Perry rushes forward, sweeping me up into a huge embrace.

After an absence of six years, the sight of his dear familiar face and the use of the pet name from our childhood is overwhelming. So much has happened to both of us since we last saw each other. He feels it too. He's holding me so tight I can hardly breathe. Then a dry cough reminds us that we're not alone.

Perry breaks away. 'Rosa, meet Dominic Tipton, our chaplain. Dom, this is my darling Rosa.'

The man's angry eyes soften as he shakes my hand
'Perry's told me all about you. He's been so excited abou
your visit – talked of little else for days.'

'We met earlier. In the chapel.'

'Ah, yes . . .'

'It's such a beautiful building.'

'Indeed.' Then there's an awkward pause before he adds
'Perry, we'll talk later. If you'll excuse me, Rosa, I must go
Evensong . . .' He hurries off.

'Was it something I said?'

'He's a bit shy with women. You'd never believe it if you
heard him preach. He's quite brilliant, you know – a
wonderful man. The sort that gives Christianity a good
name.'

'Ha, ha – very funny. What do you mean?'

'He actually practises what he preaches, unlike a lot o
churchmen I've come across.'

'Really?'

'About eight years ago, not long after he took over a
Billings's chaplain, he singlehandedly persuaded the counci
by sheer force of personality to give him premises and finan
cial support to run a Christian drop-in centre for homeles
old men in the town. Word has it that he does an awful lo
of good down there.'

'Sounds quite a guy.'

'The evangelical young in the university love him. He'
practically a cult figure.'

Through the archway I could see Tipton trudging toward
the chapel.

'Right now he looks as if he's carrying the weight of th
world on his back.'

'He's a bit preoccupied at the moment, poor chap. It's
ﾚe new Master – Hugo Mortimer. He's busy pressing all
ﾞom's buttons.'

'Sir Hugo Mortimer the geneticist?'

'That's the one.'

'What's the problem?'

'Hugo wants to turn Billings into the premier college in
ﾚe university for the study of genetics and related sciences.
ﾞis plan is to scale down the Arts Departments and phase
ﾞme out altogether – starting with Theology, Dom's
ﾞbject.'

'Can he do that?'

'He's trying his best. He also wants to get rid of our funny
ﾞd Theological Library and replace it with a state-of-the-
ﾞt temple to Genetics. Dom's trying to organise a palace
ﾞvolution, but he's not making much headway. Our new
ﾚaster likes to get his own way and he's a pretty ruthless
ﾞanipulator. Dom's far too straightforward and honest about
ﾞhat he wants. Hugo's running rings round him.'

'Is the English Department under threat?'

'I don't think so. Otherwise, why bother to tempt me
ﾞck to England with this fellowship? But Hugo plays a
ﾞep game, so who knows. In any event, I'm on Dom's
ﾞde. I think we need more things of the spirit in our ghastly
ﾞorld, not fewer.' He smiles down at me and once again
ﾞn reminded of the little boy I used to know. 'Enough of
ﾞllege politics. Let me give you some tea, and we can play
ﾞtch-up before I take you home.'

'Thanks for putting me up. Is April OK about it?'

'Are you kidding? She's dying to meet you. I hope you're
ﾞt going to be working all the time?'

61

'It's only a couple of short scenes, both shot very earl
in the morning, so I'll have plenty of free time.'

Over tea we fill in the gaps that our extensive emai
correspondence hasn't covered. I give Perry the finer detail
of my turbulent history since his departure, we have a littl
weep over Rob's death, and he tells me all about April. He
crazy about her, that's for sure.

'The first time I saw her I knew she was the one. Sh
came to one of my lectures on Derrida and told me I'd go
it all wrong. She was right, too. She has one of the be:
brains I've ever come across. That's why . . .' He stops.

'What?'

'I feel as if I'm being disloyal saying this, but I think sh
should do some part-time teaching to keep her hand in
However, she won't.'

'Why not?'

'It's partly that the kids have found it very unsettling
being uprooted and moving countries. It's led to a few behav
iour problems and she feels she wants to sort them ou
herself rather than handing them over to strangers to do i
But also she has this thing about being the perfect mothe
and she thinks staying at home with the kids is the way t
do it.'

'I didn't work when Danny and Anna were little.'

'I'm not knocking full-time mothers. Just saying it's wron
for her. She needs to use that formidable grey matter. An
with the kids being so close in age, she gets knackered
They go to nursery in the morning and I do what I can, o
course, but . . .'

This last remark makes me smile. Much as I love Perr
I know that pulling his weight around the house isn't h

strong point. Domestically, poor April might well feel she's coping with three children, not two.

'Maybe she'll talk to you about it, Rosaleen. If she does, try and persuade her to think about doing a bit of work.'

I'm not sure I want to venture through this little minefield in Perry's marriage, so I change the subject to one that's been preoccupying me for the last hour.

'So, Perrygreen, what's all this about Danny and Julie?'

'Hasn't he told you?'

'Not a word.'

'They've split up.'

'When?'

'About three weeks ago.'

'What happened?'

'Dan didn't give me any details. The only reason he told me at all was because he wanted a room in college. Normally there wouldn't be any at this time of year, but one of our students went home with glandular fever so I was able to fix him up.'

I'm trying not to feel hurt that Danny's kept me in the dark about this major piece of news. I know he's an adult now, and adults don't tell their mummies every last detail about their lives. But being excluded from the things that matter most to him is still hard to bear.

Perry sees I'm upset. 'It's for the best, Rosa. Julie isn't right for Danny. Don't get me wrong – she's very feisty, lots of spirit – but eventually he'd have been bored stiff with her. I can't see what they'd have in common once the sex thing wears off.'

'I couldn't agree with you more. I just feel a bit excluded, I suppose.'

'He's a big boy now. He has to sort things out for himself.'

'I'll remind you of that in fifteen years' time when you're worrying yourself sick about Hector's latest flame.'

'Talking of kids, I guess we'd better make our way back to the old homestead.'

'I'm dying to meet them. I can't believe it's taken so long.'

'Neither can I.'

'How's Frankie taken to being a granny?'

Perry's deeply devoted to his mother. She's a club singer – a throwback to the days of the good old variety show. Frankie is the reason he and I were brought up together. They lodged with us, and when Frankie went on tour, my parents looked after Perry. The tours were frequent and often, and Perry saw far more of my mother than he did of his own.

The Fabulous Frankie Faraday.

I'm curious to hear about her take on being a grandmother.

'She's been doing the cruise ships for the last few years but recently things have become a bit slack. So she's been here rather a lot since we arrived.'

I bet April loves that.

'She must be thrilled that you're back in England.'

Perry gives a wry smile. 'She and April don't exactly hit it off.'

I'm not surprised. If I had the Fabulous Frankie for a mother-in-law I think I'd probably end it all. Perry, of course, doesn't see it. Where Frankie's concerned, he's deaf, dumb and blind to whatever's going on.

'That's why I asked you to come here first instead of

going straight to the house. I need to ask a favour . . . Don't bring up our childhood.'

'What?'

'It's like a red rag to a bull.'

'But—'

'Moving countries is a big deal for anyone, but April was really up for it, you know. She was determined to make a success of it, and she has. She's made new friends, joined things, really got into the swing of being a don's wife . . .'

'So what's the problem?'

'I thought Frankie visiting, having another pair of hands, might give her more freedom, help her settle in, but it hasn't worked out like that. She seems to resent any suggestion Frankie makes, particularly about the kids. Frankie tries to be helpful, but April takes everything the wrong way.'

Frankie? Helpful?

Perry smiles. 'I don't know what I've done to deserve it, but April really loves me, Rosa. She knows Frankie was away a lot when we were children, and she can't bear to think of me as a little boy, struggling along without a mum. She deeply resents it on my behalf, much more than I do. She doesn't understand that Frankie had no choice. And she thinks there are things from back then cluttering up my psyche and that it's her job to bring them into the light. So any mention from you about my childhood, and she'll be probing away asking for chapter and verse. And quite frankly, it doesn't do either of us any good.'

I haven't yet clapped eyes on April, but I already know I'm going to love her. She's seen the scars on Perry's soul, and knows exactly where they come from. It sounds as if she's on some sort of healing crusade, although she'll be lucky if she gets anywhere. Perry's in deep denial about his mother. Always has been.

'I just don't want to upset any apple-carts, Rosaleen. Not tonight, when we're all together at last.'

Perry never was one for upsetting apple-carts. 'Anything for a quiet life' is his motto, which over the years has meant letting Frankie get away with everything. And now I'm getting the vibe that April is pretty strong-minded too. Poor Perry — caught between the irresistible force and the immovable object.

'Anything that happened more than twenty years ago is henceforth obliterated,' I promise. 'I am a blank slate.'

Perry grins. 'No need to overdo it,' he says. 'Come on, let's go home.'

We leave the college and walk up to Chesterton Road. As we draw level with the footbridge, I hear an earsplitting cacophony coming from one of the houses.

Perry turns in at the gate. 'Kids' bedtime,' he says, without batting an eyelid. He strides up the path, key in hand and lets himself in. 'Where are my little bush babies?'

The noise stops.

'Daddy!!' Two naked, wet children hurtle down the stairs and throw themselves at him.

'Whoa! Anybody would think I'd been away for a year.'

'Mummy says we have to go straight to bed without seeing Aunty Rosa.'

'What have you done?'

'Nothing.'

'What have you done?'

66

'We were playing big storms in the bath and the giant wave splashed out and went through the kitchen ceiling.'

Two pairs of blue eyes gaze up at Perry. I'm captivated by the accent. I know it's stupid, but I hadn't anticipated the Australian voices.

'We didn't mean it, Daddy. Please can we see Aunty Rosa and Danny? Please?'

Perry's eyes are filled with pure, unadulterated love. 'You're in luck, tiddlers. Who do you think this is?'

The eyes swivel in my direction.

'Cassandra, Hector, say hello to Aunty Rosa.'

'G'day, Aunty Rosa.' The little girl moves shyly behind her father.

'Why are you so skinny?'

'Hector! That's very rude. Apologise.' Perry struggles to keep his composure.

'Why is it rude? She *is* skinny.'

'It's rude to comment on a person's size.'

'You do. The other day you said Mrs Brewster had a bum like a garage balloon. What's a garage balloon?'

Perry is beginning to look slightly hunted. 'Barrage balloon. And anyway, that was different.'

'Why?'

'Well, for starters, Mrs Brewster wasn't actually there when I said it.'

'Mummy says it's wrong to talk behind people's back.'

Perry's patience snaps. 'Go and put some clothes on, you little beasts. Mummy's right. You're very naughty. It's time for bed.'

Two mouths open in unison.

I make a pre-emptive strike. 'When I unpack my bag,

67

there may just be a little something in there for you both. But only if you do as Daddy says.'

'And as Mummy has already said, repeatedly.'

April stands at the top of the stairs. She's dressed in shorts and a sleeveless vest. Her blonde curly hair looks as if it hasn't seen a brush for a week and her cheeks are shiny from the steamy bathroom, but even so, with her tall curvaceous figure and beautiful clear skin I can see the beauty that Perry raves about. Even though I know her to be a bit of a library lurker, April's aura is that of the great outdoors. Standing above me on the upper landing she's like an Australian Valkyrie, big, beautiful and, at this moment, in spite of trying to do the polite hostess thing, somewhat bolshie.

'Up here, you two. Pyjamas and teeth. Hello, Rosa. We meet at last.' Her eyes are a light clear grey, and when she smiles she reveals a row of perfect white teeth. 'I'll be down in a minute. Perry, give Rosa a drink. Can you manage that, do you think?'

Reading between the lines, I suspect Perry's been his usual absent self during the preparations for my visit. He may love April to distraction, but that doesn't necessarily translate into action.

He also has an irritating ability that I remember of old, of blithely ignoring any snide little digs aimed in his direction. 'What can I get you?' he says cheerfully, ushering me into the cosy living room. 'White wine, sherry, or something stronger?'

'White wine would be lovely. What beautiful kids.'

He seizes on my words. 'Aren't they just? They're always cranky at this time of day. Tomorrow you'll see what they're really like.' His eyes dare me to contradict him.

'Kids whinge at bedtime. It's a given.'
'One glass of wine coming up.' He beams at me.

Hugo Mortimer smirked at Dominic Tipton's surprise and discomfort on seeing him in the Master's pew at Evensong. It was only Hugo's second appearance in the chapel since his election. As Master of the college he was obliged to attend the Christmas carol concert and that, to date, had been the sole extent of his public religious observance.

Religion, he felt, was, even in the twenty-first century, singlehandedly responsible for many of the ills that dogged our battered old world. The sooner it was stamped out, the better. In Hugo Mortimer's bright new future, Billings College would be a magnet for the best scientific brains in the world. And now the Miller Foundation in Boston was on the point of committing vast sums to build and endow a new genetics library that would be the envy of Cambridge. All he had to do was persuade the few doubters in the Senior Common Room that the underused, practically redundant Theological Library – an endowment from the pious Horace Billings himself – should be demolished and its contents donated to the University Library, and that Theology should be struck off the list of subjects offered by the college to its students.

He wished he had the power to strike Dominic Tipton off his list as well.

How he despised the man, with his evangelical posturings and his attachment to the dismal past. Not to mention his blasted refuge in Bateman Street, which seemed such a draw for god-bothered undergraduates. Doling out soup and sympathy to down-and-outs was such a highly unsuitable activity for the chaplain of a Cambridge college. The man should quit the Gown if he wanted so badly to pursue the sinners of the Town.

Hugo cursed the constitution of the college, which said that all members of the Senior Common Room had to concur with any major change to college life. He was so nearly there. The waverers like Perry Grimshaw could be brought into line, but Tipton would never agree to the double whammy – the destruction of both his beloved library *and* the Theology Department. So Hugo had to find other methods of persuasion.

Coming to chapel was one way of psyching him out. The Trojan Horse manoeuvre: attack him from within his own citadel. Hugo experienced a grim frisson of satisfaction as he noted that the man could hardly get through the service, so evidently preoccupied was he with wondering what his godless enemy was playing at.

Relieved that Evensong was much shorter than Matins, the Master couldn't wait for the mumbo jumbo to be over so that he could zap Tipton with news of the American offer. As the congregation shuffled out, he remained in his seat, relishing the disquietude on the man's face.

Finally the organ ceased and the chapel was quiet.

'A word, Chaplain.'

'Master?'

'Just to let you know that the Miller Foundation has given a very favourable response to the plans for our new library, and I've every confidence they'll stump up the major part of the money.'

'What?'

'Since I know how upsetting you find all this business,

70

I thought I'd tell you before anyone else. As a courtesy.'

'How thoughtful of you.'

'You may choose not to believe me, but I do understand where you're coming from, Tipton. Forward progress isn't always an easy thing to come to terms with, particularly when it involves difficult but necessary sacrifice.'

'It all rather depends on your definition of forward progress, doesn't it?'

Hugo forged serenely on. He was enjoying this little exchange no end. 'With the Americans on board, and funding from college alumni and some of our wealthier parents, we'll be ready to proceed. The Hugo Mortimer Library of Genetics is now a racing certainty. It *will* happen. So I hope that when we all meet tomorrow to ratify the plan, you'll see your way to finally dropping your objections.'

'I think not, Master.' The wretched man's voice was quiet but firm.

Hugo smiled brightly. 'What a pity. We shall have to find some way of helping you change your mind, shan't we?' Mission accomplished, he turned on his heel. But as he strode down the nave, he collided with a young man carrying a stack of large hymn books. They fell to the ground, several of them via Hugo's feet.

'Whoops. Sorry,' said the young man. But he didn't sound sorry, and the glacial blue stare that he bestowed on Hugo made him feel as if he'd suddenly entered a walk-in freezer. Ignoring the excruciating pain in his big toe, where one of the books had landed on a nerve, he made for the exit as quickly as his short legs could carry him.

Outside, he found himself shivering, in spite of the hot

summer sun. The stupid boy had somehow managed to mar his small but perfectly formed moment of victory.

Dominic watched his tormentor limp out of the chapel.

'I find myself thinking distinctly unholy thoughts whenever that man comes within spitting distance,' he said.

'Don't worry, Unc,' said Lucas. 'He's not going to take away your faculty or destroy the library. It's much too big a deal. Everything will be OK, you'll see. Don't forget, you have God on your side.'

Dominic wished he had Lucas's simple and absolute faith. In his experience, The Almighty was a good deal more tricky in His allegiances, and couldn't always be relied on to support the right team.

Lucas was clucking over him like a mother hen. 'Come on, it's time you put something in your stomach. When did you last eat?'

'Breakfast, I think. There hasn't been much time today. I've been trying to mobilise support from some of the other Fellows – without much success, I have to say. None of them seems to give a damn. They're all dazzled by Mortimer's ridiculous hype. They truly believe that his vision for the college will raise our profile, and make us much more capable of attracting the so-called *crème de la crème*. It's all such rubbish. What's wrong with the intake we already have, I'd like to know?'

'Chill, Unc. Please. You're going to make yourself ill if you carry on like this.'

'I can't help it.'

'I've never seen you so stressed. You're usually so on top of things.'

'It's starting to really get to me. My sleep patterns are shot to pieces. I'm not eating properly. I don't know what's happening, Lucas.'

His nephew's face radiated concern. 'You can't let that man drag you down, Unc. He's not worth it.'

'But I have to make people realise what's going on—'

'And you will, but not right now. Right now, I'm going to make you some tea, and I'm going to make sure you eat it.'

As Dominic followed his nephew out of the chapel he reflected on the changes in his life over the past months. Who would have imagined that he'd be content to let someone look after him in this way? He was the strong one, the one who'd always done the looking after. But Lucas had the knack of seeing almost before he did himself, when the almost superhuman willpower required to fulfil his college obligations as well as run R&R, was about to crack. He'd never married – one passionate but failed affair in his youth had destroyed his faith in romance. And by the same token he'd been childless, and never watched the flowering and unfolding of a new human being – blood of his blood, bone of his bone. But he hadn't minded. His students, his parishioners, his flock, especially those at R&R, were all the family he'd ever needed. Until Lucas. Lucas was the son he'd never had. This is what fathers must feel like as they grow older and weaker, he often thought. They must experience the same sense of relief and gratitude as their sons take up the baton.

'Will you stay for supper? I could take you into Hall if you like,' he offered.

'Bit busy tonight, Unc. Things to do. I said I'd let the regulars look over some shoes I picked up in a car-boot sale this morning. Robbie the Rover badly needs new gear. All he has are those holey old trainers. He'll get trench-foot if we don't do something about it.'

Dominic tried not to feel disappointed. 'Of course,' he said. 'Why don't you go now? I can manage.'

'Not so fast. I've said I'm making you tea and that's exactly what I'm going to do.'

Dominic meekly allowed himself to be led back to his rooms.

FIVE

Kill me to-morrow; let me live to-night! You should be on
the bed by this point in the scene.'

'But Lee wants me standing. Looking down on you.'

'He's wrong. Lie here beside me – or maybe straddle
me. It'd be much more intimate, like a proper married
couple. Let's try it. If we get it right, he'll see that it works.'

Stella was driving him crazy. In the confines of her small
room, it was impossible to ignore his feelings. In anyone
else her behaviour would have been a blatant come-on, but
Stella seemed blissfully unaware of the effect her close proximity was having on him.

Or was she just waiting for him to make the first move?

But every time he made up his mind to take the plunge,
those green eyes gazed at him with such lack of guile that
he concluded he was misreading her signals in a major
way.

It had been going on for long enough.

'It's time I split,' he said. 'April'll go ape-shit if I'm late
or dinner. She's got a thing about punctuality.'

'April Grimshaw?'

'Yeah.'

'What's she like?'

'OK.'

'Wasn't she originally one of Dr Grimshaw's students?'

'A graduate student, in Australia. Yeah.'

'Much younger than him then?'

'Over ten years. Where's your essay?'

'I could do with some fresh air.' She smiled at him. 'It's stifling in here. Why don't I walk over there with you?'

His heart sang. She didn't want them to part. She wanted to stay with him for a few more minutes. And hopefully, out in the open he wouldn't feel quite so horny as he did in this tiny room. He could just enjoy being with her.

'Cool,' he said, affecting a nonchalance he was far from feeling. 'We'll have to go via my room. I need to change my shirt.'

'Sure.'

But back at his room he found Flora sitting on his bed diligently mending trousers, and next to her – horror of horrors – Julie.

'Jules?'

He saw the hurt in her eyes at the sight of Stella. Her voice, in contrast, was tightly controlled. 'Surprise surprise.'

'What are you doing here?'

'Helping Flora with the costumes.' Her eyes flicked to Stella. '*Someone* had to.'

'Oh,' said Danny, wondering how the hell she'd suddenly become so intimate with bloody Flora who, to his knowledge, had never even spoken to her before today.

There followed a very long, loaded silence, which he eventually broke. 'I need to change my shirt.'

All three women stared at him.

'Don't let us stop you,' said Julie.

Feeling like a male stripper, Danny removed one shirt and replaced it with another, conscious of three pairs of eyes fixed on his bare torso. Beneath the embarrassment was a growing anger. What was Julie playing at? Here she was, his very, very ex, hunkered down in his room. Nightmare.

'Lock the door when you leave,' he muttered.

'Sure,' said Flora. 'Are you eating in Hall, Stella?'

'Later. I thought I'd get a bit of exercise and walk over to Dr Grimshaw's with Danny.'

Julie visibly flinched. But all she said was, 'I'm taking some time off work to help Flora. So I'll see you here tomorrow morning, Dan.'

Unbelievable. She'd somehow wormed her way back, not just into his life, but even into his bloody room. For the duration of the show she'd be hanging around psyching him out. Laying on the guilt trip.

Watching him.

'Let's go,' he said to Stella.

Once Danny and Stella had gone, Julie picked up the trousers she'd been mending and continued to sew.

'That must have been awful for you,' said Flora.

'What do you mean?'

'Them being together like that.'

'I told you. Danny and I are cool.'

'I saw your face when he walked in with her.'

'We aren't going out any more. He can be with who h[e]
likes.'

'Can I ask you something?'

'OK.'

'Why did you and Danny break up?'

Julie frowned. 'That's private.'

'Sorry.'

'Anyway, what's it to you?'

Flora sighed. 'I'm Stella's best friend.'

'And?'

'Forget it.'

'If you've got something to say, then for fuck's sake say it[.]'

'She's very attractive.'

'If you like that sort of thing.'

'Most men fall for her.'

'Can't think why. No tits and a bum like a board. Loo[k]
– Danny and me split up because things had run thei[r]
course.'

'Is that what he told you?'

'We both felt— No, we didn't. All right, it was his deci[-]
sion. But nothing to do with him meeting someone else.[']

Flora's voice was gentle. 'Lee Watson wanted to d[o]
Othello specifically so he could have Stella as Desdemon[a.]
He got her to agree before committing himself to the pla[y.]
She was the first person he cast.'

'So?'

'Before this term, had Danny shown any interest wha[t]
soever in acting?'

'No.'

There was a long silence.

Eventually Julie spoke. 'Fucking prick.' She burst out crying. 'Arsehole.'

Flora extended a comforting arm. 'It's all right,' she murmured. 'Let it all out – you'll feel better.'

When the storm of tears had passed, Julie scrubbed her eyes with a tissue, thoughtfully provided by Flora, and said, 'I didn't think I could ever feel worse than I did when he dumped me, but now I could fucking kill him.'

'Of course you could,' said Flora. 'It's only natural. Look, Julie, much as I appreciate your offer of help, maybe it's not such a good idea for you to do the costumes. Seeing them together will only upset you.'

Julie jumped up.

'What are you doing?'

'I'm going to crash his posh family dinner and give him a few home truths. Let his pissing godfather see what a shit his precious godson is.'

'I don't think that's a very good idea.'

'Why not?'

'Because you need to keep your dignity. It'll look so uncool if you barge in there all guns blazing.'

'Are you saying I should let him get away with it?'

'I think you should forget Danny and get on with your life. And as Jesus says, it's much better to turn the other cheek.'

'Balls to that,' said Julie.

Light evenings are a drag. It means waiting. Endless waiting. Intolerable. Itches need to be scratched here and now. Not hours later.

But tonight there are other things to think about before the dark. Plans to be made. Decisions to be arrived at. The what is clear; it's the when and how that need more thought. Lord help me in my hour of need.

SIX

Never had Cambridge been bathed in such a glow. Walking to Perry's house with Stella, Danny forgot his Julie-guilt, forgot *Othello*, forgot how much he was looking forward to seeing his mother. Forgot everything except the here-and-now with Stella.

Not that Stella was saying much.

It was one of the things about her that with a word here and a smile there she seemed to draw everything out of you and into her magic circle of enigmatic intimacy. With very little effort she somehow made you desperate to entertain and explain, to show yourself, to please her. Danny found himself laying his life at her feet. His mum, his sister, his dad killed in a road accident, his friends Dwaine and Delroy in London, his love of music, his hopes, his fears, his dreams. She seemed to suck out his soul and reflect it back at him with her oceanic eyes.

He suddenly felt embarrassed at his outpouring.

'Here we are,' he said, pointing out Perry's house. 'Where's your essay?'

She flashed him a mischievous smile. 'Come and get it.'

Waving the essay above her head, she ran off and disappeared into Perry's front garden. Danny set off in pursuit, shot through by sudden rapture – he was young, alive, and chasing a beautiful girl down a hot, dusty street.

When he reached the garden, it was deserted. He couldn't see her anywhere. Then she appeared from behind a tree.

'Look – our special tree.'

'*Our* special tree?' Danny felt fit to burst.

Her clear voice floated over to him, singing a familiar song. '*I call'd my love false love but what said he then? Sing willow, willow, willow.* It's a willow tree.' She draped one of the delicate trailing branches around her slim body.

The Willow Song. Desdemona's last lament.

His Desdemona looked anything but tragic as she leaned against the trunk, beaming at him.

'Gotcha!' Danny ran forward and grabbed at her. In avoiding him, she stumbled and fell.

'Ow!!'

He was down beside her in a flash. 'Are you OK?' Her face was very close to his, and he could feel her warm breath on his cheek, smelling faintly of cloves.

'Help me up.' But when she tried to stand, she cried out.

'What?'

'I've twisted my ankle.'

'Grab my arm. I'll help you inside. It needs cold water to take the swelling down.' She leaned into him and he trembled as he felt her body up against his.

'Thank you, Mr Moor.'

'My pleasure . . . Mrs Moor.'

Their first private joke. Danny rang Perry's doorbell,

which harmonised wonderfully with the other jubilant bells clamouring in his brain.

'Danny Boy!' Perry's expression changed to one of concern when he saw Stella leaning on Danny's arm. 'Stella. What's up?'

When Danny explained, Perry said, 'Come in. Let April have a look at it.'

Danny was about to follow them into the kitchen, when Perry said, 'Go and say hello to your mother, Dan. If she has to wait much longer to see you, I think she'll explode.'

But the exploding mother was already in the hall, sweeping him up into a huge hug. 'Darling Dan! I swear you've grown even taller in the last two months!'

'Mum . . .' He was torn between embarrassment that Stella should hear this maternal outpouring, and pleasure at the familiar sight of his mother with her wild chestnut hair and wide smile.

'Let me look at you.' She held him at arm's length. 'I like the new hairdo. Scrumptious! I've missed you so much. It's been ages.'

'Yeah.'

'Anna sends her love and says thanks for the Good Luck card.'

'It's the big exam this week, isn't it?'

'Don't mention it. I feel so guilty. I should be at home cheering her on.'

'Rubbish. She's much better off without you breathing down her neck.'

'Gee, thanks for the vote of confidence.'

Their conversation had led them into Perry and April's sitting room. As his mother folded her tall slim frame onto the sofa, she said, 'Who's the girl?' Her voice had assumed the elaborately casual tone she utilised when she was fiendishly interested in some aspect of his life but wanted to appear uninvolved.

'Stella. She's playing Desdemona.'

'Oh . . . Is she nice?'

This was Rosa code for 'Is there something going on between you and her?'

'She's OK.'

'I arrived early so I went straight to Park Parade, but Joan Watkins said you didn't live there any more.'

'No.'

'And?'

'Don't pretend you don't know. Perry's bound to have said something. Me and Jules have split up.'

'He did mention you'd had some sort of row. Is it serious?'

'You could say so. We're finished.'

'Oh.'

Danny caught the quickly suppressed flash of relief in his mother's eyes. She'd never been happy about him and Julie. She'd tried to hide it, but he was an expert in reading Rosa Thorn. Not that she took much reading. He watched with wry amusement the emotions playing across her features as she tried to decide whether to poke and pry, or whether to wait for him to spill the beans.

'Who broke it off?' She couldn't resist.

'Me.'

'Oh.'

He waited, making a small bet with himself that by the time he'd counted to ten in his head, his mother would have asked him why.

'Why?'

He'd barely reached three.

'Things had run their course. We didn't have anything to say to each other any more.'

'I'm not surprised. I thought she was—' She stopped herself.

'Was what?' Danny knew what she was going to say.

She looked shifty. 'Was far too young for such a serious relationship.'

Danny let it go. He knew perfectly well what she really thought. In spite of her egalitarian values, when it came to her own children Rosa was a bit of an intellectual snob. She felt he could do better than a shop girl. She wanted him to fall for a clever undergraduate. Wild horses would never allow her to admit this, possibly even to herself, but it was the truth.

What Danny, in his turn, couldn't admit was that she could well have a point. Life with Julie in the past few months had become very dull. He was bored rigid by her endless capacity to chat shopping, and he felt trapped by her wish to spend every free moment together. Right from the start she'd had a chip on her shoulder about his student friends, retreating into a sulky silence whenever they started discussing work, politics, culture, anything really. She dismissed it all as pretentious crap. He knew it was a defence against her own feeling of inferiority about leaving school at sixteen with only three GCSEs, and his heart bled for her pugnacious valour on the odd occasion she'd tried to take on some cocky undergraduate in argument. As a result of trying to spare her such bruising encounters, he'd never really got close to anyone in college or in his Faculty. Julie claimed all his spare time, and although in the first flush of love, this was what he too wanted, he'd gradually become aware during his second year, particularly since being out of college and living in her house, how much it had narrowed his university experience.

The breaking-point came when he noticed that Joan and Julie had both started to drop the word *engagement* into the conversation at every available opportunity. Then one day he found a wedding magazine lying on Julie's bed. He experienced the nightmare sensation of iron gates clanging shut and at that moment knew he had to finish it.

But the break-up had been harder than he would have thought possible, not least because at one level he still loved Julie. He loved her sharp street savvy and her high spirits and the way she was always fiercely on his side against the world, no matter what. And he loved what they'd been to each other; he couldn't ever forget that. And although he wanted out, his instinct to protect and care for her remained. Seeing the damage he himself inflicted on her on that fateful evening when he dropped his bombshell, made him want to hit out and defend her against his own wishes and decisions. Like punching himself in the mirror. It was very confusing.

His mother was looking at him expectantly, but there was no way he was ready to open up to her. Not yet. And not here, with Stella being mended in Perry's kitchen. Anyway, how could he describe what he was feeling when he didn't know himself? When the inside of his head was all muddle?

'You're right. We both felt we were far too young to settle down,' was all he could bring himself to say.

His mother's amber eyes were full of concern. 'Well, if

you need to talk, I'm here,' she said. 'No need to be on your own with it.'

The temptation to revert to childhood and tell her, safe in the knowledge of her unconditional love, had to be resisted. He was a man now. He was the one in charge of his life.

He smiled. 'I'm fine, Mum, really. Or rather I will be when I've got the first night of *Othello* over with.'

'My son the actor.' She laughed, reluctantly complying with his change of tone. 'Who would have thought it.'

Who indeed, thought Danny. It was going to require all the acting skills at his disposal to get through the next few days, with Julie furiously sewing costumes in his room, a witness to his burgeoning feelings for Stella.

Then Perry breezed in and announced that Stella was to join them for supper.

SEVEN

Everyone's singing for their supper. Danny and Perry are particularly on form, sparring with each other in their own lighthearted yet combative way. Tonight Danny is heartbreakingly like Rob, whose sense of humour was one of the things I most loved about him. As the evening wears on, conversation ripples back and forth like quicksilver, and the atmosphere becomes more and more hectic as people try to outdo one another with each new sparkling anecdote.

At the still centre of this loud jollity sits Stella, the radiant focus of our feast.

'Danny's a wonderful Othello,' she says to me soon after we've been introduced. 'I've never acted before and I'm finding it quite nervewracking, but Danny's always there for me. He's so supportive and helpful.'

I'll bet he is.

Every mother revels in praise for her children. I'm no exception but I try to be suitably modest on his behalf. 'It's his acting début too, so you'll both be able to help each other.'

She leans shyly towards me. 'I love the colour of your

hair. I know it's very rude of me to ask, but is it natural? It looks like one of those Pre-Raphaelite paintings. Fantastic. You're so lucky.'

I'm unforgivably vain about my dark red hair. 'Thanks,' I say, trying for casual. 'I inherited it from my mother. It's a bit of a bore though – takes ages to dry. One day I'll chop it all off and have a nice easy crop, like yours.'

'Oh no, you mustn't!' she cries in alarm. 'That would be sacrilege.'

What a discerning young woman.

Studying her over the course of the evening I realise that while saying very little, she has an uncanny ability to draw people in. She's little more than a child, yet everyone at the table seems to be aiming their *bons mots* and pithy witticisms in her direction. I'm reminded of a group of children clamouring for adult attention. *Watch me, Mummy, watch me! Over here, watch me!*

And yet she's the youngest one here. How does she do it?

I'm also getting to know April. She's very funny and we bond instantly over Perry's little peculiarities. She's also brilliant at preventing him from monopolising the conversation with various intellectual rants that can lose his audience in a fog of incomprehension. Her tactic is to gently tease and poke fun at him until he reverts back to a more humdrum plane of existence. Tonight she has to utilise this skill quite frequently, for Perry is in full professorial flood, his mercurial mind dancing from thesis to hypothesis in a pyrotechnic display of intellect, which leaves the rest of us hardpressed to keep up as the evening wears on.

'So, Stella,' I now hear her saying. 'How are you finding my husband's teaching methods?'

Stella smiles. 'He's really good.'

'Does he do that thing with his eyebrows when you mess up? That funny kind of wobble?' She gives a demonstra tion. It's Perry to a T.

Stella bursts out laughing and nods, glancing over a Perry, who groans theatrically. 'What are you trying to do my darling? Destroy all the pathetic credibility I've strug gled so hard to gain over my students?'

But April hasn't finished. 'And does he still do that little cough before saying "Young woman, I think you'll undoubt edly find blab la bla," whenever you've made an arse o yourself in one of your essays?' Again her voice is uncan nily like Perry at his most pompous and we all fall abou laughing. She's also richly comical about the difficulties o fitting into the arcane traditions of Billings College after a much more down-to-earth existence in Sydney. Perry's right she's very bright.

In the middle of dessert, the phone rings. Perry's neares to it, but discoursing eloquently about the function of womer in Shakespeare's oeuvre with relation to Desdemona, he ignores it.

'I'll get that then, shall I?' says April pointedly. Perry i oblivious.

April sighs ostentatiously. 'Let the servants at it, then, she says, leaning over him to pick up. 'Hello? Oh, right. She gives the handset to Perry. 'It's your mother.'

Frankie's voice is so loud that everyone can hear wha she's saying as clearly as if she were on speakerphone.

'Why is it always me as has to call you, you poncy littl git?'

'I'll take this in the kitchen.' Perry slips away.

GREEN EYE

His absence breaks the festive mood, and suddenly, like air being expelled from a balloon, the evening loses all momentum. Danny is goggling in an irritatingly besotted way at Stella, April has lapsed into sudden silence, and I too seem to have run out of things to say. Perry's voice rumbles away in the kitchen. We can't hear his words but we get the general picture: Frankie's giving him hell.

'Cheese, Stella?' April says eventually.

'Actually I ought to go. Big stress tomorrow. Complete runthrough of the play in the morning and the dress rehearsal later.' She throws everyone a bewitching smile and rises from the table. 'Thank you so much, Mrs Grimshaw. That was a lovely meal. And thanks for looking after my ankle, too. Please would you say goodbye to Dr Grimshaw for me.'

'I'll walk you back,' says Danny, jumping up so eagerly that he knocks his chair over. 'Great nosh, April. Cheers. Night, Mum. Break a leg tomorrow morning with the filming.'

'And you with the dress. We'll catch up later in the day . . .' But I'm speaking to his retreating back as he hurries to support the still-limping Stella.

After they've gone, April and I exchange glances. 'Now you see them, now you don't,' she says.

'What do you know about her?'

'Not a lot.'

'So Perry's her supervisor?'

'Yes. To her and her friend, Flora.'

'Individual supervisions?' Why did I say that?

'No,' she says shortly. 'Together.'

I get the feeling she wants to change the subject, but

then her voice softens. 'Rosa, there's something I want to ask you before Perry comes back.' She stops.

'Go on.' I'm intrigued.

'I've been so looking forward to meeting you. You're such an important part of Perry's life, and . . .'

'And?'

'I feel so stupid, but I need to get it out, and I'm a bit drunk so I'll just say it. I want to know all about the bits of Perry that I never can know because I wasn't there.'

Perry was right.

'What do you mean?'

'Perry knows every last boring detail about my life before I met him, but he's really buttoned up about his own past. He rarely talks about his childhood, for example, except for the odd anecdote about the mischief the pair of you got up to. He's so closed off that it drives me crazy. And I get the feeling you're the one who knows the answers.'

There are things I know, April, but Perry's childhood pain is something for him to tell you about. Not me.

'There's no big secret waiting to crawl out of the woodwork. His childhood was difficult, but you've met Frankie so you must already know that.'

'Yes. She's quite something, isn't she?'

'That's one way of putting it. Listen, April, forget Perry's past. It's not worth going into. You've made him happier than I've ever seen him. He spent most of tea-time telling me how besotted he is.'

'Really?' Her face lights up and I see again what captivated Perry.

'Oh yes. Before he met you he was a real rolling stone – a complete commitment-phobe. I used to worry that he'd

nd up a lonely old man with no family and no one to love
im. But not any more. No worries, as you say in Australia.
ve rarely seen such a sickeningly uxorious gentleman.'

She's laughing now. 'No need to overdo it.'

'Bet he still doesn't do the washing up, though.'

'See what I mean? You do know him better than anyone.'
he smiles. 'I can see why Perry loves you. I hope we can
e good friends too.'

'We surely can.'

At this point Perry reappears. 'Where are the young ones?'

'Gone back to college.'

'So early?' His dismay is comical. 'They've hardly been
ere two minutes.'

'Big day tomorrow. Runthrough and dress rehearsal. They
eed their beauty sleep.'

'Stella hardly needs any beauty sleep.'

'Oh, I don't know. A good night's kip would do wonders
or the goblin ears and the squint,' says April, quick as a
ash.

Perry grins. 'Actually, the child needs all the good looks
ne can get because she's certainly not much of a scholar.
Ier friend Flora runs rings around her. Stella's a lazy little
nadam.'

'Really?'

'She doesn't know it yet, but she's only just scraped
nrough her prelims.'

'That bad?'

'Oh yes.'

'What did Frankie want?'

Perry groans. 'To moan about Alf. How his lack of oomph
ruining her career.'

'Not again,' says April. 'That man is a saint. One day he'll snap and strangle her with one of those sequined scarves she wears in the mistaken belief that it hides her stringy neck.'

'Steady,' murmurs Perry, and I remember how he always jumps to Frankie's defence no matter what.

Alf is the Fabulous Frankie Faraday's agent and fall guy who for over forty years has selflessly loved, cherished and supported her. He'd marry her tomorrow if she'd say the word, but she never has, so he just waits patiently for the gaps between lovers when she deigns to share his bed and credit cards.

'She's given him an ultimatum. Either he gets her a TV gig or she fires him.'

'No contest,' murmurs April.

'Don't be like that,' says Perry. 'She's just worried about her career. Now she's getting on a bit, the work's drying up. Showbiz is her whole life, you know that.'

'Why does he put up with her? She's constantly trashing him.'

'She doesn't mean half the things she says. He knows that.'

'You and Alf both let her get away with blue murder.'

'She's my mother. And she's had a tough life. Where's the tolerance, April.'

'You're tolerant enough for both of us.'

I've had it with this scintillating domestic badinage. 'I'm off to bed, folks. I have to be up at the crack of dawn. And unlike the fair Stella, I do need all the beauty sleep I can get.'

'Sorry,' says Perry. 'You don't need to hear all this.'

'True,' I say. 'But I know Frankie of old. Remember, Perrygreen – your first loyalty is to your wife. Not your mother.'

'I don't need a lecture from you, Rosaleen,' Perry says huffily.

'Which is why I'm going to bed and leaving you to it.'

'Thanks, Rosa,' whispers April. 'Sleep well.'

But I don't. I toss and turn, and have bad dreams.

The stone creatures in Berkeley Court bay at the moon, their noise unheard by anyone except themselves. They watch as a boy climbs through a mullioned window and stands upright on the sill, gazing down into the shadowy depths of the courtyard.

The creatures howl. Their old, cold eyes have witnessed many things since they first took shape beneath the chisel of a Victorian master mason with a demented Gothic imagination. They have witnessed many things. Including this.

'Don't do it,' they cry. 'Life's a gift. Don't throw it back in the face of your Creator.'

But the boy isn't listening. Arms outstretched, he pitches forward into the velvet darkness, smiling as the ground comes up to meet him.

At the end of the courtyard, the fountain bubbles and foams, heedless of the boy's fall. But the liquid gushing from the mouths of the three stone serpents has lost its usual crystal clarity.

It's now a deep and vivid crimson.

EIGHT

After several hours Flora was ready to leave, but Julie wouldn't budge. 'There's fuckloads to get through,' she said, sorting and patching and mending with a stubborn intensity.

When Danny returned he was not pleased. 'Still here?'

Flora saw that he couldn't even look at Julie. 'Fun evening?' she said.

'Fine. But now I need my bed.'

'Don't let us stop you.' Julie couldn't keep the bitterness from her voice.

'You're sitting on it.'

Flora leaped up. 'Come on, Julie, our leading man must have his eight hours.'

But Julie's eyes were fixed on Danny. 'You go. I want a word with Dan.'

Danny's grim face revealed exactly what he thought of this idea.

'Sure,' said Flora. 'Look, Julie, we've done so much tonight that I can probably finish the rest myself, so there's really no need for you to take time off.'

'Don't be daft,' said Julie. 'I'll meet you here at nine and you can show me what to do next.'

Flora faced the fact that her efforts to jettison Julie weren't working. 'Fair enough,' she muttered. 'See you tomorrow, hen.'

As the door closed behind her she heard Danny say, 'Jules, I really do need to get some kip,' and Julie reply, 'You can't stand being anywhere near me, can you?'

Please God make Danny boot her out. She tried to hear more but it was impossible, and besides, eavesdropping was bad. Dom certainly wouldn't approve.

As she walked away, she thought about Danny and Stella. She recalled how Stella hadn't been prepared to spend even five minutes helping her with the costumes and how she couldn't wait to go off with Danny. To learn lines? Yeah, right. An unexpected resentment rose up inside her. She was struggling to suppress it when, out of nowhere, came a thought.

Stella had never been truly bothered about any of the men who chased after her. She'd never actually fancied any of them.

So was it just an inability to hurt people's feelings that compelled her to go out with most of them, or something else? Flora came to a startling conclusion: Stella liked toying with men. Just for the hell of it. Just because she could.

And she liked it particularly if they had something she wanted.

It could be something small like the loan of a book, or something much bigger. Flora recalled the time Stella had had her bike stolen. She'd been devastated until a graduate engineer from Pembroke had presented her with a new one, all wrapped up in pink ribbon. He didn't receive much of a return on his investment though. Stella had dumped him two days later in favour of a Geography undergraduate from Magdalene whose father owned large chunks of Leicestershire and who'd invited her to a hunt ball.

Flora's resentment faded and she felt deeply ashamed for thinking such disloyal thoughts. Stella was kind and good. And she always accepted the gifts and favours that came her way with sweet surprise and affectionate gratitude. *Flora, look what Tom/Dick/ Harry etc's given me. Look at this cool ring/ book/ dress etc. Isn't he an angel?*

The gifts and favours that came her way with unremitting regularity.

Stella had only to express a wish in the presence of one of her admirers, for that wish to be granted. It was surprising how often Stella's wishes were expressed in the presence of said admirers. Hating herself for even contemplating the idea, Flora tested it out.

Stella was definitely coming on to Danny. So if her theory was correct, she must want something from him.

Flora didn't need to be Brain of Britain to work out what Stella wanted Danny to make her look good in her first major acting role for BADS. She needed him to be the genuinely besotted Moor to her tragically beautiful Desdemona.

The hot summer night acquired a dreamlike unreality as Flora's perceptions and certainties shifted and changed. It took an alarmingly short period of time to absorb, accommodate and reflect. She looked around at Locke Court. It was the same as it had always been, and yet utterly different.

But then she realised something else: although she felt truly shocked and an absolute bitch for thinking such thoughts about her precious Stella, if she was right, there was an upside: Stella would be concentrating exclusively on Danny for the duration of the play.

Which was good.

Her thoughts were interrupted by a commotion coming from Berkeley Court. It wasn't the usual student frolicking or the bellowing aftermath of a rugger-bugger supper. It sounded serious.

Flora ran through the elaborately carved archway. What she saw turned her legs to jelly and she had to lean against the wall.

The stone serpents were vomiting blood.

It spewed from their wide mouths, cascading into the pool beneath, which was now a great gory bath that overflowed into the courtyard, where it split into red rivulets running across the paving stones before disappearing into the grass.

And, even worse, a lifeless figure was being lifted onto a stretcher by two paramedics. A group of people including the Master hovered nearby.

'What's going on?' Flora asked.

'Looks like he jumped,' said someone.

'Who?'

'Simon Smith.'

Simon Smith. One of Dom's most fervent followers. Earnest Simon, with his thin face, thick spectacles and bible permanently protruding from the pocket of his jeans. The student who, apart from Flora herself, did more shifts at R&R than anyone, trying to persuade the dispossessed

of Cambridge to accept not only God's nourishment for
the body but also His nourishment for the soul in the form
of the Holy Bible.

Simon had jumped from his window.

'Is he dead?'

'Unconscious. They're carting him off to Addenbrooke's.
Just as well he lived on the first floor. They reckon if it had
been a second-floor window, he wouldn't have stood a
chance.'

A distraught figure brushed past her and bent over the
stretcher. 'Simon, what in God's name have you done?' It
was Dom.

'I hope for your sake he didn't do it in God's name,
Dominic. I gather he's one of your merry band. Wouldn't
be very good press for you or the Almighty, would it, inspiring
young men to jump out of windows.'

The Master.

But Dom just stared down at Simon, before turning to
one of the paramedics. 'How serious is it?'

'We need to get him to hospital.'

'May I come too?'

'Certainly.'

Then, for the first time, Dom acknowledged the foun
tain of blood. He stared at it, his dark eyes glittering.
Eventually he spoke. 'This isn't Simon's blood, is it?'

'No,' someone said. 'Simon fell onto the paving-stones.
The fountain's been like that all evening.'

Dom slowly nodded. *'And the Lord said, "Behold, I will
smite with the rod that is in my hand upon the waters that
are in the river, and they shall be turned to blood",'* he
muttered to himself.

Flora saw several undergraduate onlookers sniggering. She wanted to smack them in the face. Couldn't they see how upset he was?

'The Lord doesn't enter into this particular equation,' the Master snapped. 'Someone has emptied poster paint into the water tank that services the fountain. A tiresome May Week prank, no doubt.' He glared pointedly at Dom. 'At least, that's what I'm assuming. This is the last thing the college needs. If Smith dies we'll have to cancel the May Ball, just as the people from the Miller Foundation arrive with the expectation of a unique Cambridge experience. It's most unfortunate.'

Dom glared back. 'I'm so sorry that Simon's unhappiness has caused problems, Master,' he said. 'How selfish of him not to consult your plans before he jumped.' He turned abruptly and followed the paramedics.

Suppressed whispers alerted the Master to the fact that a significant number of his student body were avidly absorbing this hostile interchange between members of the senior Common Room. 'Show's over, people,' he said. 'I'd rather no one actually saw what happened?'

And when the group muttered a collective negative: 'Precisely. So don't go spreading false rumour. I just overheard someone say that today is Suicide Sunday which, according to tradition, for those of you who don't know, is the first Sunday after Finals, when those who've failed their exams sometimes choose to end it all. Well, such foolish talk will foster all kinds of misunderstanding. The chances are that this was nothing more than an unfortunate accident. Simon will doubtless enlighten us when he recovers, which I'm sure he will. And now may I suggest you all return to your rooms. It's very late.' He strode off toward the Master's Lodge.

How dare the Master insinuate that R&R was involved in Simon's accident? Flora burned with indignation. Her friends at the refuge were the happiest and most fulfilled people she'd ever known. Doing God's will brought great joy into every single day. If Simon had problems, it was nothing to do with R&R.

When she reached her room, she looked up the stair well and saw that Stella's light was off.

Good.

Stella was an insomniac. She often kept Flora up all night listening to music. Not any more. Stella had burned her bridges along with their last mutual lamp of midnight oil. For as Flora left Berkeley Court she'd had another thought, much more dreadful than the last.

Perhaps she, too, had been used by Stella.

For what? she asked herself. Then: *Easy. A combination of servant, sounding board, wardrobe and bank.*

The more she thought about it, the more likely it seemed

She cried into her pillow for a very long time. Afterwards she stared at the ceiling. The old lonely feeling was back It had been good having a best friend. Too good to be true She'd always wondered why someone as charismatic and beautiful as Stella would want to be her best friend.

Finally she'd worked it out. But a small part of her still rejected her conclusions. Maybe she was being ridiculous and melodramatic. Maybe the shock of seeing poor Simon Smith had made her succumb to irrational late-night hysteria.

She went back over the events of the afternoon. Had she

completely misinterpreted what was happening between Stella and Lucas at the rehearsal? She sighed into the darkness. She didn't think so. She saw what she saw. Stella was definitely flirting.

How could she? Although Flora had denied it, Stella knew exactly how she felt about Lucas. How could she betray her in such a way?

Flora swallowed the hurt and started to think. According to the new theory, Stella must want something from him.

What, precisely?

She came to an even more unpalatable conclusion: Stella wanted Lucas precisely because he *was* Flora's.

Stella had spent a year helping herself to Flora's stuff. Lucas was merely the latest thing she planned to appropriate.

Julie didn't see the ambulance speeding out of the main gate. She almost fell under its wheels, but she hardly noticed. She was far too preoccupied, rerunning her conversation with Danny. He was fucking mental. All she'd wanted to do was talk about the Ball – where they were going to meet, what time, who they were sitting with – things like that. So what if she'd also mentioned the minger he'd gone off with after the rehearsal. (OK, not a minger. To be honest the girl was a real babe with her choppy blonde hair and bedtime eyes.) Why shouldn't Julie ask about her? Danny had insisted they'd always be mates, even if they were no longer lovers. As his 'mate' therefore, wasn't she entitled to ask if he was interested in the blonde? What a bastard! He'd sworn that there was no one else, but that's not what Flora said. So she had every reason to sound him out. He had

no right to go off on one like that. No right at all. *She* was
the one who'd been shat on from a great height. She had
thought they'd be together forever. Marriage. Kids. The
works. That's what he'd led her to believe. And then he'd
destroyed it all. Pissed on her dreams. And lied about it
too. So he had no right to treat her like some irritating itch
that he couldn't be bothered to scratch. *Jules, leave it. What
I do with Stella's none of your business, right? Not any more.
Just fuck off.* So harsh. That's when she lost it. 'You two-
timing piece of shit, I hope your bollocks drop off,' she'd
screamed before slamming out.

She ran over the footbridge onto Jesus Green. Her mother
had forbidden her to cross the Green alone at night. Until
recently she'd always been with Danny after dark, but not
now. He didn't love her any more. Nobody loved her. She
was all by herself on a lonely riverbank late at night. Danny
should have seen her home. When she'd run off he should
have come after her, but he didn't care. He didn't care if
she lived or died.

And neither did she.

Her mother always told her that if she was by herself, to
stick to the river path where there were generally more people.
But the large open space beckoned. To lose herself in its
black depths seemed utterly desirable as well as being the
quickest way home. She set a diagonal course across the
grass.

Then it happened.

Her face was slammed against the trunk of a tree, and
a body was pressed so hard against hers that she couldn't
breathe.

'Scream and I'll kill you,' whispered a voice, and she felt

the point of a knife against her throat. 'Do as I say and you'll be all right. Nod if you understand.'

This couldn't be happening. She was within yards of her own front door.

'I said nod if you understand, cunt,' the voice hissed.

Julie nodded.

'Wrap your arms round the tree.'

Julie obeyed. She tried to think but her brain was scrambled. Hands were pulling down her jeans and fumbling round her buttocks, squeezing and kneading them. She could hear breathing, harsh and laboured. Then there was the sharp sound of a zip and something hard and fleshy was touching her bare skin. And all the time there was the muttering. Things she couldn't hear. Didn't want to hear.

Then, unbelievably, came another sound. Barking. And something furry rubbed up against her leg. In the distance a voice shouted, 'Bozo! Here, boy! Good boy.'

But Bozo was not a good boy. What he'd found was far more interesting than anything his master had to offer. He gave a series of short yelps and jumped up and down.

Her attacker snarled and kicked out. The dog started growling.

All of a sudden the pressure pinning her to the tree disappeared. She felt a sharp pain on the back of her hand. Then nothing. She turned and saw a black-clad figure in a balaclava, running towards the river. In a lightning reflex action she pulled up her jeans and straightened her clothing.

Just in time.

Seconds later, an elderly man materialised out of the darkness.

'Bozo – here, boy!' he called. Then: 'Oh, hello there, young lady. I'm so sorry. Is he bothering you!'

It was now, as danger receded, that terror kicked in. She was aware of a high whining in her head and her legs seemed boneless. She leaned back against the tree, forcing the bark into her spine in an effort to bring herself back to normality.

'No,' she said. 'What a lovely dog.' She wondered if the man noticed her wobbly voice and whether he could see her trembling.

'Are you all right, my dear?'

His concern nearly finished her off.

'Yeah.'

'Are you sure?'

He had such a kind face. She wanted to collapse into his arms and pour out the whole story. But something was stopping her. What was it? Embarrassment? Shame? But why should *she* be ashamed? She was the victim here. That disgusting pervert had . . . She opened her mouth to speak, but what came out was, 'I've just had a row with my boyfriend. He's left me here on my own, and I feel a bit nervous. I live on Park Parade. Could you walk me over there, do you think?'

Why did she not tell the old boy the truth?

'Only too delighted, my dear. What a naughty boy. I'd be very cross with him if you were my daughter. You shouldn't be alone out here at this time of night. Not with this rapist chap on the loose.'

What she should be saying now was, 'Talking of rapists, can you call the cops, please?'

But she didn't.

GREEN EYE

All the way across the Green she tried to say the words, but they wouldn't come. When they reached her front door she thanked her kindly saviour, pretended to put her key in the lock, and then waited until he'd disappeared before collapsing. She slid down onto the doorstep, teeth chattering, body shaking. She couldn't go into the house. Not yet. She couldn't risk bumping into her mother. She couldn't face her. Couldn't face telling her what had happened. It was too horrible. Too humiliating. And her mother would go mental with her for crossing the Green alone. She would shout. And she couldn't cope with being shouted at, not at the moment. She felt sick as the cold of the porch tiles sank through to her bones. She took some deep breaths, trying to calm herself, but her mind was all chaos and confusion – the knife against her throat, the hands on her buttocks, the insane whispering. It was utterly unreal and yet at the same time unbearably real. She couldn't get her head around it. She wanted to crawl into her bed but she couldn't face the normality of life behind the neat front door. So she stayed curled up and shivering in a kind of feverish limbo as the minutes ticked by.

When she finally moved she was stiff with cold in spite of the warm summer night. But she'd made a decision.

She would tell no one what had happened.

Not the police. Not her friends. And not her mother. Particularly not her mother.

She'd finally worked out why. It was nothing to do with shame or embarrassment.

The maniac hadn't actually raped her. He'd groped her and touched her bum with his nasty little prick, and it had been really, really horrible and disgusting and terrifying. But that was it.

The act of rape had not taken place. Not technically. Not at all.

All that had happened was that some sicko had perved on her. That's all. Wasn't it?

If she reported it to the police, her mother would have to know.

And that would be a complete disaster. She'd never be allowed out alone ever again. And if she did go out, the rules and regulations would be overwhelming. It didn't bear thinking about.

And there was another thing: Mum wouldn't even answer the door to the postman in her dressing-gown. She'd go through unspeakable agony if the family name got into the papers over a rape allegation. Not to mention if the rapist was caught and Julie had to testify against him. She pictured Joan in court, her thin little body hunched in horror as she watched Julie tell the world about her attack. For Mum would be there, however agonising it was. She was always on Julie's side, no matter what. She'd never let her little girl go through it unsupported, that was for sure. Julie's heart contracted in a sudden rush of love for her mother. She couldn't put her through such an ordeal.

Life would be unbearable if she told the police.

It happened in seconds. She could forget it in seconds. She would *make* herself forget it.

It was forgotten. No one would ever know. She was way strong enough to deal with this by herself.

She opened the front door and rushed straight up to the

bathroom, where she vomited so violently that she thought she'd split open her throat.

'Julie, are you all right?' It was her mother, outside the bathroom door.

'Yeah,' she croaked. 'Dodgy burger. I'm fine now – having a shower. See you in the morning.'

Her shower lasted the best part of an hour. Even after the water ran cold Julie couldn't stop scrubbing herself. Nor could she stop staring at the cut on her hand.

The rapist's tag.

Incomplete. Interrupted.

She hoped he hadn't been watching from the shadows and seen where she lived.

She hoped he wouldn't come back to finish the rape.

What rape?

The Lord will smite with a scab the crown of the head of the daughters of Zion, and the Lord will discover their secret parts.

MONDAY 20 JUNE

NINE

People think filming is glamorous. They should try rising at half past four in the morning to go through costume and make-up before starting work as soon as day breaks so as not to inconvenience the good folk of Cambridge as they go about their daily business.

We're in Trumpington Street, by the Fitzwilliam Museum. The sight of the huge white trucks, looming out of the grey dawn, the tangles of cables and lights and the absurd number of people needed to shoot the briefest of scenes between two actors, gives me the usual tingle of anticipation in spite of the fact that I'm still half-asleep.

In *Law Lord*, the aristocratic police detective has an estranged wife (me) with whom he's trying to achieve a reconciliation. I'm an art historian, and in the scene we're shooting I'm leaving the Art History Faculty in Scroope Terrace and being accosted by my penitent husband outside the Fitzwilliam.

The upside of this early rising is seeing Buster Jones, the director, and Jeremy Antrobus who plays Roddy Langham, the detective. We had a lot of laughs in the last series and I get on particularly well with Jeremy, which can have its problems when it comes to corpsing at crucial moments on set.

Jeremy's already in make-up by the time I arrive at the truck, which serves as both wardrobe and make-up.

'Darling! What a godforsaken hour! How come you look so gorgeous, while I'm a dead ringer for dear old Charlie Laughton in *The Hunchback?*'

Nothing could be further from the truth. Jeremy's the classic Greek god public-school type with regular features that never look less than perfect. Think Anthony Andrews in *Brideshead Revisited*. The joke is that his father was a street-cleaner from Acton, and far from being brought up on the playing-fields of Eton, Jeremy learned life's lessons very early on in the gutters of Gunnersbury.

'So aren't you the Little Miss Superior! Too good to slum it at the Garden House Hotel with the rest of us.'

'Actually I'm staying with my oldest friend. He's a don at Billings College.'

'What fun, darling.'

Fun doesn't remotely describe the atmosphere at Chesterton Road. April and Perry were barely speaking by the time we finally went to bed last night. No wonder I had bad dreams. They're having a drinks-party this evening for members of the Senior Common Room and friends, including the Master. It's their first major stab at entertaining since they arrived in Cambridge, and to say April is in a tizz about it would be the understatement of the century. So last night, when Perry announced that he had an unmissable committee meeting in the afternoon, thus saddling April with all the party preparation, she quite rightly, in my opinion, lost it. I suspect he chose to reveal this in front of me, in the hope that good manners would keep her quiet. No chance. When I offered to help, it only made matters worse. April snapped, 'No way. You're our guest. This party was Perry's brilliant idea. The least he could do is help prepare for it.'

All in all I'm quite glad to be missing breakfast chez Grimshaw. *Grim* being the operative syllable here.

Jeremy's still burbling. 'I suppose staying with a Cambridge don is all good research for your character, my little art-historical blue-stocking. Is he a fuddy-duddy old academic, this friend of yours?'

'He's your typical absent-minded professor. Most of the time he doesn't even know what day it is, but when he's back on Planet Earth, he's great fun. You'd like him. He hasn't changed that much since we were children.'

'Good Lord, you've known him forever.'

'He's like a brother really, though we've lost touch a bit in recent years. He's been working in Sydney. He wasn't even able to come to Rob's funeral, and I met his wife and two children for the first time yesterday.'

'Is she Australian?'

'Yes.'

'Nice?'

'Very. They're clearly crazy about each other – most of the time. But today I suspect things might be a little strained. They're throwing a drinks-party tonight and Perry's doing a vanishing act instead of helping. April's furious and I'm caught somewhere in the middle.'

'Sounds very wearing, darling. Pack your bags and come to the Garden House.'

'Don't tempt me.'

Just then, a fraught young runner clutching a clipboard pops his head round the door. 'We're ready for you now.'

As I leave the truck I spot a lone figure cycling along Trumpington Street in the dawning light.

Dominic Tipton.

Why's he up and about so early in the morning?

Hugo Mortimer opened the door of the Master's Lodge and inhaled great mouthfuls of sweet early-morning air.

'Out you go, Dawkins,' he instructed his small fat pug.

Dawkins waddled unwillingly across the grass and relieved himself against a red-hot poker. The great outdoors was vastly overrated as far as he was concerned. Within seconds he was back on the doorstep, panting with effort. Hugo sighed. Like himself, the animal was exercise-phobic. Its greatest efforts were expended shunting between basket and food bowl. An early-morning walk along the Backs would do them both good, but it wasn't going to happen and they both knew it.

'After today, Dawkins, things will be different. When the Fellows finally approve my plans I'll have much more time. Then you and I will embark on a stringent keep-fit regime that will astonish everyone.'

Dawkins gave him a withering look and padded indoors. Hugo ventured onto the lawn and gazed back at the Lodge. After a year as Master of Billings College, he still felt immense satisfaction at his new position. The lodge with its grandiose turrets, long narrow windows and heavily carved friezes encapsulated that satisfaction. Whoever lived in such a building was undoubtedly someone to be reckoned with. His favourite

116

bit of the house was the arched doorway, flanked on either side by two pillars, each topped by a stone wolf, fangs bared against all intruders. He liked the wolves. Inside his pudgy body, he too was a lean and rampant predator, ready to destroy all opposition.

This afternoon, the Fellows would finally consent to the demolition of the Theological Library and to parting with its obsolete contents – the first step towards the construction of the Hugo Mortimer Library of Genetics.

Suffused with wellbeing, Hugo bared his own yellowing fangs at the wolves as he stepped back inside the lodge.

'Say your prayers, Tipton,' he said. 'Not that your imaginary friend in the clouds will be much help.'

Something was wrong with Julie. Joan felt it in her water. It had to be bloody Daniel Thorn. He'd hurt her again in some way. When Julie had rushed straight up to the bathroom last night, Joan ached to comfort her daughter. But Julie wouldn't let her. Joan had gone to bed and listened miserably to the girl's weeping. She was wide-awake worrying, long after the noise had ceased, when suddenly it hit her. Setting aside an eating disorder – Julie was far too fond of her food to be suffering from that – there was only one good reason why a healthy young girl should start vomiting. And it was nothing to do with dodgy burgers.

This morning Julie was very pale.

'You'll be late for work,' said Joan.

'I'm not going.'

'Do you still feel sick?'

'I'm taking a couple of days off to help with the costumes for Danny's play.'

Joan couldn't believe what she was hearing. 'You're what?'

'You heard.'

'You're squandering your precious holiday allowance helping him when he's treated you like dirt?'

'It's not like that.'

'Where's your pride?'

'I'm not helping him. I'm helping Flora, the girl who's doing costumes. It's nothing to do with Danny.'

'Does he know?'

'Yes.'

'Oh, Julie.' How would Julie ever recover if she kept hanging around that waste of space? Not for the first time Joan wished that he would vanish in a puff of smoke. She took a deep breath. 'It's not food poisoning, is it?'

'What?'

'The reason you were so sick last night.'

Julie turned even paler. Joan's heart sank. It was just as she feared.

'Don't know what you're on about.' She wouldn't look at her mother.

'I think you do, Julie.'

'I told you – it was a dodgy burger.'

Anger and intense shame flooded through Joan. History was repeating itself. Her children were the result of a five-year relationship with a married man who swore untruthfully that he'd leave his wife. She'd spent the past twenty years convincing herself and everyone else that she was a respectable widow. It was the one thing she'd been adamant would never happen to Julie. The words tumbled out before she could stop them. 'Stop lying,' she said. 'You're pregnant, you dirty little trollop. Don't deny it.'

'Don't be stupid.' Julie grabbed her bag and made for the front door.

'I'm talking to you, madam!'

But Julie was gone.

Joan was beside herself. Reaching for the phone, she dialled a number. 'Scott? We need to talk.'

Stomach rumbling, Billy Wizz staggered down Bateman Street, desperate for the bowl of porridge waiting for him at R&R. Once at the gate, he looked up at the shabby peeling porch over which hung a tattered banner: *Come inside for Rest and Relaxation with The Lord.*

Rest and Relaxation? That's what it used to be like before Preacher Man took up residence. Now *Repentance and Retribution* was more like it.

Still, listening to Preacher Man's thunderings was a small price to pay for a hot meal and somewhere to hang out all day. Added to which, there was always top totty dishing out the grub, and plenty of lads wet enough behind the ears to be tapped for fags and even the odd quid for a tinny when Dom wasn't looking. He wondered why Dom didn't resent Preacher Man trespassing on his territory. He was the genuine article when all was said and done. Preacher Man was just an old Bible-bashing loony. But then that was Dom – the loonier folk were, the more he seemed to like them. Billy remembered watching him, Flora and Lux once, coaxing Barmy Al down from the roof where he'd taken himself after one of his funny turns. They were such a team, the three of them – Flora and Dom hanging out of the window, trying to tempt him down with cigarettes, and when that failed, Lux running along the roofridge like

Spiderman, and gradually persuading him down. And then the three of them, fussing round old Al, patting and stroking him until he was calm again. Afterwards he'd seen them all laughing with relief as they relived the more hairy moments of the incident. Billy felt jealous. He wished he had friends like that – friends who worked and played and joked together, who each knew what the other was doing before they even did it. Friends you could rely on and trust.

'Morning Billy. Come on in.' It was Lux, beaming like an angel in the doorway. Why a good-looking young bloke like Lux wanted to spend his time ministering to the likes of him, was beyond Billy. But never one to look a gift horse in the mouth, he limped up the weed-strewn path, a big smile stretched over his toothless gums. 'Wotcher, Lux,' he said. 'No chance of a bite or two before prayers, I suppose?'

Lux smiled. 'No chance, Bill,' he said. 'You know the rules.'

Inside, Billy could hear Preacher Man: '*Woe unto them that are mighty to drink wine, and men of strength to mingle strong drink.*' Then Dom's gentle but firm voice: 'Thank you, Sidney. Will you join us all in morning prayers now?'

Billy sighed. Why couldn't Dom do his prayer thing after breakfast? Then Billy, full of eggs, porridge and strong sweet tea, could have a bit of shut-eye and let all the God stuff drift over his head.

'Come on, Billy, time for daily worship.' No longer an angel, but more like an officious little devil, Lux steered him into the meeting room where a motley crew of vagrants, all well-known to Billy, were on their knees, heads bowed as Dom began praying. Barmy Al lifted his head briefly and gave Billy a sly wink. Billy winked back, trying to ignore the void in his tummy. Prayers had only just started. It was going to be a while yet before he could tuck into a plate of food.

In the kitchen, Flora stirred her catering-size pan of porridge, oblivious to the hot lumps flying up and burning her hand. Preacher Man's ranting was a fitting accompaniment to her own turmoil. She should have given R&R a miss today, and had an extra couple of hours in bed before the dress rehearsal. But after her revelations of the previous night, she'd badly needed to see Lucas.

He always looked at his most gorgeous in the dawn light, and when it was only the two of them, he would invite her up to his room for a quick coffee before they started work. But today he hadn't come anywhere near her, merely waved absentmindedly as he swept the floor of the meeting room.

And when, finally, he'd poked his head around the kitchen door, it wasn't to chat.

'Can you get me a ticket for *Othello*? I told your friend Stella I was coming. I promised her I'd be there, and I don't have time to go up to Billings and buy one.'

A high-pitched humming started up in her head, and a sour, sick churning in her gut.

'I didn't know you were a fan of Shakespeare,' she said.

He grinned. 'Well, there you go. You learn something new every day.' He looked more closely at her. 'Not a problem, is it?'

'No,' she said.

'Cool.' And then he'd gone again.

The humming in her head was replaced by a sudden

strong pulse, battering remorselessly at her right temple. *Stella had asked him to go and see* Othello?

She became aware of an acrid smell. Burning porridge. She turned off the gas and stared into the bubbling depths now flecked with brown. Spoiled, she thought. All spoiled. She transferred the porridge into another pan. Then she rummaged around the chaotic cutlery drawer until she found what she was looking for.

A sharp knife.

She plunged it into the bottom of the discarded pan and scraped it repeatedly across the burned surface, watching the blackened bits curl up as she did so.

TEN

Danny was ten years old again, and he'd just won a prize on the rifle range at the Bank Holiday Fair on Hampstead Heath. He was choosing a doll for little Anna, who was giddy with excitement. There were two dollies on offer: one dark, the other fair. As he dithered, Anna said, *Danny, look!* and Danny saw that the dark-haired doll's vacant blue eyes were spouting a great waterfall of tears, which gushed down its smooth plastic cheeks and onto his shirt, soaking it through. Then his dad was there. Alive again. *Watch me, Dan. I'll show you how to shoot properly.* But instead of aiming his rifle at the targets, he turned the gun on himself and before Danny could stop him, he pulled the trigger. There was a loud bang; and then Danny was back in his room at Billings College.

Someone was hammering on his door.

'Wake up, sleepyhead.'

Danny, still raw from the dream, groaned as reality kicked in. Too much reality. 'Hang on,' he shouted. He threw on a dressing-gown and opened the door. There stood Flora and Julie.

'I'm off for a shower,' he mumbled, grabbing his clothes

'Great dressing-gown,' said Flora.

Danny winced. The dressing-gown had been a Christmas present from Julie – a Calvin Klein effort from the expensive boutique where she worked. She'd given it to him the night they were reunited after the Christmas Vac. He remembered parading up and down in a catwalk parody And then Julie removing it, saying she wanted to see what was stirring beneath its designer folds. Now, as he caught her eye, he knew that she too was remembering.

'Can we talk?' she said.

Why wouldn't she just accept that it was over? Talking was pointless. He was about to deliver a curt reply when he saw the tension in her pinched face, and a surge of guilty pity killed his anger stone dead. But he still couldn't face her.

'I'm a bit rushed. Catch you later.' He ran upstairs to the bathroom, feeling her eyes burning into his back. He felt like a shit. He *was* a shit. But what was the point in flogging a dead horse? The sooner Julie accepted that he wasn't going back to her, the sooner she'd be able to move on and find someone else. Someone who'd be much better for her than him.

Why did she have to look so sad?

Later, in Hall, as he ploughed his way through a rubbery fried egg and a slice of over-cooked bacon, his thoughts turned, inevitably, to Stella. How easy she was to talk to. On the way back to college after leaving Perry's last night he'd found himself telling her all about the Grimshaws. How his mum and Perry had been brought up together because Perry's flaky mum had put her career as a singer

ay above childrearing. How much Perry adored his mum,
i spite of her neglect. How Rosa had thought that Perry
ould never marry because he was too much under
rankie's thumb. How surprised everyone was when he'd
nally got it together with April, and how touching it was
) see his devotion to his kids. Stella listened, saying very
ttle, her magnetic green eyes drawing him out to further
onfidences.

By the time they'd reached her room, Danny was in a
ate. Panic and desire had jostled together in his head. Would
ie invite him in? If she did, it would mean only one thing.
. thing that he both longed for, yet feared. He'd sworn to
ilie that there was no one else. And in all honesty, he didn't
ant another involvement. Not yet. He wanted a summer
ith the lads, and no girlie emotional shit whatsoever.

But when Stella looked at him he knew he would do
hatever she asked.

In the event, nothing happened. She'd unlocked her
oor and turned to face him. '*Good night, good night.
Ieaven me such uses send, not to pick bad from bad, but
y bad mend.* Thanks for walking me back, Danny.' She'd
iven him one of her heartstopping smiles and then a
noment later he was looking at a closed wooden door,
ying to make sense of his feelings. He was still trying now
1 Hall as he demolished his greasy breakfast, when suddenly
e felt something tickling the back of his neck.

'*Alas, why gnaw you so your nether lip?*' There she was,
norning-fresh and more beautiful than ever.

'Do you always speak in Shakespearean quotations?'

'Only when I'm suffering from dress-rehearsal nerves.'
he sat down on the bench, face inches away from his, and

Danny had to stop himself from leaning forward and kissin
her perfectly glossed lips.

'We could do lines again if you like.' The green eye
gazed hopefully into his.

Danny swallowed hard. 'Lee wants us onstage in te
minutes.'

'So why don't we go to our marital bed and run throug
our scenes until everyone's ready to start? People are boun
to be late. Flora's never been on time in her life. Neithe
has Shareef.'

Danny couldn't think of any valid objection to lying or
a bed with Stella, so they made their way to the Fellow
Garden and lay down under the canopy of the vast doubl
bed, which dominated the centre of the stage.

Which is where Julie found them some time later, whe
she entered the garden carrying armfuls of costumes.

Danny told himself that there was no good reason wh
he shouldn't be going through lines with Stella. And n
good reason why they should not be participating in thi
innocent activity stretched out on Desdemona's bed.

But it didn't feel innocent.

Julie didn't think it was either, judging by the look or
her face.

Then Flora appeared. 'Julie, let's make camp under tha
tree. I can help when I'm not onstage. Emilia isn't a hug
part so I'll be with you most of the time.'

Shareef's squeals shattered the air. 'Lee, admit it. It's
set to die for. Look how the gold thread in the canopy'
catching the light! Exquisite! I can't wait for my parents t
see what I've done. My mother's like me. She has a ver
highly developed aesthetic sensibility. She'll adore this.'

'Stop yakkin', Sharon – you're doin' my head in. OK, people, let's kick off or we won't get through before lunch. Places, please.'

Stella held out her hand for Danny to pull her up. The sun flooded the garden with hot summer light.

Dominic watched Lucas serving mugs of sweet tea to a group of dishevelled old men who were playing dominoes in the corner of the meeting room. Every day he gave thanks to God for the miracle of the boy's re-appearance, shabby rucksack on his back, with his tousled blond hair and all-embracing smile. *The Prodigal returns, Uncle. Kill the fatted calf.* From that moment Dominic had lost completely the intense loneliness that had become such second nature to him that he hadn't even been aware of its existence.

And Lucas's devotion to R&R, if anything, exceeded his own. Over and above their normal activities he regularly organised fundraising events, was gradually redecorating the building, and had visited all the Christian associations in the other colleges and persuaded many new people to join them. Since he'd arrived, R&R had acquired twice as many volunteers. Dominic was filled with gratitude and hope. For the first time there was a future to plan for that didn't just involve himself. He didn't like admitting it, but before Lucas the strain of combining his chaplaincy of Billings with his teaching commitments while at the same time running R&R, was becoming too much. Although only forty-eight, he'd sometimes felt like a hundred and five. But now Lucas had taken over the day-to-day running of the refuge, a great weight had been lifted from his shoulders.

He couldn't believe how much in accord they were. Both

wanted to promote a simpler way of living, where the haves willingly provided for the have-nots, and pleasure came from sharing and helping others rather than exploitation and the accumulation of possessions. He knew it was a largely futile exercise, trying to hold back the remorseless tsunami of greed and cupidity which threatened to swamp all that was good in the world, but with Lucas at his side, he felt he had the strength to keep on trying.

In spite of Hugo Mortimer.

Today he couldn't stop thinking about the forthcoming college committee meeting, and what Hugo would be trying to do. The man was a destructive force, however well he dissimulated in the name of progress. The Fellows of the college must be made to understand exactly what they were doing by signing away the library, and scrapping the Theology Department.

'Why so gloomy, Unc?' Lucas loomed over him.

'Wondering what to say at the committee meeting this afternoon. I can't seem to think straight at the moment.'

Lucas laid a hand on his shoulder. 'It'll be all right, believe me,' he said. 'These things have a habit of sorting themselves out.'

The feel of his nephew's hand, heavy on his jacket, and the boy's comforting words, so calm and reassuring, almost made Dominic weep. 'Bless you, Lucas,' he said. Then he remembered something he'd been meaning to ask for some days. 'How are you getting on with Flora?'

'She's great.'

'She likes you very much, you know.'

'She's a very special person. I'm very fond of her.'

'And?'

'And what?'

A wave of disappointment washed over Dominic.

'Are you matchmaking, Unc?'

Dominic laughed. 'You noticed?'

Lucas smiled. 'You can't make people fall in love, you know.'

'She likes you a lot. I've seen her looking at you.'

'She's just a friend.'

'I'm not so sure *she* feels that way.'

'Really?'

'You'd better make your position clear. I don't want her hurt.'

'I'd never hurt Flora. She's a wonderful person with wonderful qualities, and one day she'll be a wonderful wife. But at the moment she and I are just good friends. That's what both of us want.'

Lucas clearly felt it was time to end this particular conversation. He wandered back to the games players and congratulated Billy Wizz on winning the dominoes tournament. Dominic watched absentmindedly. Lucas hadn't told him exactly what he wanted to hear, but neither had he completely ruled it out of court. The phrase *at the moment* stuck in his mind. Yet something in his nephew's eyes made Dominic think the boy wasn't being completely honest. Young people, in his experience, could be particularly secretive about their love lives, and only declare themselves openly when they were sure the other person was as committed as they were. Flora was perfect for Lucas. Who knew what the future might bring?

* * *

VENA CORK

'*Come down and sit in the dust, O virgin daughter of Babylon, sit on the ground; there is no throne: for thou shalt no more be called tender and delicate. Thy nakedness shall be uncovered, yea thy shame shall be seen; I will take vengeance and I will not meet thee as a man.*'

ELEVEN

April's day was fast disappearing down the toilet. The kids were so hyperactive that she decided they'd simultaneously developed Attention Deficit Disorder in the night. And Perry had sloped off to Billings straight after breakfast.

Then the cleaner cancelled. And the nursery phoned to say that they had a burst pipe and would be closed for the day.

If only she hadn't refused Rosa's offer of help.

She spent the morning lurching from squabbling children, to house cleaning, to the preparation of nibbles for the party.

And underneath it all was something else, nagging away like bad toothache. Something she'd rather die than confess to anyone.

Perry and the rest of the world saw her as bubbly April, never short of an opinion, or a witty riposte, always game for a laugh. Confident, competent April. And it was all true. In most areas of life, April shone. She'd bounced into Cambridge a mere three months ago, and already she was chairperson of the Parent-Teacher Association at the children's nursery, she'd started a book group at the local library, and she'd joined the Billings College Women's Tennis and Athletics clubs and taken part in several competitions. She possessed a strong belief in self-improvement which, added to a formidable brain and healthy good looks, was a winning combination. If you weren't much good at something you could always improve if you worked at it, she believed. Parenthood, for example. It was a struggle, but one that she knew she would win eventually.

But there was one area of her life over which she had no control, where she felt as helpless as a baby.

She'd never understood why someone as handsome and clever as Perry had fallen in love with her. Half the eligible women at the University of Sydney had been after him, so she'd been stunned when he'd asked her out. He could have had the pick of the bunch, but he'd chosen her. She hadn't ever told him how she felt – she knew that fit and feisty was much more to his taste than doe-eyed and dependent. She let him think he was doing all the running, and even when she allowed herself to be caught, she never confessed. She liked to think she had it under control most of the time, but even now, after more than five years of marriage, the insecurity was still there, ever ready to surface in spite of all evidence that Perry adored her and had never looked twice at anyone else.

Until this girl.

April had never seen Perry behave as he had last night when that girl had invited herself to dinner. In her saner moments she was able to recognise that her hostility towards any female to whom Perry addressed more than two words had its root in her own neurosis, which she knew full well was, predictably and boringly, to do with the fact that her father had walked out on the family when she was twelve years old. But this girl was different.

Perry's response to this girl was different.

April knew, in the deepest part of her being, that here was something worthy of her hysteria. This was not a false alarm. This was what she'd been in training for from Day One of her life with Perry.

'I don't like pasta. I want a sausage. With my own little stick.' Hector tipped his lunch on the floor and started skidding round on the mess. Cassandra meanwhile had already seized a party sausage, rammed it into her mouth and then jabbed the stick into Hector's arm. The resultant wailing was so deafening that April didn't hear someone come into the room until a familiar voice said, 'Anything I can do?'

That girl again.

In her kitchen.

She was kneeling down and talking to the kids in her low, musical voice, and, unbelievably, they'd shut up. Moreover, the expression on Hector's face was one of dawning adoration.

April felt like plunging her vegetable knife into the girl's cutesy crop.

'Who are you?' Cassandra, at least, retained a vestige of suspicion.

'Stella.'

'That's a funny name.'

'It means star.'

'Have you fallen out of the sky?'

'Perhaps.'

133

'You do twinkle,' said Hector dreamily. 'You twinkle like in the song.'

Pass the sick bag.

'Why do you know us?' Cassandra again.

'Your daddy is my teacher.'

'My daddy isn't here. Mummy says he's never spigging here when he should be.'

'I came to dinner last night when you were asleep and I left some make-up in your bathroom, and now I need it for a play I'm doing.'

'What's a play?'

'A story. Where people pretend to be other people.'

'What's your story about?'

'About a silly man who was so jealous of his wife that he killed her.'

'What's jealous?'

April finally found her voice. 'That's enough, Hector.'

Stella beamed at her. 'I did ring, but no one heard. The door was open so I just came in. I hope you don't mind.'

'That's OK.'

'I don't suppose you noticed my mascara on your bathroom shelf?'

Her physical proximity made April's skin crawl. 'No.'

'I'll get it for you,' said Hector.

This was a first. Hector never offered to help anybody with anything.

'It's OK, little one,' Stella said. 'I know the way.' She slipped noiselessly from the room. The kids stared at the space in the air previously occupied by her body.

'Close your mouth, Hector, or you might swallow something nasty,' snapped April.

Within moments Stella was back, waving a small black cylinder. 'Got it,' she said. 'Thanks a lot, Mrs Grimshaw.' She ruffled Hector's hair. 'What lovely kids. You must be very proud of them. If you ever need a babysitter . . .'

'That's very sweet of you, but we normally use the girl next door.' April spoke between gritted teeth. The sight of the three blond heads so close together had conjured up a nightmare vision of the future: Stella talking to some unspecified person. *Yes, we do look alike, don't we. But they're not mine. They're my stepchildren. From my husband's first marriage.*

She jerked herself back to reality. Stella was speaking. 'I'm off. Lee says we're to rest before the dress rehearsal. Thanks again. I'll see myself out.'

And then she was gone.

'Twinkle twinkle little star,' sang Hector.

Cassandra pouted. 'I don't like that lady,' she said. 'I think she's pooey.'

April knelt down. 'Have another sausage, possum. In fact, why not have several.' She gave her daughter an extra big hug.

Later, passing Perry's study, she noticed that on his desk was an envelope, addressed to him. It was propped up against a book so that he couldn't fail to spot it.

One of April's more unnecessary activities that morning had been to tidy and dust this very desk.

There had been no envelope at that point.

After the runthrough, Flora had excused herself to Julie. 'Gotta split for an hour. I'm doing a lunch-time shift at R&R.'

'R&R?'

'The refuge in Bateman Street. Dom runs it.'

'Who?'

How could the girl not know Dom?

'The college chaplain. I thought you'd know that, what with your mum working in the office.'

'My mum's got her life, I've got mine. She don't tell me nothing what happens in this place. She knows I'm not bothered. She knows it drives me mental when she starts rabbiting on.'

'Dom's a great man. You should come to R&R one day. You'd find it very inspiring.'

'Yeah, well. I ain't into religion.'

'You should see the good work he does with the home-less.'

'Then tell him to do something about those smelly old piss-heads who hang around the bus station. They're a total fucking disgrace.'

Flora sensed she was onto a losing wicket in her bid to rouse Julie's social conscience. In any event, she realised that Julie had more pressing things on her mind. At the end of the runthrough, Stella had made a quick exit, alone, and Danny, looking more than a little put out, had slouched away muttering into his mobile. He didn't give Julie a second glance. Flora had seen the misery in the girl's eyes.

Stella hadn't said where she was going. She usually let Flora buy her lunch, but today she was off without a word, like a rat up a drainpipe. Flora was suddenly possessed with the absurd notion that she was meeting Lucas. She recognised it as irrational – why on earth should Stella suddenly be meeting him? She hardly knew him. But the more she hought about it, the more it got to her. She had to know. She'd told Julie a fib. She wasn't on duty at R&R, but Lucas was. If Stella had arranged to see him, that's where they'd be – in Lucas's room, at the refuge. The thought made her rantic.

But when she arrived at R&R and looked for Stella's oike, it wasn't there. Lucas was though, and gave her the smile that, as usual, melted her insides. He was handing out sweets to a group of old men. One of the things she loved about him was his habit of offering sweets to the homeless, in the belief that they were a realistic distraction from the pleasures of alcohol.

'Flo! I was just thinking of you.'

'Of me?' Her spirits rose.

'Did you get that *Othello* ticket?'

The bloody ticket again. She felt it burning a hole in her pocket and wanted to rip it into pieces in front of him.

'I must be there for the first night, you see.'

'Why?'

Lucas grinned. He was standing very close to her. 'Why do you think? I want to see you strut your stuff. So have you got it?'

'Yes.'

'Great. How much do I owe you?'

'It doesn't matter.'

'Sure it does. I always pay my debts.' He felt in his pocket. 'Shit, my money's in my other jeans. Come upstairs and I'll get it for you.'

Flora loved his room. It was very simple – just a cupboard, a chest of drawers, a wooden chair, and a futon which served as bed at night and sofa during the day. And it smelled of

Lucas – musky and spicy with a hint of pear drops. She'
taken several photos of it one morning when Lucas was awa
somewhere, and stuck them in one of her Lucas albums
Sometimes she'd look at them and imagine how she'd redec
orate the room when she lived there with him. As his wife

'Take a pew,' said Lucas, indicating the futon.

She went hot all over when he sat down next to her
'What's this?' she said to cover her confusion, picking u
a book that was lying on the floor beside her.

'It's an illustrated Bible I found at a car-boot sale the
other day. It only cost me fifty pee. It's fantastic. Look a
these plates. They're all Old Master reproductions. See thi:
Botticelli Virgin? Isn't she perfect? And this one by Bosch
– this is one of my favourites – his vision of Hell. It's so
detailed. It must have terrified people way back when he
painted it. Given them a really good reason to be good.'

Flora was hardly able to focus, so aware was she of hi:
arm leaning against hers.

'And this,' he said, turning to a painting by Rubens o
Delilah cutting off Samson's hair. 'Poor Samson, completely
unmanned by love.' He shook his head. 'All his strength
was useless against that female black magic . . .'

The voluptuous bodies in the painting made Flora fee
quite faint. Why was Lucas showing her such things? Wha
was he trying to tell her?

Then it came to her: he was shy. He came across a:
supremely confident, but maybe it was all an act. Showing
her this sexy painting was a way of signalling how he reall
felt about her. He wanted her to make the first move, wanted
to be sure she liked him before confessing his own feelings
In that case, it was up to her not to disappoint. Her hear

as hammering in her chest as she tried to summon up the
ourage to kiss his beautiful mouth.

Then she heard a familiar voice.

'Am I interrupting?' In the doorway stood Stella.

Lucas jumped. 'Stella. What can I do for you?'

She pouted. 'That's a tough one. Let me think about it.'

Flora felt as if someone had thrown a switch and instan-
aneously disconnected the current between herself and
Lucas. 'What do you want?'

Stella raised her eyebrows in surprise. 'You, of course,
idiot,' she grinned. 'Julie said you were here. Lee's starting
the dress rehearsal early. He asked me to find you.'

'Oh.' Flora felt stupid. Wrong-footed. Confused. Silence
echoed round the shabby sunlit space. 'I'd better come then.'

'Yeah.' Stella leaned, unmoving, against the doorframe.

'I'll catch you up,' said Flora finally.

Stella looked from her to Lucas, a faint smile on her
lips. 'See you outside, then. Bye, Lucas.' She clattered off
down the stairs.

'Bummer,' said Lucas. 'But no sweat – I'll see you later,
OK?'

It wasn't OK. She couldn't cope with this seesaw of
emotion. Up and down from second to second. She couldn't
stand it.

'What do you think of Stella?' There. She'd said it.

Lucas stared at her, unsmiling. 'She's great. But then
she would be – she's your friend and you have very good
instincts' He peered through the window. 'She's waiting.
You'd better go. Did you say you'd got that ticket?'

'Yes,' said Flora. She pulled it from her pocket and gave
it to him.

'Cheers. How much do I owe you?'
'Have it on me,' said Flora dully.

Elbowing his way through the lunch-time drinkers in th
Eagle, Danny saw his mother straight away. She was in th
centre of a rowdy group, telling some animated tale tha
had everyone in stitches. The man laughing loudest was
famous face: the actor Jeremy Antrobus. Danny felt sudden
awkward and young. When his mother had suggested lunc
he hadn't bargained on the rest of the film company bein
there. He was steeling himself to join them when his mothe
spotted him. She waved, said something. Everyone stared
Danny wanted to sink through the floor. But to his immens
relief, his mother grabbed a large straw bag and made he
way across to him.

'I thought we'd have a picnic on the Backs,' she beamed
'Get some fresh air.'

They made their way down Senate House Passage, ove
Garret Hostel Lane Bridge and found a spot on the banks o
the Cam where they could watch all the punts jostling fo
position in the crowded river against the stunning backdro
of King's Chapel. There was a holiday atmosphere in the air
students and tourists alike enjoying the bright June sunshine

'How was the filming?' he asked.

'Good, apart from the excruciatingly early start. All
want to do now is sleep. How I'll survive Perry's party tonigh
I really don't know. How was the run-through?'

'Terrible. I forgot most of my lines, and the ones I remem
bered sounded like they were being spoken by a larg
wooden plank.'

'First run-throughs are always awful. The dress rehearsa

ll be better.' She looked at him quizzically, a look he
new of old. She was on a fishing expedition. 'Unless, of
ourse, your mind's not really on the job . . .'

'Why shouldn't it be?'

'I thought that maybe playing opposite the lovely Stella
ight be a tad distracting.'

'Mum . . .'

'OK, OK – I know. None of my business.'

'Too right.'

'It's just that you seemed quite smitten last night at Perry's.'

'No.'

His mother laughed. 'Danny Thorn, you couldn't take
our eyes off her.'

Danny sighed. Once his mother got her teeth into some-
ing, she never let go. And this week's something was
early his love life. He also knew that the questions about
tella were not idle chit-chat. She had an opinion – which
e was undoubtedly about to share with him.

'So what happened with Julie? You don't have to say if
ou don't want to . . .'

That was another of her tactics. Ask a question about some-
ing unrelated, but something she nonetheless wanted to
now, and catch him on the hop so that he'd say something
nguarded.

'. . . but you do know I'm here for you, if you need a
ounding board.'

His mother was good to talk to, but at the moment he
eeded to sort his life out for himself. Anyway, she was his
other. He couldn't share the ins and outs of his sex life
ith his bloody mother.

'Things are a bit complicated, Mum.'

'Try me.'

'Not now.'

'Fair enough.'

There was a short pause. Danny thought he'd got aw: with it. He should have known better.

'I hope you were kind to Julie when you broke it off.'

'Kind?'

'I hope you let her down gently.'

Danny laughed. 'There's no gentle way of breaking c a long relationship. I did my best not to hurt her.'

'What does she feel about you and Stella?'

'There is no me and Stella.'

'Be careful, Dan.'

'What do you mean?'

'I don't know.' Rosa frowned. 'Just a feeling in my gut

Danny groaned. He could really do without his mother mystical gut.

'You didn't like Julie, did you? I bet you're thrilled bits that we've broken up.'

'Dan!'

He was being unreasonable, but he couldn't stop himsel All the self-disgust he was feeling spilled out over his mothe instead.

'You thought she was a bit of a slag.'

'Danny!'

'There's a lot more to Julie than you ever gave her cred for. She really loves me, you know, and I feel like sh dumping her.'

'Danny, I never said I didn't like Julie—'

'You'd disapprove of any girl I went out with. You ju can't cope with me having adult relationships.'

GREEN EYE

His mother looked as if he'd punched her in the face. 'There's nothing adult about you at the moment.' She stood up abruptly. 'I'll see you later.'

Danny watched her stomp off. He knew he should apologise, but a part of him was perversely glad he'd alienated her. It meant he could get on with his life without interference. He refused to feel guilty. What was it about women that conjured up that emotion so easily?

Martine Daumier and her new boyfriend Sven had cut class. Mr Russell at the Russell School of English regularly sent them to sleep with his long-winded and unnecessary perorations into the intricacies of English grammar. This morning it had been the function of the adjectival clause in the structure of the sentence. So on this lovely June afternoon, they decided that their studies would be far better served if they conducted a one-to-one *viva voce* in the Cambridge University Botanic Garden.

They had picked out a particularly private spot near the winding stream in the bog garden to test-run their theory, and Sven was just making very satisfactory inroads into Martine's clothing, when they first heard the noise. It came from behind a large clump of ferns. Sven was up for ignoring it but the sound acted like a bucket of water on Martine's libido.

'*Écoute*, Sven.'

'Martine, *chérie*. Let me show you how I feel about you.'

But Martine couldn't concentrate with the pitiful moans ringing in her ears. '*Ça suffit*,' she said and, jumping up, made her way through the ferns.

'*O Mon Dieu*,' she whispered.

A girl lay face down on the ground, skirt round her waist, pants round her ankles. Ugly purple bruises had already begun to develop all over her legs. At the sound of Martine's voice she turned her head. 'Help me,' she whispered, stretching out her hand.

On the back of it, Martine could see a zigzag slash, still bleeding profusely.

TWELVE

Back at Perry's my plans for some serious shut-eye before the party are well and truly scuppered. Chaos reigns. The children run around naked, shooting at each other with giant water-pistols, the living room looks as if it's been ransacked by a tribe of baboons, the kitchen is covered in half-prepared food, most of it on the floor, and in the middle of it all sits April, puffing on a cigarette.

'I didn't know you smoked,' is all I can think of to say.

'I don't.'

I bribe the kids to stay in their room with chocolate and a DVD, and make April a cup of tea. Then I do a lightning tidy of the living room, sweep the kitchen floor and load the dishwasher before finally saying, 'What's up?'

April points to an envelope on the table, smeared with avocado dip and tears. I pull out two tickets and a short note.

Dear Dr Grimshaw,

It was so kind of you to invite me to dinner last night. I'd like you and Mrs Grimshaw to have these tickets for Othello *as a small thank you.*
  Best wishes, Stella

'She seems very appreciative,' I say carefully.

'Doesn't she just,' says April.

'Why are you so upset?'

She waves the envelope at me. 'Look.'

I look. It's written in pink Biro, the style florid and girlish.

'The "i" in Grimshaw has a little circle above it instead of a dot,' I venture. 'Isn't that a sign of some character defect? I'm sure I once read that somewhere.'

'Dr Grimshaw.'

Sorry? 'I think I might be missing the point here, April.'

'Not *Dr and Mrs Grimshaw*. Why isn't it addressed to both of us? And why didn't she give it straight to me when she came round this morning? Instead, she sneaked into his study behind my back and left it there for him to find.'

'But the tickets *are* for both of you.'

'That's where she's so clever. She's excluded me without excluding me, if you see what I mean.'

'I'm sure she didn't mean to.'

'I know what I know, Rosa.'

'What are you saying? That she's after Perry?'

April looks as if I've smacked her in the face. 'Why? Is that what *you* think?'

It's a minefield. 'No, I don't. I just thought that was what *you* thought. And if you do, then stop right now. Even if

146

she does have some sort of adolescent crush on him, so what? Perry loves you. You know he does.'

'Does he?'

'Is the Pope Catholic? Let's get going on this party, or people will think they've come on the wrong day.'

Now she's got things off her chest, she feels better and we start to make inroads into the mess, and prepare the house for the party. It takes us a couple of hours, at the end of which we're shattered.

Then we hear the key in the door. April's face lights up. 'It's Perry. He must have finished early.'

She's potty about him. I can see it in every line of her body. I remember when the sound of Rob's key could make my heart do a little jig. Days long gone. *Don't think about it, Rosa.*

Then I realise that her joy has been replaced by dawning horror.

'Not much of a welcome, I must say.'

The doorway is filled by a swaying figure in five-inch white stilettos. A blast from my far distant past.

The Fabulous Frankie Faraday.

She squints shortsightedly across at me and I remember that although she's as blind as a bat, she refuses to wear specs or contacts.

'Bugger me, if it isn't our Rosa. Bloody hell, girl, you look like a long drink of water wi' nothing on. You want to put a bit of flesh on them bones, or by the time you're my age no man'll look at you twice. You're no spring chicken any more, you know, and now you're a widow, you mun' cultivate your assets or mark my words, you'll end up a lonely scraggy old bag.'

'Nice to see you too, Frankie.'

No danger of anyone not looking at her twice. Although she's well into her sixties, her stridently golden hair is swept into a tottering French pleat secured by a diamanté slide. Her electric-blue eyelids are thickly lined with black kohl, and the bloom on her cheeks is most definitely not the bloom of youth. She's wearing a low-cut polka-dot two-piece in egg-yolk yellow, which at one end displays her crêpey cleavage and at the other her bony knees and thighs freckled with liver spots.

April finally speaks. 'I wasn't expecting you.'

Frankie crushes her in an ostentatiously affectionate embrace. 'Didn't Perry tell you? He'd forget his head if it were loose, that lad. It's what comes of being so clever, I suppose.'

'How did you get in?' April doesn't bother to hide her displeasure.

'Didn't he tell you that, either? He doesn't tell you much, does he, that husband of yours. He had a key cut for me on my last visit – when he said that I was to regard his house as my house. Now, where are my precious babbas?' She sweeps out of the room and upstairs, where Hector and Cassandra come rushing out of their room, shouting, 'Granny Granny Granny! Hooray!'

'She's popular with someone then,' I whisper.

'Oh yes,' says April. 'They love her. She spoils them rotten. What the hell is she doing here? She knows we have a full house this week.'

As we speak, Frankie's saying in a voice that carries all the way down to where we are sitting, 'Poor chickabiddies, has Mummy made you stay in your room all day? Never

148

mind. Granny's here now. Let's see whether there's something in my suitcase for my special little sweethearts.'

'Perry?' April is already on the phone. 'Guess who's here – apparently at your invitation. Your mother. With a large suitcase. Joke? I wouldn't joke about a thing like that. I need you to come home and deal with her. I don't care whether you're voting for the whole of Billings College to be demolished. If you're not back soon I might just book the next flight Down Under and you'll have to organise your party yourself.' She slams down the phone and turns to me. 'He claims he didn't invite her. Says she must have misunderstood something he said. Bastard. I don't believe him.'

'Come on, April. Perry's not perfect but he's no liar.'

'When it comes to her he is.'

From my long-ago experience of living with Perry and Frankie, I have to admit that she's right. Frankie has a way of twisting Perry round her little finger. He's never been able to deal with her lethal combination of neglect and protestations of eternal love.

Then April brightens. *'You're* here!' she exclaims.

'I believe so. To the best of my knowledge.'

'So she can't stay.'

'Why not?'

'You're using the spare room.'

But right on cue Frankie's voice booms down from above. 'Rosa, come and shift your bits and pieces.'

April and I stare at each other.

'Sorry, I didn't quite catch that,' I shout back.

'I can't sleep on this camp bed in the babbas' room. Not with my back. You're younger than me. You'll be as right as ninepence.'

April gasps. 'I couldn't possibly ask Rosa to bunk in with the children,' she roars up the stairs.

'She doesn't mind, do you, pet?'

Yes, I do. I mind very much. But even though she'd die rather than admit it, Frankie's an elderly lady. With a bad back. It would be downright churlish of me to kick up a fuss.

'It's fine, Frankie, I'll be up in a minute.'

April is apoplectic. 'I'm so, so sorry. She's completely impossible.'

'She always was.'

Then the colour drains from her face, leaving it the colour of porridge. 'Oh my God,' she says.

'What?'

'She'll be here for the party.'

'Horace Billings would turn in his grave if he knew what you were planning. He established this college on the staunchest of religious principles. He saw it as an earthly paradise, a place of enlightenment and scholarship with the teachings of God and the Bible at the core of everything. If you remember, he even originally wanted it to be called Eden College. You only have to look at the Billings Archangels to know how he felt. They were his idea, you know – not Saxby's. And he donated his collection of devotional literature to the college in good faith. He would be mortified to think that we'd relinquish it without a second thought.'

'Just as well he's not here then, Dominic.' Hugo was at the end of his patience. The Fellows, give or take the odd waverer like Perry Grimshaw, whom he could collar over

150

tea and surely persuade to toe the line, would vote over-whelmingly for his proposal. Only the chaplain categori-cally refused to budge. 'Will no one rid me of this turbulent priest?' he hissed under his breath.

'Dominic, the books will be much better off in the University Library.' A new voice interrupted. 'That building's in a dreadful state. It was only thrown up as a temporary measure to house the collection when the main library became so overcrowded. And in the UL, many more students would have access to these books. We don't need them here any more, particularly if we scrap the Theology Department.'

Hugo smiled. His creature had spoken. Douglas Baines, the college librarian, was one of his first appointments on becoming Master. Douglas couldn't wait to see the back of the Billings Bible and all the other musty old volumes. Electronic forms of communication were the only things that really interested him. Putting the Billings College Library online was the main reason he'd been hired.

'Why not swallow the whole library, book by book, Douglas?' snapped Tipton. 'Chew it up, spit it out, and have an end to it. I'm sure that would earn you a few brownie points.'

Hugo suppressed a smirk. Douglas was such an ambi-tious little arse-licker that he'd probably do just that if asked. He viewed the serried ranks of the Senior Common Room slumped in various attitudes of boredom and dejection.

'One way or another, this matter must be settled today,' he said. 'The Americans and the parent and alumni spon-sors are all coming up for the May Ball. It's vital we present a united front. Dominic, if you can't see your way to voting for my proposal, I suggest you might like to reconsider your position.' He paused before delivering his major broadside. 'Perhaps being chaplain of this college is no longer something you value particularly. We're all very aware that with your work in the town your loyalties could be seen to be somewhat divided. Not to say overstretched. None of us would wish to see your health suffer.'

'Are you implying that the refuge interferes with my position as college chaplain?'

'I ought to mention that if it's deemed in the best interest of the college, I do have it in my power to relieve you of your responsibilities.'

A couple of the Fellows gasped. Hugo tingled with satisfaction. That'll shake them up a bit, he thought. Like the sun rising and setting, being a Fellow of Billings was a lifelong condition, ended only by decrepitude, dementia or death. Short of being accused of gross sexual misconduct or murder, no one had ever been given the push. It simply wasn't done. But he was a new broom. It was time to show them all how thoroughly he was prepared to sweep clean.

'I've been browsing through the college statutes,' he said. 'Fascinating. I found a most interesting sub-clause buried away in one paragraph, dating right back to the original constitution. I intend to ask my friend William Grace to look it over, but it seems pretty categorical. It says that if a Fellow is bent on a course of action considered detrimental to the wellbeing of the college, then the Senior Common Room is at liberty to decide whether or not that person should remain a Fellow of this college.'

A stunned silence followed. It was very hot in the

committee room. Two flies which had been buzzing around for several minutes landed on Hugo's bald and sweating head. He brushed them away. If only, he thought, it was possible to do the same with the wretched Tipton. Still, his little bluff had certainly set the cat among the pigeons, and when William did look through the constitution as he'd promised, who knows what he might find.

'Oh, I say, Hugo. Steady on, old chap. That's a little extreme, don't you think?' It was Giles Winchelsea, the oldest and most longstanding Fellow in the college.

'Desperate times, desperate measures, Giles.' Hugo was at his most regretful.

'I'd be very loath to see you take such a drastic step. It would create a dangerous precedent.' Surprisingly it was Perry Grimshaw, the new boy, sticking his head above the parapet. And to Hugo's fury a rumble of support rippled round the room.

But he knew when to back off. 'Tea-time, I think. Give everyone a moment to review the various options. Chef tells me he's prepared one of his choicest spreads for our delectation, so I suggest we move through to the Saxby Room. Then later, when we're all feeling refreshed, we can continue our discussions and, it is to be hoped, reach a conclusion that will be satisfactory to all.'

He rose and everyone followed his example. Greed chased relief in the eyes of the Fellows. For a while, at least, they could forget their disagreements and concentrate on the far more enticing question of food. The spread laid on for committee meetings was a high spot of Senior Common Room life: tea served in a silver Samovar said to have been looted from the Winter Palace by a White Russian émigré in 1917, masses of tiny triangular sandwiches, mouthwatering Viennese pastries, chocolate fudge cake and the famou Billings College scones. Hugo's tastebuds wept in anticipation of the clotted cream and homemade strawberry jam.

Pausing at the door to the small panelled dining roon used by the Fellows when they didn't wish to eat at High Table, he announced, 'I told Chef we'd serve ourselves The staff are having the afternoon off in lieu of the extra hours they'll be working on the night of the Ball.'

Afterwards, no one was quite sure what happened wher he opened the door. For those near the back of the group it was the sound which first alerted them – high and whining like a thousand electric saws. For the others it was the fee of it. The assault on bare arms and faces. And for Hugo Mortimer, in the doorway, it was the heaving blackness swarming over every inch of the small room. Over the dainty cakes and sandwiches, over the dishes of clotted cream and jam. Over everything.

Flies.

Millions of them. Fruit flies, houseflies, bluebottles – a Glastonbury of flies, indulging themselves in the ultimate flyfest.

As Hugo waved his arms, swatting and batting the air in a frantic attempt to close the door on the devastation, Dominic Tipton muttered something in his ear. He was, unbelievably, smiling.

'What?' roared Hugo. 'What are you saying, Tipton?'

'*And there came a grievous swarm of flies into the house of Pharaoh, and into his servants' houses, and into all the land of Egypt: the land was corrupted by reason of the swarm of flies.*'

Hugo thrust him aside and stormed off, pursued by his own honour guard of flying insects.

And I saw another angel come down from heaven, having great power. And he cried mightily with a strong voice, saying, Babylon the great is fallen, is fallen, and is become the habitation of devils, and the hold of every foul spirit, and a cage of every unclean and hateful bird.

'Therefore shall her plagues come. Death and mourning and famine.'

THIRTEEN

The dress rehearsal had started well. The addition of set and costumes combined to give the actors a quickening excitement. All their efforts were at last coming together.

But then came the Second Act.

At the last minute, a small flight of steps had been erected on the side of the stage for Desdemona to disembark from her plane onto the island of Cyprus. Lee moaned that the structure was completely unnecessary, since it would only be used once, but Shareef had insisted. 'You said I had *carte blanche* with the set. You promised.'

'Yeah, but—'

'You're so visually illiterate sometimes, Lee. It's one of your fatal flaws. Trust me, the steps are a brilliant way of establishing Desdemona's significance to Cassio. Work with me, hon.'

Realising it was quicker and much less hassle to submit, Lee had agreed and the steps were duly built.

Cassio had just declaimed, '*Hail to thee, lady! And the grace of heaven, before, behind thee, and on every hand, nwheel thee round,'* when a cracking, groaning sound before, ehind and on every hand was heard, which effectively rowned out Desdemona's gracious reply. Cast and crew atched, helpless, as the rickety structure buckled and then ollapsed like matchwood. The fair Desdemona tumbled irough the air and pitched onto the ground where she lay iotionless.

'Ohmigodohmigodohmigod.' Shareef was hysterical.

Flora, emerging from backstage at a run, was the first at tella's side. 'Stella, are you OK?'

Stella opened her eyes. 'What happened?'

'The stairs collapsed. You fell.' Flora looked around, full f indignation. 'Whoever cobbled this thing together ought ） be shot.'

'Oi!' It was Melvyn Stubbs, the Billings College maths rodigy, who fancied himself as a bit of a carpenter. 'It was ool. I checked it myself after lunch.'

Lee examined the damage. 'When you checked it, Melv, ne old son, you didn't happen to hack through this piece f timber in a fit of techie absentmindedness?'

'What?' Melvyn peered at the wreckage of his work. One f the main supporting struts was broken. 'Fuckin' 'ell. I wear to God it wasn't like that when I left it.'

'You could have killed someone, you pillock.'

'I'm tellin' you it was good.'

'Yeah yeah.'

'Sod off, Lee. If you don't believe me you can fuckin' epair it yourself. Wanker.' Melvyn flung his hammer onto ie grass and walked off.

Flora gently took Stella's arm. 'Try to stand up. See if nything's broken . . . How's that?'

'Fine, I think. Wow, Flo, it's just as well you did you usual thing and missed your cue, or you'd have copped as well. You're supposed to be with me on the steps b then.'

'I know,' murmured Flora. 'Lucky, or what?'

Shareef was at his most dramatic. 'If you ask me, it look like it's been deliberately tampered with. See? It's been cu right through.'

'Don't be ridiculous! That's a horrible thing to say snapped Flora.

'Yeah, Sharon,' said Lee. 'It's Melvyn's crap carpentry that's all. He don't know the difference between a saw an a screwdriver. I knew I shouldn't have let you persuade m to ask him to do the job, eyelashes or no eyelashes. He's fuckin' disaster. So, Stel, you OK now, babe? Can we ge on?'

'Give her a minute, Lee.' Danny had joined Stella, wh leaned against him looking fragile and shaken.

Flora glanced over at Julie. She was staring at Stella, an clutching Iago's knife so tightly that her knuckles were bone white. Flora would have given a lot to know what she wa thinking.

But Stella's fragility was cutting no ice with Lee. 'She' cool, incha, Stel? She don't wanna be here at midnight an neither do I. I wanna get through this and go for a pint.'

Stella managed a brave smile. 'The show must go on I'm fine, Danny. Honestly.'

'That's my girl,' said Lee. 'Places, people! Act Two, Scene One!' He turned to Shareef who was still muttering abou sabotage and conspiracy. 'Shut your cakehole, Sharon Anybody'd think it was you what fell.'

Shareef's voice was heavy with accusation. 'Lee, some of us could have been killed here tonight.'

'Only me or Stella,' said Flora softly. 'We're the only two who use those stairs.'

She stumbled woodenly through the rest of the dress rehearsal. After it was all over, everyone went to Danny's room to change out of their costumes. Everyone except Flora, who headed off in the direction of Bacon Court.

'Where are you going?' asked Julie. 'I need your costume. I'm getting everything sorted, ready for tomorrow night.'

'If I tell you, promise you'll keep it to yourself?' muttered Flora.

'Sure,' said Julie, eyes wide with curiosity.

'I feel really embarrassed, stripping off in front of all the blokes,' Flora said. 'I'll change in my room and then bring it back. Is that OK?'

A flash of scorn registered in Julie's eyes, but all she said was, 'Sure. I'll wait for you.'

When Flora returned, Julie was the only one still there, arranging everything on rails in order of appearance.

'You look knackered, Julie,' Flora said. 'Why don't you go and find the others. They're off to the pub. I'll finish here.'

The party's going with a swing. Watching April weaving her way in and out of the groups of chattering people, her face animated as she dispenses Pimms from a crystal jug, it's impossible to equate her with the distraught woman that I'd discovered earlier. Perry follows my gaze. 'Isn't she wonderful?' he says.

'Yes, she is. And you should tell her so on a frequent and regular basis.'

'What do you mean?'

'She's not sure you love her.'

'Is that what she's been saying?'

'She didn't have to say anything. I could just tell.'

'Bollocks.'

'Is it? She's not the only one who saw the way you were looking at that Stella girl last night.'

'What? You are joking, I hope. Credit me with some professional integrity. Stella's my student.'

'So was April.'

'April was a graduate student. Not the same thing at all.'

'Look me in the eye and tell me you're completely indifferent to Miss Stella Whatsit.'

'I am completely indifferent to Miss Stella Whatsit.'

Perry and I have never been able to lie to each other. Not about anything that matters.

'Care to take that one again?'

'I love my wife more than life itself. I really do. I'm crazy about her. And I'd never cheat on her – especially with a nineteen-year-old student. You're letting that dramatic imagination of yours run away with you. Look, forget Stella. What with all the various Grimshaw dramas, we haven't had much chance to talk about you. How are things? Really?'

I'd better let it drop. It's none of my business anyway.

'Good, in many ways. My career's back on track, the kids are healthy and doing well. I thought I'd never recover after Rob died, but of course one does. Life goes on.'

'I still feel lousy, not making it to the funeral.'

'Yeah. Bastard.' I give him a playful nudge. 'Seriously, though – it's OK. It was much too expensive to come just for one day.'

'Doesn't stop me feeling bad, though. Particularly since I don't expect your parents were there, either.'

'What do you think?'

'I'd hoped that the only good thing to come out of Rob's death might be a reconciliation.'

'Mum wrote. She said that now Rob was dead we could put the past twenty years behind us, and that I was welcome to visit.'

'Well, that's good, isn't it?'

'Just me. Not the children.'

'You have to be joking!'

'Unfortunately not.'

'I still can't believe they'd be like that. They were always so good to me.'

'I think my dad preferred you. He could do all those boy things that I wasn't interested in.' I took a deep breath. There was a question I'd always shied away from over the years since my marriage. 'Do you still see them?'

'It's mostly Christmas cards and the odd phone call.'

He's holding back.

'Have they met April and the kids?'

He won't meet my eye.

'Come on, Perrygreen. Spit it out.'

'Once. Just after we arrived back. They were on holiday in Norfolk and they popped in on their way home.' He's hating this. So am I.

'Did they ask about me?'

'I can't remember.'

'That means no.'

On learning of my engagement to Rob, my father had cast me into outer darkness. My mother had chosen him over me, and I haven't seen either of them for more than twenty years. I thought I'd come to terms with it, but now, hearing that my parents have seen Perry's children, have petted and kissed and made a big Northern fuss of them, I realise I'm not so sure. I should have left well alone. I brought this on myself. For a moment I want to scratch Perry's eyes out, but then I look at him and remember my childhood and how close we were. It isn't his fault my father's a racist bigot.

'I'm sorry,' he says miserably.

I hug him. 'I'm just glad to be here now. You really are very dear to me, you know, little brother.'

'Likewise,' he says, hugging me back. Then, in typical male fashion, finding too much emotion too much, he says, 'I think I should rescue Hugo. Frankie's had him cornered for the last twenty minutes. God knows what the implications are for my brilliant career. Come, Rosaleen, time for you to meet Billings's head honcho.' He leads me through the crowded room to where a nattily dressed portly man in his fifties, balding pate gleaming, is trapped between Frankie and the wall. He isn't my idea of a scientist. Far too florid and exquisite. Hazarding a guess at this man's profession I'd plump for something in the arts. Antique dealer, ballet critic – something along those lines. Yet Hugo Mortimer's discoveries are legendary. They've revolutionised the study of Genetics, not just in Britain but in the entire world.

However, at this precise moment his brilliant mind is clearly light years away from concocting the next Nobel Prize theory. His eyes have the glazed patina of the recently deceased. When he sees us approaching 'drowning man' and 'straw' are the words that spring to mind.

'So I said "Alf, if you can't get me the work, then I'm off. I could have found another agent years ago – as you well know, I've had enough offers – but I didn't. I stuck with you".'

'Bravo,' mutters Mortimer.

'Call me a sentimental old fool,' says Frankie, clutching at his arm with a scarlet talon, 'but that's just the way I am. Loyal to a fault, you see.'

'Oh, I do. I do indeed.'

'It doesn't do the bugger any harm to get a boot up the bum now and again,' Frankie continues. 'Shows him who's boss. Mark my words, tomorrow he'll be on the blower, contract in hand, begging me to go back.'

'Let's hope so,' the Master murmurs, seizing Perry. 'Ah, Perry, there you are. You didn't mention that your delightful mother was to grace your little gathering—'

'Hasn't Sir Hugo got a lovely speaking voice, Perry?' Frankie simpers. 'It's what I always wanted for our Perry, Sir Hugo. Spent a fortune on elocution lessons. Waste of bloody money. You can take the boy out of the North, but you can't take the North out of the boy.'

The Master's eyes gleam. 'How true, dear lady.' He turns to Perry. 'I had no idea you had such close connections with the world of popular culture, my boy. We must persuade your mother to perform for us at some point. Perhaps later in the year, as a Christmas treat.'

Watching him, I see why, apart from his formidable brain, Hugo Mortimer has made it to the top of the tree. He's a twenty-first-century Machiavelli. I know exactly what's going through his mind at this moment: how he can best use his newfound knowledge of Perry's dreadful mother to his advantage.

'You mustn't let that Northern twang influence you when it comes to giving my lad promotion, though,' Frankie wobbles on her stilettos and I realise that she's had more than her fair share of Pimms, 'or you'll have me to answer to. We're very close, you see, me being a widow and him an only child. Just the two of us against the world – that's how it's always been.' She gives a plucky little smile.

I don't know about the widow bit. The absent Mr Grimshaw, as far as I remember, had not so much died as decamped, and hadn't stayed long enough anyway to put a ring on Frankie's finger. And as for Frankie and Perry against the world, I remember Perry as a small boy weeping and clinging to her as she prepared to depart on yet another extensive tour, and her brushing him away like an annoying fly. *Bloody hell, Perry, get your grubby little paws off me dress. You'll ruin it. And for Christ's sake put a sock in it, you mardy little bugger. No goodbye kiss from me until you shut your cake-hole. Nobody loves a Moaning Minnie.*

Perry cuts in. 'Hugo, may I introduce Rosa Thorn. She's in Cambridge filming a TV series.'

'Fascinating,' says the Master eagerly. 'Your glass is empty, Rosa. Come, let me get you a refill and you can tell me all about it.' He beams at Frankie. 'Do excuse me, Mrs Grimshaw.'

'Miss Faraday. But you can call me Frankie.'

'It's all been most illuminating, Frankie. I had no idea

the world of cruise-line entertainment was so intriguing. Perry, I need a word later. About the incident this afternoon.'

'He didn't offer to get *me* another drink,' I hear Frankie saying as he steers me away.

Earlier, Perry had updated us about the committee meeting. He had us helpless with laughter as he described it in the manner of a 1950s sci-fi movie, with the perplexed scholars of Billings trying to escape from *Invasion of the Alien Flies*.

I knew what he was doing. It was a familiar Grimshaw ploy. By turning it into a funny story he was hoping to divert April from giving him hell over his mother's unexpected appearance. His plan had worked. She was gripped.

He said no one was any the wiser about who had put the flies in the Saxby Room, but the Master had tracked down the source: a consignment being used in various experiments had gone missing from one of the university science labs. Perry suspected that Mortimer was a bit rattled. First the attempted suicide of an undergraduate, and the business with the fountain of blood. Now the flies débâcle.

'Does he think there's a connection?' April had asked.

'He's just jumpy about the Americans. If he stuffs up their visit he won't have enough funding to build his library. Not that it'll be built anyway, if Dominic doesn't cave in.'

'I thought you didn't want to vote for it either,' I said.

'I don't. All other things being equal, I'd support Dom, but I have my career to think of. Eventually I'd like a Senior Fellowship. That means choosing my fight carefully. I don't want to put Mortimer's back up unless I have to. Anyway,

Dom's OK. It only needs one Fellow to vote against the proposal for it to bomb.'

'One dissenting voice can defeat the whole project?'

'Oh yes. If I were Dom, I'd lock my bedroom door at night.'

At this point the first guests had arrived and our conversation had been curtailed. Now, I think I'll try and work out what makes Mortimer tick.

'I don't see the chaplain here tonight,' I say to him.

He grimaces. 'Parties aren't quite Dominic's thing.'

'Has he been at Billings for long?'

'Ten years. Appointed by my predecessor when the previous God Squaddie developed senile dementia. He'd had it for some time apparently, before anyone noticed any difference. Tells you something about religion, doesn't it?'

'You sound as if you disapprove.'

'It's a childish and outmoded concept, peddled by grown men who should know better. Caused more trouble than anything else in human history. The sooner it's abolished the better. In fact, let's stop talking about it right now. Tell me about you. What is it that you're doing in Cambridge? Is it something for the television, or for one of our delightfully eccentric British films?'

I fill him in on my activities, finishing with my bad news: Buster Jones revealed to me this morning that budget constraints have led to the May Ball scene being cut. Instead I'm merely to be filmed in a ballgown, canoodling with Jeremy in a penguin suit on Clare Bridge over the Cam.

'I so wanted to go to a May Ball, even if it was only a fictional one.'

I haven't particularly taken to Hugo Mortimer, but now to my astonishment he comes up trumps. Big time.

'As it happens, I was taking my Senior Tutor but she's had to cancel on me. Would you care to come in her place?'

'Are you serious?'

'You'd be doing me a service. I'm hosting a table of potential sponsors for our new college library, and a woman's touch, particularly a woman as attractive as yourself, would be an enormous asset.'

So near and yet so far.

'It's on Thursday, isn't it?'

'That's right.'

'Oh dear, I have to leave on Wednesday. My daughter's in the middle of her A Levels.'

'What a pity. Must you go?' He sounds genuinely disappointed.

I do a rapid calculation. After tomorrow, Anna doesn't have any more exams for the next ten days. And also, if I'm nice to the Master, it might earn Perry some brownie points.

'I'm sure I can organise something.' I give him my best smile. 'I'd love to come.'

He beams. 'Splendid.'

'You're taking her to the Ball, Sir Hugo?' It's Frankie. She's come up behind us. Several more glasses of Pimms have evidently found their way down her throat in the few minutes since we last spoke. 'Can I come too?'

'Unhappily, that isn't possible, dear lady.' Hugo backs away. 'The tickets are all sold out.'

'So how come *she* gets to go?'

'Rosa is replacing my partner, who's unable to come owing to a last-minute invitation to lecture in the Lebanon.'

'Surely you can dredge up one ticket for little old me. You're the bleeding boss. You can do what the 'ell you like.'

'If only,' murmurs Hugo, with feeling.

'I'm surprised you didn't ask me in the first place. I would have thought you'd want someone with a bit more glamour and sophistication than our Rosa.'

The Master titters nervously, glancing apologetically in my direction. Looking at Frankie's face I remember, with a sinking sensation, her lightning mood changes. Particularly when she's had a few.

Now she's scowling. 'I get the picture. Well, you can sod off. I wouldn't touch your buggering Ball with a bargepole.'

Her voice is loud. The people round us fall silent. April, a bright smile plastered across her face, elbows her way through the curious crowd. 'Please excuse my mother-in-law, Hugo. She hasn't been well . . .' She tries to steer Frankie away, but Frankie shrugs her off.

'I don't need you apologising for me, madam!'

Perry appears. 'Come on, darling. Time for a lie-down.'

Her mascara is beginning to run. The black rivulets follow the deep creases on her cheeks. 'They're being nasty, Perrykins. Don't let them be nasty to your poor old ma.'

'Nobody's being nasty, Mum. You're tired. You need a little sleep.'

He leads her gently away, and the general hubbub starts up again with renewed vigour.

Danny had never been so drunk. Or felt such a heel. What had he done? It so wasn't meant to be like this. He needed to think. Get things straight. He staggered to the river and gazed into its cold glassy depths. Maybe a swim might clear his head.

'Careful, pal. Not a good idea to get too near the edge. Not in your condition.' A friendly arm was guiding him to a bench. 'Are you all right?'

'Never better,' mumbled Danny. 'Never better. Just have a little rest, then go home.'

'Right you are, then. Cheers.'

His rescuer disappeared into the darkness, leaving Danny alone with his muddled thoughts.

The dress rehearsal, apart from the collapsing stairs, had been a million times better than the run-through. Afterwards, Lee had marched them all down to the Maypole for a celebratory pint.

Everyone was exhausted but content. The set looked good, the sound cues worked. Most people remembered most of their lines and most of their entrances and exits, most of the time.

They had a show.

Even Stella's cheeks were flushed with excitement.

The only fly in the ointment had been Julie. As they walked over Jesus Green and along Park Parade to the pub, Flora had said, 'You look exhausted, Julie. You've worked twice as hard as anyone today. Didn't you say you live along here? Maybe you ought to get to bed. Big day tomorrow.'

Yeah. Give me a break, Jules. Go home.

But with a quick glance in his direction she'd said, 'I'm completely wired. I couldn't possibly sleep.'

'Too right, and anyway I owe you a pint, girl,' said Lee. 'You've well and truly saved our bacon, innit, Sharon?'

'You surely have, hon,' said Shareef. 'No way are you snuggling up in your little bed yet awhile.'

Once in the pub, Danny had been ultra-conscious of her presence, monitoring his every word and gesture. He'd wanted to squeeze in next to Stella, but couldn't bring himself to do it under Julie's penetrating gaze. He couldn't even speak to Stella without feeling like a complete shit. The only thing to do was to get drunk. But for some reason the alcohol didn't appear to be working. So he had to drink twice as much.

It had seemed like a very long evening.

And then, as they all walked back to college via Julie's house, she'd said, 'Danny, will you come inside? I need to tell you something. It's really important.'

This had precipitated a cacophony of raucous comments from the rest of the group, but by now something strange had happened: Danny hadn't minded. He hadn't minded at all. For Danny had become Mr Mellow. He'd realised somewhere between the Maypole and Park Parade that life was too short to be filled with stupid complications. Life was simple. Life was easy. Life was to be enjoyed. Life was not something to agonise over. Life was love and there was enough love in this beautiful world for everyone to love everyone. Love wasn't like a tap that you could turn on and off. Love was like the air we breathe and there was an endless supply of it. There was enough love to go round everyone. There was certainly enough love in him to go round everyone. He had enough love in him to service the whole world. He *was* love, a love god . . .

The alcohol was finally working.

'Fuck off, you dirty sods,' he'd said. 'I'll catch you later.'

He'd caught Stella's eye. She'll have to wait, he'd thought. Her turn will come. But not now. Right now he owed it to Julie, his poor sweet little Julie, to hear what she had to say. He'd treated her like shit. Dumped on her from a great height. The least he could do was listen properly to her. He owed her that much at least. He couldn't stomach what he'd done to her. Couldn't bear her pain. He'd told her what he wanted and then he'd bolted. But now was the time to make it up to her. Stella would have to wait. Everything comes to her who waits. There was enough love in him to go round everyone. Enough love for everyone.

He'd followed Julie into the house,

'Be quiet,' she whispered. 'We don't want to wake Mum.'

Danny was with her on that one. The last person he wanted to bump into was Julie's mum. Even in his loved-up state he couldn't stomach a bellyful of Moaning Joan.

Julie led him upstairs into her room. And then something happened that he wasn't expecting. The familiar smell of her perfumes and potions, the sight of the frilly bed canopy and the stuffed animals arranged on the pillow hit him like a punch in the gut. All of a sudden he was crying. It was so sad. So very, very sad. How different a place looked when love had left.

She'd drawn him down onto the bed. 'Why are you crying?' She touched his face. 'Don't cry, Dan. Please don't cry.'

'I'm so sorry,' he'd said. 'I'm so sorry, Jules. I didn't want to hurt you.'

'I know you didn't.' Then her arms were round him and she was kissing away the tears, and the smell of her had taken Danny back to the beginning. He'd found himself kissing her back, feeling her soft, warm skin under his fingers, feeling the familiar curves of her body, feeling her becoming aroused by his touch, becoming aroused himself. Feeling the two of them coming together like it always used to be, skin on skin, slippery with desire, burning with the need for each other. And then there was no stopping. No way back.

Afterwards, he lay there watching the familiar room spin round. *What have I done? What have I done?* He'd tried to move but Julie's arms were entwined round him, like jungle creeper, poison ivy, trapping him, holding him down. Her eyes had gazed into his, and he'd felt his soul being sucked away.

It was all his own fault.

He'd recognised that, even in his drunken haze, and he was appalled.

He'd finally found the strength and courage to pull away from her. 'Fuck, Jules, I'm so sorry.'

'So you keep saying. But it doesn't matter now.'

'You wanted to tell me something. What was it?'

'That doesn't matter either.'

His head was spinning. He had to get out. In one movement he'd wrenched himself off the bed.

'What are you doing?'

'I have to go.'

'No, you don't. Not now. Stay with me, Danny.'

'That shouldn't have happened.'

'You still love me. You've just proved it. Don't say it shouldn't have happened.' Now she was beginning to cry.

'This was a big mistake.'

He'd run from the room, down the stairs and out of the

ouse, trying to block out her sobs. But in his mind he still eard them as he headed down Park Parade towards the ver.

Now, minutes later, sitting on the bench, he was onscious only of guilt and shame. He couldn't blame the lcohol. He wasn't so pissed he hadn't known what he was oing. He hadn't given the slightest thought to what his ehaviour would lead Julie to believe. He had no self-ontrol. He was a pathetic low-life, no better than an animal. t least the first time he'd hurt her, it had been an honest nd sober expression of his feelings. But this thing he'd one tonight, this was the behaviour of a complete shit.

He left his bench and knelt down by the river's edge gain. He could see his face reflected in the water. The pples contorted his features, breaking them up, making iem shift and fragment. That's what he was: a shifty, ifting, shiftless figure who couldn't control his dick.

And then something slammed into his back. A fist. It nocked him flat onto his face. Gasping, he turned over nd found himself looking at Scott Watkins.

Julie's brother.

The marine. Hellbent on demonstrating his compre-ensive grasp of martial arts.

Danny didn't even try to defend himself. In some perverse ay he gloried in the attack. He deserved it. He lost all nse of time as the punches rained down.

Finally it stopped, leaving Danny a barely conscious mass f pain. But he still felt glad. Glad he'd taken his punish-ient. Maybe it would go some way to making up for what e'd done.

Then Scott spoke. It wasn't a long speech, but it was

very clear. He spat out the words, turned on his heel and vanished into the darkness. What he said filled Danny with despair. He lay on the riverbank, head swirling with alcohol, pain and a sick incredulity.

His punishment was not over.

It would never be over.

TUESDAY 21 JUNE

FOURTEEN

It's the morning after the night before and April and I are clearing up the mess. Perry, meanwhile, is arranging with painstaking care a breakfast tray, complete with pink rose in silver vase. As he carries it upstairs I catch April looking at him with wry resignation.

'What's with the tray?' I ask. 'Is Frankie ill, or just hungover?'

'She's never hungover. She has the constitution of an ox. Perry's giving her breakfast in bed because that's what he always does.'

'After her performance last night, she should be on her hands and knees, scrubbing the floor in penance.'

'I wish.'

Later, after Perry's gone to college, and the house is restored to normality, Frankie, sensing the clean-up's finished, finally appears. Today she's very gold. Gold sandals, a gold jersey top over white Capri pants, and large gold hoop earrings. Her hair, equally gold, hangs long and loose over her shoulders.

'Hellfire, you two look rough this morning,' she says to April and me as we slump over coffee at the kitchen table. 'April, pet, you mun' take some of my heavy-duty handcream. Your mitts look like summat nasty on a butcher's block.'

'Thanks, Frankie. How kind,' says April, with granite eyes.

Frankie's oblivious. 'I thought I'd take my grandbabbies shopping this morning,' she says. 'Buy them some decent clothes.'

'They already have plenty of decent clothes,' says April between clenched teeth. 'And they're at nursery now.'

'Alf's preparing my new portfolio,' says Frankie, 'and some shots of me and the kiddies would go down well with the cruise brigade – glamorous granny and what have you. They'll probably think I'm Mum not Gran, but that's no bad thing. When they find out, they'll be stoked. They like to identify, you see, poor old dears. But I can't have the babbas looking like tramps. Alf wouldn't like it. If there's one thing he hates, it's sloppy.'

April's about to lose it. Big time.

'I thought you'd dumped Alf?' I say hastily.

'What gave you that idea?' she asks. 'He needs bringing to heel, that's all. Men do occasionally. Surely you realise that, Rosa. By now he'll be fixing up my TV deal and tonight he'll be on the blower begging me to go home. I shan't, of course. Not yet. Let him stew a bit longer. Anyway, I fancy doing this May Ball malarky, so I'm not going anywhere till after that. But I still won't have long to organise this photo shoot.'

'I don't think I want Cassandra and Hector to appear in publicity photographs. I'll have to consult Perry,' April says stiffly.

'No need, pet. I've already asked him. He's right chuffed.

Says you've never bothered to have any decent photos taken. Not proper studio shots. Rosa, do you remember that lovely one of me and Perry, when he was a babba? The one in the silver frame with me in the organza frock and the angora bolero?'

I remember. When Frankie was away, which was most of the time, Perry used to take it out of the frame and sleep with it under his pillow.

'It were such a beautiful photo. I often wonder where it got to.'

I could tell her, but I don't. Over time, Frankie's face became so mottled and stained where Perry had kissed it good night that eventually it almost vanished. Then one day, when she'd broken a solemn promise to come to school Prize Day and watch Perry collecting at least four prizes, he'd torn it into tiny bits and thrown it on the fire.

'Frankie, I really do have to discuss this with Perry.'

When Frankie realises that April is serious, her mouth twitches with annoyance. She doesn't like being thwarted. 'He'll only tell you what he told me. If you must, you must – but make it soon. I need to arrange a date with my photographer. He'll do anything for me, of course, but he does need a bit of notice.'

'Perry's home for lunch. Is that soon enough?'

Frankie's pencilled eyebrows shoot up. 'Didn't he tell you, pet?'

'Tell me what?'

'He's not back till later this afternoon. He said he had a supervision wi' one of his students.' Her eyes gleam. 'I were a bit surprised, I must admit. I thought he'd finished this term's teaching.' She beams at April. 'Isn't life odd. Once you were Perry's student, and now you're cleaning his house while he's off giving the other bright young things what-for. It must feel a bit funny.'

'Not in the least.'

Frankie smiles. 'He's very lucky to have such an under-standing wife, isn't he, Rosa? There's not many women would be as trusting, knowing that a man with his looks and charm spends so much time with all those gorgeous, clever young girls.'

I'd forgotten exactly how much of a monster Frankie was.

'Perry knows exactly how lucky he is to have April,' I say quickly. 'It's obvious to everyone that he adores her.'

'Of course he does. Our April's a poppet. What's not to adore?' Frankie somehow makes it sound like an insult. 'Is that the time? I'm off for a bit of retail therapy. Work hard, girls.' She bustles out. After she's gone there's silence for several seconds.

'Don't let her rile you. That's what she wants,' I say.

But April isn't listening. 'One day I'll swing for her,' she mutters. 'And I'm not kidding.'

Hugo and Dawkins surveyed the efforts of the workmen who were erecting the vast marquee in Bacon Court. It was a magnificent sight. This was Hugo's first May Ball as Master and he was determined it would go down to posterity as the best ever. He gazed up at the cloudless heaven and willed the weather to hold. Rain would be a disaster. But despite the early hour, the air hung hot and still. Two days to go and so far, so good.

And today he was giving lunch to William Grace, from Trinity Hall, and a world expert in the field of contract law.

William was dying to get his hands on the Billings College statutes. Hugo had asked him to confirm what he suspected – that there was at least one sub-clause hidden away in the constitution which would clobber Dominic Tipton.

Dawkins started yapping. Hugo tore his eyes away from the billowing marquee and saw Tipton himself, hurrying across the grass with the beautiful young man from the chapel on Sunday. Hugo frowned. He was pretty sure the boy wasn't a student. Though not desperately interested in his undergraduate population, he did vaguely recognise most of them.

'Good morning, Dominic,' he called cheerily.

The chaplain came to a halt. 'Is it?'

'I'm having a working lunch in the Master's Lodge with William Grace today. Do you know him?'

'Lawyer. Trinity Hall.'

'That's right.'

'Only by reputation.'

'He's so looking forward to examining our statutes.'

'I'll bet he is,' muttered Tipton.

'He thinks it's highly likely there'll be a way of breaking the impasse in which we seem to find ourselves.'

'For pity's sake, Master! Stop this business right now. You cannot destroy Billings College history and tradition in such a cavalier way.'

Hugo smiled. 'I think you'll find I can,' he said.

Then the young man spoke. 'Catch you later,' he said to Tipton and, ignoring Hugo, he turned and walked away. Hugo saw the chaplain's eyes soften as the young man spoke.

'Well, Chaplain, *à bientôt*. Heel, Dawkins!' And he trotted off with a breezy, 'Bravo, lads. Keep up the good work,' to some workmen who were struggling with a particularly recalcitrant tentpole.

It later occurred to him that he still hadn't established the identity of Tipton's young companion. But then a thought occurred.

'Perhaps he's Tipton's bum boy,' he said to Dawkins.

It would make sense. Tipton had never been married, and the boy was exceptionally good-looking. As he let himself back into the Lodge, Hugo wondered in what way this particular scrap of information might be useful.

It was the laughter that first alerted Flora. She heard it echoing down from the landing above.

Stella's landing.

Stella's voice.

Lucas's voice.

She closed her door quietly and leaned her forehead against its wooden solidity. Her heart and head were pounding in unison. Several minutes passed before a knock brought her back to reality.

It was Lucas, with Stella beside him. His smile faded as he took in her appearance. 'Hey, Flo – you look wasted.'

Flora forced a smile. 'Got bladdered after the dress rehearsal last night. Don't tell Dom. He'd kill me.' She looked from one to the other. 'You two off somewhere?' She tried to sound casual and unconcerned.

Lucas laughed. 'No. We just met on the stairs. We're both competing for your attention, Ms Popular. Stella wants you to go to breakfast with her, and I've come to ask a favour. Could you do my shift this morning? I've got some stuff to do for my uncle.'

Met on the stairs indeed. Lucas had passed her door without knocking and carried straight on up to Stella's room. *He'd gone to see Stella first.*

'I can't. I'm busy.' It was the first time she'd refused him anything.

'What?'

'Sorry.'

'But what are you doing that's so important?'

Another first for Flora: the first time she'd disapproved of Lucas. It was none of his business. Her refusal should have been enough. What's more, she didn't like the inference that someone like her couldn't possibly have more important stuff to do than he did.

'Things,' she said, determined not to go into specifics. Anyway, there were no specifics. In reality her morning stretched emptily ahead for several hours.

'Like breakfast with me.' Stella smiled at Lucas.

His blue eyes were cold. 'Fine,' he said, and stomped off down the stairs.

'Someone got out of bed on the wrong side this morning,' said Stella, staring after him. 'I'm starving, Flo. Let's go to some breakfast.'

'Actually, I don't feel too well.'

'You poor thing,' said Stella. 'Hangovers are the pits. Maybe you should go back to bed.'

'What was Lucas doing on your landing?'

'Thought you lived further up, I suppose. Can I borrow your dining card?'

Flora handed her card over. 'Could you bring me back some toast and juice?'

'Actually, I'm not coming up to my room again. I'm

going straight into town after breakfast. But I will if you want.'

'It's OK,' said Flora.

'I could ask someone else to bring you something, if you like.'

'Forget it,' she said.

'OK, babes. See you.' Stella was already halfway down the stairs. 'You'll feel better after a kip,' she shouted blithely.

Flora gazed down the stairwell at Stella's rapidly retreating back. Then she went back into her room to think.

Julie had locked her door.

Joan could hear her crying. 'Let me in, Julie,' she said.

No response.

'Whatever's wrong, you can tell me. I'm your mother.' Joan hoped Julie would be the one to say the dreaded 'P' word. She herself couldn't face bringing it up again after the girl's vehement denial last time.

She tried again. 'Was that Danny with you last night?'

No response.

'Your brother said it was. I think he might have had a word. I don't know for sure because he had to go back to barracks very early this morning.'

'Scott talked to Danny?'

'I believe so.'

'About what?'

Joan felt a fit of vagueness coming on. Scott's nocturnal activities were not something she cared to contemplate. 'I don't know.'

Suddenly the door opened and Julie pushed past her.

GREEN EYE

'Where are you off to?'
But all she heard was the front door slamming.

*The Lord is slow to anger and great in power; the Lord will
not lead the guilty unpunished. His way is the whirlwind
and the storm, and clouds are the dust of his feet.*

FIFTEEN

Danny's torso was a mass of pain.

His torso. Not his face.

He had to admire Scott's expertise. The beating had been designed to hurt rather than damage. And Scott had clearly calculated that Danny would be too ashamed to blab to anyone, so by leaving the face alone, he'd ensured that no awkward questions would be asked. He was spot on. Danny knew he ought to get himself checked out by a doctor but he couldn't face the explanations.

Scott had been crystal clear as to why he was doing what he was doing. He'd said Julie was pregnant. With Danny's baby.

Bile rose in Danny's throat.

His child, who must, ironically, have been conceived during their last painful days together as a couple, when they hardly ever made love, lay snugly in Julie's womb.

Waiting to pop out and shackle him to her forever.

Only now, with that prospect in view, did he properly realise how over it really was with Julie.

Except that it wasn't. It would never be over. Not if she was having his baby.

He was going to be a father. Impossible. He was scarcely more than a baby himself.

Suddenly he wanted his mum. Badly. His mum would make it better. It was what she did.

But this was something he had to sort out for himself. He had done what a man does. Now he had to bear the consequences like a man.

His thoughts were interrupted by a knock on his door.

'I know you're in there, Dan. I saw you through the window. I left my sewing kit in your room yesterday and I need it.'

Julie.

Danny couldn't believe it. Less than twelve hours ago, he'd shagged her in a moment of drunken sentimentality, and then soon afterwards, he'd been beaten senseless by her Neanderthal brother. Yet here she was, behaving as if nothing had happened. Yattering about sewing kits.

And carrying his child inside her.

He wanted to be anywhere but here, but he was lumbered. Lumbered forever with his deep shame and even deeper resentment. Lumbered forever with her.

He put on a T-shirt to hide the bruises, and opened the door. Julie scowled up at him, tiny and frail, and touchingly belligerent. He could see her heart fluttering like a trapped bird beneath her top. Her vulnerability tore him in two, and his hostility vanished like a morning mist.

'Julie, I'm so—'

She pushed past him and he winced as her arm knocked against one of his bruises. 'I left it by the window.' She glanced around. 'There it is.'

'I know what you're—'

'Sorry to barge in, but there's still a couple of costumes to fix before tonight.'

'I know—'

Suddenly, she rounded on him. 'What *do* you know? Fuck all, that's what. You know fuck all, Danny Thorn.'

He caught her arm. 'We have to talk.'

'About what, exactly?' Then her face hardened as she looked beyond him to the door. 'Anyway, I wouldn't want to cramp your style.'

There stood Stella. 'Am I interrupting?'

Julie pulled away from him. 'No.' He wanted to curl up and die. 'See you, Dan,' she said.

Then Danny was alone with Stella.

'Was it something I said?'

Danny sighed. 'Don't ask.'

'I thought we could rehearse,' she said. 'I'm still confused about our last scene. I keep forgetting my lines.'

This time yesterday, Danny would have been ecstatic at the idea.

'I'm rather pushed at the moment,' he said.

'But I was hoping you'd be able to put your finger on my weak spots.' She smiled.

Does she know what she's doing when she makes remarks like that?

'If I dry this evening, it'll be your fault,' she teased. 'Do you want to be responsible for that?'

What Danny wanted was to kiss her creamy flower face. But a thing with Stella was now out of the question. And anyway, even if he were free as a bird, the bruises covering his body made him wince at the thought of close physical

contact. He tried to invest his voice with a firm maturity.
I really do have things to sort out.'

'Oh, pants,' she murmured.

But she didn't seem too bothered. In spite of his other
preoccupations, Danny couldn't help feeling fed up that
she was taking his knock-back so lightly.

'Sorry,' he muttered.

'You know where I live if you change your mind.'

And then he was alone again. He lowered himself
gingerly onto the bed, fighting a desire to sleep. It was
impossible to imagine that in a few hours' time he'd be
playing the Moor of Venice to all and sundry, including
his mother.

Right on cue, there was another knock on the door, and
the sound of his mother's voice.

'Danny?'

He froze.

She knocked again. 'Dan? Are you still in bed? I'm taking
you to lunch. You haven't forgotten?'

Even though his bruises weren't visible, his mother would
suss that something was wrong. She always knew when he
was in trouble. She'd tease and squeeze it out of him and
then give her usual forceful opinion about what to do. But
this time he couldn't risk being influenced by her. He had
to work it out for himself first and then present her with
his decision.

He lay rigid until she went away.

As her footsteps faded, a hot tear slid down his cheek
and into his ear. She had such high hopes of him. What
would she say when she knew he'd messed up so badly?

*   *   *

189

Flora brooded in bed all morning. When she eventually got up, the first thing she did, from longstanding habit, was to drag herself over to the window and check the entrance to Dom's staircase in the hope of catching a glimpse of Lucas visiting his uncle. Ninety-nine times out of a hundred she was unlucky.

But not today.

There he was.

Dom's rooms were arguably the best in Cambridge, being situated in the Billings Gatehouse with an unparalleled view over the town. And a door at the end of his corridor opened onto a flight of steps that led up to the walkway on which stood the Billings Archangels. It was forbidden to students, but Dom had promised to take her up there one day for a closer look, not only at the view, but also at the angels themselves, who, he said, were even more impressive close up than they appeared from ground level.

Now Flora saw Lucas and Stella on the walkway, leaning against the parapet, two golden additions to the heavenly host already *in situ*. They were laughing and talking and Lucas was caressing the carved robes of the Archangel Michael.

They seemed very comfortable together. At one point, Lucas put his hand on Stella's back and led her to another bit of the parapet, gesticulating with his free hand to the town below. Stella leaned in towards him, and Flora was reminded of the glossy University admissions brochure, depicting brilliant and beautiful students standing amid the brilliant and beautiful architecture and gazing towards the brilliant and beautiful future guaranteed by the possession of a Cambridge degree.

She seized her camera, which she always kept handy in

case the opportunity of snapping Lucas occurred. But her hands were trembling so much that she couldn't focus properly. She threw the camera down and fell to her knees.

'Please, God, what should I do?'

When she next looked at the Gatehouse, the walkway was empty.

Except for Raphael, Gabriel and Michael, who guarded the gates of Billings with their usual celestial equanimity.

My son has stood me up. He's probably off somewhere with the delectable Stella. Belatedly, I try his mobile. It's on message.

I'm flouncing through Billings in a mild tantrum when I see April. If I'm put out, she, judging by her face, is in a complete fury. She's heading in the direction of Perry's rooms.

'April?'

'Want to see a woman strangle her husband with her bare hands?'

In Berkeley Court she bangs on Perry's door, oblivious of the curious glances thrown in our direction by passing students. Perry answers almost immediately.

'What's wrong?'

'I could ask you the same question.'

'What do you mean?' Perry knows full well what she means. He's as shifty as a one-eyed polecat.

'When I go to collect my children from nursery today, guess what – they aren't there. In fact, they haven't been there for a good hour. Their grandmother has taken them away. "How did you know it was their grandmother?" I ask. "You can't just hand them over to a complete stranger without parental permission." "But we did have parental permission," they say. "The lady told us to phone your husband, which we did, and he said it was fine".'

'Oh,' said Perry. 'That.'

'I felt like a complete dork,' said April.

'I didn't think.'

'You never do. Not where she's concerned.'

'Don't start.'

'I told her that I didn't want them leaving nursery early, so what does she do? She nicks off behind my back and asks you. And it doesn't occur to you to check with me that it's OK?'

'She said it was fine by you. And in any case, I don't have to ask your permission to let my own kids leave nursery early,' says Perry shirtily.

'You should have checked.' I can't resist pitching in with my five-pennyworth.

'Shut up, Rosa,' snaps Perry. 'This is none of your business.'

Too true.

'You're right. I'm off.'

But April says, 'Stop! You're my witness.'

'Witness to what?' Perry's shouting now.

'She witnessed me tell Frankie not to take them shopping this morning and now she's witnessing you once again putting your mother before me.'

'Oh, for Christ's sake! My mother wanted to take her grandchildren out for a treat. What's the problem?'

'See what I mean, Rosa?'

I wish I'd carried on my own sweet way, sulking about Danny's defection.

'The problem is that she always undermines me and you always let her.'

'The problem is that where she's concerned, you're bloody paranoid. She says you won't let her buy the kids some clothes.'

'Oh, I see. You can't be bothered to pick up the phone and speak to me about it, but you've obviously had a good old chat to her.'

'She called me. She felt very hurt.'

'Well, that makes two of us. She said my children looked like tramps. Bear me out, Rosa.'

'It's true, Perry.'

'You must have misunderstood. All she wanted—'

'Wise up! She wasn't buying them new clothes out of the goodness of her heart. She just wanted to tart them up for her cheap little portfolio. Well, over my dead body. She's not exploiting my kids.'

'It's a great idea. It'll be good to have some decent photos of them for once.'

'So,' says April, 'at least I know where I stand now. Your priorities are quite clear.'

'For Christ's sake, woman, don't be such a diva.'

'It's not me that's the diva, Perry. The sooner you realise that, the better for all of us.' She opens the door and sets off across Berkeley Court.

Perry calls after her but she keeps going. He turns to me. 'I can't ever seem to get it right with her and Mum, Rosaleen. I don't know what to do.'

Sometimes Perry is such an idiot.

'Yes, you do,' I say, and follow April.

When she and I arrive back at the house, the kids greet us at the door.

'Look at my pretty new dress,' squeals Cassandra, twirling

round in a lilac satin party frock, with matching lilac ribbons in her hair, which has been curled into long ringlets.

'Granny says a man's going to take our photograph,' says Hector. He's immaculate in a miniature man's suit complete with bow tie. His thatch of thick blond hair has been parted and plastered flat to his scalp.

April and I gaze at them, dumbfounded.

'*The Village of the Damned*, circa 1960,' she mutters.

Frankie emerges from the sitting room. 'There you are. I thought you'd emigrated. All right, April? You look a bit peaky, pet.'

April walks past them into the kitchen without a word. The disingenuous smile playing round Frankie's lips vanishes when she sees my face. 'She's very highly-strung for an Australian, isn't she?'

I glare at her.

Her piggy eyes glare defiantly back. 'That lad of yours stood you up, has he?'

After a long, liquid lunch, courtesy of the college kitchens and the superb Billings wine cellar, Hugo finally produced the statute books, open at the relevant pages, and good old William got down to business, humming and muttering happily as he worked.

As time ticked past, Hugo realised that he was bored. For the moment he was surplus to requirements, a passive acolyte in the temple of William's expertise. 'Might as well leave you to it,' he said to his friend. 'No sense in me sitting here watching. I could be preparing my welcoming speech for the Yanks.'

William looked up, eyes glazed. 'What? Oh, yes. Certainly, old chap. I'll give you a shout if I strike gold.'

But when Hugo rose to his feet, something didn't feel right. There was a buzzing in his ears and the ground was shifting alarmingly. And his face, in fact his whole body had started to burn. He sat down again heavily.

William looked up. 'Steady on, old boy. Didn't think you'd drunk that much over lunch.' Then his eyes widened. 'Good Lord, Hugo, what's the matter with your face? It's covered in red blotches.'

Hugo knew very well what was the matter.

Nuts. He was allergic to nuts.

Chef and the kitchen staff were fully aware of the problem. In fact, since Hugo's arrival, all recipes containing nuts had been banished from High Table and the Master's Lodge.

So how come his throat was closing and he was feeling very ill indeed?

'Bathroom cupboard,' he croaked. 'Top shelf. Syringe of adrenaline in oblong red case. Quick.'

William might have possessed one of the finest minds in the university, but in a crisis he flapped. It seemed like ten thousand years before he finally reappeared, clutching a red box.

'Inject my thigh,' gasped Hugo.

'Who, me? Oh . . . ah . . . are you sure? I've never—'

'Do it. Or I'll die.'

But William also had his peculiarities. Needle phobia being one of them.

He strove manfully to do as he was told. He pulled down Hugo's trousers fairly successfully. He even managed to take the syringe out of its box. But when he tried to jab the tip of the needle into Hugo's thigh, the blood drained from his cheeks. 'Sorry, old boy,' he gasped. His eyes rolled upwards and his tall spindly figure swayed alarmingly over Hugo.

With the last of his strength, Hugo seized the syringe. He plunged it into his leg and then he waited, hoping against hope that the adrenaline would do its job.

Behold the Lord will take firm hold on you and hurl you away, O you mighty man. He will roll you up tightly like a ball and throw you into a large country. There you will die.

SIXTEEN

The afternoon sunlight poured through the stained-glass windows, bathing Dominic in a shaft of rainbow light. Over in the Master's Lodge, by now the deed would have been done.

William Grace would undoubtedly corroborate Mortimer's interpretation of the constitution, and thus enable the man to implement his sorry scheme. So now Dominic could only pray for divine intervention to save the library, the sacred space which, as much as the chapel itself, embodied the soul of Billings College.

It was the anger he found hardest to bear – the intense animosity he felt towards Mortimer. It was a new sensation, taking him in directions that he did not like and of which he did not approve. He was used to dealing with his generalised indignation at a greedy world that cared much for possession and little for dispossession. He was able to utilise these feelings for the good: they were what fuelled his crusade. But the rage he felt against Mortimer was different. It was personal, and he couldn't cope with it, didn't know

where to put it, carried it around on his back like a sack
of iron bars weighing him down.

He suddenly became aware of movement at the back of
the chapel.

It was Shane Bennett, one of the kitchen staff. Shane
was one of the few college servants who attended chapel,
although Dominic feared his words of wisdom fell on stony
ground, since Shane was what in less politically correct
days would have been known as 'a bit simple'.

'Shane?'

The boy rubbed a sleeve over smeared and snotty cheeks.
'I din do it, Chaplain. I wouldn't. They think I'm too stupid
to know, but I'm not.'

'Slow down, Shane. Do what?'

Shane's eyes were wide with indignation. 'They said I
must of put something nutty in Master's dinner. But I never.
I know nuts make Master sick.'

Dominic's heart thumped behind his ribs.

'Chef give me the sack. What will my mum say?'

'Is . . .' Dominic could hardly form the words. 'Is the
Master dead?'

'She'll be very cross,' moaned Shane.

'Is the Master dead?' He found himself shouting.

Shane cowered away from him.

'Shane, I'm sorry. I didn't mean to frighten you.'

'Want to go home now.'

'Of course you do. I'll come with you and explain things
to your mum. She won't be cross.'

'Really?'

'Really. Now what's happened to the Master?'

'Chef said that he took some medicine that made him

better real quick and then Chef said it was my fault and sacked me. But I never.' He started to cry again.

Mortimer was still alive.

'Let's get you home.'

But before he guided the young man out of the chapel, Dominic mounted the pulpit and turned the pages of the large and ornate college Bible until he found the page he was looking for. *So they took soot from a furnace and stood before Pharaoh. Moses tossed it into the air and festering boils broke out on men and animals.*

As he closed the Bible, a great sigh escaped him.

'Pardon?' said Shane.

'God,' he said, 'moves in a mysterious way. Never forget that, Shane.'

After he'd taken the boy home, he returned to the chapel and prayed for forgiveness.

All she'd wanted was to talk to Perry without the Wicked Witch of the North hovering round on her broomstick. She had to tackle the problem of Frankie head on. She was damned if she'd spend the rest of her marriage coming runner-up to his mother on Perry's list of priorities. In her book, being an also-ran was not an option. This would never have happened back home. Moving hemispheres had clearly weakened her more than she realised. Back home she wouldn't have tolerated this situation for five minutes. Where was her fighting spirit? Where was the woman who campaigned long and hard for the rights of the indigenous people of Australia? Where was the girl who, aged fifteen, had singlehandedly secured the dismissal of a bullying teacher at her school? Where was the feisty chick who broke it off with a longstanding boyfriend because he refused to choose between her and the vast quantities of cocaine he regularly shovelled up his nose? It was time for this person to put in an appearance. It was time to take a stand. Her ancestors had tackled the New World with courage and resilience, triumphing over massive adversity. Now she would conquer the Old World as represented by old Frankie and her devious manipulations.

But having this showdown at the house wasn't feasible. Frankie would stick her oar in and muddy the waters. And there was also Rosa. True, Rosa was on her side, but no one likes conducting their marital post-mortems in front of witnesses.

So she'd stormed round to college, to beard Perry in his den.

And there she'd seen him, coming out of his rooms with that girl. They were standing very close together – far too close – well within the eighteen-inches personal exclusion zone, and talking so intensely that it was as if the rest of the world didn't exist.

Her worst fears incarnating in front of her very eyes.

She'd followed them as they left college and walked down to the river. She wasn't even worried that they'd see her. They were so wrapped up in themselves that they were completely oblivious of their surroundings.

The only time they'd emerged from their cocoon was when Perry bought ice creams.

She'd found this the most painful thing of all. It was such an intimate gesture. She watched, heartsick, as he handed over a double cornet to the girl who, gazing up at him, stuck out her long pink tongue and delicately licked the creamy concoction. April had wanted to snatch it out of her hand and ram it into her face.

For a second she'd contemplated crashing into their little idyll. *Hi, darling! Supervision going well? Didn't know river walks were part of the service. Whoops, my hand slipped. Oh dear – doesn't look like she can swim.*

But all the earlier fight had gone out of her. It was one thing tackling Perry about his mother. This was something else again. And she'd known that there was no way she could confront them. Because if she did, it would make the whole episode real. As long as she kept it to herself she could pretend it hadn't happened. Pretend it was someone else coming out of Perry's room with Stella in tow. In fact, if she had a sleep, she might be able to persuade herself that it was all a dream.

So she'd returned home.

The house was hot and silent. Frankie had taken the children to meet her photographer friend. April was glad. It gave her time to go through Perry's things without being disturbed.

The image of Perry and Stella eating ice cream capered in front of her like a ghoul on a ghost train. She became increasingly frantic as she rifled through his desk, his bank statements, his clothes. The fact that she failed to find anything merely confirmed her suspicions that he was a conniving bastard who'd go to any lengths to protect his secret life.

Just as she'd finished, she heard Frankie and the children.

'Mummy,' shouted Hector. 'Look at me!'

Leave me alone.

Then she felt guilty. I mustn't take it out on the children, she thought. It's not their fault.

Plastering a smile onto her face she emerged from the bedroom and walked to the top of the stairs.

She gasped. 'Hector, what's happened to you?'

'Can't you tell, you silly mummy? Granny took me to the barbers to make me into a proper boy. He used some things called clippers. They buzzed.'

His thick hair had gone. In its place was a short back and sides of monumental severity, rigid with gel, a ramrod-straight parting carved expertly through one side.

'Doesn't he look like his daddy?' Frankie walked upstairs, face wreathed in smiles.

Her painted face was almost level with April, and the younger woman could smell the heavy, sickly odour of L'Heure Bleu in which, as always, her mother-in-law was drenched. She'd heard about the red mist that people were reputed to see when in the throes of extreme rage. She'd always assumed it to be a metaphor.

Not any more.

I'm fed up.

I went to a *Law Lord* costume-fitting earlier, for my May Ball gown. It's a gorgeous creation which, if I say so myself, makes me look pretty hot for someone in their fifth decade. And guess what? The bloody wardrobe woman won't let me borrow it for the Billings Ball. So I'll have to shell out for a dress I'll probably only wear once, which couldn't possibly be as nice as this one.

To add to my irritation, I still haven't hooked up with my elusive son. He did eventually respond, but his call came when I was in the middle of my fitting and I only picked up the message afterwards. He claims he had an extra rehearsal, and that he'd texted me. He was puzzled that the message had somehow failed to get through.

Yeah, right.

It isn't like Dan. He's usually pretty reliable and also, in spite of his cool dude attitude towards me in public, I know how much he misses family and home, even after two years away, and I know he was looking forward to our lunch.

That was then. This is now.

Ever since I arrived he's been weird. Obviously the break-up with Julie hasn't been easy, but that's not all. Something else is going on. I just can't fathom what it is, and Danny certainly isn't giving me any clues. When my children were in the throes of full-blown adolescence, I thought that communication was difficult. It was a piece of cake compared to this grown-up-away-from-home stuff. You don't see them for weeks, and when you do, they've changed utterly.

Or is it, on the contrary, that they've changed infinitesimally, but in such a way that you can't fathom it? Like in dreams, where you're in a place that you know well, yet something's imperceptibly different so that you can't find your way around any more. And you can't work out what the something is that's different.

Yes, I know I'm being melodramatic, as usual, but there's a truth in there somewhere, screeching to get out.

Maybe it's as it should be. Danny's a big man now, with his own life to lead. He doesn't need me breathing down his neck, monitoring his every emotional move. But it's hard to detach. After Rob's death I feared our little family was on the verge of falling apart, but we came through with a greater understanding of each other than ever before. Closer than most families ever manage.

That's why Danny's distancing antics hurt.

I suppose I thought in some way that as the years passed our relationship, without denying the parent-child thing would evolve into a more equal, adult friendship where we could confide in each other as we would with other friends.

But Danny clearly has no wish to confide, or even to see me at the moment.

This visit is not turning out the way I thought it would. And I wish the old maternal alarm system would catch up with logic and reason, accept that life has moved on and turn itself off, instead of nagging at me that Danny's in some kind of trouble.

Oh well, if my son doesn't need me, maybe my daughter would welcome a call.

'Hi, Anna.'

'Hi, Mum. How's it going?'

I won't get into a huge thing with her about Danny. Not when she has an exam tomorrow. 'Fine. Just checking you're OK.'

'Josh is still fussing, and the revision's more or less on schedule. How's life chez Grimshaw?'

'Peachy. I'm April's only defender against her loathsome ma-in-law.'

'Not the Fabulous Frankie?'

'Yes indeed. She turned up out of the blue yesterday and turfed me out of my room. I'm sleeping with the dynamic duo. Not very restful – to put it mildly.'

'Stuff A-Level English. I'm catching the next train. I have
to meet the Fabulous Frankie.'

Frankie is a living legend to Danny and Anna – a part
of my mysterious childhood. They've never actually met
her, but feel somehow they know her.

'She's even worse than I remember,' I grumble.

'How's Perry?'

'Irritatingly sorry for himself.'

'What do you mean?'

'When push comes to shove, a husband should put his
wife before his mother.'

'And he doesn't?'

I haven't realised until now how cross I am with him.
But my feelings are between me and him. To say more
to Anna would be inappropriate.

'Do you mind if I stay on an extra day?' I ask. 'After
tomorrow's exam you haven't got another one for a week
at least . . .'

'Whassup, Mum? Met the Man of your Dreams?'

'I wish. Actually I've been invited to the Billings May
Ball.'

'So you *have* met the man of your dreams.'

'No, just Perry's boss – the Master of the college. Wants
me to help him entertain some rich Americans.'

'Is he fit?'

'Couldn't be less fit if he tried. So is that OK?'

'Go for it.'

'Are you sure?'

'Are you kidding? What are you going to wear?'

'I haven't a clue. All I know is that it's bound to cost a
bomb.'

'Go to Julie's shop. She'll give you a discount.'

Anna gets her brains from me.

'Anna, you're a genius. Listen, I've got to go. Good luck for tomorrow morning. I'll keep all my toes and fingers crossed. Love you.'

'Love you too, Mum.'

Julie's shop.

If the mountain in the form of Danny won't come to Mohammed, then Mohammed will go to the mountain in the form of Julie. One way or another I'll get to the bottom of Danny's odd behaviour.

And, with any luck, I'll get a posh frock on the cheap as well.

My conversation with Anna has taken me back to Perry's house. I ring the bell, but no one answers. Judging by the commotion inside, no one's heard. 'It's Rosa,' I shout through the letterbox. 'Let me in!'

I hear a chair being dragged across the floor and someone climbing onto it. The door opens and Cassandra's shocked little face peers at me. 'Granny fell,' she sobs.

Frankie is draped across the bottom of the stairs. April stands at the top. The kids are wailing in Dolby Surround Sound.

I kneel down beside Frankie, her make-up garish against a chalk-white face.

'Is she dead?' asks Hector tearfully.

Could be. But when I feel for a pulse, my wrist is seized in an iron grip. 'She tried to kill me.'

Not dead. Merely suffering from a terminal dose of malice.

April glares down at us.

Frankie's resurrection gathers pace. 'You pushed me downstairs, lady,' she hisses. 'Don't deny it. The kiddies saw you.'

Hector takes a momentary break from bawling and nods importantly. 'You did, Mummy. We saw you, didn't we, Cass?'

Cassandra continues to wail. 'I didn't see nuffing.'

Hector kicks her. 'You're such a girl,' he says scornfully, before resuming full bellow mode.

Still April says nothing.

Frankie's eyes bore into her. I can see some rapid calculation going on. 'I expect it was an accident, pet,' she says finally. 'I dare say you lost your balance. As you know, I'm not one to bear grudges so we'll say no more about it. Help me up, Rosa.' She staggers to her feet and makes for the sitting room.

I go upstairs to April. She's shivering. I put my arm round her. 'How about a stiff drink?' I suggest.

'I didn't push her.'

'Of course you didn't.' I try to sound convincing. The look on her face is one I remember of old. It's the one my children used to wear when they were frightened of being caught out in some piece of mischief.

SEVENTEEN

Flora lay on the grass in the Fellows' Garden and tried to concentrate on Lee's warm-up exercises. They were intended to relax everybody before the show, but his portentous delivery was having the opposite effect on her. All through the rehearsal period, she hadn't quite absorbed the implications of what she'd done in agreeing to act in *Othello*, having never before set foot on a stage. And latterly she'd been preoccupied by other things. But now, listening to Lee exhorting her to breathe deeply and articulate the syllables *maa mee moo*, the nerves finally kicked in.

She was about to humiliate herself in front of a paying audience. Which would include her parents.

Flora lived with the knowledge that her existence was a matter of indifference to her father and a grave disappointment to her mother. The worldly, sophisticated pair had never understood how they'd produced someone so plain and gauche. Her father who, even after twenty-five years of marriage, doted on her glamorous mother to the exclusion of all else, hardly bothered to acknowledge her at all. But to her mother, she was a constant source of irritation and exasperation. Large, clumsy, blue-stocking Flora, so totally unlike the daughters of her society friends with their sleek frivolity and shallow charm.

But when Flora revealed that she was acting in the BADS May Week production, Meredith Mainwaring was, for once, lavish in her approval. 'Darling, how marvellous,' she'd trilled. 'At last! A bit of the Mainwaring oomph! We simply must catch your first night. Be sure to leave a couple of tickets for us on the door. What do they say in theatrical circles? Break a leg!'

Flora thought wistfully that it would have been nice if her parents had offered her tea before the show or dinner after it. Or both. But she understood that they probably had more important things to do. After all, the main reason they were coming to Cambridge was to attend the May Ball as special guests of the Master. And she couldn't compete with that. She didn't really mind. She was so excited at the thought of seeing them for the first time since Christmas that nothing else mattered. And she so wanted to make them proud of her.

But now the moment was almost upon her, she felt dizzy with fear. What if she dried? Or tripped? Or missed her cue? She'd never face her mother again. She tried to look on the bright side. If she gave a truly dazzling performance, it might permanently change the way her parents viewed her.

But judging by Lee's pronouncements on her attempts so far, that was hardly going to happen.

And then there was Lucas. If she messed up, what would

he think? He'd be comparing her with Stella, who would undoubtedly capture all hearts with her stunning rendition of Desdemona the doomed.

But then she remembered: firstly that there were other things in her life far more important than her performance in *Othello*, and secondly that God was on her side.

All would be well. She would come out a winner. It was in the bag.

'Mee mii moo maa,' she intoned.

Julie struggled to manoeuvre the costume rail into the Fellows' Garden. None of the cast came to help. Snotty arseholes, she thought. Granted, they were doing the pre-show warm-up, but even so, it would only have taken a moment. Her stomach dive-bombed as she spotted Stella and Danny lying on the grass doing the wanky voice exercises, their arms lightly touching.

'Want some help?'

It was the fit bloke she'd seen talking to Stella and Flora after rehearsal the other day. He angled the clothes rail so that it moved easily through the narrow gateway. Close up, he was a real stud muffin. Made Danny look like Peter Plain. A brilliant idea occurred: if Danny saw this hunk chatting her up he might feel jealous.

'I don't think I'm strong enough to push it over the grass,' she said helplessly.

He flashed her a toothpaste-ad smile. 'You're Joan's daughter, aren't you?'

'Yeah. How did you know?' Julie felt absurdly pleased that he recognised her.

'I sometimes leave messages for my uncle in the college

office and I've seen your photo on Joan's desk. It doesn't do you justice. I'm Lucas, by the way. My uncle's the college chaplain.' Then he waved and smiled at someone.

Julie followed his gaze and saw Stella. *The bitch is everywhere.* She was about to launch her most toxic scowl, but then she caught eyes with Danny so she treated Lucas to a sexy smile instead.

After they'd pushed the rail behind the stage, she was desperate to keep him talking a little longer to make sure Danny got the point.

'Are you a student?' she asked.

He laughed. 'Not likely. Mr No Brains, that's me. I help my uncle with his Christian refuge in Bateman Street.'

'Flora was telling me about that. It's a shelter for the homeless, right?'

'Yeah.'

Julie had no time for the homeless – they stank of booze and piss, and behaved unpredictably. It was entirely their own fault they were on the street in the first place. However, that was not what Lucas would want to hear, and right now she needed him to like her.

'That's great.' She searched for the right phrase – the kind of expression Danny and his snotty friends would use. 'Much more meaningful than being a student. Helping those less fortunate than ourselves innit. Fantastic.'

'If you're interested,' said Lucas, 'you could volunteer?'

'Yeah?' She tried to sound enthusiastic. 'Cool.'

He grinned. 'Have a sweet.' He pulled out a bag of sweets and thrust it towards her. She didn't like boiled sweets, but she took one anyway, hoping Danny was watching as she slid it suggestively into her mouth.

Lucas continued his sales pitch. 'Come and see us and we'll fix you up with some shifts. I can tell you're a really caring person. You'll love it – it's such a cool place.'

Gazing into his deep blue eyes Julie was almost tempted. But then he spoiled it by clasping his hands together and saying thank you to God for bringing her to him. Right there, out loud, in the middle of the garden. She was very relieved to find Danny wasn't looking after all. What she absolutely didn't want was for him to think she was getting involved with some Jesus freak. She willed Lucas to piss off, and to her great relief he did. Having finished his chat with the Almighty, he treated her to a final drop-dead gorgeous smile. 'I'll see you at R&R.' Then he loped off, the sun glinting on his golden mane.

Tragic, thought Julie. What a waste. A waste, and also the last thing she needed. She'd already had to tell Flora that religion was not her thing. Now Lucas would be breathing down her neck, trying to convert her at every available opportunity. Every time she came into college, she'd be scared he'd loom round the corner waving his Bible and spouting crap.

Except that after *Othello* was over, she'd be gone from Billings. If she couldn't be with Danny, she didn't want to come within five miles of the bloody place.

But then again, that situation might change.

She could make it change.

She reviewed the awesome idea she'd had earlier. Right decision or wrong decision? Right for her yet wrong, full stop. She knew she wasn't perfect, but up until now her sins had been pretty small-scale. She could look at herself in the mirror with a fairly clear conscience. But what she was contemplating would definitely take her over to the dark side. The more she tried to get her head around it, the more confused she felt.

Confused and now something else. Weird. Strange. The green lawn was dropping away beneath her feet and although she could see the actors, could reach out and touch them even, she felt that they weren't real – that she was the only real thing. The only real thing in the entire universe. She stood, petrified, as the world shrank, the sunshine disappeared, everything went dark and she was transported back to the moment when, face up against a tree, she had struggled to free herself from the monster on Jesus Green.

Not again.

Ever since Sunday this horrible thing had kept happening, ambushing her when she least expected it. This time it was particularly strong. She struggled to make it go away by pinching herself repeatedly until finally the sensation of pain superseded the sensation of obliteration; the nightmare faded and once more she became aware of the afternoon heat caressing her skin.

But she felt distinctly wobbly. In mind as well as body.

Maybe this was a sign that she should forget her great idea. Leave it well alone.

Lee had brought the warm-up to a close and was waving the actors in her direction. Time for costume and make-up. She noticed, as they strolled towards her, that Stella and Danny were still joined at the hip.

Flora dashed ahead of the others. 'What did Lucas want?'

'Nothing. He was helping me with the costume rail.'

'Did he leave a message for me?'

"Fraid not. Do you know him well?'

'We work together at R&R.'

'He's just asked me to be a volunteer. But I can't be arsed with no religious shit. No offence, Flora.'

'None taken,' said Flora absently. 'Come on, Julie. Things to do.'

Julie relaxed momentarily. Let someone else take the strain. Make the decisions.

We're having an early meal with the children, before April, Perry and I attend the opening night of *Othello*. But what should be a nice cosy supper feels like a bad nineteenth-century Scandinavian play. April's not talking, Frankie's sighing and wincing a lot and Perry – well, I don't know what's up with Perry. I've never seen him so tense. The kids, spooked by their parents' general lack of focus on them, are behaving appallingly – throwing food, shouting and running round the room instead of sitting at the table. I'm itching to step in, but it's one of life's unwritten rules: never chastise friends' children. At least, not within earshot of their doting parents. Try and pretend that the creatures cavorting in front of you and producing a decibel level well in excess of average health and safety levels are dear little souls exhibiting normal childish high spirits, rather than the first symptoms of a deranged psychopathology.

'Shut the fuck up, you little turds.' Frankie's had enough.

Silence for a beat, then Hector starts chanting, 'Fuck fuck fuckie fuckie fuck fuck.'

Cassandra joins in.

Perry looks across at April, clearly expecting her to leap into her usual masterful mummy mode. But she hardly seems to have registered anything. I feel a rising impatience. Why is he being so wet? OK, so normally he sits back and lets April do the disciplining. But can't he see she's not herself?

Eventually he rises to the occasion. 'Hector! Cassandra! Don't ever let me hear either of you use that word again.'

'Granny used it.'

'Granny's a grown-up.'

'So it's OK for grown-ups?'

'No, but—'

'Then why don't you tell Granny off?'

'Grown-ups don't tell each other off.'

'Granny told Mummy off when Mummy pushed her downstairs.'

'*What?*'

A deathly hush descends.

Then Frankie leaps in. 'It was an accident,' she says, somehow implying the exact opposite. 'No harm done, is there, April, pet?'

April doesn't respond.

Perry says, 'Go upstairs now, please, children. I'll run your bath in a minute when I've had a word with Granny.'

'You *are* going to tell her off!'

'Daddy's going to smack you, Granny!'

'That's enough! Granny's babysitting tonight. I just want to check that she knows all your routines. Now upstairs right this minute or no bedtime story.'

The children, astounded by their father's uncharacteristically stern tone, troop off obediently.

Once they're out of earshot, Perry says, 'What's this all about?'

'Honestly, pet, it's nothing.' Frankie gestures dismissively, giving a lighthearted laugh that modulates into a frail little gasp of pain. She clutches her arm.

'Nothing? Let me see.'

'I said it's nothing.' But she nonetheless allows him to roll up her sleeve and expose two or three nasty abrasions.

'What happened?'

April sits rigidly upright in her seat. I don't even know whether she's listening.

'She didn't mean it,' says Frankie insincerely. 'She was walking along the landing towards the stairs and she tripped and knocked into me, didn't you, pet?'

Finally, April looks at her. Their eyes lock. 'Yes. That's right. I overbalanced. As you say, Frankie, no harm done.'

Frankie's eyes harden. 'No. Although it's just as well I'm not working at the moment. My poor legs are battered black and blue.' She extends one of her spindly legs. There is indeed extensive bruising along the shin. 'I'm lucky to be in one piece. In spite of appearances, I'm no spring chicken any more.'

Is Perry aware of her game-playing? Game-playing? What am I saying? The woman's covered in bruises. She's not making it up. No, but whatever the truth she's definitely trying to drop April in it with Perry.

Will he fall for it?

He looks from his mother to his wife and back again. Eventually he speaks. 'All's well that ends well. Thank goodness you weren't more badly hurt, Mum. It's my fault, darling,' he says to April. 'You've been saying for weeks that we ought to replace that worn carpet at the top of the stairs, and I've been putting it off.'

I see the thwarted rage flash across Frankie's face.

Perry's clearly wondering why April hasn't responded to his lifeline. 'Frankie doesn't blame you, darling. No one does. Are you OK?'

'I'm fine.'

'You don't sound it.'

'I'm fine.'

Frankie stares at April, eyes narrowing. 'You don't look fine. You look proper peaky, pet. I think perhaps you had more of a shock than I did.'

What's she up to?

'Maybe you shouldn't go to the play tonight. You needn't waste the ticket. I could use it instead.'

'I really am OK, thank you, Frankie.' April turns to Perry. 'And after entertaining not only Othello but also the lovely Desdemona the other night, I wouldn't miss this production for the world.'

Perry isn't looking at her any more. 'You could always go later in the week.' He's mumbling into the table.

'I'm fine. And I'm coming tonight. End of.'

Why is she so aggressive? Why is he so sheepish? There's a complex unspoken conversation going on here. Married couple semaphore. I remember it well. Sometimes, whole issues can be covered by a mere shrug of the shoulder or lift of an eyebrow.

Frankie, meanwhile, has probably fully taken on board for the first time the horror of an evening alone with Hector and Cassandra in their present mood. 'I know I said I wasn't bothered, but I've changed my mind. It's a long time since I've seen a bit of Shakespeare. And,' she gestures towards me, 'I'd like to see how your Danny shapes up. If I have a shufty on t'first night, I can give him the benefit of my professional advice – stand him in good stead for the rest of the run. Can't you get a babysitter, Perry?'

'Not at such short notice.' April cuts across her.

But Frankie's making cow eyes at him.

He gets up. 'I'll give Karen a ring,' he says.

What Frankie wants Frankie gets. In a couple of minutes Perry's back. 'We're in luck,' he says.

'Hooray,' says April.

'I'll go and titivate.' Frankie jumps up, then, remembering she's an invalid, limps feebly towards the door. 'The fall's left me quite shaky,' she says pitifully. 'It'll do me good to get out. Take my mind off it.'

Then there were three.

Until April, brittle as spun sugar, says, 'I'd better get ready too. Can't let the side down, can I?' And off she goes.

Perry and I face each other over the table.

'I ought to bed down the troops.'

'What's going on, Perry?'

He looks cornered. 'What do you mean?'

'Frankie's winding April up like a clockwork toy and you're letting her.'

'I told you – April's always moody when Frankie's around. She sees her as some kind of threat. Ridiculous, I know, but there it is.'

This man's ostrich head is so far in the sand that any minute now he'll open his eyes and find himself back on Bondi Beach.

'I know you don't want to hear this, Perrygreen, but Frankie really doesn't wish April well.'

'Bollocks.'

'It's true.'

'No. April's behaving very badly. She got used to having me all to herself in Australia and she's not prepared to share me occasionally with my poor old mum who has no one except me.'

I remember when we were children how angry I would be on Perry's behalf when Frankie had yet again let him down, and how Perry would brush aside my rage and devise the most elaborate and unlikely scenarios to explain why Frankie had made one of her casually cruel remarks, or shrugged off his pitiful attempts to get her affection, or forgotten his birthday, or failed to participate in some other important event in his life.

I can talk till I'm blue in the face about Frankie's skulduggery. He's not going to listen. Nothing changes.

'April needs your support, and as far as I can see, she isn't getting it.'

Perry's eyes blaze. 'Frankie bends over backwards to be nice to her.'

'Perry, tell me you're joking.'

'If anyone's behaving badly, it's April. All that sulking over supper. And what's all this about her pushing Frankie downstairs?'

'An accident. You heard.'

'Yes, I did, and for someone who you claim doesn't wish my wife well, Frankie seemed pretty keen to defend her.'

There's no point me trying to tell him what Frankie was

219

doing. I can't prove it. I can't prove anything except my own dislike of Frankie. And besides, I'm on dodgy ground here. I saw the look in April's eyes this afternoon when Frankie was lying at the bottom of the stairs.

'All I'm saying is that you'd do well to remember the bit in the marriage service about forsaking all others and clinging only to your wife.'

'Piss off, Rosa,' says Perry.

That went well.

From now on I'll confine my worrying to my own son, whose imminent appearance as the Moor of Venice is causing little explosions of fear to erupt inside me.

Hugo smiled at himself in the bathroom mirror as he exfoliated his pink scalp with something delicious from Jo Malone. His ordeal earlier in the day had left him a bit wobbly but it hadn't stopped him making several telephone calls to his colleagues in the Senior Common Room.

William's perusal of the statutes had been a raging success. He'd unearthed a tiny sub-clause that stated unequivocally that if there was any long-term question mark over the mental competence of a Fellow, then that Fellow would be barred from voting in matters of major concern to the college.

All Hugo had to do, therefore, was to demonstrate that the Chaplain was bonkers.

It wouldn't be difficult. The chaps and chapesses in the Senior Common Room were a pretty conservative bunch and Tipton was already regarded as unacceptably vulgarian by many of them. They felt his work at the wretched refuge in Bateman Street was worthy enough in itself, but distinctly unbecoming to a respected academic and Senior Fellow of a Cambridge college. They thought he was deluded even to imagine he could combine the roles, and they were also currently concerned that Tipton's Tramps, as they were known behind his back, were not staying in their proper place down in the town, but increasingly finding their way up to Billings. The consensus was that the poor were always with us, but it was preferable that they and their problems remained at a safe distance from the college. Several times in recent months Stanley Gordon had had to boot out various ripe specimens who were wandering round the courtyards claiming to be looking for the Chaplain. And only two weeks ago there had been an incident that shocked many of them to the core. Preacher Man, the local hellfire loony, had come into college and hung around the entrance to Tipton's staircase for nearly two hours, scowling and snarling at everyone who passed, particularly the female students. But then, just as Gordon was about to call the police and have him forcibly removed, Tipton had appeared. He'd upbraided poor Gordon for not even offering the man a drink of water, and had then taken him into Hall and given him dinner.

Taken a tramp into Hall. To High Table, no less.

It just wasn't on.

It would be a piece of cake to convince the Fellows that Tipton's activities were the result, not of charitable compassion, but creeping insanity.

'I rather think we've cracked it, Dawkins,' he chortled. 'Now be a good boy this evening, and don't torment the cats – you know they always get the better of you. I must go and show my face at this wretched play.'

Shakespeare, along with God, was, as far as Hugo was concerned, an over-rated anachronism.

EIGHTEEN

He hovered near the entrance to the Fellows' Garden, watching the audience congregate and waiting for Lucas.

'Are you all right, Dominic?'

It was Millicent Eddington, Reader in Modern Languages. She was the fourth of his colleagues to ask him that question in the last half-hour.

'Of course I'm all right. Why shouldn't I be?'

'No reason,' said Millicent hurriedly, and darted away.

He caught the eye of another of his colleagues, a Physics don, who was also going to the play. The man immediately looked away, but not before Dominic saw something that looked very much like pity in his eyes. What was going on?

Maybe Lucas had taken his seat already. He hoped this was not the case. He badly wanted to dissuade him from seeing *Othello*.

Lucas was a handsome young man with a young man's blood in his veins. Dominic saw how he looked at the female volunteers who passed through R&R. And that was as it should be. Young men had urges. But Lucas needed someone who would love and support him in his mission. Someone like Flora. At present Lucas still maintained they were just good friends, but that could change. Given time and opportunity, the friendship between them could develop into something far deeper.

Which was why the thought of Lucas watching *Othello* filled him with deep unease.

When Flora had brought Stella Grainger to the refuge, Dominic had been taken aback to register the spark between her and Lucas, and he knew instantly that his hopes for Lucas and Flora would be shattered if this girl was added to the mix. She was very beautiful and very charming. He'd seen her around college. Always followed by a trail of drooling youth.

But not Lucas. Not if he could help it. He would not stand by and see the boy bewitched and beguiled by the girl's doubtless heart-wrenching portrayal of the hapless Desdemona. He knew only too well the potency of play-acting. He'd fallen for the only girl he'd ever loved after seeing her spirited interpretation of Hedda Gabler in an OUDS production at Oxford when he was an under-graduate.

A prime example of something that had ended extremely badly.

The play was about to start. Maybe Lucas had decided not to come after all . . .

But there he was, loping across the grass. 'Hi, Unc. Didn't think this was your bag.'

Dominic's heart swelled with love. 'Lucas. A word.'

'Make it quick, Unc, or I'll miss curtain-up.'

Dominic suddenly realised that he hadn't thought

through exactly how he was going to prevent Lucas from seeing the play. He couldn't say, 'Don't go in there because you'll fall for Desdemona, and all my plans for you and Flora will go up in smoke.' He definitely couldn't say that. So what exactly could he say?

Lucas was glancing surreptitiously at his watch. Dominic panicked. He had to speak. He opened his mouth but the words that came out bore no relation at all to what he really wanted to tell the boy.

'The devil is in there waiting to steal your immortal soul.'

Lucas blinked in surprise. 'Where did that come from?' He grinned, clearly thinking Dominic was joking. 'You taking over from Preacher Man tonight, then?'

'If you want drama, the stories in the Bible are far more engrossing than any play.'

Lucas laughed uneasily. 'Wassup, Unc?'

Having, it seemed, adopted Preacher Man's persona, Dominic didn't know how to extricate himself. He found himself saying, 'Theatre is a corrupting force designed by Satan to seduce people away from God.'

Lucas finally seemed to take him seriously. 'You're wrong, Unc,' he said. 'To fight the devil, a man must go down into the pit.'

'But—'

'Trust me.' And then he'd vanished into the Fellows' Garden.

To his horror, Dominic wanted to cry. He knew his reaction was disproportionate, but he couldn't help it. His boy was courting disaster. He clasped his hands in silent prayer, not caring that several latecomers were desperately trying to avoid looking at him.

'Please God, shield Lucas. Lead him not into temptation—'

'Competition to the main event, are we, Dominic?'

It was the Master. He didn't look remotely like someone
who'd recently had a near-death experience. He steered his
female companion past Dominic towards the Fellows'
Garden, where the audience had fallen silent in response
to the sound of rapid machine-gun fire. 'Come, Lady
Latimer, the play begins. We must leave the chaplain to
his devotions. They're clearly extremely urgent since he
feels moved to perform them here in the middle of Locke
Court.'

Dominic suppressed the unChristian wish that during
the performance the Master might absentmindedly help
himself to a proffered chocolate from the large box clutched
in his companion's bejewelled paw. And that the chocolate
might, in its hidden centre, contain a nut.

'Keep up your bright swords, for the dew will rust them.'

Is this my son, this charismatic man who speaks with
such authority? Is this my Danny?

Being an actor myself, I'm more aware than most of the
transforming power of art, but Danny's particular transformation has taken me by surprise. I've only ever seen him
performing with 3D, his group. But this is a different ball
game. Acting, the ability to convince people that you are
somebody other than yourself, is like alchemy: you either
have it, or you don't.

I've been a bundle of nerves ever since we took our
places on the hard plastic chairs set out in the Fellows'
Garden. Before the play began I tried to divert myself by

bridging the conversational gap between April on my left and Frankie on my right. This required major diplomatic skill, since they both persisted in addressing their remarks solely to me, and not each other, and Perry, sitting next to his mother, had stopped talking to anybody.

It should have been enough to distract me, but it wasn't. Within minutes I'd reduced my copy of the flimsy programme to a crumpled mess of print, making it almost impossible to read either the cast list or the earnest and convoluted Eng-lit rationale from the director about why he'd chosen to set the play in twenty-first-century post-war Iraq rather than Renaissance Cyprus.

As time ticked closer to curtain-up, I forced myself to assimilate and appreciate the details of the set – a huge tented canopy under which a vast bed piled high with bright silk cushions dominates the stage. I even managed a care-free wave for the Master as he took his seat right at the last minute, accompanied by a fat woman in a pink pashmina.

Underneath, I was in agony.

But immediately Danny, resplendent in the uniform of a five-star American General, started to speak, I relaxed.

He *is* Othello.

He's never shown the slightest interest in acting up until now, and to be honest I'd have a fit if he ever seriously contemplated it as a profession, but I'm still dead chuffed that he's got what it takes. He's inherited some of my genes, after all.

For a student production it's not bad. The director has concentrated on clarity. Even the minor characters have been coached in how to point up the meaning of the language. I'm particularly amused by Bianca the Whore, played for some reason by a boy, who succeeds in blatantly upstaging everyone whenever 'she's' onstage. Now I can relax about Danny, I'm really enjoying myself. Particularly since Frankie, who's been very restless – fanning herself with her programme, shifting in her seat and sighing a lot – has at last shut up. I'd have taken bets that Shakespeare wouldn't do it for dear Frankie, and her reaction to the first ten minutes of the play seemed to bear me out. But now she's as silent as the tomb. I sneak a sideways look at her.

'That I do love the Moor to live with him, my downright violence, and storm of fortunes, may trumpet to the world,' Desdemona tells her father. And Frankie's with her every step of the way. She's bolt upright, eyes glued to the stage, rigid with concentration.

As is her son.

Perry can't take his eyes off Stella.

And April can't take her eyes off Perry. I don't think she sees more than a fraction of what's taking place on the stage.

By the time the interval arrives, I feel I've been attending two different productions, both playing simultaneously.

Both tragic.

Frankie suddenly says, 'I'm off. I can only take so much of this amateur Shakespeare malarky. Besides, I'm expecting a message from Alf and I can't keep my flaming mobile on in here. Ta ta for now, folks.'

She teeters away, her spiked heels doing a great job of aerating the Fellows' lawn.

'Pity she didn't remember how badly amateur Shakespeare malarky affected her before we shelled out for a babysitter,'

April mutters. She looks around. 'Where's Perry?' Her voice is suddenly shrill.

'Over there, talking to that nervy-looking bloke. I think it might be the director.' I recognise him from my illicit peek into rehearsals on the day of my arrival.

When Perry returns, he says that Lee Watson's invited us to stay for a drink after the show.

'He's one of my brighter students. Bit of a rough diamond, but he should go far. I've got a lot of time for Lee.'

'You've got a lot of time for a lot of your students, haven't you?' April's tone holds a challenge.

'What do you mean?'

They eyeball each other.

'I'm just saying that you always do the best for your students.'

'A ringing endorsement, my darling. How kind of you.'

I've never pegged sarcasm as part of Perry's make-up. Not until now.

I'm relieved when the second half begins and I can lose myself in the fictional unravelling of a doomed relationship.

Her parents hadn't come. Two seats in the front row next to the Master remained yawningly empty throughout the show, their *Reserved* signs staring mockingly up at her. She tried to ignore the lump in her throat that had threatened to prevent her from saying her first few lines. It didn't really matter. It wasn't that important. They'd probably had to go to dinner with Daddy's computer billionaire colleague who lived in a mansion outside Cambridge. She knew Daddy was very anxious to get him onside for some important business deal. What was a silly college production compared to that? Or maybe she'd misunderstood Mummy. Maybe Mummy had said they were coming on another night. All in all, there was bound to be a very good reason why they hadn't turned up.

'Be thus when thou art dead and I will kill thee, and love thee after. One more, and that's the last.'

Flora watched Julie as Othello kissed Desdemona long and deep. Too long. Too deep. The girl looked devastated, but when she saw Flora staring at her, she grimaced towards Stella. 'She ain't that great tonight,' she whispered.

'What?'

'She's a bag of nerves. Look – she's wriggling around like a fucking eel. Lee's going to be well pissed off. I wonder what's up? Maybe she and Danny had a row before the show.'

'Do you reckon?' Flora peered at the lovers on the stage. 'She seems the same as usual to me.'

She watched Stella trying to control her twitching, writhing body as she lay stretched out on the big bed. She was close enough to see the expression on her face as she pleaded with her husband to let her live. And then she observed closely her agonised efforts to remain death-still after Othello finally did the deed and smothered her.

Flora had to admire her capacity for dissimulation.

Danny downed his third glass of warm white wine in the space of as many minutes, his brain buzzing. The cathartic effect of being the Moor for three hours had left him in a state of euphoria bordering on frenzy. The high he was experiencing was easily as powerful as when he played a gig with 3D. Awesome.

He'd never fallen for the Cambridge Experience. Never really got what it was about. Always seen himself as an outsider, not quite sure where he fitted. But tonight, for the first time, he fitted perfectly. He was part of something bigger than him, part of something going back hundreds of years, an attempt to make sense of the world through scholarship and art.

It wasn't just the act of performing. It was everything – the gradual sinking of the evening into night, mirroring the mood of the unfolding tragedy; the rapt expressions on the faces of the audience, sitting in the beautiful garden; the sight of his mother in the gathering twilight, her expression, as always, conveying her inner feelings so vividly, as she lived through each harrowing moment of the inexorable advance towards the horror of Act Five; the heady perfume of night-scented stock, her favourite summer flower, redolent of home, flooding through the garden, mixed with the sharp metallic smell of adrenaline on the stage.

And most of all, the intimate looks and whispers exchanged between him and Stella as they waited behind set to enact the final collision of the two doomed lives. Particularly the moment at the props table when he was collecting his army issue knife, the instrument of his own death. She, without any trace of self-consciousness, had stood in her underwear, arms raised, and gestured wordlessly for him to slip on her nightdress – Desdemona's shroud. And when he'd done it and they were as close as two people could be, he'd bent down and kissed her lightly on the lips.

He knew he would remember that moment for the rest of his life – standing in the sheltering comfort of a warm Cambridge night, bursting wide open with a love of life and of the beautiful girl standing beside him. Even the fact that, minutes later, when they were playing out their final scenes, Stella seemed somewhat distracted didn't faze him. Even when she rushed off after the curtain call without even changing her costume, none of these things was able to curb his elation.

He'd had a brief bad moment during the post-show drinks when his mother had given him a huge hug. He'd let out a yelp of pain as she squeezed his bruised torso, but he'd fobbed her off with a tale of a minor injury caused during a stage-fight. After that he'd been swallowed up in a 'darling you were marvellous' half-hour.

Now, as he listened to the animated chatter around him in the garden, he tried to retain that earlier euphoria. He saw April being a good college wife, buzzing around like a blue-arsed fly, talking animatedly to all the right people, and wondered what was up with her. She'd hardly stopped to congratulate him on his performance before asking with frantic urgency if he'd seen Perry. Danny was puzzled. He'd never seen her so brittle. But he hadn't clapped eyes on his godfather since spotting him in the audience during the play. Truth to tell, he felt a bit miffed. He'd been looking forward to Perry's assessment of his performance.

The thought of Rosa caused his excitement to splutter out like a spent firework. After she'd finished socialising, Rosa would be back, wanting to know why he'd cut lunch. He had no wish to tell more lies, but he still wasn't ready to talk about Julie.

He was beginning to wish he could be Othello on a permanent basis – a character in a play. Fiction was simple. You lived. You died. There was cause and effect. Stories had a beginning, a middle and an end. And there was never any real harm done. The next night, Desdemona lived and loved once more, and the whole process began again.

'Danny, can I ask you a favour?'

It was Julie.

'Will you see me home?' Her voice was flat and dull. 'I'm scared of going on my own. Another girl's been attacked in the Botanic Gardens. It was in today's paper. I wouldn't ask you, but . . .'

Everything in him screamed *no way*. If he left now he'd miss seeing Stella when she came back from wherever she'd been hiding herself since the end of the play. And walking Julie back to her house, where he'd recently disgraced himself so thoroughly, filled him with unspeakable horror. She was bound to do her clinging-vine routine, and now, with the pregnancy, she'd got the perfect weapon in her armoury. In fact, she was probably only asking him in order to reveal the glad tidings and bind him to her forever. And he couldn't face that. Not yet. Not tonight. He needed a walk with Julie like he needed a dose of the clap. All he wanted was to find Stella and continue where they'd left off backstage. He had to stop himself from shouting, 'Piss off,' in Julie's face. 'Piss off, you manipulative bitch. Who do you think you're fooling? Afraid of going home alone? When were you ever afraid of going home alone? You were climbing out of your bedroom window and going clubbing when you were fifteen years old. Or so you say. Leave me alone. I don't want you. I don't want anything more to do with you. I wish I'd never met you.'

Then his conscience kicked in. What a selfish, self-centred bastard! He no longer had the right to dream about Stella. Or to think of Julie as some pathetic nuisance standing in his way. She was the mother of his child. He was a complete shit, who couldn't even do one small thing like seeing her home. What sort of a man was prepared to let a vulnerable pregnant woman cross a dark and dangerous park on her own late at night with a rapist on the loose?

'Sure,' he said.

And with a heavy heart he realised that, far from being a situation to avoid, far from leaving it to Julie to set the agenda, this was the perfect opportunity for him to face up to his responsibilities and do what he should have done hours ago: talk to Julie about the baby.

'Do you want to go right now?'

'If that's OK?'

He steered her round the edge of the garden where it was darkest so no one would see them together. Particularly his mother. He didn't want to confuse her even further until he'd sorted things out.

As they walked over the footbridge onto Jesus Green Julie was uncharacteristically silent. One of the things he'd loved was her colourful, rapid-fire delivery in which opinions, images, whole conversations she'd had with people were reproduced in vivid detail with extraordinary relish. And if she was pissed off about something she'd normally pitch straight in without thinking twice, showering the unlucky recipient with a torrent of recrimination and abuse.

Not tonight. She walked, head down, seemingly hardly

aware of Danny's presence beside her. He willed himself to talk about the pregnancy, but the more he tried to form the right words, the more tongue-tied he became.

Eventually it became intolerable. 'It went off all right tonight, didn't it?' He tried for bright and breezy.

'Suppose so.'

'It was great of you to take time off work and help Flora.'

'Was it?'

'She'd never have managed without you.'

She stopped abruptly. 'You know why I did it.'

He couldn't think of any response.

'Don't you?'

'I—'

'To be near you. That's the only reason. I couldn't give a fuck about your shitty costumes and your shitty play.'

'Jules, I'm gutted about last night. I shouldn't have done it. I'm sorry.'

She looked up at him, and he could see in her eyes the world of hope that she was struggling so hard to mask. 'So why did you?'

'I – I was pissed.'

'And when you're pissed you shag any chick that comes within pulling distance, do you?'

'No! It was you . . .' He trailed off, aware that he was getting into a tangle.

'But you don't want *me* any more. I don't mean anything to you.'

'Not true. When I went into your house, I remembered stuff . . . about you and me . . .'

'Stuff that made you love me again?'

'No. Yes. No . . .'

'What? What are you trying to say, Danny?'

'I do love you, but . . .' He watched the light dying in her eyes.

'But not like you love her.'

'Who?' Danny couldn't bring himself to acknowledge what she was talking about.

'You know who. Stella bleeding Grainger.'

'I hardly know her.'

'For fuck's sake, Danny.'

He swallowed hard. They were walking again, across the diagonal path leading to Park Parade on the other side of the Green. It was properly dark now, with only one isolated lamp in the distance to show them the way. In spite of her fierce words he felt Julie draw closer to him. She kept glancing around and he realised she really was nervous. This was not just a ploy to get him on his own. He gulped in a mouthful of warm night air. It was time.

'Jules, I know about the baby.' He felt her tense up and move away from him. But she said nothing, just kept on walking, head down.

'Julie?'

Finally she stopped. 'Do you have a thing for Stella Grainger? Yes or no?'

Danny's heart was pumping hard. She deserved the truth. 'Yes. Not love, though. It's something . . . I don't know what. But it doesn't matter any more. Whatever it is, I'll get over it. You and me and what we're going to do about this baby – that's what matters now.'

'You have feelings for her.'

'Jules, listen.'

But she was running away from him across the Green.

He ran after her, but emotion had given her feet a turbo-boost. He caught up with her in time to have the front door of her house slammed in his face.

'Thou hast played the harlot with many lovers, yet return again to me,' saith the Lord. *'I find more bitter than death the woman who is a snare, whose heart is a trap and whose hands are chains.'*

WEDNESDAY 22 JUNE

NINETEEN

Sandra Bullimore hurried down Peas Hill and turned into St Edward's Passage on her way to Trinity College, where she worked. Mrs Matson had said that today she could do the common parts instead of her normal bedder's job, as that would help her finish by nine. She hoped so. Unless she and her daughter Gemma caught a fairly early train, they wouldn't have enough time to cover the whole of the West End in their search for the perfect wedding dress.

She didn't like going down St Edward's Passage this time in the morning, when everything was so quiet and deserted. However, there was a lovely dress shop somewhere at the end, along King's Parade, and she just wanted a quick butcher's in the window; finding her mother-of-the-bride outfit was proving a right pain.

Sandra shivered. It was a creepy place at best, with the mouldy old church and its crowded churchyard. The low wall, in her opinion, didn't put half enough space between passing shoppers and the ancient dead festering away under the crumbling gravestones. What's more, she'd heard stories about Gothic masses being held there, where everyone had to wear black. Now call her old-fashioned, but that wasn't normal, was it? What with that and the Haunted Bookshop, St Edward's Passage gave her a bad feeling. It was a place where people meddled with things they didn't ought to. She couldn't stomach religion – it gave her the heeby-jeebies. She was very glad Gemma wanted a register office do.

Then she heard something.

A voice. Someone was calling to her.

That was another reason. The churchyard was an ideal place for homeless layabouts to kip down for the night, and to pester poor folk going about their lawful business. It wasn't right. The police should do something. As a lone woman, obliged by the demands of her job to be out at such an unsocial hour, she deserved at the very least to feel safe. Heart fluttering slightly, eyes fixed firmly ahead, she kept going. If anyone thought they could intimidate her into parting with one penny of her hard-earned cash just so they could squander it on a can of cheap booze, they were much mistaken.

It was then that she heard the other noise: a strange scraping and rustling. In spite of herself she cried out and stopped. She glared defiantly around. Nothing. Stupid woman, letting her imagination run away with her. She set off again. In the silence, the sound of her own heels clicking on the ancient paving was suddenly unnerving. She quickened her pace. Nearly out onto Kings Parade. Nearly there.

She was level with the churchyard when a figure reared up from behind the wall.

'Please . . .'

It was a girl. No older than Gemma. Her skimpy clothing was ripped and torn, her face grazed as if she'd been dragged along the ground, and her eyes looked as if they'd seen the pit of hell.

'Please . . .' she said again, and then collapsed, face down, arms outstretched, along the wall.

Across the back of her bloodsoaked hand, a zigzag slash was gouged into the flesh.

With trembling fingers Sandra took out her mobile and dialled 999. 'He's done it again,' she informed the operator, cloaking her terror in righteous rage. 'He's raped another one. It's time you lot pulled your finger out and did something. It's a disgrace.'

'Happy is the man whom God correcteth: therefore despise not thou the chastening of the Almighty.'

Surveying the group of men gobbling toast and porridge, Dominic wondered whether anything had penetrated. He doubted it. Only Lonny Betts, who'd gambled away his livelihood and with it his home and family, seemed to accept God's just punishment with appropriate joy. A bit too much joy, Dominic thought, as Lonny interrupted his sermon with yet another cheery comment.

He pressed on. *'They that plough iniquity and sow wickedness reap the same. By the blast of God they perish and by the breath of His nostrils they are consumed.'*

'I just nearly fucking perished, by the breath of Preacher Man's nostrils,' interjected Lonny. 'One hundred per cent proof, it is. Don't anyone put a lighted match under his fat conk or we'll all go up in flames.'

Preacher Man pushed his face into Lonny's. 'Woe unto

thee, Lonny Betts,' he said. 'It is an evil thing and bitter that thou hast forsaken the Lord.'

'Shut it, wanker,' said Lonny cheerfully.

Dominic prayed for patience. He had a dreadful headache and couldn't think straight, which was probably why he was preaching such a highly unsuitable sermon. Maybe he really had been invaded by the spirit of Preacher Man, as Lucas had joked last night. But to spout hell and damnation to these poor souls who, more than anyone needed his love, understanding and compassion, was a step too far and nothing like his usual doctrine of peace and love. He grimaced. He'd read the odd psychology text and acknowledged to himself exactly what he was doing. Preacher Man didn't come into it. This untypical urge of his to brandish the wrath of the Almighty was really aimed, not at his shambling old reprobates, but at Hugo Mortimer. Even the thought of the man made his fists clench. His behaviour filled him with dismay. He'd better pull himself together double quick. He needed to be on top form if he wanted to outsmart the Master.

He looked across at Lucas, who was feeding the flock with his usual good humour. He suspected he'd made a fool of himself outside the Fellows' Garden yesterday evening. He suspected his nephew thought so too. He hadn't yet spoken to the boy this morning. He wanted to ask about the play, but he couldn't quite face it after his somewhat bizarre behaviour last night, so he kept his distance and tried to concentrate on his miserable sermon which, now he'd started, he supposed he ought to finish.

'*Man is born to trouble as the sparks fly upward—*'

'Talking of sparks,' chortled Lonny, 'Fag-Ash Fred set fire

to his beard again last night. Fell asleep in a skip with a Benson and Hedges still in his gob, silly cunt. It really took hold this time. They had to cart 'im off to A&E. He was hoping they'd keep 'im in for a few days, but no such bloody luck. He was back out on the streets before you could say nicotine fix.'

'Your porridge is getting cold. Eat up, Lonny.' What he really wanted to do was take a leaf out of the man's own book and say, 'Shut it, Lonny.'

Then his mobile rang. Who'd be calling at this early hour? It was the Master.

'I was chatting to Donald Hodges last night,' he said. 'He suggests you might like to pop in for a check-up later today.'

Donald Hodges, the college GP?

'But I'm not ill.'

'I sincerely hope *not*, my dear chap. But some of us are rather concerned. We feel you may have been overdoing things lately. We think it would be a good idea if Donald gave you the once-over.'

'We? Who's we?' He knew he was blustering, but he needed a moment to think. The Master wanted him to see a doctor. On the face of it, this was the action of a concerned friend and colleague.

But the Master was no friend of his.

'Several of the Fellows have observed that you haven't seemed yourself recently.'

'Like who?'

The Master was at his most vague, 'Oh, you know . . .'

'So?'

Mortimer's voice oozed concern. 'So they're worried about you.'

'I'm very touched, but I'm perfectly well. Fit as the

245

proverbial fiddle. I certainly don't need a check-up.' He tried to inject vigour into his tone, inserting a carefree laugh at the end of his sentence for added authenticity.

The laugh plummeted into a sceptical silence. Eventually, the Master spoke. 'Of course, my dear chap, you must do as you see fit . . .'

There's more. Wait for it.

'By the by, I thought you might be interested in William Grace's findings.'

Told you.

'Something rather intriguing . . .'

'What?'

'Apparently, if a Fellow of the college is in any way considered mentally compromised, he can't vote on college policy.'

Mentally compromised?

'Oh.' He broke out into a sweat, his hand so clammy he could hardly grasp his mobile.

'The Fellows must also deliberate on whether to relieve him of his Fellowship. And, unlike our normal procedures, the decision goes by majority rather than unanimous decision, with the Master, for his sins, having the casting vote. Interesting, don't you think? So far in our long and distinguished history, this clause has never been invoked. But I suppose at some point it may become necessary to do so. Though not in my time, I sincerely hope.'

So that was it. He was to withdraw his objections to the Master's plans or face the prospect of being declared a raving lunatic by his colleagues and slung out on his ear.

He dismissed his own earlier concerns about his state of mind. He was as sane as anyone else in the Senior Common Room. Much saner than some he could mention. No doctor would pronounce him insane since he manifestly wasn't. Then he remembered: Dr Donald Hodges was a very old friend of Hugo Mortimer. They'd been at Winchester together.

'Dominic, are you still there?' The smarmy voice buzzed in his ear.

'Yes.'

'Fascinating, don't you think, these arcane little gems from our esteemed founder?'

He couldn't speak.

'Well, I'll let you get on with your good works. Don't forget now – Donald's door is always open.'

Then there was the sound of the connection being cut. It was several seconds before he removed the phone from his ear.

'Cheer up, Father,' carolled Lonny. 'It might never happen.'

He slipped it into his pocket. 'Oh, but it has, Lonny. It surely has. *The thing which I greatly feared is come upon me, and that which I was afraid of is come unto me.*'

'Bummer,' said Lonny. 'Any more porridge in that pan?'

'Where did you go after the play? It's a simple question.'

'And I gave you a simple answer. For a walk.'

'Until two in the morning?'

'Is there a law against it?'

'But . . .'

'What exactly are you accusing me of, April?'

A direct question. Her chance to be equally direct. But she couldn't do it. She couldn't bear to hear the answer.

'It's just that it's not like you to stay out half the night without telling me.'

'Maybe I'm not as bloody predictable as you like to think.'

'I wish *I* could disappear whenever I felt like it, instead of being stuck at home looking after your children.'

'Why are you trying to lay this guilt trip on me?'

'People only feel guilty if they've got something to feel guilty about.'

'For fuck's sake!' Perry was suddenly bellowing.

'Don't shout.'

'I'll shout as much as I fucking want.'

This was not Perry. Not the loving and affectionate Perry she was used to. Perry didn't lose his temper. Perry liked a quiet life with no hassles. April knew she ought to back off, but she couldn't. She didn't seem able to control the bitter words spewing from her mouth.

'This week you've done what you like, when you like and how you like. Meanwhile I'm looking after your kids, dealing with your mother, and throwing parties so that you can float around being the great professor.'

Why were you walking by the river with Stella Grainger?

Why did you buy her ice cream?

Were you with her tonight when you should have been here with me?

That's what she wanted to say. Instead, all this other stuff was coming out.

'It was your choice to be a stay-at-home mum. And much good it's done you.'

'What do you mean by that?'

'Don't get me started.'

'I've had it up to here, Perry.'

'You and me both! It's come to something when I can't have my own mother in my own home without having to

248

put up with your endless bitching. When I can't even go for a walk without you giving me the third degree. I'm telling you, April, I can't take much more.'

He left the bedroom and seconds later she heard the front door slam.

She flung herself on the bed, weeping loudly, not caring who heard.

Some time later, her door creaked open. 'All right, pet?'

The last person she needed. The mother-in-law from hell. Hovering over her, like one of the Furies.

'Go away,' she bellowed. 'Go away go away go away!'

Then she felt a stinging pain on her cheek. It stunned her into silence.

'Nothing like a good slap for hysterics. Works every time.'

'Get out.'

'Pin back your lug-holes and listen to me, madam.'

Something in Frankie's voice made April do as she said.

'Stop meithering our Perry. He can't be having it. Men don't like to feel they're permanently in the dog-house, and only let out now and again on a short leash. They panic. Then they scarper.'

'It's not like that between me and Perry.'

'If you want to hold on to him, you'd best start making him feel good about himself, instead of like something that's come in on the bottom of your shoe. Remember, if you don't, there's plenty as would. He's a good-looking fella – quite a catch.'

Her words made April feel hollow inside. Hollow and even more horrible than she did already. And she didn't trust Frankie an inch. What was the woman playing at?

'Is this some kind of sick joke? Handy marital tips from

the woman who's tried her best at every available opportunity to clobber this marriage?'

'I don't know what you mean.'

'I may be new to the UK, but I'm not wet behind the ears. You've done everything you can to come between me and Perry.'

'I don't need to come between you. I'm there already – whether you like it or not. Perry and I have a special bond. He always said, right from being a lad, that we came as a package, him and me, and that any woman he married would have to like it or lump it. *You're* the troublemaker, not me.'

'I'd like you to leave my room now.'

Instead, Frankie sat down heavily on the bed. 'Look, pet, I know our Perry. He likes things to be calm and peaceful so he can get on doing his thinking and what-have-you. He can't stand upset. And I'm telling you straight, if he gets too much of it he'll sling you out.'

'You wish.'

'I don't, actually. Whatever you think, I have your best interests at heart.'

'You've a funny way of showing it. And for your information, the only time Perry and I have any major rows is when you're around.'

Frankie regarded her with narrowed eyes. 'That may well be so, but this time I'm not the only bone of contention. Am I?'

'What do you mean?'

'I think you know.'

It felt like a fist, squeezing her heart. But she had her pride. If Perry did have another woman, the last person whose shoulder she'd cry on would be Frankie.

'I get it. You hear us rowing so you up the ante by making insinuations about our marriage. But it won't work. You know nothing about me and Perry, so piss off.'

Frankie stared down at her. Then she shrugged. 'Well, pet, when you're left looking after two small kids on your own, don't say I didn't warn you.'

After she'd gone, April stared at the ceiling and tried to ignore the creeping black doom which filled the room, insinuating itself into every corner.

It's going to be a searingly hot day. Even at this hour I can feel the heat building up as I trudge back to Perry's after doing my second and final scene for Buster. I've said a fond farewell to Jeremy and the rest of the cast and made the usual promises to meet up for a drink in London. I can't believe I've finished. I'd thought my mind would be totally focused on my work this week, but somehow it's come and gone with me hardly being aware of its passing. I ought to catch up on some sleep, but on the other hand, I have to make sure I utilise my time to the best advantage. Primarily I have to find Danny. Last night after the play, he was too busy meeting and greeting his adoring public to spend more than a few moments with me, but during our brief chat I was struck by how evasive he was. Today I won't be fobbed off. Danny, watch out. Your mother's about!

But if, on the other hand, he continues to play Colin Clam, and I get nowhere with him, then maybe Julie will be more forthcoming. I shall go to her shop. No harm in that, is there? In any case, I have a valid reason for invading her place of work: the purchase of my very own ballgown. Having spent several hours in the gorgeous creation worn by my character, having draped myself winsomely over the parapet of Clare Bridge and walked hand-in-hand with Jeremy, suitably handsome in penguin suit, down Garret Hostel Lane in the misty dawn, I am determined that my real life début at the Billings Ball will be equally glamorous, even if my date does look like the Pilsbury Dough Boy.

Julie's shop is just the place to make my dream come true. And she and I might manage a fruitful exchange at the same time.

By the time I reach Perry's it's eight o'clock. On my previous two mornings this has been a moment of maximum volume chez Grimshaw, with the kids screaming at each other, April screaming at the kids, and Perry playing the 'Ride of the Valkyrie' in a vain bid to absent himself from the din.

Today, the house is eerily quiet. The Screamers must be having a lie-in. But when I go into the kitchen, they're sitting at the table eating cereal. In my short acquaintance with the little treasures, I've never seen them so subdued.

'What grown-up children you are – making your own breakfast,' I say brightly.

Hector's tone is withering. 'Of course we didn't. We're far too little. We might cut ourselves or set something on fire.'

'Or pour boiling water over ourselves,' chips in Cassandra.

'Mummy made it before she went back upstairs to quarrel with Daddy.'

'Before Daddy ran away.'

There's not a lot you can say to that.

'May I join you?'

'Yes. But you're not allowed muesli. That's ours. It's special. Mummy makes it just for us.'

Cassandra's autocratic tone reminds me of someone.

'Where's Granny?'

'Daddy said we mustn't disturb her 'cos she's got a multi-grain.'

'My grain, stupid,' sneers Hector.

For a moment I think Cassandra will deck him with her cereal bowl, but instead she subsides listlessly in her chair and picks her nose.

'I'll just have cornflakes then, should I?'

'Are you divorced?' Hector's tone is severe.

'No.'

'Do you have a husband?'

'Not any more.'

'Why not? Did you quarrel?'

'No. He died.'

'Sebastian's mummy and daddy had such big quarrels that Sebastian says they needed two houses, so they got divorced. Sebastian lives with his mummy and only sees his daddy sometimes. When mummies and daddies quarrel, does that always mean they're going to get divorced?'

I look up from my cornflake preparation. Two pairs of anxious eyes bore into mine. Cassandra's lip is trembling and Hector's freckles stand out against his pale face. I don't know what's been happening here whilst I've been swanning around Cambridge in the BBC's glad rags, but these children are upset. For the first time I see the vulnerable little babies beneath the precocious monsters.

'Of course not.'

'Did you ever quarrel with your husband, before he was dead?'

'You bet. If we hadn't, we'd have been perfect – and nobody's perfect.'

They ponder this nugget of wisdom.

'Look at you two – you're always quarrelling.'

'Aren't.'

'Are.'

'Aren't.'

'Are.'

Their little faces crack into identical smiles and they start to giggle.

'Doesn't mean you want to live in different houses, does it? Everybody quarrels sometimes. Even your mummy and daddy. But they love each other very much, and they'll soon make friends again, you'll see.'

Cassandra slips down from her chair and climbs onto my lap. 'Do you think so?' She snuggles against me and sticks her thumb into her mouth.

'I know so.' I cross all my fingers under the table.

'I'll show you my new computer game if you like,' says Hector nonchalantly.

'Great,' I say.

He goes over to the door. 'I'll call you when it's set up.' His gaze is critical, but the tone is kind. 'You'll probably find it quite difficult to understand at first,' he says. 'But don't worry – I'll explain and then you'll be fine.'

'Thank you,' I say humbly.

My plans for the morning recede rapidly into the distance.

TWENTY

Flora, knocking repeatedly on Stella's door in an attempt to rouse her, thought about the previous evening. The moment the curtain had fallen, Stella had rushed offstage complaining that throughout Act Five she'd had a burning, itching sensation all over her body. It was utterly unbearable, she'd said. Flora had whisked her back to her own room where she'd exclaimed in horror at the angry red rash covering Stella's lily-pale skin. Then she'd lent her some expensive shower cream, and after Stella had spent an age under a restorative cold jet of water, had smoothed cool calamine lotion into the affected areas.

How lucky that she happened to have a bottle handy.

Finally, she'd examined Desdemona's nightgown.

'Itching powder. You can see it, if you look closely. What a nasty trick, Stel! Someone's really got it in for you.'

'Like who?'

'Search me. Everybody loves you. Although . . .'

'Yeah?' Stella was wide-eyed.

'No – I'm sure I'm wrong.'

'Go on.'

'It's a really bitchy thing for me to say.'

'Tell me.'

'Julie . . .'

'Your little helper?'

'Yeah.'

'But I hardly know her.'

'She's Danny Thorn's ex.'

'So?'

'Maybe she thinks you're after him and it's some kind of weird revenge attack.'

Stella laughed. 'Why would she think I'm after him?'

'I can't imagine,' said Flora. 'With you being lovers in *Othello*, I suppose.'

'But that's just acting.'

'She's probably a bit confused. She's not all that bright.' Flora smiled. 'You are both very convincing. You're brilliant, Stel. I can't believe it's the first thing you've acted in.'

'Cheers, Flo.'

'I can also see that any ex-girlfriend of Danny's would be really jealous, seeing you snogging his face off – he's so gorgeous.'

Stella shrugged. 'I suppose.'

'He likes you – anyone can see that. Julie certainly could I've noticed her watching you both. She thinks Danny's got a thing for you and she's gutted, I can tell.'

'So she sprinkles itching powder on my costume?'

'Who knows?'

'It's not my fault she and Danny broke up. I didn't even know him till we started rehearsals.'

'Poor kid. She's crazy about him.'

'I was in agony, Flo.'

'I never thought she'd pull a stunt like this.'

'What good did she think it would do?'

'Perhaps she thought that if you mucked up his opening night, Danny would go off you and run back to her.'

'But I'm not even *with* him.'

'Maybe that's the problem: the uncertainty. Maybe if you *were* going out with him she'd be able to accept that he'd dumped her and move on.'

Stella's green eyes opened wide. 'So if I pulled him, I'd actually be doing her a favour – helping her get her shit together.'

'I suppose you would.'

Stella jumped up. 'My skin feels much better. I'm going back to the drinks thing. You don't mind, do you?'

Stella's way of saying that she doesn't want me tagging along.

'I'm coming too,' Flora said. 'I promised I'd have a drink with Lucas.'

My way of saying, 'Hands off my bloke.'

'Oh,' said Stella. 'I see. I was just wondering . . .'

'What?'

'Well, I can't put that itchy nightie back on and my clothes are in the wardrobe room.'

'I'll go up to your room and get you something else, should I?'

'I don't have my door-key. It's in my jeans . . . Can I cadge something off you?'

'Help yourself.'

But Stella was looking awkward. 'I don't suppose I could

borrow that top you're wearing? Only, it's quite small . . . You're so much bigger than me that most of your stuff wouldn't fit, but I could wear that top as a dress . . .' She trailed off.

And it just so happens that this is the most expensive garment in my whole wardrobe.

The new, cynical Flora took off her top. 'Be my guest. It'll suit you much better than me anyway.'

She knew it was the last she'd see of it, but she hadn't minded. Instead she'd experienced a surge of intense energy.

And today, on this bright, hot morning, as she hammered on Stella's door she felt it again, even more strongly. It was time to look after number one. If she didn't, who would? Certainly not her nearest and supposedly dearest. Her parents couldn't even pick up the phone and explain why they had missed the play.

'Wassup?' Stella stood in her open doorway, tousled and bleary. 'I was having a lie-in. I didn't get to bed till really late.'

'May Ball shopping, that's what. For something irresistible to wow Danny Thorn. My dad sent me lots of dosh the other day, remember? And I want to treat you to an outfit.'

Stella's face sprang to vivid life. 'Really?'

'What are best friends for?'

'Give me five. And be an angel – make me a coffee.'

'Where should we start?' asked Flora when Stella was finally ready.

'What about *Belle et Beau*?'

'*Belle et Beau*? The most expensive shop in Cambridge?' *And also the place where Julie worked.*

'I suppose it is, but their clothes are to die for. I saw a

mega-cool dress in the window the other day . . .' Stella's face crumpled. 'But anyway, I couldn't possibly let you spend that sort of money on me.'

Flora bowed to the inevitable. 'Daddy sent cartloads of cash. *Belle et Beau* sounds a great idea.'

'Are you sure?'

'Absolutely.'

But Stella's face had fallen again. 'Actually, forget it. The sort of clothes you buy there need really expensive accessories, too.'

Flora laughed. 'That's why we're going for shoes and bags too – the whole shebang.'

Stella's face shone. 'Really?'

'You bet.'

'You angel.'

Flora was pretty certain Stella didn't know that *Belle et Beau* was where Julie worked. As they approached the shop, the adrenaline kicked in. This would be the first meeting between the two since she'd told Stella that Julie was responsible for the itching powder. She must be developing a taste for danger.

The shop was in King Street, but such was its reputation among wealthy undergraduates and dons that nobody minded straying from the beaten track around Market Square and Petty Cury. Inside there were three floors, stark and simple in design, a perfect backdrop for the exquisite clothes on display. The bottom two floors were for women. Stella, a world-class shopper, had, within minutes, scooped up armfuls of garments. Flora loitered behind a pillar, waiting for the fateful moment. It took longer than she thought.

But eventually Stella staggered up to the girl guarding the changing rooms, with all her booty.

'Four garments only, madam.' The bored intonation was Julie's.

Flora watched realisation hit both girls at the same time.

'Julie! I didn't realise you worked here.' Smiling beatifically, Stella looked her up and down. 'What a shame they don't let you wear the clothes.'

'Catch me in this crud. Like it's so middle-aged. My mum loves it. She'd buy fuckloads here if she was rich.' She lowered her voice. 'I'd watch it if I were you. The manager gets really fucked off if she thinks people are pissing about and not serious about buying.'

'Sorry?'

'*Top Shop* might be more up your street.'

'Oh, we're buying. Aren't we, Flo?'

'Hi, Julie.' Flora crept into Julie's field of vision.

'Flo's treating me.'

Julie's eyes bored into Flora's, but all she said was, 'You did great last night, Flora. I meant to tell you after the show, but I couldn't find you. I left early.' She glanced at Stella. 'Danny took me home. He wouldn't let me go on my own. Not with this rapist about.'

Stella's smile was diamond bright. 'He's such a great guy, isn't he? Do anything for anyone. I've got to know him really well in the last couple of weeks. You build up such an intimate relationship when you're acting together.'

Julie's composure was showing signs of cracking, and Flora could see the snooty manager peering over. 'We must try this stuff on,' she said. 'I'm doing the lunch-time shift at R&R so I haven't much time.'

Stella eyeballed Julie. 'Sure,' she said. 'Let's hope no hidden extras come with them. Like itching powder, for example.'

Julie glared back.

'Come on, Stel,' said Flora quickly.

An hour later, when they made their purchases, Julie had disappeared. Flora was glad. She'd decided she wasn't quite yet ready for Armageddon.

Anna's exam will be finished soon. All morning, as I've played with the mercifully subdued Screamers, I've been mentally cheering her on while at the same time feeling utterly helpless. When your children are four years old their needs are straightforward. If they're hungry, you feed them; if they're tired you put them to bed; if they're distressed, you kiss them better; if they're curious about something, you explain; if they can't do something, you show them how.

But when they grow up, they have to manage all by themselves. *And usually you're the last one to know exactly what it is they're trying to manage.*

Finally April takes over and I go in search of my son. I won't call his mobile and give him an excuse to put me off. I'll go straight to his room.

When he opens the door I'm shocked. He looks terrible. Not terrible as in exhausted after playing the Moor for three hours last night. Terrible as in being eaten away inside.

'Hi, Mum.' His tone is listless.

'I've been here since Sunday and we've hardly seen each other. I thought we could do lunch today since we didn't make it yesterday.'

'I'm not showered or anything.'

'I can wait.' I barge past him and plonk myself firmly down on a chair. He knows when he's beaten and trails off to perform his ablutions.

I glance around. Although I've been visiting his university rooms for nearly two years now, it still seems odd to be in the place where he lives, and for it not to be home. Unfamiliar posters cover the walls – mostly bands he's into that I don't know about. And there's a large pinboard plastered in art postcards. This is a new departure. In spite, or perhaps because of his father being an artist, he's always professed indifference to painting and sculpture. Not any more.

And most touching of all, somehow, the scrawlings on a whiteboard stuck to the outside of his door that I'd noticed when I was waiting for him to open up – messages from friends, social arrangements, jokes, earnest reminders about supervisions – evidence of a life that I know nothing about.

But it's a life that Danny doesn't appear to be enjoying at the moment. Unhappiness pervades the room. My mother's instinct tells me I'm right, and when Danny returns from his shower I know it. Abject misery is written all over his face.

'What is it, my darling?'

I think he's going to tell me to mind my own business. But then his face crumples and he's sobbing in my arms. And saying sorry.

Why apologise to *me*?

I murmur comforting meaningless sounds. I can't remember the last time I did this. He's never been one for tears. Even when Rob died he kept most of his grief inside, and concentrated on being strong for me and Anna.

But now he's in pieces.

Eventually he starts to talk. He tells me all about his slow and painful falling out of love with Julie. How he gradually realised they had nothing in common. How everything about her had started to rub him up the wrong way, and how he felt more and more trapped. He told me how his irritation had infected their physical relationship. He didn't fancy her any more. It was a major effort to make love. He felt deeply ashamed at feeling such things. Julie had done nothing wrong. She was as she had always been. It was he who had changed. He was desperate to keep his love alive. He fought to preserve it. He denied what was happening and tried to make things like they once were. To feel what he once felt.

He failed.

He tells me about the evening he finally dumped her. She didn't believe him. She clung so hard when he tried to leave that he'd had to forcibly peel her fingers off his arms. He says she still hasn't accepted things. Her latest ploy is getting involved with the costumes for *Othello*.

Even though I could have predicted that this outcome was inevitable, and from my point of view, desirable, my heart still bleeds for both of them.

Such pain.

But Danny's misery seems out of proportion. However sad he is for Julie, he should by now be starting to enjoy his freedom.

'What else, Dan?'

He pulls away slightly.

'Why were you saying sorry just now? What do my feelings matter in all this? There's something else, isn't there?'

'I think I'm falling in love again.'

I know what's coming. 'Do I know her?'

'Stella.'

What a surprise.

'So why all the misery? Falling in love's supposed to make you happy.'

'I told Julie there was no one else.'

Fair enough, but his unhappiness still seems excessive. After their initial upset, people who do the dumping are usually massively relieved. I think there's something else bothering him. However, I'll run with what he's giving me for now.

'And was that true? How did you feel about Stella three weeks ago?'

'I hardly knew her. I'd seen her around college, thought she was a bit of a babe, but that's all.'

'Then you've nothing to feel guilty about. You told Julie the truth as it was at the time. It's awful for her that you've fallen for someone else so soon, but you couldn't help it. When love strikes you don't have a choice. It just happens.'

Is this nugget of maternal wisdom doing any good? Who knows?

'However, I do think it's a good thing to take things slowly. How does Stella feel about you?'

'I don't know. Sometimes it's like she really likes me. Other times she's quite distant.'

'Have you told her how you feel?'

'She must know. It's blindingly obvious.'

'Maybe you should leave it until after the Long Vac. Get

a bit of distance. Don't forget, you're acting out one of the great tragic love stories of all time with this girl. It's sometimes hard to separate the play from the reality. That's why so many actors have affairs. It's like a temporary madness that doesn't necessarily mean anything in the long term.'

His voice is dull. 'Yeah. You're probably right.'

That was easy. Too easy. I was right. There *is* something else. He's still holding back.

'And?'

'What?'

'Come on, Danny Thorn. I haven't been your mother for all these years without picking up a thing or two about the way your mind works. What else is bugging you?'

This is it. The big one. The thing he's finding it impossible to tell. The thing that makes him, in the middle of his misery, apologise to me.

'Spit it out. You're making me nervous.'

He slowly raises his eyes to mine. 'I've really messed up, Mum.'

'Now I *am* worried. Put me out of my misery.'

'Julie's pregnant.'

For some reason, this is the last thing I'm expecting. The shock makes me stupid. 'Is it yours?'

Danny just looks at me.

'Sorry, Dan. Of course it would be.'

No wonder he's devastated. Prospective father to a baby whose mother he no longer loves. Saddled.

'Is she having it?'

'I don't know. She won't talk.'

'What do you want?'

'I want to wake up and find it's a dream.'

'Well, it isn't, so what are you going to do about it?'

'I don't know, Mum! Get off my back. I knew I shouldn't have told you.' He leaps up and paces the room. 'That's it, isn't it? I'll never get away from her now. I'm really up shit creek.'

It's hard not to agree with him.

'You must make Julie tell you what she wants. The sooner the better. Right now. I'll come with you.'

'No. This is my mess – I'll sort it. She's at work now anyway, but she's coming in to do costumes again tonight. I'll talk to her after the show.'

'Promise?'

'I promise. In any case, I have to know before tomorrow evening.'

'Why?'

He sighs. 'Because even though we've split up I promised I'd still take her to the May Ball. And I have to know where I stand if I'm going to spend all tomorrow night carting her round the festivities.'

He looks completely forlorn.

'Oh Danny. What a mess.'

'Tell me about it.'

TWENTY-ONE

Perry didn't come home for lunch. She'd tried his college phone, tried his mobile. Nothing.

She knew where he was and what he was doing. He was in his room at Billings with Stella. Doing all sorts of things that he'd never done with her.

'Mummy, I've asked you three times to kiss Fluffy Bear. Why won't you listen?' Cassandra's plaintive voice seemed to be coming from a long way off.

She made a decision. Frankie was lolling on the sofa reading *The Stage*.

'Can you mind the kids for half an hour?' April asked.

Without waiting for a reply she left the house and ran up the road to college. She noticed with detached interest that her limbs were trembling and her face was wet with tears. In Berkeley Court she hammered on Perry's door. No answer. Instead of relief she felt even worse.

Why were his curtains closed in the middle of the day?

She pressed her ear against the window. Was that a noise she could hear inside the room? She knew it. They were in there, the two of them – screwing themselves stupid and laughing at her.

'He isn't here. I saw him earlier heading towards town.' It was Dominic Tipton. 'Are you all right?'

She sagged against the window. 'Was he . . . with anyone?' 'No.'

She could have kissed his gaunt cheeks for being the one to dispel her ridiculous fantasy. She realised how strange she must appear – ear glued to Perry's window, weeping.

'I'm sorry,' she said. 'It's just that . . .'

'Come,' he said. Then he gently steered her through the college and out onto the street.

'I'm fine,' she said.

'You're upset, April. Can I help?'

'No. Really, I'm fine.'

His eyes were kind and full of concern. 'I'm taking you home.'

She was too wrung out to protest.

They walked back to the house in silence. She hoped she hadn't embarrassed him too much. Outside his professional persona he was a shy man, particularly with women and since she knew that he was at his most comfortable when ministering, she was very touched and grateful that he didn't propose God as the answer to her problems. They were walking up her path and she was wondering whether she could bear to ask him in for a cup of tea, when her front door was flung open.

'Next time you want to bugger off and leave me with the brats, I'd thank you to give me notice. I do have a schedule, you know. I can't just drop everything to suit you—'

GREEN EYE

When Frankie saw Dominic, her tone underwent a miraculous transformation. 'Pardon my language, Vicar. My daughter-in-law didn't mention that you were popping by.' She scowled at April. 'And since she doesn't see fit to introduce me, I'd better do it meself. I'm Dr Grimshaw's mother – Frankie Faraday.'

She gave him her special look – the one that said it was inconceivable the recipient hadn't heard of her. But then the look shifted and was staring beyond them to the gate, where a fat perspiring man on the far side of middle age was toiling up the path, staggering under the weight of two enormous suitcases.

'Look what the cat dragged in.' Her voice was harsh.

April recognised the man from the one time she'd met him. At her wedding. It was Alf Rimmer – Frankie's long-suffering agent, long-time lover and allround stooge.

He regarded Frankie with tired eyes that sported their very own set of cabin trunks.

'So where's the bloody contract?' she snapped.

'There is no contract.'

'Then sod off – pardon my French, Vicar – and don't come back until you've got something for me to sign.'

April noticed that a van had backed up to the gate. From it, a woman had emerged with a table lamp, a portable TV and several small cardboard boxes.

'There is no contract. Not for the TV series . . . and not for you and me any more.'

'What the flamin' hell are you on about?'

'I'm finished with you, Frankie, love.'

'Don't be so bloody silly.' Then Frankie registered what he was carrying. 'What are you doing with my good cases?'

'It's the rest of your clothes.'

'You what?'

'I can't do it any more, Frankie. I don't want nowt else to do wi' you.' He looked, as if for reassurance, at the woman labouring up the path with the lamp and the TV.

'But you're my agent, even if you *are* bloody useless. You can't leave me.'

'I just did.'

'Watch my lips, sunshine. You don't leave me. If there's any leaving to be done, it's me what does it.'

'Not this time.'

'But you love me.' Her face is a picture of incomprehension.

Alf took a deep breath. 'Not any more.'

The colour came and went on her face. 'You don't do this to me. No one does this to me.'

April and Dominic were pushed aside as Frankie lunged towards the hapless Alf. But then the woman stepped forward. She was small and stocky, with bright red cheeks.

'Consider yourself officially chucked, luv. As of now. So back off.'

April thought that Frankie would explode. 'What the hell is it to do with you, you sweaty slag?'

'Frankie, this is Doris. My fiancée.'

Frankie snorted. 'And I'm Biffo the Bear.'

'It's true.'

'Since when?'

'Since you didn't bother to get in touch for two month till the other day when you wanted something.'

'Who is she when she's at home?'

'I met her in our local library. She's the Chief Librarian.'

'Spare me the pathetic details.'

'We love each other, Frankie. And unlike you, she wants to be my wife. We're getting hitched next week.'

For a moment everything stopped. Then vivid imprecations spattered all over the garden as Frankie cursed Alf from one end of the universe to the other.

April now knew from whom her children had inherited their formidable lungpower. The noise was excruciating. There was only one thing to do, and it gave her intense satisfaction to be the one to do it.

She slapped Frankie hard across the face.

The noise ceased. 'What the hell did you do that for?'

'Nothing like a good slap for hysterics. Works every time.'

Doris had retreated down the path to the van where he was gathering fresh boxes and parcels to her vast bosom.

Alf persevered. 'I'm sorry, Frankie, but I've had it. When I met Doris, I realised how daft I'd been to put up wi' your shenanigans all these years. Now I'm getting on I need a bit of peace. I'm retiring from the Business. Me and Doris have bought a place in Spain.'

The words hovered in the air above Chesterton Road. When Frankie finally spoke, her voice was sweet as syrup.

'Poor Buggerlugs. What a selfish cow I am. I've been so busy with my family commitments that I've left you to fend for yourself for far too long. That's what comes of trying to spread myself too thin. But that's me – generous to a fault. Always putting myself before others. Neglecting my own precious boy in order to help Perry and April. But don't fret, I'll make it up to you. We'll have a little holiday, just the two of us, should we? Where should we go? Tenerife?

Majorca? You choose – anywhere but Cyprus. You know
can't stand Cyprus.'

'Frankie, did you hear what I said?'

'I get it. You wanted to show me how fed up you were
so you cooked this up. All power to your elbow, Alfie boy
it's a clever do.' She nods towards Doris. 'Although you
could have picked less of a moose to play her part. She's
not very convincing as a love rival.'

'Frankie—'

'Fancy going to so much trouble. It shows how much
you care. Well, it's worked. You can stop pretending now
Joke over.'

'I'm not pretending.'

Frankie smirked. 'No?'

'If I find any more of your stuff I'll send it on.'

April could almost hear the penny drop in Frankie's
brain. A storm of emotion flickered back and forth across
her painted features and it seemed as if millennia passed
before she finally spoke. When she did, her voice was
Vesuvius, the night before the destruction of Pompeii
April registered the alarm on Dominic's face and realised
it must mirror her own.

'You think you can just turn me out of my own home—

'It's not your home, Frankie. It never was. It's the place
you came whenever you ran out of better offers. Well
I've had the locks changed. You're not welcome any
more.'

Doris appeared beside him. 'That's the lot, Alf. We should
be on our way.'

He put his arm around her shoulder. 'I'm done, girl
Let's go.' He turned to Frankie. 'Take care, love.' He touched

her cheek. 'There was a time, you know, when I worshipped the ground you walked on.'

Then he turned to April. At his words, in spite of the boiling hot day, the blood in her veins ran cold.

'Look after her, April. You and Perry are all she's got now.'

Xam ok. Messd up q.3. In pub, bit pissd. Xxx

Anna's text is wonderfully straightforward. Her exam's over for better or worse, and her sole task in the next few hours will be to remain upright.

If only Danny's problems were so easily solved.

Over lunch in a Greek taverna behind Market Square we talk up and down and round the subject, covering all the angles. I try to be openminded and evenhanded. Danny must make his own decisions without being influenced by my views.

If indeed I knew exactly what they were.

But I do know. I just can't face admitting it, even to myself. *I want this baby not to exist.*

There, I've said it. I don't want this unplanned-for, uninvited child ruining my son's life. Or Julie's. I've seen a hundred TV dramas where girls get as far as the abortion clinic and then decide at the last minute to go ahead with the pregnancy, however dreadful their situation. And how it all comes right in the end.

Real life's not like that. The consequences for both Danny and Julie don't bear thinking about.

I can't say this to Danny. My role here is to be a soundingboard for all sides of the argument. It's his life, his decision. Before he sees Julie, he must be clear about his own views. And whatever he decides, I have to support him.

But he's floundering. He says it's impossible for him to decide one way or another until he's talked properly to Julie. We go round in circles, until eventually there's nothing left to say that hasn't been said a million times already. We both stare dumbly at the wooden table, fresh out of words.

Eventually he says, 'I'm knackered. I need a kip before tonight's show.'

'I have to do some shopping, so I'll stay in town. Call me tonight when you've spoken to her.'

After he's gone I walk over to King Street. I'm going to see Julie. I know I should leave it, but I can't. Danny said Julie was on the pill when they were together, and that the pregnancy is a piece of monumental bad luck.

Maybe. Maybe not. Maybe it's a piece of monumental bad behaviour. What better way to hang onto my son?

I want to look into her eyes when she talks to me.

When I arrive at *Belle et Beau* I see her straight away. And she sees me. We stare across the posh frocks, and she knows that I know.

She comes over. 'Hi, Rosa. Long time no see.'

'Julie, I'm so sorry to hear about the—'

'Yeah, well. Shit happens.'

'I'm really sorry.'

Her china-blue eyes are hard. 'Are you?'

Somehow I've been wrong-footed. 'It's very upsetting. Especially when you've been together for so long.'

'Was it me or clothes that you wanted?' She's not giving anything away.

'Both. I wanted to see you, but I also need a dress for the Billings May Ball. I gather you and Danny are still going together?'

She's picking furiously at a loose thread on an embroidered waistcoat hung on the rack next to us. 'Yeah. Even though we're having a break, we're still good mates.'

Having a break? Surely she means, 'Even though we've broken up,' doesn't she?

Either she's gone into total denial, or she isn't upset any more. And why would that be?

But no matter how I probe, she reveals nothing. I'm wasting my time.

It's my own fault she won't confide in me. Although I've had plenty of opportunity to get to know her, I've never really tried. Not really. If I'm honest, I've always regarded the relationship as a temporary thing. I now see my impersonal courtesy through Julie's eyes. I think about her various visits to Consort Park and realise how much, under the brash, couldn't-care-less exterior, she was striving to fit in. And how I didn't help her. How I persisted in treating her with the formal politeness extended to a comparative stranger rather than the laidback, inclusive warmth meted out to family and close friends. I've repeatedly sent out signals that said, 'Back off.' Hardly surprising therefore, that she should now do exactly that.

I feel deeply ashamed for my lack of generosity.

I also face up to my own manipulations. Despite all my guff about children making their own decisions, I have, over the months, very definitely tried to steer things towards an outcome that I considered suitable – in this case Julie becoming a sweet memory from Danny's golden youth.

I owe her a big apology, but that would require a heart-to-heart session that isn't possible here in the scented and hushed boutique. All I can do for the moment, therefore, is concentrate on my other reason for being at *Belle et Beau*. And who knows, maybe, if I'm nice enough during our joint quest for my dress she might forgive me a little and open up about the pregnancy.

Eventually, after an age of unreciprocated chit-chat on my part, I choose a floor-length dress in pale green silk with a fitted bodice, bootlace straps and a very full skirt. It's fantastic, but even as I hand over my hard-earned cash I know that this particular garment will be forever associated in my mind, not with Billings May Ball, but with the nightmare of Julie and Danny's baby.

I'm about to have one final shot at bringing up the pregnancy when she says, 'You've never liked me, have you?'

How does one respond to that? With the truth? Hardly. The girl might now be part of my life for a very long time. I wouldn't want this lying between us down the years.

'My dear girl—'

'Don't patronise me. I'm not stupid. You think Danny's too good for me. I saw it in your eyes the first time we met. My mum saw it too. She says you're a toffee-nosed bitch who thinks her precious son's been slumming it.'

'I thought you and Dan were too young to get so serious about each other, that's all.'

'I bet you're well chuffed now we're having problems.'

'No. I think it's very sad for both of you.'

'Don't lie,' she says.

'Especially now you're pregnant.' There. I've said it.

The manager looks our way, frowning.

Julie is seething. She grabs my elbow and propels me to the door. 'If there's nothing else I can help you with, madam, let me see you out.'

GREEN EYE

Then I'm on the sunlit pavement, with the door shut firmly behind me. I move to go back in, but I see from the expression in Julie's eyes on the other side of the glass that this would not be a good idea.

TWENTY-TWO

He was helpless in the face of female hysteria. To be subjected to two bouts in the same day was unspeakable. Perry Grimshaw should put his house in order. Both his women were out of control. First April, who he'd previously thought of as a cheerful and level-headed sort, peering through Perry's window and bawling like a baby, and then the one in Chesterton Road, who turned out, incredibly, to be Perry's mother. Sixty-five if she was a day, but dressed like a prostitute with her wrinkled breasts hanging out of her tight mini-dress, her ridiculous high-heeled shoes and her cheap jewellery. And the way she spoke to the fat man – it didn't surprise him one bit that the poor chap had found solace elsewhere.

He'd wanted to slip away, but the gateway was blocked by the man's van, so he'd had to stick it out. And then to cap it all, April seemed to think that, as a man of the cloth, he'd be the best qualified to calm her mother-in-law down. She enlisted his help in guiding the woman up to her bedroom, and then asked him to stay while she tried to contact Perry, who was evidently having a Scarlet Pimpernel day. Having seen both women in action, Dominic wasn't surprised.

Rational conversation proved impossible so he took refuge in his Bible, hoping that the sound of his voice might eventually soothe the woman into silence. The book fell open at the book of Zechariah, and he tried to calm his own shattered nerves, still reeling from the Master's phone call, by reading out the prophesies and exhortations as beautifully as he could.

'What did you say?' The woman had finally stopped weeping. 'Read it again. That last bit.'

'Woe to the worthless shepherd, who deserts the flock! May the sword strike his arm and his right eye! May his arm be completely withered, his right eye totally blinded.'

She sat up. 'Too bloody right.'

'I beg your pardon?'

'This Bible baloney makes a lot of sense.' She clawed at his arm. 'An eye for an eye. Isn't that what it says in there?'

'Indeed, but—'

'Getting your own back. Do you believe in that?'

He thought about the Master. 'God is not completely averse to the idea of retribution. In certain circumstances. Turning the other cheek isn't always the answer. It can sometimes be taken as a sign of weakness. However—'

She interrupted, nodding decisively. 'Maybe I should come to your church. Find out about the real God. The big tough guy – not the mardy old bugger dished up to us when we was kids.'

Don't say he had a convert on his hands.

He wasn't sure that he wanted this particular convert.

Particularly since her interest seemed only to be roused by the vindictive thunderings of the bloodthirsty Old Testament. However, he had himself to thank for that. When the Bible had fallen open at Zechariah, he could easily have flipped forward to the Beatitudes. *Blessed are the Peacemakers.* The Sermon on the Mount was far closer to what he really believed. But today he'd taken an alarming relish in articulating all the cursings of the prophet.

However, part of his job was to save souls, and Lord knows there were few enough of those around nowadays. He couldn't afford to turn one away.

'I run a refuge for the homeless down in the town. We also have Bible study groups which you may find interesting. You'd be very welcome to come along at any time.'

He didn't get to hear her reply because at that moment, Perry appeared.

'April's told me about Alf,' he said immediately. 'I'm so sorry, Mum.'

'After everything I've done for him an' all,' Frankie whispered, sinking back against her pillow. 'Would you believe it – marrying that scheming lump of offal. There are some reet evil folk in the world, Perry.' Her eyes filled up and her lip trembled.

Dominic tensed. He didn't know whether he could take another outburst.

But then she sat up. 'Still, I were going to give him the boot anyhow. He's been holding my career back for long enough. And he won't get away with it. When I've finished, no one in the Business will touch him with a bargepole. He'll soon find out you can't treat Frankie Faraday like a used sanitary pad.'

GREEN EYE

As her mouth opened and closed, Dominic was mesmerised by the red lipstick smeared over her teeth. It reminded him of a bird of prey that had just ripped open the throat of a hapless woodland animal. But with Perry's arrival, her interest in God appeared to have evaporated so, unnoticed by either of them, Dominic left her recounting her tribulations with enormous relish, and crept downstairs. As he passed the kitchen he saw April. She was gazing into the hall. Her eyes met his, but there was no spark of recognition. She was in another world. Not a very pleasant one, judging by the expression on her face. He opened the front door and almost ran down the path in his eagerness to escape.

Back in college, he headed for the library. He needed to visit the place which, even more than the chapel, gave him an abiding sense of peace and order. He needed to sit in its quiet spaces, surrounded by ancient volumes of theology, and allow them to soothe all his troubles away.

As he walked towards Augustine Court, he became conscious of a heaviness in the air. The sky had turned to pewter and the elaborate Gothic façades of the buildings were bathed in a strange yellowish light. In the distance towards Newmarket, banks of ragged black clouds loomed over the horizon. Then he noticed something else: the birds had stopped singing. It meant only one thing – an impending storm. Hurrying through Berkeley Court, he caught sight of the stone creatures leaping from the walls. In the eerie light they seemed to leer and threaten, and once he even thought he heard savage laughter. Was he going mad, as the Master had insinuated? Possibly. Only mad people imagined that cold stone could laugh. The air hung hot and heavy like a thick curtain, and he could almost feel his body pushing it aside as he moved through it.

When he reached the library he was sweating profusely. With relief he pushed open the heavy wooden door and let the musty air envelop him. Wiping his face, he stumbled into the nearest chair.

Then he stiffened. Something was different. The acoustics. The muffled quality of the booklined room had disappeared. Instead, the atmosphere was clearer. Sharper. He looked around.

Yard upon yard of empty shelving yawned back at him, and at the far end he saw numerous packing cases stacked on top of each other. Two men stood on the balcony which ran round the room. They were removing books from the shelves and placing them into yet more packing cases.

A great weight descended on his chest, and he found himself fighting for breath. He wondered if he was having a heart attack. He thought it entirely possible that he might be dying. He must have been making noises, because the men looked round in concern and rushed down the stairs towards him.

'All right, mate?'

Eventually the pain subsided and he was able to speak. 'What are you doing?'

'Shifting this lot.'

'Shifting?'

'Into storage.'

'On whose authority?'

'Sir Hugo Mortimer.'

Ignoring their concerned faces, he staggered out into the

courtyard, the image of the ravaged shelves beating on his brain, a sorrow so intense pulsing through him that he felt he might shatter into tiny pieces.

Then rage superseded grief. It propelled him back through the college, past the marquee, past the fountain, past the statue of Horace Billings, past the chapel. At some point he realised that someone was beside him: Lucas.

'Unc? What's up?'

He shrugged off the boy's restraining arm and powered through the double doors into Hall. The Master was presiding at High Table, surrounded by many of the Fellows. A pair of strangers flanked him. Both wore gold-rimmed spectacles and tweed suits.

Mortimer's Americans.

Dominic strode down between the long tables of under-graduates and stopped at the dais. He dimly registered that Mortimer looked both appalled and apprehensive.

Behind him, Lucas was saying, 'Leave it, Unc.'

'On what authority have you started dismantling the library? The committee hasn't yet ratified any such move.' He was aware of the appalled faces of his colleagues, and the excited murmur of undergraduate voices. But he didn't care.

'The decision's a mere technicality, Tipton.'

'Not to me it isn't.'

'Would you be kind enough to escort the chaplain back to his rooms, young man. And perhaps a call to the doctor would be in order.' Mortimer turned to the American on his right. 'I do beg your pardon,' he murmured. 'The Reverend Tipton isn't himself.'

Dominic opened his mouth to continue but Lucas was

283

dragging him away, past all the shocked faces and out into the air.

'Be cool, Unc. Please.'

He was taken aback by the anxiety in the boy's eyes.

'He's destroyed the library. There are men in there, at this very moment, packing books into boxes.'

As he spoke, he felt a spot of rain. Then another. And then something hard and sharp struck him in the face. Hailstones, millions of them, relentlessly battering himself and Lucas. Within seconds they were both drenched. He raised his eyes to the heavens. Listened to the thunder rumbling round the sky. Saw the jagged prongs of lightning illuminating the Billings Archangels as they stood guard on the Gatehouse. And then he began to laugh.

'What's so funny?'

'*And Moses stretched forth his rod towards heaven, and the Lord sent thunder and hail. And the Lord rained hail upon the land of Egypt.*'

Lucas stared at him, water dripping off his long dark lashes, blond hair plastered to his skull. And then, after a long moment, he laughed too.

She watched the hail pounding on the window. The weather mirrored her mood exactly. She knew that her perpetual anxiety about Perry was irrational, and normally she was able to rise above it. But not this time. Apart from the fact that she'd actually seen him walking by the river with that girl, Perry was quite unlike his normal self. After he'd persuaded Frankie to have a nap, he'd come to the kitchen, where she was making flapjacks with the kids in an attempt to put some kind of normality back into their day. He'd made himself a coffee, without saying a word. At first she thought he was continuing their row of the morning, but after he'd ignored a question from Cassandra and a remark from Hector, she realised that he was present in body only.

'Are you and Daddy still having a blue?' Cassandra's little face was anxious.

'No, of course not. We're not quarrelling, are we, Perry?'

'What?'

'We're not quarrelling any more.'

Perry managed a wan smile. 'No, Cassie. We're not quarrelling. I'll be in my study if you need me, April. I gave Frankie a pill so she should sleep for a while, but when she wakes up, let me know.'

He was polite. Too polite. April felt hollow inside. She followed him to his study.

'Perry . . .'

He seemed surprised to see her, as if he'd forgotten she existed. 'Yes?' He wore the patient expression usually reserved for nervous undergraduates.

'This business with Frankie and Alf . . .'

Perry's face darkened. 'I'd like to wring his fat neck.'

'Do you think they're really finished?'

'Looks like it.'

'All those years down the pan. What a waste.'

'Waste is a life half-lived. Better to cut her losses and start again before it's too late.' The emptiness in his voice made her shiver.

She didn't ask what he meant. His easygoing good humour had vanished. And with its disappearance, all the warmth in her life drained away. Suddenly she didn't want to interrogate him about his day. Suddenly she didn't want to know what he was up to.

He was still talking, and she could hear a challenge in his tone. 'Naturally Frankie will stay with us until she's on her feet again.'

There were three things in life that April most feared.

One: Something happening to the kids.

Two: Perry leaving her.

Three: Frankie living with them on a permanent basis.

The increasingly likely prospect of number two occurring put number three into its proper perspective. And anyway, if he left her he could take his bloody mother with him.

'Naturally,' she murmured.

Perry looked as if he didn't quite believe what he was hearing. Then the incredulity faded. 'Was there anything else?' He spoke as if to a stranger.

'No,' she said. 'I'll call you when supper's ready.'

'I shan't be eating in.'

'Oh.' She couldn't bear to ask why not. What was happening to her? She'd suddenly become a complete coward.

'I promised Lee Watson I'd watch the play again and give him notes.'

'Won't it be cancelled because of the weather?' She trembled at the sight of his frantic expression.

He peered out of the window. 'It's easing off already. The sky's blue over there. It's a summer storm. Over in a flash.'

'Good,' she said, mouth dry. 'There are so few performances it would be a pity to have to cancel one.'

'I think I'll go over to college now. Once the rain stops they'll need help drying off the seats.'

'Can't the stage staff do that?'

The irritation in his eyes belied his calm voice. 'I expect they could do with an extra pair of hands.'

Normally she'd have countered with the fact that she too could do with an extra pair of hands. Now she merely said, 'I'm sure they could.'

But he was already grabbing an umbrella and plunging out into the receding storm.

'I'm sorry, April.'

The voice came from the top of the stairs.

Frankie.

In her dressing-gown, without her make-up and with her yellow locks straggling loose over her shoulder, she was a dead ringer for Bette Davis in *Whatever Happened to Baby Jane?*

'I'm sorry,' she said again.

For some reason it made April more frightened than anything that had gone before.

She hadn't thought that the word 'sorry' was part of Frankie's vocabulary.

TWENTY-THREE

When Flora opened the door, there stood Lucas, soaked to the skin. His small, dark nipples, seen through the wet shirt plastered to his body, made her insides go all fluttery. When she spoke, her voice emerged as a faint croak. 'You'll catch pneumonia out there. Come in. I'll find you a towel.'

He examined her, frowning. 'You're tall for a girl, and your hips are very slim. Don't suppose I could borrow some jeans and a T-shirt?'

Her body went into meltdown. He hadn't touched her, yet it felt as if he were exploring her most intimate places. 'Sure,' she whispered, and started delving in drawers to hide her fiery cheeks.

'Here,' she said, after she'd regained her self-control. 'These might fit.'

When she looked round, he had his back to her and he'd removed his wet things.

All of them.

He was achingly beautiful.

'Towel,' she said, and dived into another drawer. How

awkward she felt. How young and inexperienced he must think her.

And he'd be right. She'd never even seen a naked man before, not in the flesh. He wrapped the towel around himself and turned, smiling. She found herself moving towards him. She tried to stop, but her treacherous body just kept on going. 'Oh Lucas,' she said. 'Oh Lux . . .'

And then she was pressed up against him, feeling the taut muscles beneath his satin-smooth flesh, kissing his soft lips.

But something was wrong. He was pushing her away. His face registered shock, and something else that she refused to think about. 'Don't, Flo,' he said.

She felt the blood pumping in her ears. 'Why not?' She hated herself for even asking.

'I respect you too much to do something we'd both regret.'

Flora knew that making love to Lucas was something she'd never regret. It was what she'd been dreaming about ever since he arrived. The loitering around R&R, after her shifts had finished, the extra shifts she'd done in order to spend more time with him, the long talks about God that she'd initiated, all added up to one thing: getting as close as she could to him. It had just about been enough to keep her going until he asked her to marry him. This, and also the secret things: the three albums of photos, the Lucas memento box to which she added stuff almost daily, and the full and frequent account of everything he said and did written in a beautiful leather-bound book that she'd bought on the market.

And now, with one stupid move, she'd gone and blown it all.

He was already throwing on the T-shirt and jeans.

Flora wanted to die.

'I think you're great, Flo, I honestly do, but at the moment I'm not really into relationships with women.'

'Why? Are you gay?'

He laughed. 'Hell, no. I love women. That's my problem. I don't want to get into anything that's going to distract me from all the plans Uncle Dom and I have for R&R. Right now, there's the building expansion, and the outreach work, and the stall on the market for selling Bibles and T-shirts. There's no time for a serious relationship.'

'I could help you—'

'You already do.'

'I could work on the stall, do some of the outreach work.'

'There's something else. You know there is.' He sighed. 'We've talked loads of times about how we don't believe in sex before marriage.'

'Yes, but—'

'I know that if I had a serious girlfriend I wouldn't be strong enough to resist temptation, so I've decided it's better for me not to bother at the moment.'

Flora went hot and cold all over. They'd had many conversations about the promiscuity of today's youth, and how sleeping with people cheapened sex and turned it into a commodity, and how the only meaningful sexual relationships were those within marriage. So what must he now think of her, jettisoning her principles for the sake of a quick grope?

'I'm so sorry, Lucas.'

He stroked her cheek. 'Hey, I'm flattered. Any man would be.'

'Don't lie. Nobody fancies me.'

'Why do you always do yourself down, Flo?'

'Well, you don't fancy me, do you?'

'You're a very special person.'

'We both know what that's code for.' Then she heard footsteps outside on the stairs.

Lucas glanced towards the door. 'Let's pretend this never happened,' he said. 'I will if you will.'

And before Flora had a chance to reply, he'd gone.

Let's pretend this never happened.

He wanted to deny the existence of her love. It was like he was denying her existence too. She stared dumbly down at the carpet. But then she heard the sound of voices outside in the court. She went to the window. Lucas had emerged from the staircase.

He wasn't alone. He said something to his companion that made her laugh. As they walked across the court together, she touched his shoulder in a casually intimate way.

Stella.

Always Stella.

Danny was taking her for a drink after the show. That had to be good news, didn't it? She'd have to tread carefully. She daren't mess up, not now she had another chance with him. Everything hinged on her not blowing it. Like she almost did this afternoon when his mother walked into the shop. Rosa was nosing around like crazy, but Julie hadn't given her a damn thing, even when she'd come right out with it about the supposed pregnancy. Her heart had nearly stopped but she'd pushed Rosa out of the shop

and still managed not to give anything away. She didn't
trust Rosa. The woman was the last person she'd ever
confide in. Underneath the sympathetic concern, there
was only one person Rosa was interested in protecting,
and it wasn't her.

Thank fuck the performance was nearly over. It had gone
on forever. The cast were suffering from what they kept
calling 'second-night blues', and even she, who couldn't
give a shit about any of it, could see that their acting was
dull and lifeless compared to last night. So boring. You
needed an interpreter to understand more than two words
in every ten.

She peered through the curtain. Danny was waving his
knife around and mouthing off. She didn't mind when he
was onstage. He was well good. Easily the best. She could
sometimes even get what he was on about. The bit about
not normally being jealous, but once he was then he
couldn't control himself – that was spot on. She glared at
the slag on the bed. Her chest was heaving up and down.
She was supposed to be dead. She could at least make the
effort to look it.

After the show, she waited for Danny. It took ages before
he was ready. His godfather had turned up again and was
farting about giving them all the benefit of his advice.
Especially the slag. He seemed to have an awful lot to say
to her. In fact, now he was walking off with her, still giving
it large. Julie saw Danny staring at them as he came towards
her.

She produced her prettiest smile. 'Ready, Dan?'

For a split second it was like he didn't know who she
was, but then he said, 'Ready as I'll ever be, babe. The

others are going to the Maypole, but I thought we'd go somewhere where we won't be disturbed.'

He wants me all to himself.

It would all come good, she just knew it.

But of course, it didn't.

For a start, he didn't touch her. Danny was mega touchy-feely, and it had always felt so good to be with him because he'd made it very clear to everyone that she was his girl. He'd put his arm around her, hold her hand, stroke her face, plant little absentminded kisses on her cheek while he was talking to other people. He knew she felt stupid next to his clever friends and this was partly his way of reassuring her. Making sure she knew how important she was to him. Making sure they all knew it, too. He was sensitive and considerate and light years away from the boys she'd been out with before, who were all like Scott – bone-headed morons who wanted a pint and a fuck in that order and weren't remotely interested in her as a person. Danny wasn't like that. He'd really listen to her, and ask all the right questions, and she'd told him things she could never have imagined telling any guy. She told him everything. He knew everything. Everything.

But now, he parked himself across the other side of the table and it felt like there was a million miles between them. She ached to touch him. If only she had the words to explain how she felt. She knew she wasn't brainy like his friends and she knew she didn't fit into his arty-farty family. Staying with them was like negotiating your way round a foreign country, trying to interpret their strange ways. But she was a quick learner. She might not know much about boring Shakespeare, but in the last year she'd looked and listened and picked up fuckloads about the weird little signals and codes that told the snotty classes you were one of them. *I can change, Dan. I can be whatever you want me to be. Just love me again.*

'I meant what I said last night, Jules.'

'About what?'

'The baby. If you don't want it, then I'll support you through the abortion. And if you do, then you won't be on your own.'

She felt the first beginnings of a thaw in her arctic despair, but she needed to pin him down. 'What do you mean, I won't be on my own? Are you saying you'll marry me if I decide I want to keep it?'

His body stiffened, but after a moment he said, 'If that's what's best.'

Somewhere deep inside her, joy bubbled up. She did her best to quell it. *Not yet, Julie. Not yet.* 'But what do *you* want, babe?' she said.

He shook his head. 'It's your decision. It's not my body that has to deal with this mess. But I helped make it and I want you to know that I'll take my share of responsibility.'

'It's not a baby to you, then? Just a mess?'

His voice was suddenly sharp. 'You know what I mean.' The air between them quivered.

'Babies cost money. You're a student. You don't have any money.'

His eyes closed momentarily and she saw a small muscle flickering in his lower jaw. 'I'll leave university and get a job.'

He still loves me. He must. Otherwise he wouldn't be willing to make such a sacrifice. 'You'd do that?'

'If that's what it takes.'

'You'd fuck up your whole future?'

He shrugged. His dark eyes, ringed with kohl that he hadn't properly removed after the play, were dull, and there were smudged shadows below them. He looked like he hadn't slept for days.

But he's offering himself to me. Offering his life to me.

She'd got what she'd so badly wanted. So why did she feel so awful?

She forced herself to confront it. 'But you said you didn't love me any more.'

Her words hung between them. He wouldn't look at her.

The coldness came again, rolling down like mist on a mountain. 'You don't love me, Danny.'

When his eyes finally met hers, they were desperate. 'I did once. Maybe I will again. I'll try my best.'

'Don't strain yourself.' The words were out before she could stop them.

Watch it, girl. This ain't no way to win him back. Be cool.

But his voice was kind. 'I just meant that maybe this last month has been some kind of madness on my part, and that soon everything will be the way it was.'

'That's what I said when you dumped me.'

'Yes.'

She wished he didn't sound so sad and hopeless. She wanted to take him in her arms and kiss him better, but instead she found herself saying, 'What about Stella?' She cursed her own stupidity. Why remind him of that bitch? But it was an itchy scab that she couldn't stop picking.

'Stella's not an issue.'

So how come you looked so gutted, when the slag was talking to your godfather earlier?

She didn't want his pity. If he married her, it had to be because he loved her. Which, at the moment, it was fucking obvious he didn't. But if he married her, she'd *make* him love her again. They'd have their own place, where no one would come between them and she'd have things perfect for him and the baby.

Julie, there ain't no baby.

She'd almost convinced herself that there was.

Yesterday, when he'd come out with all this shit about her being pregnant, she'd genuinely started to speak up, to tell him he'd got the wrong end of the stick, but then the words had died in her throat. As he'd babbled about doing the right thing, her mind had instantly grasped the implications of the situation. *This might be the way to get him back.*

If she said that she wanted the baby, Danny could be hers for the taking.

She'd been filled with a wild hope. But at that point, she hadn't quite had the bottle to come out with the lie. *But neither could she bring herself to tell the truth.*

Keeping quiet was a way of buying time. Time to contemplate whether or not she could go through with such a monstrous deception. Time to see whether Danny was still prepared to make good his promise, having slept on it. And tonight, twenty-four hours later, she had her answer. He'd more or less said he'd marry her.

If there was a baby.

If there was no baby, he'd be off without a backward glance.

She couldn't lose him all over again. Far better to keep quiet, get married and show him what a great wife she could be. That's what they did in other cultures. Arranged marriages and all that shit where the couple didn't always love each other at first. Some people said they often worked out better in the end.

If he marries me, sooner or later he'll find out I've been lying about the baby.

If I got pregnant for real he'd never know – but what if I don't?

It won't matter, because by then I'll have made him love me again. Oh yeah? How?

Make him love me again. It was all so vague. She needed specifics. What exactly could she do to make it happen – and soon? Her mind scrabbled frantically for the answer. At first there was nothing, then, very dimly, the outline of an idea took shape.

'Dan, I don't know what I want at the moment. I sure as hell don't know whether I'm ready for marriage.' She tried not to see the relief in his eyes.

'There's not much of a margin with these things. If you want an abortion, Jules, the sooner the better.'

'A day won't make much difference. Let's just chill until after the Ball.'

'The what? Oh shit – the Ball. I keep forgetting.'

'I don't. I've never been to a May Ball, and I'm really looking forward to it. Will you do something for me?'

'If I can.'

'Forget the baby for twenty-four hours and just try to enjoy being at the Ball with me.'

He smiled wanly. 'It's a deal. No more baby-talk for twenty-four hours. And after that, you'll tell me what you want to do?'

'I promise.'

For the first time that evening, he reached out and gently stroked her hand as it lay on the table. Tears sprang to her eyes and she turned away so he didn't see them.

Dawkins, performing his late-night business in the Master's Garden, sniffed the air appreciatively. The storm had freshened everything up, washed away the old stale smells, leaving only new and interesting ones.

And the thing he could smell at the moment was more interesting than anything he'd come across for a long time. Rank and juicy, it called to him from the hedge at the bottom of the garden. He'd eaten well that evening – a particularly high game pie that even the old fart couldn't stomach. So it was quite an effort for him to traipse all the way to the far end of the garden. But it was imperative to investigate the wonderful smell, so he waddled towards it as fast as his stubby legs would carry him.

The closer he got, the more enticing the aroma. Behind him he heard his Master calling him. He turned and saw the old fart, standing on the porch, the mellow light from the Lodge streaming out around him, the two cats weaving round his legs. Dawkins ventured a contemptuous growl. When the dog's away, the cats will play, he thought. They'd never accepted that whatever they did, he would always be *numero uno* in the Lodge. No matter. Let them have their brief moment. He'd deal with them later.

'Dawkins! Here, boy. Here! Bonio time!'

He was tempted. From the black depths of the garden, home looked especially inviting. But for once he ignored his master's voice. Sometimes a dog had to do what a dog had to do. He forged on down the manicured lawn, confident that his fat little body had by now disappeared into the darkness and was incapable of being spotted.

The smell was very pungent now. He was almost on top of it. Then he heard something: a movement in the hedge. And there was a different smell. A stink. Acrid and sharp, it momentarily obliterated the other one. He felt the fur on the back of his neck rise, and gave a low growl. He stood very still. Should he turn back? But as he dithered, he was once more aware of the delicious odour. He'd come so far it seemed foolish and a tad cowardly to abandon the adventure now. So, more alert than he'd been for several years, he plunged into the hole in the hedge from which the intriguing smell emanated.

These are the words of him who has the sharp double-edged sword. 'I know where you live, where Satan has his throne. Repent therefore.'

THURSDAY 23 JUNE

TWENTY-FOUR

In my dream I'm a little old lady reciting *Green Eggs and Ham* to a cherubic child who lies in bed, big beautiful brown eyes – Danny's eyes – drinking in my every word. But then the child's nose becomes a snout, she starts squealing, and I see that my granddaughter is, in fact, a pig and that it's my job to turn her into prime organic pork chops. I whip the pillow from under her and press it onto her face. The noise increases. I don't understand. I'm suffocating her – it should be diminishing. But instead it intensifies until it sounds as if a whole farmyard is trying to escape from under my murderous fingers.

Then I'm awake. But the high-pitched cacophony is still assaulting my eardrums.

It's the Screamers. They pummel me with their tiny fists.

Cassie sees I'm awake. 'You said they'd stop. You said they'd stop.'

'Calm down, Cass. Stop what?'

'They're at it again.' Hector's voice is fierce, but his eyes are full of panic.

I realise that even though the children have now stopped bellowing, there's still considerable noise in the house.

It comes from downstairs. April and Perry. Snarling at each other like two pit bulls.

'You two stay here and I'll go and see what's up.'

'Can't we come too?'

'Best not.'

'Why?'

'Because . . . because I say so.' I escape before they bombard me with more questions and accusations.

The dreadful sound comes from the living room. I make my presence known. 'Your children are in a state of abject terror. They think you're killing each other. I was rather beginning to wonder, myself.'

They both turn, faces white and strained.

'Oh shit. Poor kids.' April pushes past me and runs upstairs.

'What's going on, Perry?'

He collapses onto the sofa, head in hands. 'It's all such a mess.'

'Want to talk about it?'

He looks at me with bloodshot eyes. 'Why doesn't she believe me?'

'What doesn't she believe?'

'That I spent the night on the sofa because I came in late after the play and didn't want to wake her.' His tone is too defensive. If he can't even manage to persuade me, no wonder April isn't falling for it.

'How late?'

'Oh . . .' He waves a vague hand. 'Dunno really. Quite late.'

Evasive or what?

'If I say I spent several hours discussing the play with Lee Watson, then she should take my word for it.'

'Why? You're not even doing a good job of convincing me.'

'Rosa!'

'It's true.'

'Thanks for the vote of confidence.'

'Don't get moody. Tell me the truth.'

'I am.' He can't look me in the eye.

'Perrygreen, I've known you since you were six years old. You looked just like you do now, the day you stole my favourite Noddy book and dropped it down the loo.'

There's a long pause. Then he says, 'I love April. I adore her. And I love my family. I dearly love all of them. But something's happened over the last few days. I don't understand it, I don't want it, but I have to go along with it. It's big, Rosaleen. Big.'

I could thump him. 'You're shagging Stella Grainger, so don't try and elevate it to something deep and meaningful.'

'I am not!'

Such righteous anger.

'Well, something's going on and that girl's slap bang in the middle of it.'

He crosses to the window and stares out over the dark garden. To avoid looking at me? 'I just want to be with her, Rosa. I can't explain it. It's like a physical pull whenever I'm in her vicinity. I want to be with her, talk to her, listen to anything and everything she has to say. I know it's wrong. I know that, even though I haven't touched her, I'm somehow betraying April. But I can't help it.'

'Yes, you can!' Now it's me who's shouting. 'Stop making a mystery out of it. You want to shag her. As yet, your conscience hasn't quite given you permission. But you will. You'll find some way of justifying it to yourself. And meanwhile, you're denying April the evidence of her own eyes and pretending *she's* the one at fault. You'll destroy your marriage if you're not careful.'

'I've no intention of destroying my marriage.'

'Stella's probably pegged you as a stepping-stone to a good degree. I've seen girls like her in action before. She's a user. She's been using Danny too.'

'What?'

'Though what she wants from him, God only knows. Maybe she hopes to add a black boyfriend to her extensive collection.'

'She wouldn't do that.'

'Wouldn't she just! Anyway, Dan has other problems, so Stella will be taking a back seat from now on as far as he's concerned. Which leaves the field free for you, I suppose.'

'You don't get it. Whatever I'm feeling, the question of me sleeping with Stella doesn't arise. Apart from anything else, she's my student. I do have some integrity.'

'You mean, if she weren't your student then it would be OK to cheat on your wife?'

'I am *not* cheating on my wife. I'm merely saying that there's something here that I need to explore.'

'Oh please! Cut the psychobabble. If you go on like this you'll be in Stella's bed before the end of the week.'

At that moment, there's a loud noise in the hall. Something falling. Perry opens the door. Behind it lies Frankie.

'Not the stairs again, Mother.'

'It's that daft rug you keep in the middle of the floor. Didn't I say it was an accident waiting to happen?'

She struggles to her feet. Perry puts out a hand but she won't let him anywhere near her. The expression 'tight-lipped and ashen-faced' isn't one I'd normally use for Frankie. In general, her mouth is always open and gagging to give everyone the benefit of her valuable opinion. But now she's pinched and silent. Without another word she starts back upstairs. She must have overheard Perry's row with April. She couldn't *not* have heard it – the whole street could probably submit *The Grimshaws' Marital Upsets* as their specialist subject in *Mastermind*. But why is *she* so upset? She's been stirring up trouble between them ever since she arrived. I thought she'd be singing 'The Hallelujah Chorus', mission accomplished.

'Are you OK, Frankie?' Perry, too, is bewildered by his mother's uncharacteristically low-key exit.

'No,' she mutters, without a backward glance. 'No, I'm not.'

As she disappears from view, Perry sighs. 'Remember the time we ran away to Blackpool?'

'We only got as far as the corner shop before my mum caught up with us.'

'Fancy another attempt?'

'In your dreams, sunshine. You've got stuff to sort.'

'Why are you always right, Rosaleen? It's very boring.' He glances upstairs where his entire family are busy being upset in various locations. 'I'm off out now. I may be some time.'

'Perry . . .'

But he's gone.

* * *

Hugo was a morning person. He liked the fresh promise of a new day, and this new day promised to be one of the best. Tonight, the Billings May Ball would be the jewel in the crown, enhancing all his other achievements. The list of wealthy parents and alumni willing to contribute to the library fund was growing daily. The inducement of free tickets to the Ball had worked wonders. Hugo laughed to himself at the parsimony of extreme wealth: willing to donate thousands to the college, but still greedy for a freebie.

And then there were the Americans. Yesterday they'd more or less intimated that their foundation would provide the bulk of the money. It had, admittedly, been a low moment when the ghastly Tipton had stormed into Hall and berated him like a lunatic, but in some ways he felt that this had ultimately worked to his advantage. The Americans were impressed with his coolness under pressure, and when he'd explained the background, they were suitably outraged that one religious fanatic should try to impede the march of forward progress.

He finished shaving and patted his face with his favourite cologne, smiling at himself in the bathroom mirror. With the personable Thorn woman as his consort for the Ball, tonight would be the clincher. By this time tomorrow, it would all be in the bag.

He strolled down to the kitchen to feed the animals, but there was no sign of any of them. Ming and Mong had probably been mousing all night and wouldn't be interested in breakfast, but where was Dawkins? He was a lazy animal and usually had to be tempted out of his basket next to the Aga with much petting and doggy-choc inducements. However, the basket was empty this morning. Then he remembered: the silly creature had given him the run-around last night so he'd shut him out. The poor thing had spent the night in the porch. The little chap wouldn't have liked that – he loved his home comforts. Better go and put him out of his misery.

He threw open the massive oak door and stepped out into the garden. It was a glorious morning. Yesterday's storm had washed the world clean. All the heavy stickiness had disappeared, leaving everything pulsating with life. The grim grey façades of the college buildings seemed to have mellowed and softened, and his wolves on top of their pillars on either side of the front door, caught by the morning sun, smiled rosily down on him. As for the Master's Garden, even Hugo, not the world's greatest fan of natural beauty – give him the perfection of a gene pattern seen through a microscope any day – was dazzled by the richness and profusion of the borders. The very grass seemed more intense, an emerald carpet spread out before him, still spattered with dew.

And something else.

With the onset of middle age, Hugo had bowed to the inevitable and acquired a very expensive pair of designer spectacles. But this morning they still lay in their case on his night-table. Which meant that his view of the garden was somewhat Impressionistic. So the strange humps at the far end of the lawn remained just that – strange humps.

Until, that is, he came within spitting distance. Then he screamed.

The scream was long, loud and continuous, and very quickly brought his housekeeper out of the Lodge. When she saw what he was looking at, she screamed too.

Arranged in a neat line, unblinking eyes gazing skyward, lay Dawkins, Ming and Mong.

Very still. And very, very dead.

Among the prophets of Jerusalem I have seen something horrible. I will make them eat bitter food and drink poisoned water.

TWENTY-FIVE

Tidying the chapel after early-morning Communion, Dominic was giddy with fatigue. Had last night really happened? He feared it was so.

But it wasn't all bad. After making his ignominious exit from Hall, he'd let Lucas take him back to his rooms, where he'd gone to bed and fallen into a deep sleep. At three in the morning he'd awoken, desperate for water. On his way to the tiny kitchenette, he'd seen a rug and a pillow on the sofa in the sitting room. Lucas must have stayed over, bless him.

So where was he?

The door was slightly ajar. As was the door to the Gatehouse. On impulse, he'd mounted the stone stairs leading to the walkway. It was a moonless night, but the sodium glare from the town still cast enough light to see the Guardian, the Messenger and the Healer, their massive, intricately carved wings unfurled, cascades of curls streaming down their backs, the beauty of their faces when seen in such close proximity, quite dazzling.

But tonight they were not alone. Tonight there was a fourth angel.

He was balanced on the edge of the narrow parapet alongside Gabriel, arms outstretched as if ready for flight, hair ruffled by a light breeze. Dominic's stomach lurched.

'Don't!' he'd cried. 'Don't leave me, Lucas!'

Lucas had turned, an ethereal smile on his face. 'Hey, Unc. Why would I want to do that?' Then he'd leaped lightly down beside Dom. 'You're shivering. Let's go inside.'

'What are you doing?' With the image of Simon Smith's shattered body hovering in front of him, Dom could hardly bring himself to say the words.

'I like high places – always have. Dad used to take me to the top of the tallest building in every place we visited, and I'd write down the name in my *Big Buildings Book*. I've still got it. I'll show you some time.'

Lucas never talked much about life before Dominic. Dominic's brother, Nicholas, was an engineer – a bridge-builder – whose wife ran off with an architect when Lucas was five, never to be seen again. Nicholas refused to do the expected thing and send Lucas to boarding-school. Instead, the two of them had lived like gypsies, travelling the world, building bridges. But when Lucas was eighteen, Nicholas had been killed. He'd slipped and fallen from the top of a suspension bridge which he'd been constructing. Dominic met Lucas for the first time at the funeral. He'd expected the boy to come and live with him, but Lucas had announced his intention of continuing his world odyssey. Dominic had done precious little to dissuade him. His nephew was legally of age, and Dominic had been far too preoccupied with setting up R&R to relish dealing with a rebellious adolescent. He'd contented himself, as a trustee and executor of Nicholas's estate, in making sure his nephew's bank account had sufficient sums of money paid into it at regular intervals. Then, last Christmas, Lucas had turned up out of the blue, bursting with the evangelical fervour of untried youth, and begging to work with him at the refuge. Dominic had initially been sceptical, such passionate avowals often being of a self-combusting and shortlived duration, but he'd set aside his misgivings and welcomed his nephew with open arms. And in the succeeding months, to his great joy and surprise, he'd found a dear son and trusted companion, whose strong beliefs seemed to increase rather than fade away, the longer he worked at R&R.

And he, in his turn, had come to love Lucas. It was the first time since his failed affair as an undergraduate, that he'd loved a specific human being. In spite of his skill as a preacher, and his passionate championing of the have-nots, he found it hard to articulate, let alone value, his own emotions. He'd never thought of himself as someone who was particularly lovable, or indeed deserving of love, but it didn't bother him. His own lovability wasn't an issue. Other people were what mattered. Until Lucas arrived, a generalised love of humanity, and his specific love for God had been more than enough to keep him going. Now, each day, he gloried in the complex network of protective and loving feelings awakened in him by his nephew.

But the episode on the walkway made him experience, all over again, the downside of loving. *The monstrous and terrible fear of loss.*

Back in his rooms, Lucas had made him a hot drink. 'How are you feeling after last night?'

'I made a fool of myself in front of the whole college. The Master would be perfectly justified in having me committed.'

'Rubbish. You've brought it out into the open. People will now realise exactly what he's trying to do to Billings.'

'No.' He'd been overwhelmed by the futility of his task. 'It's over, Lucas. The library's done for. My Department will be next.'

'Stop worrying. God won't let you down. He knows how important this is. He'll have a plan to sort it, you'll see.'

Sometimes Dominic felt slightly uncomfortable when Lucas talked about God as if he were a wise old professor who lived next door. It seemed inappropriately childish for a man in his twenties. But then, he'd heard many young evangelical Christians doing the same thing: behaving as if God were incarnated amongst them, ever-ready with solutions and strictures to guide and help them towards salvation and away from damnation. The faith of these wide-eyed youngsters seemed very black and white and not at all the grey hinterland in which he often found himself. But maybe this was the way forward, this open and frankly-stated inclusion of God into everyday life. Maybe this was the way to shore up a dying faith, rather than the middle-of-the-road middle-class C of E Christianity that considered it tasteless to shout about God in public, and that would rather die than foist its beliefs onto others.

'It could be, for instance,' Lucas was saying, 'that His plan is for all those students who heard what you said in Hall last night to mount a campaign to save the library.'

Dominic envied the boy his certainty. Personally, he couldn't quite see it. He hadn't noticed any particular

314

affection for the Theological Library amongst the under-graduate population of Billings, and couldn't envisage the sudden onset of religious zeal that would make them want to save it. He looked across at his nephew, naïve belief in God's power to change things for the good writ large over his face. It was time he had a serious talk with Lucas. His own problems could go on the back-burner for now. He had a few things he needed to get off his chest.

'I've been thinking a lot recently, Lucas, about all that travelling you did after your father died. I feel very guilty about it. Anything could have happened to you. I should have made much more effort to stop you from going. Made it much clearer that you had a home here with me.'

'But nothing did happen to me. I'm here and I'm fine.'

'Nevertheless, I failed you, and I want to apologise. I'm so sorry.'

'Hey – don't stress, Unc. You did what you had to do. So did I. I couldn't have settled here then. I needed to split.'

'But why?'

Lucas had smiled, but Dom saw the pain in his eyes. 'I thought that if I kept moving I could run away from Dad's death.'

'So what changed your mind?'

'I learned that you can't really run away from anything.'

'Is that why you came back?'

'I realised the thing I was looking for had been here all the time.'

'And what was it?'

'To heal myself I needed to heal others. I remembered your work with the refuge and I realised that that was what

I wanted to do, too. Before I left, you'd said I was welcome to come and live with you. So I took a chance that you meant it and came back.'

'You'll never know how much I've valued your help and companionship over the past months.'

'Hey, Unc. Don't go all soppy on me.'

Dominic had felt swamped by emotion. 'I couldn't manage without you now.'

'You don't have to. I'm not going anywhere.'

Today, in the chapel, remembering this conversation, Dominic felt the emotion welling up again. To have such support after all the solitary years was more than he'd ever expected or deserved.

Then the quiet serenity of the moment was broken by a loud crash as the chapel doors were flung open.

'The police are on their way, and when they arrive I'm sending them straight to you. Did you honestly imagine you could get away with it?'

He turned round. There stood the Master, dressed in maroon silk pyjamas, literally hopping up and down on his fat little legs. The colour of his face matched his nightwear. He looked dangerously close to having a stroke.

'Hugo, show some respect. You're in God's House.'

'Fuck God. Fuck your non-existent crapulous excuse for most of the shit that goes on in this rotten world. What harm did my poor little animals ever do you?'

'I don't know what you're talking about—'

But the Master wasn't listening. 'You killed my pets and I'm going to make sure they lock you up and throw away the key. Then we'll see how well your God protects you.'

After that, he left.

'*And the Lord did that thing on the morrow, and all the cattle of Egypt died,*' said Dominic quietly, and with a heavy heart.

All morning, April felt horrible. Perry hadn't returned, and Rosa had also disappeared without a word. *Why? What had Perry told Rosa that he couldn't tell her?*

The kids were in the back garden. She'd insisted that the latest quarrel between her and Daddy was nothing to worry about, but she didn't think they were convinced. Not if their behaviour was anything to go by. This morning they were particularly cranky, and after a nasty incident involving Cassandra's favourite jumper and the kitchen scissors, April had turned them both out of doors, saying they weren't welcome back inside until lunch-time. Listlessly she watched them hitting each other with delphiniums they'd ripped out of the flowerbed. Not that she cared. Let them destroy the whole garden. It was a ghastly metaphor for the destruction of the paradise that had been her life as little as a week ago.

She wondered why Frankie wasn't glorying in the upset. But all her mother-in-law had said so far this morning was that she intended to use the Grimshaws' phone for some business calls. She'd been in Perry's study for ages. April could hear her strident tones through the half-open door. In an attempt to ignore her own gnawing anxiety, she started to eavesdrop

Frankie's calls all ran along similar lines:

'Is that Pizza Hut, Church Road? I'd like to order five Super Supreme Pizzas, five portions of garlic bread and three bottles of Coke to be sent to 54, Walton Street. You are the Wigan branch, not the one in Warrington, aren't you? Good. Half an hour? Ta muchly.

'Is that the Kashmir? I'd like to order a takeaway meal to be delivered to 54, Walton Street. Ten portions of tandoori chicken, eight mixed vegetable curries, eight aloo ghobi, seven lamb biryani, ten portions of pilau rice, twenty poppadoms and three raita. That's it. Forty minutes? Cheers.'

After about ten fast-food orders, the script changed.

'Humphreys Fine Furnishings? I'm a local landlord and I need to furnish one of my properties very quickly – today, in fact. I've heard that your store can deliver immediately, is that right? Good. In that case I'd like to order a kingsize bed, a three-piece suite and a dining table and eight chairs. They need to last, so I'll take your most expensive items . . . Pink leather sounds just the job. Excellent. If you come up to scratch, I'll be using you to equip several other properties as well. The address for delivery is Rimmer, 54, Walton Street, Wigan. Credit card number? Certainly. Five zero five nine . . .'

After that she phoned three more furniture shops, several florists and a series of clothes catalogues before coming through to the kitchen.

'Any chance of a cuppa, pet? I'm parched. All that yakking doesn't half play pot with the vocals.'

'I couldn't help overhearing—'

'Sorry, it's the trained voice. Projection, you see. Vital for the stage, but you can't switch it off. A bugger if you want some privacy for your doings.'

'All that food – and the furniture?'

Frankie's voice was hard. 'If there's one thing I've learned, pet, it's that you can't let folk walk all over you.'

'No, I suppose not. But . . .'

'It's an eye for an eye in this shitty old world of ours. That vicar said as much yesterday. If someone dumps on you, you dump right back on them, but worse. Let them know that if they fuck you over, then they'll frigging well pay for it.' Her harsh bark of laughter contained no warmth. 'Alf Rimmer will know that by now. The fat bastard will have enough takeaway food to feed an army, and by the time he's paid for it, the furniture will be rolling up. I'd love to see his face when he takes delivery of that three-piece suite. Especially since he's allergic to leather and hates pink. And I do so hope that old boot he's banging suffers from hay fever.' She gave another grim laugh. 'Mind you, if she didn't before, she will once she's got all those lovely flowers from Alf.'

'From Alf?'

'You didn't think I was paying with *my* credit card? The bugger was in such a hurry yesterday that he forgot to ask for it back.' She looked at her watch. 'Hellfire! I should have gone on a shopping spree first and maxed it out before he twigs what's going on. Mind you, he's such a gormless article it probably won't occur to him.' She laughed again. 'And if he thinks it's over by the end of today, he's got another think coming. Those catalogues take weeks to deliver stuff. He'll be getting little reminders of Yours Truly well into the New Year.'

In the few months April had known Frankie, her mother-in-law's tactics had tended towards the oblique – nastiness hidden under disingenuous disclaimers, so that April could be accused of misinterpretation, and end up in Perry's eyes as the aggressor. But this was undisguised, unrepentant malevolence. Hell did indeed have no fury. She shivered at the thought of what that fury could do if it were turned on her with truly serious intent.

But at present, Frankie seemed to regard her as a sister-in-arms, equally wronged by perfidious man. 'For what it's worth, pet, I think our Perry's being a total arse.'

April wasn't ready to badmouth Perry to his mother, however inexplicably hurtful she found his present behaviour. 'I don't know what you mean.'

'I heard you at it again earlier.'

'That was just a bit of a tiff.'

'Then I'd hate to see a fullblown argy-bargy. Come off it – you've been at each other's throats ever since I arrived. It's that girl. You know it and I know it, so stop playing silly buggers and let me give you some advice.'

She was the last person whose advice April needed – particularly after witnessing her attack on poor Alf. But Frankie was going to give it to her anyway, so she sat back and braced herself.

'She's out to get him. And if you don't pull your finger out, she'll succeed.'

April's misery was complete. Up until now she'd tried to convince herself that her own neurosis was causing her to misinterpret everything. But now Frankie had put it into words, it was a reality.

'She might want him but it doesn't mean he wants *her*,' she said, unable to keep the hostility out of her voice.

'He wants her, all right.'

'In that case she's welcome to him. If he wants her, then he doesn't want me. And I don't go where I'm not wanted.'

'Don't be so soft! You've got to fight for him.'

'Like you fought for Alf yesterday?'

Frankie's lips became a thin purple line. 'That's different. For starters, me and Alf don't have young babbas. How do you think they'll feel if their mam and dad become another divorce statistic? If you ask me, they're already frigging disturbed.' She gestured into the back garden, where the children had dismantled their Wendy House and thrown the bits all over the lawn. Now Hector was hammering the trunk of a tree with a piece of wood while Cassandra sat beside a small pile of decapitated dolls, systematically removing their limbs.

'Oh God! I'd better see to them!' April opened the back door.

'Wait!' Frankie's tone stopped her in her tracks. 'You're a good wife to our Perry.'

'You've changed your tune.'

'I didn't think you were, but I've changed my mind.'

'Don't claim to have my best interests at heart, because I'm sorry, Frankie, it won't wash.'

'I don't want my boy to do something he'll regret for the rest of his life. He still loves you. You've just got to make him see it, that's all.'

'And how do I do that?' April despised herself. In spite of everything, she wanted to hear what Frankie was proposing. She must be more desperate than she'd realised.

'Make him see what he'd be missing if he left you.'

'Like how?'

Frankie looked her up and down. 'I've seen snaps of you in Ozzie Land before the wedding, when you first met our Perry, and you were a right pretty lass. But I'm going to be blunt, pet. You've let yourself go since having those babbas.'

'Thanks a bunch,' muttered April. Whatever her stated intentions, Frankie still couldn't resist sticking the knife in.

'I'm only saying it for your own good. A man likes to come home to a sexy wife, who's taken a bit of trouble with her appearance, and who looks pleased to see him. He doesn't want some harassed harpy with dirty hair, no make-up, broken nails and shabby jeans telling him what a neglectful bugger he is.'

April gripped the edge of the table. This was all she needed – a lecture on grooming and man management from the Fabulous Frankie Faraday.

'This is the twenty-first century, Frankie, not some cosy fifties' idyll where men were men and women were glad of it. Perry and I are an equal partnership. It isn't dependent on me being the obedient little Hausfrau stroke geisha, waiting at home for the master's return.'

'You're not listening, pet. If you want to get him back, that's exactly what you've got to be for a while.'

'Oh, go to hell!' April finally snapped. She opened the back door. 'I'm going to count to three hundred,' she bellowed to the kids. 'If that garden isn't tidy by the time I've finished, there's no lunch.'

When she turned back, Frankie had gone.

April stared at her reflection in the chrome trim on the Aga. What if Frankie was right? What if it *was* all her fault? What if, in her attempt to be the perfect mother, she'd driven Perry to seek comfort elsewhere?

And what could she realistically do to put a spanner in Stella's irresistible works?

TWENTY-SIX

He treated himself to a latte and a slice of chocolate cheese-cake from the café by the river near Magdalene Bridge. Expensive comfort food.

The text message from Julie winked up at him from his mobile. *Am kping it. Did u mean what u said?*

He bit viciously into the cake. All around, people were having fun. The afternoon river was crowded, punts and other craft jostling for position, people shouting good-natured insults to each other across the water. One rowing boat contained a family – mum, dad, and a small boy. The child was having one mother of a tantrum. It seriously threatened the stability of the boat. Nothing his parents said or did made any difference. The mum clung desperately to the side, clearly expecting at any moment to find herself on the bottom of the Cam.

Family life.

'Cheer up.'

Stella had materialised from nowhere. She took a bite of his cake. He thought he'd never seen anything quite so

sexy as the faint down of golden hairs on her arm. He ha
to sit on his hands in order to stop himself stroking i
brown, summer smoothness.

If only he could stay forever in this sunny place by th
river, feeding her mouthfuls of cake.

He finished his coffee and stood up. 'I'm off to Perry'
to see my mum.'

'Mind if I tag along?' said Stella. 'I'm going back t
Billings anyway.'

As they strolled along the riverbank, she linked her arn
in his. 'I don't see why we have to cancel a performance
just because of the Ball,' she said. 'We could have done i
this afternoon instead. I'll miss strutting our stuff togethe
tonight.'

'Yeah,' he muttered, tonguetied with lust and misery.

She walked with him all the way to Perry's gate. 'Se
you at the Ball?'

'I love you, Stella.'

It just slipped out. *Idiot*. What had possessed him? Wha
would she say?

Like some corny Hollywood movie, time slipped int
Slo-mo as she gazed up at him.

And then they were interrupted by a vision in a scarle
dress, the brevity of which did no favours to the spindl
legs protruding from beneath the scanty skirt.

'It's our Danny, isn't it?'

His first encounter with the Fabulous Frankie. His mun
always said she had an uncanny knack of barging in at th
wrong moment.

'I saw your performance the other night, pet. Blood
good. Nice to see a proper blackie playing *Othello*. I use

to work with the Black and White Minstrels years ago. I always thought they looked a right bunch of silly articles, with all that boot polish on their faces.' She turned to Stella. Her smile didn't reach her eyes. 'And you're the lass he smothered. Not a nice way to go. She didn't deserve it, that Desdemona. Unlike some.'

Go away, Frankie. Now. The last thing he wanted was an *Othello* debriefing from a batty old woman. But he needn't have worried.

'Well,' she said, 'I must love you and leave you. I'm off to try and blag a ticket for the Ball. It's time I saw exactly what goes on at one of these lah-di-dah do's.' She walked past them, glaring at Stella, who met her gorgon gaze with sweet equanimity.

After she was out of earshot, Danny said, 'I bet she gets one, too.'

Stella's green eyes followed Frankie as she retreated into the distance. 'Yeah.'

He was desperate to get things back to where they had been, but he could feel the moment retreating as rapidly as Frankie's absurd high-heels click-clacking up the road towards Billings. 'Stella—'

'Can I have a glass of water? My mouth's really dry.'

'Sure.' It was as if she hadn't heard what he said before Frankie's untimely interruption.

When he took her into the kitchen, April and his mother looked like they'd smelled bad drains. April muttered a greeting. Rosa said nothing.

What was their problem?

He filled a glass with water and handed it to Stella. He'd never known his mother to be unnecessarily rude. *The root of good manners is care and concern for others, particularly guests in our home* was one of Rosa's most stringent maxims, drilled into him and Anna since babyhood. But her response to Stella was the most blatant piece of blanking he'd seen for a long time.

'I'll be in the living room, Dan. Don't be long,' she said. Then she walked out.

April, on the other hand, watched, mesmerised as Stella gulped down the water. The silence in the kitchen was broken only by the sound of swallowing.

Eventually Stella handed the glass back to him. 'I'm off. See you at the Ball.' She smiled at April. 'Are you looking forward to tonight, Mrs Grimshaw? Dr Grimshaw says that you've bought a fab dress.'

Danny was impressed by the way she was ignoring the weird hostility directed towards her. He thought it very mature. April and Rosa might act like spoiled kids, but Stella, half their age, was clearly above such petty bad behaviour.

He thought at first April wasn't going to reply, but after a moment she said, not taking her eyes off Stella, 'Yes, I am. Very much.' She indicated a pink orchid, stem wrapped in foil, which lay on the dresser. 'That's my corsage. Perry sent it to mark our first Billings Ball together.'

Stella's smile widened. 'How romantic. I hope you enjoy yourselves.' She turned to Danny. 'Laters.'

Then she was out of the door and flying down the path at warp speed. He didn't blame her. The welcome she'd received would be enough to chase anyone away. Or was it from him she was escaping? To avoid responding to his brain-dead declaration at the gate.

Feeling like shit, he dragged himself into the living room.

'Has she gone?' Rosa's tone was curt.

'Why were you both so rude?'

'You don't want to know.'

'Yes, I do.'

'Leave it alone, Dan. And you'll leave her alone too, if you've any sense. Now, tell me, what's happening with Julie?'

The Constable, perspiring freely after climbing two flights of stairs, looked familiar.

'PC Mears, Reverend Tipton,' he said, producing his warrant card. 'May I have a word?'

As the man emerged into the light of the sitting room, Dominic recognised him. In his work at R&R he liaised regularly with the local police, who often brought men to the refuge to be fed and watered. He was pretty sure he'd seen this particular policeman trying to tempt a drunken Robbie the Rover in through the doors of R&R a few weeks ago, with the promise of a bowl of stew.

'It's Sir Hugo Mortimer,' said the Constable.

Every which way he turned, that man was there.

'He's had a bit of a nasty experience, I'm afraid. His dog and his two cats were found dead this morning.'

'So I gather. What's that to do with me?' *As if he didn't know.*

'They'd ingested a quantity of rat poison.'

'And he's implying that I have something to do with it?'

'Look, Reverend, I'm a great admirer of yours. What you do at R&R deserves a medal, but it's my duty to ask you some questions, so I beg pardon and hope you'll excuse me.'

'Of course. Duty is the thing that keeps us on the right path, even in the darkest of times.'

'Sir Hugo claims that poisoning his animals is the culmination of a series of malicious incidents perpetrated by yourself against him.'

'The man's mad.'

PC Mears coughed. 'That's what he's saying about *you*, sir.'

Dominic struggled to suppress his anger. If he started ranting, the policeman would think Mortimer was right, and that he was indeed a raving nutcase. 'He doesn't seriously imagine I'd poison his pets?'

The Constable's embarrassment grew. 'There are several other incidents.' He consulted his notebook. 'Polluting the Billings College fountain with red paint, disrupting a committee meeting by introducing a swarm of flies into the proceedings, and contaminating his food with traces of nuts, in the full knowledge that he has a potentially fatal nut allergy.'

Stay cool. Stay calm. Stay collected.

'And has the Master any proof of these ridiculous accusations?'

'No, Reverend. If he had, I'd be obliged to place you under arrest. But I'd be most grateful if you'd tell me where you were yesterday between the hours of eleven p.m. and six a.m. this morning.'

'Asleep in bed.'

PC Mears looked agonised. 'Can anyone confirm that, sir?'

'Of course not! Wait – yes, my nephew, Lucas Tipton. I wasn't feeling too well last night, so he stayed here.'

'What's your nephew's address?'

'He lives in the flat above R&R.'

PC Mears carefully wrote it down and then said, 'That's all for now. I'm very sorry to have bothered you, Reverend. If anything else transpires, I'll be in touch.'

After he'd gone, Dominic felt the need for some air. He went up to the walkway over the Gatehouse and stared out over the college. Last-minute preparations for the Ball were in full swing. Apart from the giant marquee in Bacon he could also see a smaller marquee in Thomas More and a very professional-looking wooden dance-floor in Locke. In Augustine, his poor library was being draped in fairy-lights by two excited students who wobbled precariously on ancient college ladders, while over the other side, several fairground stalls and a carousel had been set up. He turned his back on the college and looked instead at the river. Then he heard his name being called from the pavement below.

'Don't do it, Vicar. It's not worth it.' A cackle of witchy laughter followed.

It was Perry Grimshaw's ghastly mother. The soul he ought to be saving. His spirits sank even further.

'Don't do what?'

'Jump. Don't jump!'

'I wasn't—'

'Just my little joke.'

'Oh. Very amusing.' He bared his teeth in what he hoped resembled a smile. Perhaps he ought to invite her up for tea – but he just couldn't face it. God would have to wait a while longer for Frankie Faraday to be returned to His bosom.

'I'm on my way to see Whatsisname.' She seemed to imagine he'd know who she was talking about. When he didn't respond she clicked her fingers impatiently. 'You know, Whatsisname. Mastermind – bloke in charge.'

'Hugo Mortimer.'

'That's the one.'

Dominic's favourite person.

'I'm going to persuade him to part with a ticket for the Ball. Be a good boy and point me in the right direction.'

'You may not find the Master in the best of moods.'

'Why's that then?'

'This morning, his two cats and his dog were found dead in rather unpleasant circumstances.'

'Oh.' She frowned, but then her face cleared. 'So now's definitely the moment to stick my oar in. Get 'em when they're down – that's what I always say. Thanks for the tip off, Vic.'

After she'd gone he prayed for guidance about Frankie Faraday's conversion. But the Almighty had clearly decided to keep His own counsel and maintained an uncompromising silence on the subject.

TWENTY-SEVEN

Months ago, Stella had suggested they share a double ticket. 'Who needs guys to take us to the Ball? We're twenty-first-century chicks. We do our own thing. The price is horrendous – a hundred quid. Stick it on your card. I'll pay you back later.'

Back then, the thought of her and Stella together at their very first May Ball thrilled Flora beyond reason. She did feel guilty for a while after buying the ticket. Dom thought the Ball a frivolous waste of money – money that could have been given to charity or used for R&R. But the temptation was irresistible. After all, even Jesus was known to have attended various festivities – wedding celebrations and so forth.

Stella was a perfectionist when it came to sartorial matters, and as her foil, Flora, too, was expected to cut the mustard. It was clear that Flora couldn't be trusted with this task herself. Stella sat her firmly down and made up her face with painstaking care, using her own precious cosmetics. She deliberated endlessly over the best style for Flora's hair, and even lent her a necklace and some earrings. In short, she was the perfect girlie chum to have on hand when getting ready for one's first ball.

Flora basked in the pampering, ignoring the little voice in her head which suggested that this was one of the ways in which Stella maintained her hold. That the shortlived but intense barrage of attention was designed to make her Stella's willing stooge for weeks afterwards, humbly grateful that this charismatic girl should expend so much time and energy on plain, insignificant her.

Then she felt sickened by this ever-present inner voice that now rubbished everything Stella did. What if she was completely wrong? What if, over the last few days, she'd had some kind of brainstorm? Maybe it was her own stupid inadequacy that made her read treachery into Stella's attitude towards Lucas. Maybe Stella thought she was helping Flora by being so nice to him. Maybe she saw it as an inclusive gesture, welcoming him to their friendship.

Stella had now transformed Flora's brown rats' tails into a sleek and shining curtain, and was beaming with pleasure. 'You look really hot. Like some pop princess.'

Flora realised she was clenching her jaw so hard that her teeth were hurting. It was time to confront her confusion once and for all. She stared into the mirror at Stella, exquisite in the pale yellow dress they'd bought from *Belle et Beau*, beautiful face bright with excitement at the successful makeover of her friend.

'Stell, do you like Lucas?'

Stella, running the straightening tongs through Flora's hair for the final time, said, 'He's OK.'

'But nothing special?'

'No.'

'So you don't like him – you know – like that?'

Stella laughed. 'No.'

'He's a really fit bloke.'

'Bit too calendar boy for my taste.'

She took the plunge. 'So, so why are you always coming on to him?'

Stella removed the tongs from Flora's hair. 'Are you serious?'

'Can't you see how hurtful it is?'

'I don't come on to guys—'

'But—'

'And I really can't help it if they come on to me.'

'Are you saying that's what Lucas has been doing?'

'What am I supposed to do? I don't want to be rude, especially since he's your mate.'

'You *know* I'm crazy about him.'

'Actually, I don't. You said he was just a friend.'

Flora's head began to pound. 'Yes, but you knew that wasn't true.'

'You need to seriously chill, Flo.' Stella's concerned gaze met Flora's.

Flora looked down at her freshly painted nails, and tried to banish the image of two golden figures leaning over the parapet on the Gatehouse.

'Look, don't stress over a guy – it's not worth it. It'll spoil your evening. I said we'd meet the others in the JCR. Let's go.' Stella grabbed her tiny, but highly expensive, bag and slipped her feet into matching strappy sandals. 'Are you coming or what?'

Flora sat stock still. Her face, in spite of Stella's efforts, looked plain, the make-up sitting on top of it like a garish mask and the poker-straight hair dragging down her already lugubrious features. 'I'll catch you up.'

'Don't spoil things, Flo. We've been looking forward to this for ages.'

Flora couldn't bring herself to reply.

Stella walked to the door. 'Sulking's very uncool, you know.'

After she'd gone, Flora continued to stare at her reflection.

The manager was gutted that she'd taken yet another afternoon off work, but Julie didn't care. She needed the extra time. Everything had to be perfect. She'd been slaving away for hours, locked in her bedroom. And it had all worked out just as she'd planned. She surveyed herself in the mirror and was confident that she'd be giving Danny exactly what he wanted.

She heard Mum lurking about on the landing, gagging for a glimpse.

She knew that now she'd taken the irrevocable step, there was no way back. She hadn't meant to say a word, not until everything was in the bag, but there'd been no option.

Mum had cornered her over lunch. 'Time for a chat, missy.'

She'd needed one of Mum's 'chats' like she needed a slap from a wet fish. 'I've got shitloads to do. I don't want to keep Danny waiting.'

'It's about him that I wanted to talk.'

'Oh.' She'd tried not to sound defensive. Mum's moaning about Danny had made her misery over the past weeks a million times worse.

'I still don't begin to understand why you're going to a ball with a boy who's treated you so disgracefully.'

'No, he hasn't.'

'He used you, Julie. He took your virginity and then left you without a backward glance.'

Took your virginity. In her whole life this was the closest reference Mum had ever made to sex. She never mentioned *those things*, as she called it. This had suited Julie fine. She and her friends had discussed sex endlessly since the age of ten, but talking about it with Mum struck her as a cringe-making ordeal comparable to walking naked through the streets of Cambridge.

'I know what the two of you were up to every night for all those months. I let it go on because I thought you were as good as engaged. I thought he was an honourable boy. How wrong could I be? In the old days, what he's done would be regarded as breach of promise.'

'Give it up, Mum! You know nothing about it.'

'Don't I?' Mum had taken her hand. It was an untypical gesture that set loud warning bells ringing. 'The other day I asked you a question, Julie . . .'

'What?'

'I'm your mother. There's nothing you can't say to me.'

'I don't know what you're talking about.'

Mum had dropped the hand as if scalded. 'Have it your own way. But when that thing in your belly puts in an appearance, don't expect me to rally round and give you both a home. I have my reputation to consider. I'm an employee of a highly respected Cambridge college. I'm also landlady to certain undergraduates of that college. While they're under my roof I'm *in loco parentis*. How would it

look if they had to share houseroom with my tart of a
daughter and her bastard brat?'

Bastard brat?

She'd almost forgotten that it was Mum who first raised
the idea that she might be pregnant. And she clearly hadn't
given up on it, in spite of Julie's denial. Maybe it was a
good omen, showing her that what she wanted to do was
OK.

OK? Hardly.

She was suddenly overwhelmed by the ramifications of
her proposed deception. It wasn't just Danny she'd be
fooling. It would be Mum, Scott – everyone. But then she'd
had a vision of Danny's face: his dark velvet eyes and dreamy
smile. She'd hung on to him by the skin of her teeth. And
it was this mythical baby that had done the trick. If she
admitted that it didn't exist, she'd lose him again – and that
she couldn't bear.

She took a deep breath and plunged in. 'How did you
know I was pregnant?' *No going back now.*

'I heard you being sick one night and put two and two
together.'

Put two and two together and made five. Once again
she'd been transported back to Jesus Green at midnight
feeling the body pressed against her and smelling her own
fear. Then arriving home, rushing to the bathroom and
heaving her guts up. She heaved now as she remembered.

Mum's face had creased in concern. 'Are you all right
lovie? Feeling a bit queasy? Let me get you something
Dry toast always did the trick for me.'

The switch from Nazi interrogator to loving mum was
too much. As the girl registered the worry lines around her

mum's eyes and mouth, she felt suddenly ashamed at how, over the years, she'd made fun of her petty respectability with its cheap china, plastic chair-covers and obsessive cleaning routines. Poor Mum. She'd brought up two kids singlehanded, with no help from anyone. All she'd ever wanted was a good life for her family.

If Julie married Danny, she could make sure that Joan achieved at least one of her ambitions: a Cambridge graduate for a son-in-law. Surely that was a good enough reason to keep up the deception?

'Toast would be great.'

As her mother went through her meticulous and unvarying toastmaking routine, she'd chattered on. 'I've been wondering what's the best thing to do. We can't have anybody round here knowing. I might phone Aunty Beryl. You could stay with her till the baby's born. Then when you come back we'll say you married some lowlife that walked out on you. No, wait, that doesn't sound very respectable, does it? Maybe we'll say he died and you're a tragic young widow. Maybe he was in the army with Scott, and got killed in Iraq – died for his country . . .'

She hadn't been able to take any more.

'Mum – Danny and I are back together.'

Stainless steel toast-rack poised in mid-air, Mum had stopped, her face a picture of disbelief. 'What?'

'You heard.'

'After all he's put you through?'

'I told him about the baby and he wants to marry me.'

'Oh.'

He had mentioned marriage. Kind of. And after tonight, there'd be no question of it.

'So the young man's prepared to face his responsibilities. Well, I am surprised.'

Julie suppressed a smile. From being the big bad wolf, Danny had suddenly become the knight in shining armour. Mum would have to take back all her nasty cracks. It would require mega shit-eating.

Then she'd been filled with love and shame as her mother asked the one question – the only question – that really mattered. 'But, after all he's done, how can you be sure he really loves you?'

She'd smiled extra-brightly. 'He wouldn't ask me to marry him otherwise, would he? Listen, when he comes, don't mention the baby. Not tonight. We can all talk another time.'

With every word, she knew that she'd passed the point of no return.

She'd left Joan then, and gone upstairs to start her complex preparations. At some point, with trembling fingers, she'd taken the plunge and texted Danny. *Am kping it. Did u mean what u said?* Minutes later she got her answer. One word. *Yes.*

And now she was ready. Ready for her very first May Ball. With her future husband.

Julie Thorn . . .

Mrs Daniel Thorn . . .

After giving her dress a final tweak, she opened the bedroom door. Mum was outside, pretending to polish the banister.

She braced herself for the inevitable criticism. Her appearance never quite made the grade. There was always something wrong – wrong colour, wrong style, hair too messy, skirt too short, top too low.

But for once Mum was speechless.

And for once she was impatient for feedback. 'Well?'

Then the doorbell rang.

She couldn't wait for him to see how hard she'd tried to give him what he wanted. She flew downstairs and flung open the door. There he was, six foot three and drop-dead gorgeous in a dinner jacket, his beautiful face, with its high cheekbones and polished skin, dark against the white evening shirt.

She was tonguetied, as his eyes swept over her. For a long moment they stood, frozen on the doorstep, and then he bent down and took her in his arms.

'Oh Jules,' he whispered. 'What have I put you through? I never meant to give you so much grief. I'm so sorry.'

'Am I beautiful enough for you tonight?'

'Of course you are. You always were.'

Safe at last, revelling in his familiar smell, she looked up at him and saw that his eyes had filled with tears. 'It's OK,' she said. 'It don't matter any more. Let's go party.'

'You're so beautiful.'

She trembled at his words, and at the touch of his fingers on her bare skin as he struggled to pin the orchid on the slippery silk of her dress.

Everything was going to be all right.

He'd come in soon after Danny had gone. She was sitting in the kitchen with Rosa, trying to fight the cotton-wool feeling in her head that had replaced coherent thought. Rosa, too, was uncharacteristically subdued. Apart from an outburst over Stella's bare-faced cheek in coming to the house, she'd been strangely silent, and when Perry

appeared she'd immediately jumped up and said, 'I'll tak
the kids onto Jesus Green if you like, April. I could d
with some fresh air and it'll tire them out before th
babysitter arrives.'

'Thanks.' She didn't know whether to be grateful or sorry
Being alone with Perry suddenly seemed scary. What migh
he say?

But he didn't say anything. Not about the rows and upsets
anyway. He asked her what she'd been doing all day, mad
enquiries about Frankie and the children, and said tha
he'd been sorting out courses for the next academic yea
It was as if this morning had never happened. Perry ha
always been non-confrontational, but this was a *tour de forc*
of avoidance. Should she go along with it? Or should sh
bring them both back to reality?

She couldn't face it. Not tonight. Tonight she wanted t
go to the Ball and show the world what a perfect coupl
they were: successful academic Dr Peregrine Grimshaw wit
his elegant and adored young wife. So she'd played along
and they'd even shared a complicit glance when Franki
had come barging in, raging about the gross selfishness o
Hugo frigging Mortimer, who wouldn't part with one lous
ticket for a poor old lady who didn't have a damn thing i
the whole world to look forward to any more.

Now, much later, here they both were, decked out i
their glad rags, and he was telling her she was his preciou
and extremely desirable darling. And it really did seem lik
he meant it.

What was she supposed to think?

But why think at all? *Carpe diem.* Save misery ti
morning.

Then, without warning, their bedroom door was flung open.

'Can somebody do up my flaming zip? I've eaten a few too many chokkies since I last wore this bugger.'

Jessica Rabbit meets Lily Savage in a floor-length sheath dress with dangerously plunging neckline, made up of millions of deep purple sequins.

'Mum . . .'

'Get a move on. It's time we were off.'

April found her voice. 'But you don't have a ticket.'

'So?'

Perry's voice was gentle. 'Frankie, they're very strict about gatecrashers. There's no way you'll get in without one.'

'You can take me in with you.'

'I'm afraid that's not possible.'

Frankie's face reminded April of Hector in the seconds before a major tantrum. She braced herself for the onslaught. But instead, her mother-in-law's face crumpled and she turned to April. 'You don't know what it's like, being old, pet. People don't care any more, you see.' She shook her head pitifully. 'No, they don't. Not even your own children, them as cause you such pain and agony when they're torn from your poor body. They don't give a monkeys. As far as they're concerned, you're just an empty can of petrol discarded on the hard shoulder of life – neither use nor ornament. One day you'll understand what I mean.' She patted Perry's arm. 'Good night, son,' she said, voice breaking slightly. 'I think I'll turn in. Off you both go. Enjoy yourselves. You can tell me all about it in t'morning. Be sure to remember every detail. With my poor health, it'll probably be the last chance I get, to hear about such goings-on. Do you have any Horlicks, April, pet? It helps get me off to sleep. It's a small pleasure, but at my age small pleasures are all you've got.'

A knot of tension formed in April's gut. She knew what Frankie was doing: she wanted Perry to dump his wife and in an excess of filial pity, take her instead. Did she really imagine he'd do such a thing? The knot intensified as she realised that nowadays, she couldn't with any confidence say that he wouldn't. Where Perry was concerned, Frankie usually got her way.

But when he spoke, she was suffused with guilty joy. 'May Balls aren't all they're cracked up to be, Mum. They're actually quite boring – too much loud music and too much inebriated youth. As you say, with your fragile health you're much better off having an early night. We'll give you chapter and verse tomorrow.'

His voice was cheerful, but firm. He turned to April. 'Time to go, darling. The Master will kill us if we're late.' He smiled at Frankie. 'See what I mean? It's all boring duty. Hugo wants us on parade in the Lodge to impress the Americans.' He stepped past Frankie onto the landing.

'But I want to go to the Ball!' Frankie bawled, unable to believe she hadn't got her way. 'You have to get me in.'

'Sorry, Cinders,' he said. 'Maybe next year . . . if you're still with us.'

'Still what?' April and Frankie chorused in unison.

'In the land of the living. Come on, darling.'

April floated downstairs. Everything was going to be fine.

As he circulated among his guests, smiling, chatting and glad-handing, he took pride in the fact that no one who wasn't privy to his tragedy could possibly detect that he was a man in deep mourning. He'd told the housekeeper to dispose of the empty dog-basket, ostensibly because of space issues during the drinks party. In reality because every time he saw it he burst into unmanly tears. He looked around the panelled drawing room at the suits and satins clinking champagne flûtes and braying at each other. Although his party had only been going for half an hour, it seemed like an eternity. How would he make it through the long night ahead? May Balls were interminable enough when one was on top form, but tonight . . .

Why did that maniac choose today of all days to murder his precious darlings?

The answer, of course, was glaringly obvious. Because today *was* today – the most important day since his election as Master of Billings College. Tipton had done it in order to sabotage his plans. More fool him. The Mortimers were made of sterner stuff. Hugo hadn't got where he was today by allowing personal problems to interfere with the bigger picture. The Americans were almost in the bag. The glamour of a Cambridge May Ball would clinch the deal. By tomorrow the Miller Foundation would be on board. If that pathetic priest thought Hugo Mortimer would go to bed and pull the covers over his head, he was grossly mistaken. There'd be time enough to mourn when tonight was over.

And by then, Dominic Tipton would be languishing in Fulbourn. In a fair and just world, of course, it would be a police cell, not a mental institution. Why did the police claim there wasn't enough evidence to arrest the man? One of the gardeners had admitted to leaving a

shed door open last night – a shed in which rat poison
was stored – but had the police dusted it for prints? No
They seemed to think that all three animals might have
strayed in there by accident. That they'd wolfed down the
poison in some macabre animal suicide pact, and then
come and laid themselves out in a line on the lawn to
die. Absurd! And why had they only sent one bone-headed
Constable to investigate? He'd got the impression that
the man thought it was *he* rather than Tipton who was
the unstable one. Tomorrow he planned to telephone the
Chief Constable.

He would get justice for Dawkins and the cats.

His spirits lifted as he spotted Rosa Thorn. She looked
very stylish in her Romany way. All bangles and beads and
green floating draperies. And that wonderful chestnut hair
What a stroke of genius, asking her to hostess for him. Bill
Miller, chairman and founder of the Miller Foundation
had already pounced on her, and embarked on one of his
more tedious tales of life as a billionaire. Rosa, he was
pleased to see, was looking suitably enthralled. He went
over to them.

'Bill, I see you've met Rosa,' he beamed. 'She'll be sitting
next to you at dinner. Rosa, my darling, you look divine.
He kissed her on the cheek in a way that suggested inti
macy. Would she play along? She shot him a quizzical look
but didn't pull away. He was vastly relieved. The Miller
Foundation was very hot on family values, and he didn'
know whether he'd adequately sidestepped Bill's leading
questions about his unmarried status. He'd implied a tragi
past that was too painful to discuss and Bill had backed off
But it was only a temporary respite. Squiring a woman like

Rosa Thorn was just what was needed to keep the old boy satisfied. He hoped she wouldn't let slip that they'd only just met. Damn! He'd better square it with her before she put her foot in it.

'Bill, let me introduce you to our Senior Classics Tutor.' He grabbed old Harry Brooks who was tottering past. 'Harry, meet Bill Miller, chairman of the Miller Foundation. Bill says he visited some very interesting archaeological sites in Turkey last year. I told him you'd be fascinated to hear about them.' He left them to it and steered Rosa into his study.

'This is rather delicate, Rosa. Bill Miller seems to think you and I are, how should I put it? Stepping out together.'

She laughed uproariously. He was more than a little miffed. Surely it wasn't that unlikely that he and she might have a relationship?

When she saw his face she quietened down. 'Sorry, the champagne's already gone to my head. What's the problem?'

'I need to keep him on side if I'm to get his foundation to stump up.'

'And?'

He forged on. 'He appears to set enormous store by the institution of marriage . . .'

She looked at him, a smile beginning to twitch up the sides of her wide, generous mouth. 'Are you proposing, Hugo?'

He tried to contain his irritation. 'I'm just saying that if he asks about our relationship, you don't . . .'

Comprehension filled her amber eyes. 'Don't reveal that we only met once, briefly, a couple of days ago?'

He nodded.

'Are you asking me to tell a big fat lie?'

'Well, just . . .'

'Be economical with the truth?'

He nodded again.

'That's quite a price to pay for a May Ball ticket. I won't lie, Hugo, but I will try and steer him off the subject.'

Ungrateful woman. But she was all he'd got, so he'd better try and keep her sweet. He forced a smile. 'My dear, I shall be forever in your debt.' He leaned forward to give her a grateful peck on the cheek but she moved away.

'We're neglecting your guests,' she said.

He felt no more than two inches high. Humiliated by some jumped-up little actress. Well, no one got away with treating him like dirt. From now on, he'd be keeping a very careful eye on her son. As one of a minority of black students, the boy probably found Cambridge quite alienating. Who could tell what forms of anti-social behaviour that might lead to?

As Master he'd be waiting to deal with Daniel Thorn's first big mistake.

More in sorrow than in anger, of course.

TWENTY-EIGHT

Dominic gazed gloomily at the gaudy charade unfolding below him. The Ball was in full swing now even though it was still early. He was trying desperately to psych himself up for his annual dark night of the soul. By tradition the chapel had always been kept open in case any revellers wanted to give thanks to God for the end of exams. Then, some years ago, two undergraduates were caught copulating on Saxby's carved altar, and there'd been a proposal to lock the place up. Dominic had vigorously opposed this idea. On such a night it was more important than ever that people had a place to come and pray. So the chapel remained open, on the understanding that he was there to police it. Not an easy task. He sighed, recalling last year when he'd had to restrain one excessively drunken undergraduate from attempting sexual congress with the statue of Sir Thomas More.

At least this year he'd have company. When he'd asked Lucas to help, the boy had agreed immediately. Now, as he waited on the Gatehouse walkway, he saw his nephew approach Stanley Gordon, who stood on the pavement below, beefy arms folded over barrel chest, maroon bowler rammed firmly in place. The Head Porter categorically refused to leave the security of the gate to the hired heavies. 'There ain't nobody but me who I'd trust not to be fooled by the many people trying to crash the Billings Ball,' he would say to anyone who'd listen. 'As far as I'm concerned, this is my sacred responsibility. I guard this gate with my life.'

He could see Gordon shaking his head before Lucas had even spoken.

'Would you let my nephew through, please, Stanley. He's on chapel patrol with me,' he called down.

Gordon peered up at him. 'Oh, I see. Sorry, Chaplain, I wasn't told.' His voice was grudging as he said to Lucas, 'In you go then, son. But you must remain in the chapel with your uncle for the duration, on account of you don't have a ticket.'

'Can't you give him a security badge?' Dominic called. 'It would make life much easier for both of us.'

Gordon's sigh was audible even up on the walkway. 'If you insist, Chaplain. Come into the lodge, son. I'll have a rummage round. I dare say there's a spare one somewhere.' He glared up at Dominic. 'If I'd been informed of this earlier, of course, I could have had one ready and waiting.'

While Dominic waited for Lucas, he stared out over Bacon Court. He deplored the hedonistic excess below. Dante's Circles of Hell. The bass notes of the incredible cacophony issuing from the huge marquee reverberated through his whole body. He'd be amazed if anyone came away from the evening without a severe case of tinnitus.

Even at this early stage, many students were in an advanced state of inebriation, staggering around, clutching at their partners in an attempt to stand upright. No wonder, he thought, looking at the continuous bar running round the outside of the marquee. It groaned under the weight of every conceivable kind of alcohol. Over in a corner, a competition was in full swing to see who could down the most Alcopops in the shortest time, and quite near the entrance to his staircase, a young girl, usually one of his most serious and sensible Theology students, dressed in something that had to represent at least half a term's grant, had pulled her companion down onto the grass, undone his trousers and appeared to be massaging his genitalia. And it wasn't even dark yet.

He'd seen enough. He turned back to the street. Below him, Stanley Gordon was repelling yet another potential gatecrasher. Her voice made Dominic wince.

'I'm Dr Grimshaw's mother. He said he'd leave my ticket at the Porter's Lodge. The silly article must have forgotten. If you let me through, I can get the flaming thing off him and show you.'

'Sorry, madam. No ticket, no entry. More than my job's worth. Now, if Dr Grimshaw could verify your story . . .'

'And exactly how do I contact him? Frigging telepathy? He's in there already, whooping it up. And before you ask, I've tried his mobile. It's switched off. Don't you recognise me? I've been farting in and out of here like a gigolo's dick for the last two days.'

'Beg pardon, madam, but I can't be expected to re-member everyone what passes through these gates.'

She sounded astonished. 'You don't remember *me*?'

Gordon scowled.

In the midst of his yearly May Ball gloomfest, Dominic had to smile. Watching the crashing waves of the woman's mighty ego smash against the equally mighty cliff of Stanley Gordon was an entertaining diversion.

But the porter's scowl had modified into a frown of concentration. 'Come to think of it, madam, your face *is* familiar. Not from round here, though.'

From his eyrie, Dominic could sense the cogs of opportunity turning in the woman's brain.

When she responded, her voice was coy. 'Maybe you know me from somewhere else.' She struck a theatrical attitude and hummed a few bars from a popular song of an early 1960s vintage.

Then something truly astonishing happened: for the first time in the annals of Billings College, Stanley Gordon smiled. And not just a half-hearted smirk. This was a cheek-splitter which bisected his vast purple face. 'I know who you are!' His excitement was extreme. 'I don't believe it! You're the Fabulous Frankie Faraday!! My missus and I used to come and see you every year regular as clockwork in Clacton. Them were the days. I'll never forget them shows – they don't do 'em like that any more.' He looked at her fervently. And *you* were the cat's pyjamas. Frankie Faraday! Well, I never! Wait till I tell the missus.' His voice was thick with yearning. 'I don't suppose I could have your autograph?'

Frankie's smile was bright as Blackpool Illuminations. 'Course you can, pet. It's always a pleasure to meet a fan.'

Gordon disappeared into the Porters' Lodge, emerging seconds later with pen and paper, which he thrust at her.

Her timing was exquisite. About to sign, she paused, pen hovering in mid-air, before pouncing. 'I dare say you can let me in now, can't you, pet? Since you can vouch for me?'

Dominic willed Gordon to hold on to his much-vaunted integrity.

'Never let it be said that Stanley Gordon barred the door to the Fabulous Frankie Faraday. Any problems at all – send for me. It will be an honour and a privilege to sort them out.'

Frankie gave him a kiss on his mottled cheek, which was now a deep shade of beetroot. 'What's your first name, pet?'

'Stanley.'

Frankie declaimed her message as she wrote. *'Stanley, you're a star. You saved the day. Bless you, pet. All the best, Frankie Faraday. Kiss, kiss, kiss.'*

Dominic would never have believed it possible. Stanley Gordon, scourge of Billings, outwitted by such a woman.

'What's up, Unc?' Lucas had come up behind him.

Dominic smiled ruefully. 'I'm observing corruption at first hand. It gives off quite a stench. If you're ready, I think we should go to the chapel.'

Some May Ball. This should have been the fulfilment of a fantasy. Instead I'm looking at the possible sabotaging of my son's life. It's at times like this that I most miss Rob. He'd know what to do. His thinking was always much clearer than mine. But he's dead, and I can't get my head around any of it.

After we're settled at the Master's table, I look around for Danny. I can't see him at first, and then I spot him making his way across the room, with a girl in a yellow dress.

Stella.

Stella? What's he playing at? Where's Julie? But then they come closer.

It is Julie.

Her dark curls are gone; in their place a blonde, urchin crop. Identical to Stella's. As is her outfit.

The only difference between Julie and the real Stella, already seated at their table, is the colour of their handbags.

All around, people are nudging, whispering and pointing. Danny ignores them. Julie looks radiant.

And Stella? She just smiles her irritatingly secret smile.

Danny sees me and shrugs. His face is blank, his shoulders stooped. I want to rush over to him, but that would only compound his embarrassment. My heart bleeds for both him and Julie. She must be feeling pretty desperate to turn herself into a Stella clone. She obviously knows that Danny still doesn't love her, in spite of the pregnancy. What she doesn't know is that her new look won't make a jot of difference to how he feels. It doesn't work like that.

This pregnancy is a disaster. Before any irrevocable decisions are made, I have to speak to him. And to Julie.

I can't abnegate my responsibility as a mother and collude with him on the spurious premise that now he's twenty and technically an adult, he's old enough to run his own life. It's his whole future we are talking about here. First thing tomorrow, I'll contact Joan Watkins.

Having made my decision, I feel more able to focus on

my task for the evening: entertaining Hugo Mortimer's guests.

Billings Hall is unrecognisable. The theme is the Cole Porter musical *Anything Goes*, and the room's decked out like a 1930s' cruise-liner, with bunting and lifebelts, waiters dressed as sailors and a dance band on the raised dais normally occupied by High Table. It looks fabulous, but on balance I'd rather be in the small marquee in Thomas More Court where a buffet supper is being served. I'm sure it's much more fun in there. Although there are lots of tables for students in here, including the one with Danny, Julie, Stella and the cast from *Othello*, the ambience is far grander and more formal, with a preponderance of the Senior Common Room and their guests. I look across at Perry and April, sitting with other Billings Fellows and their partners. April is glowing. Perry's paying her massive amounts of attention, and she's clearly loving it. But I'm not so sure about him. His behaviour is loud and over the top, and when I catch his eye he looks away.

I'm doing my best to sparkle for Hugo Mortimer's Americans, but it's uphill work since they all appear to have left their sense of humour at the bottom of Boston Harbour. The other two couples on our table are not much jollier. Both are parents of undergraduates, invited in the hope that they'll contribute substantial amounts to the Library Fund. Both, coincidentally, have children in *Othello*. The completely silent Middle Eastern pair are the parents of Bianca the Whore, currently screaming with camp laughter and throwing bread rolls at Lee Watson, whilst the others belong to Flora, the girl who played Emilia. Not that these two seem remotely concerned with their daughter's

activities. Their main preoccupation seems to be with drop
ping names, which they do relentlessly throughout the meal
They have no plans to see the play, and leave tomorrow
for their *hice* in France. '*Cap Ferrat – do you know it?*'

I can't resist doing some meddling on Flora's behalf
'What a shame you can't postpone your departure for a day
and see the show. You'd love Flora's performance. She's
very good.'

'Really?' The woman couldn't have sounded less inter
ested.

Poor Flora. No wonder the girl looks so lost and forlorn
Tonight she's made a big effort with her appearance. If only
she looked less miserable she'd actually be quite pretty.

Stella gives no sign of being fazed by her lookalike. A
at Perry's on Sunday, she's the still centre around which
everything swirls. I have a sudden revelation. Her aston
ishing beauty is like the surface of a lake. It reflects back
to people their own preoccupations. And though constantly
on the point of revealing hidden depths, in reality it give
up little, while remaining, nevertheless, a bottomless source
of fascination.

Only Flora and Julie seem immune. Flora is virtually
silent, and Julie is radiant, her eyes never leaving Danny
Not once do I catch her glancing in Stella's direction.

Bill Miller claims my attention for the next few minutes
so it comes as a shock when the music stops abruptly and
I see Danny talking to the bandleader. Next thing, the band
plays a small fanfare and Danny takes the microphone.

'Julie, will you come up here, please.'

There's a ripple of excitement as Julie, blushing and
bewildered, walks up onto the stage. Danny kneels down

ulie Watkins, will you marry me?' The ripple turns to a
oar. Fists are thumped on tables and there's whistling and
cheering. Then a shushing noise as everyone waits for Julie's
response.

Eyes shining, beyond words, she nods. And then to the
accompaniment of more cheering, Danny slips a ring onto
her finger before standing up and kissing her. Then he turns
back to his rapt audience. 'Ladies and gentlemen, would you
raise your glasses, please, to my beautiful fiancée. To Julie.'

Everyone shouts, 'To Julie!' Then there's a huge round
of applause as the two of them finally leave the stage.

He's done it now.

Passed the point of no return.

The whole college has witnessed him commit himself
Julie.

'Are you all right?' Bill Miller's voice comes from a great
distance.

I try to get a grip. 'I'm fine. That's my son up there.'

Bill's shrewd grey eyes assess me. 'Not a welcome
announcement?'

Rob always used to say that family stuff stays in the family.
I attempt a smile. 'I'm delighted. Julie's a lovely girl.'

Bill isn't fooled. 'Waiter! A double brandy over here,
please.'

Danny and Julie are coming across to our table. I down
the brandy in one shuddering gulp.

'Congratulations,' I say, and embrace them both.

'Maybe we should go and give her a bit of moral support.'
April's heart went out to Rosa. She hadn't realised that she
was quite so anti-Julie. Perry had just set her straight.

'The last thing she needs is us fussing round, looking
if someone's died. Rosa's a thesp. She may not *be* hap
about it, but her way of coping is to *act* happy.'

'Well, she's not doing a very good job of it.'

'Forget about Rosa. Concentrate on your husband. Ha
I told you how delectable you are?'

'Only about five hundred times. How much booze ha
you put back tonight?'

'I'm drunk on love.'

'And at least six glasses of bubbly.' She couldr
remember when she last felt so happy. Perry was his o
loving self again. She didn't know why he'd reverted ar
she didn't care. It was enough that he had. Why had sl
allowed her stupid jealousy to concoct such a ridiculo
scenario between him and that girl? She must have be
mad. Perry was potty about her. He always had been. Ar
this time she'd learned her lesson. She would never aga
allow herself to indulge in such hysterical and damagi
fantasies.

It was nearing the end of the meal. Some people we
already leaving. Perry had just asked her if she'd like to
and dance when she became aware of another commotio

'Oh no,' Perry groaned, slumping down in his seat.

There, larger than life, in that unspeakable dress, w
his mother. Being manhandled onto the dais by a cou
of prop forwards from the college rugby team.

'How the hell did she get in? On second thoughts -
don't want to know.'

April was furious on his behalf. Much as he loved Frank
and wilfully ignored her shortcomings, Perry was sav
enough to try and keep her separate from his professio

fe. He'd already had to endure her bad behaviour at his
arty. For her to show him up in front of the whole college
ould be a humiliation too far.

'Music, Maestro, please.' Frankie stood centre-stage,
urple sequins glittering.

The bandleader laughed uneasily, but made no attempt
› raise his baton.

Wrong move.

'Surely you know who I am?' Her voice was strident, and
nose who hadn't been aware of what was going on, now
arted to pay attention. She threw her arms open wide as
to embrace the entire universe. 'I'm the Fabulous Frankie
araday and I'm going to give all you tight-arsed scholars
bit of a treat.' She turned back to the bandleader. 'Do
›u know "Save All Your Kisses for Me"?'

The man nodded, faintly.

'Get a move on then – my public awaits.'

The band struck up and Frankie was away. Her voice
as a good semi-tone sharp and there were several intakes
˙ breath as she repeatedly failed to hit her notes.

Finally it ended.

For a moment or two, anyway.

There was a smattering of applause, and underneath it
pril could hear surreptitious sniggering.

'Thank you, ladies and gents. And now for my next song,
l like to give you that old Elvis favourite, "Wooden Heart".'

Perry swore quietly. 'This one will run and run,' he said.
he's on a roll. That's it for the duration.'

'You dark horse, Perry. Fancy keeping your talented
other such a secret,' smirked Ricky Cardew from the other
le of the table.

357

April winced. The rivalry between Perry and Ricky i
the English Department was generally good-humoured
but occasionally threatened to spill over into somethin
darker. Ricky satirising Frankie could turn things genuinel
nasty.

'Piss off, Cardew,' said Perry. 'I need some fresh air, Apri
Come on.'

'The Master looks like thunder,' she said. 'Shouldn't w
do something?'

'Big black mark on *your* end-of-term report, Perry, m
old son.'

April willed Ricky to stop stirring. She lowered he
voice so that he wouldn't hear what she was saying. 'Hug
knows Frankie didn't have a ticket. I really think it migl
be politic to get her off that stage. After what happene
to Dawkins, he's barely holding it together. He won
thank you if your mother puts a spanner in the worl
with the Yanks. He's not a nice man, Perry. I don't tru
him.'

Perry's eyes glittered. Voice slurring slightly, he said, 'Yo
know what, April? If you're so concerned, you do som
thing. I've had it up to here.'

Then he bolted.

'Trouble in Paradise?' Ricky's eyes were brimming wit
mischief.

In an instant Perry had ruined her evening. Why th
violent moodswing? Perry didn't do moodswings. It wasn
who he was.

She rushed after him, but by the time she entered Bacc
Court, he'd disappeared.

*   *   *

GREEN EYE

*'Behold I am against thee,' saith the Lord of hosts; 'and
I will discover thy skirts upon thy face, and I will shew
the nations thy nakedness, and the kingdoms thy shame.
And I will cast abominable filth upon thee and make thee
vile.'*

TWENTY-NINE

After Danny's bombshell, Flora slipped away. All her plans had come to nothing. Danny was, as of this evening, officially off-limits, so Stella would now undoubtedly turn the full force of her charms onto Lucas. She glanced over to the Master's table where her parents were sitting. Danny's mum caught her eye and she felt a bolt of sympathy shoot towards her. She somehow knew that the woman hadn't fallen for her parents' brand of schmoozing. She felt sorry for her. When Danny had announced his engagement, his mother, for a brief moment, looked as if her world had come to an end. Then she'd smiled joyfully, as if she'd been waiting for this particular piece of news since forever. But even from across the room Flora could see that her eyes were full of tears.

Her own mother didn't believe in tears except as a means to an end. She hadn't yet apologised for missing *Othello* nor did Flora expect any explanation to be forthcoming. Neither of her parents had sought her out this evening. She'd thought they might come and say something nice about her appearance, because thanks to Stella's efforts she knew she looked as good as she ever could. But not a word. Just a quick gesture of acknowledgement, before sweeping off to dine with the people who really mattered.

Who didn't include her.

She was engulfed by desolation. There was no one for her to party with. Not her parents, not Stella, who was currently choosing dance partners from a pool of at least ten guys clamouring for her attention, and not the man to whom she'd been foolish enough to give her heart

He wasn't even at the ball.

As she walked through Thomas More Court, dodging various couples snogging on the grass, she noticed a light in the chapel. Suddenly her misery fell away. Why did she say that she had no one? She had God. He never let her down. He'd be waiting for her in the chapel. That was where she really belonged.

The chapel was wonderfully peaceful after the mayhem outside. The only light came from the sconces above the choir stalls and the flickering candles on the altar. She had come home. As she knelt down to pray, she heard a movement by the altar.

She looked up. There stood an angel in dazzling robes, golden hair a bright halo surrounding the beatific face, outstretched arm holding a glittering staff.

And the angel came in unto her and said, 'Hail thou that art highly favoured; the Lord is with thee: blessed art thou amongst women.'

'Hi, Flo.'

Lucas. Wearing a white surplice, and extinguishing one of the candles on the altar with a brass candle snuffer.

'What are you doing here?'

'Helping my uncle.'

'Oh.' She remembered their last encounter. Remembering her throwing herself into Lucas's arms and him pushing her away.

'What are *you* doing here? I thought you'd be partying.' Lucas was staring at her. It made her skin go all hot and prickly. She felt at a disadvantage on her knees – it somehow reminded her of the earlier fiasco – so she stumbled to her feet.

'You look great.'

She didn't know how to respond. 'Stella did my hair and make-up,' she babbled, before realising that she really didn't want him to think about Stella.

But he didn't seem to notice. 'Are you hungry?' he asked.

'I've just had dinner.'

'Then come and watch me eat.' He took off the surplice. Underneath, he wore a black dinner-jacket, with a large silver cross gleaming at the neck instead of a bow tie. She shivered.

Her dark angel. She wanted to pray. But she also wanted Lucas.

God or Lucas? No contest.

'OK,' she said. God would understand. 'What about Dom?'

'What *about* Dom?' The man himself emerged from the vestry.

'Flora and I are going to get some supper. We'll bring you something back, if you like.'

Dom's face was all angles and planes in the dim light. 'If I'm to last out the night I could do with a decent meal.'

He smiled, his dark eyes flickering from one to the other. 'Off you go, then.'

Lucas grinned. 'Cool. I shan't be long, though. Come on, Flora.'

And then they were outside, plunged into noise, colour and confusion.

Flora took him into the small marquee. He piled his plate high, and then they sat on the grass outside and she watched, mesmerised, as his strong white teeth ripped into chicken drumsticks and hunks of ham. She wished he'd take more time over it, so they could be together for longer, but then she felt selfish. They'd left a hungry Dom in the chapel all by himself.

But soon Lucas had finished and was pulling her to her feet. She thought they were going back to the chapel, but instead he took her to Bacon Court. Serious hip-hop was blasting out of the marquee.

'What about Dom's food?' she shouted.

But he didn't hear. 'Let's have a quick dance,' he said, and guided her inside. There she gave herself up to the throbbing beat of the music and was unaware how much time had passed until he shouted into her ear, 'I need some water. Back in a minute.'

She continued dancing, unwilling to descend from the euphoria that had gripped her, but after a while, she began to wonder where he was. She was also incredibly hot and needed water too. She fought her way past the gyrating bodies into the fresh air, and looked around. No sign of him. Grabbing a bottle of water from the bar, she gulped it down, pouring the dregs over her face.

Maybe he'd gone back to the chapel.

When she put her head around the door, Dom was reading in one of the choir stalls.

'Is Lucas back?'

He looked surprised. 'No. Isn't he with you?'

She didn't want to drop Lucas in it. 'He must still be queuing for your food. I'll go and see.'

But there was no sign of her dark angel in the food marquee. It was almost empty now, with just a few people helping themselves from the chocolate fountain. The only angelic presence was an eight-foot-high ice sculpture, a replica of the Archangel Michael, largest of the Billings Angels, flaming sword dripping slightly, angelic features now somewhat indeterminate as the heat in the marquee took its toll. By the time the night was over, he'd be little more than a celestial lump in a puddle.

Where was Lucas?

She went to the JCR and peered through the fug. Hookah pipes were being smoked up one end while up the other a large group was gathered round a roulette wheel. No luck. She tried Berkeley Court, with its fire-eaters, jugglers and various other street-theatre acts, but he wasn't there. She cut through into Augustine. Although it was the largest court in college, the crush of people here was intense, but as far as she could tell, he wasn't on the carousel, swings or dodgems, nor was he riding either of the two donkeys or the camel, or playing arcade games. She heard shrieks coming from the Bouncy Castle, but he wasn't there either.

Maybe he'd gone back to the big marquee and was looking for her. She ran back to Bacon Court and scanned the frenetic dancers inside the tent. She saw a group of people from the *Othello* production, among them Lee and Shareef,

Melvin the techie, the guy whose name she could never remember who played Brabantio, and Danny and Julie, all bumping and grinding along to Dr Dre. Melvin beckoned her over, but she pretended not to notice. Where was Lucas? She'd searched everywhere now. She considered phoning him, but then decided not: she didn't want to appear clingy.

She hadn't checked Locke Court.

In Locke a wooden dance-floor had been laid over the grass. Psychedelic light patterns were projected on to the wall of the court behind it, covering the gloomy grey stone with fantastical colours and amorphous, changing shapes. This was the cheesy corner. Couples clung to each other as Katie Melua sang about the closest thing to crazy she had ever been.

Then she spotted him.

His eyes were closed, an expression of rapture enhancing his perfect features. One arm was wrapped, tentacle-like, round his partner. The other tenderly stroked her choppy blonde hair.

Flora's energy drained away. It was replaced by something cold, hard and unyielding. The ice Archangel Michael might be melting, but she was made of sterner stuff.

When he'd proposed in front of all those people, she thought she'd died and gone to heaven.

He'd told everyone how much he loved her.

And that was what ruined everything.

If only he'd kept it private, it would have been all right. If only he'd kept it private, there would always have been a bit of her that didn't quite believe him; that would have held out until the moment they were pronounced man and wife.

But it was the way he did it. The way he told the whole world. It not only convinced them, it convinced her too.

A man who did that would love her no matter what. Even if she'd lied to him, he'd still love her. He'd said he wanted to marry her, for fuck's sake. He'd said he wanted to spend the rest of his life with her.

Surely it wasn't just because of the pregnancy? Not in this day and age, when half the female population had babies without getting married. No, the baby thing had merely focused his mind. He'd realised in the last couple of days that he couldn't live without her, and that he wanted – no, needed – to marry her.

She felt weak with tenderness at the sacrifices he was prepared to make. To give up university and get a job to provide for them. What a truly good person he was. But thinking about his goodness had caused a tiny black cloud to appear in the clear sky of her good fortune. Danny was a saint.

She wasn't worthy of him. She was a lying bitch who was marrying him under false pretences. She hated the thought of starting her marriage with such a big lie. She wanted to be able to look him in the eye, knowing that she was keeping nothing from him. The lie was making her feel dirty and deceitful.

Horrible.

Even if she got pregnant straight away so that the lie wasn't a lie any more, it wouldn't make any difference: *she* would know the truth, and it would stand between them forever.

And another thing: *if she was completely honest, she didn't want him to quit university.*

Although she slagged off his friends and called them a load of boring old geeks, in reality she was proud that such a clever guy wanted her.

'*My husband's a Cambridge graduate.*'

'*My husband stacks shelves in Asda.*'

No contest.

And, with a Cambridge degree he'd get a much better job that would pay him far more dough than he would with the four A Levels which would be all he'd have if he left Billings.

The more she thought about it, the more she hated the lie. But if, as she now believed, he truly loved her, it wouldn't matter what she'd done. It wouldn't make any difference to him. He'd understand how she had got into the situation. How she had wanted to set him straight when he said he knew about the pregnancy, but how she couldn't find the words and how, once the lie started, she couldn't stop it. He'd understand.

He'd do more than understand. He'd be so relieved he didn't have to leave university that he'd cover her with grateful kisses and thank her for saving his entire career.

The thoughts swirled round her head all evening; she couldn't get rid of them. All the time they'd supposedly been having fun, all that time a little voice had been nagging away. *Tell him. Tell him now. Just do it.*

So, finally, when the little voice got too much, she did.

The two of them were in a swingboat, swooping through the air. Danny had made it go so high she was convinced she'd fall out. 'Stop, Dan, stop! I'll puke if you carry on.'

And he'd slowed it right down and said in the gentle voice he now used when speaking to her, 'Sorry, babe. I forgot. Don't want to damage Thorn Junior, do we?'

Tell him.

'You won't,' she found herself saying.

He shook his head. 'Better safe than sorry.'

'It's OK.'

'What is?'

Just do it.

'You won't damage Thorn Junior.'

He grinned. 'How do you know? A mother's instinct?'

Tell him.

Tell him.

'Because there ain't no Thorn Junior.' Her words drifted into the festive air and were lost in the general merriment.

Danny brought the swing to a standstill. 'What do you mean, Julie?'

In spite of the hot summer night she became aware of a small, cold spot in her belly. A cold spot, which second by second grew until it covered her whole body, making her shiver uncontrollably. Why was Danny looking so weird and horrible?

Too late to turn back now. 'It was all a big fuck-up. My mum heard me being sick and she thought I was pregnant. She must have blabbed and somehow it got back to you, but when you asked me about it, I couldn't bring myself to tell you it wasn't true because I thought a baby might make you come back to me. But now I know you love me anyway, baby or no baby, so I had to tell you. I couldn't let you leave university and ruin your future – *our* future . . .' She waited for a response but none came. 'I just want to be honest with you, Danny.'

He was utterly still. She was reminded of a carved wooden statue she'd once seen on a school trip to the Museum of

Mankind in London. All around was music and colour and laughter, but the swingboat now floated in a bubble of deep silence.

'Say something, Dan. Please.'

Below them, the dodgem cars squealed and wheeled and hurtled into each other. Bursts of laughter intermittently drifted up to where they sat.

'Dan?'

It was properly dark now. Behind Danny, the fairy-lights on the side of the library glittered and twinkled. She caught sight of his mother, gypsy hair streaming behind her, trotting across the court on a donkey, an elderly man with glasses running alongside her, trying to keep up.

'Look at your mum, Dan.'

But his eyes remained fixed on her.

'Please . . .'

Still he said nothing. Then, after an age, he climbed down from the swingboat and walked away.

She followed, distraught, almost falling as her dress tangled itself in the ropes. 'Wait, Dan . . . I'm sorry. I'm sorry I lied. But I told you why. So we won't be starting off our marriage with no secrets. That's good, innit?'

Abruptly he stopped and glared at her. 'Do you honestly think I'd marry you now?'

'Danny—'

'After what you've done?'

'But you said you loved me. You said you *wanted* to marry me.'

'Not any more.'

She clutched at him, but he shrugged her off and walked away. 'Fuck off.'

'Dan, please—'

He was moving so fast she couldn't keep up with him. The carousel had stopped and the surging tide of people getting off and more people getting on seemed to be deliberately preventing her from catching up. It was a nightmare. His broad back had disappeared. She was dimly aware that she was hitting out as she pushed through the crowd.

'Hey, Julie.' Somebody thrust a bottle of champagne into her hand. 'Eat, drink and be merry, for tomorrow we die.' It was James, one of the students who lodged with her mother. He was with a group of his mates, all of them completely bladdered.

'Piss off.'

He laughed. 'I like your new look.' He ruffled her hair, then peered at her. 'You're upset. Why are you upset?' He gestured to his friends. 'Julie's not having a good time. That's not right. She's the best-looking chick at the Ball and she's not having a good time. That's a crying shame. Come on, babe, drink up.'

'No!'

'But we want to toast your engagement.'

'There is no engagement. He just dumped me.'

'You have to be joking! Why? What a complete arse. Where is he? Do you want me to hit him for you?'

In spite of herself, she laughed. James was well-known for his peaceable good nature. He could no more hit anyone than fly.

He grinned. 'That's better. Drink up. Best way to forget your troubles. We'll look after you, won't we, fellas?'

They crowded round, clucking over her like a bunch of old hens. She looked for Danny, but couldn't see him. He as gone. She took a long swig of champagne, and then nother.

'Want to dance?' James swayed above her, a sloppy smile n his face. 'Come and dance with us, Julie. Did you know 've always fancied you? That's why I came to live in your ouse. It's true – ask anyone.' He looked soulfully into her yes. 'In fact, I think I may be a little bit in love with you. 'd really like it if you came and danced with us. Please, ulie. You know you want to. How can you turn down such great bunch of guys?'

The champagne was by-passing her stomach and going traight to her brain, and as her head swirled, her mood ifted. James and his friends liked her. They liked her a lot. 'hey thought she was pretty. The prettiest girl at the Ball. Maybe she would dance with them. She loved dancing. Dancing and drinking. They were easily the best way to orget your troubles.

Fuck you, Danny. You're not the only fish in the sea. Not he only pebble on the beach. Other people still like me even ' you don't. I'm going to have some fun.

'OK, Jamie boy, let's dance,' she said. 'I'll dance with ou, and I'll dance with your friends. I'll dance with the hole world.'

She went with them to Locke Court, and she did exactly nat, reeling from partner to partner like a spinning top. he danced to Abba, she danced to Queen, she danced to Gloria Gaynor, Diana Ross, and many more.

'You're a loser, Danny Thorn,' she said. 'You don't dump ne – I dump you. I'm much too hot for you to handle. ou've missed your chance now. Get used to it.'

THIRTY

Lucas had been gone for a very long time. It was unlik
him to be so thoughtless . . .

Dominic's eyelids felt heavy. He looked at his watcl
Hours to go. Staying awake through a whole night becam
harder every year. He'd thought that this time, Lucas woul
be around.

'Tipton, if there is a hell, I'll make sure I bloody we
see you in it.' It was the Master, standing in the arche
doorway.

'Hugo—'

'Don't "Hugo" me.'

'You're drunk.'

'I don't want you peddling your superstitious claptra
in my college any more. I'm going to kick you out, an
I'm going to get rid of this place, too.' His gestu
incorporated the whole of Saxby's chapel. 'I'll have
deconsecrated, and turned into a new JCR bar. What
you think of *that*?'

Dominic had hoped that the past few hours of qui

contemplation would fortify him against Mortimer and his machinations. He was wrong. This was the last straw.

'Get out!' he shouted, pushing the man through the door into Thomas More Court. And then, without quite knowing how it got there, he found his fist making contact with the Master's pendulous jowls.

He'd never been in a fight before. Even as a small boy he'd steered away from physical violence. To initiate it was both extraordinary and exhilarating. He was hardly aware of Mortimer's reciprocal punch. Or of the pop-eyed party-goers nearby.

He'd tasted blood. It felt good. He wanted more, but Mortimer was walking away.

'Now who's the coward?' he shouted. 'Come back!' But the Master was striding towards Locke Court without a backward glance.

Dominic's indignation grew, and with it a desire to settle things once and for all. He followed Mortimer and saw him go into the Fellows' Garden. He was about to tackle him again, when his eye was caught by two of the dancers gyrating together on the dance-floor.

Lucas and Stella Grainger.

All the fight went out of him. Lucas was clearly having the best time in the world, grinding suggestively up against that hussy. Heartsick, Dominic turned away.

He no longer felt like confronting Mortimer, but he couldn't bear the idea of going back to the chapel. Not yet. He knew that if he did, the thoughts would start crowding in, and he wasn't yet ready to deal with them. So he wandered from place to place like a soul in torment. And tonight Billings College did indeed resemble hell, with the infernal music, drunken leering faces and acres of exposed female flesh. He lost all track of time. At one point it seemed to him that he'd become trapped on the carousel in Augustine Court, which was whirling round, out of control, unable to stop, and that soon he and everyone else would be flung off into darkness and infinity, lost forever in spiralling chaos.

And then it all stopped.

No more music. No more light.

As if God Himself had pulled the plug.

There was a moment of silence and then a babble of enquiry.

After several minutes of confusion, the voice of one of the student organisers boomed through a megaphone into the darkness. 'Bit of a problem with the generator, guys, but no sweat, it's being fixed as we speak.'

Problem with the generator? Dominic smiled wryly. '*And the Lord said unto Moses, "Stretch out thine hand toward Heaven that there might be darkness over the land of Egypt, even darkness which may be felt"*,' he whispered.

When the lights go out all over Billings I take the opportunity in the confusion to slip away from Bill Miller, who has just started to probe my intentions towards the Master. There's a gleam in his elderly eye which doesn't quite square with Hugo's notion of him as Mr Right and Respectable, and I'd swear that he pinched my bottom when I dismounted from my donkey-ride earlier.

I want to talk to Danny, but the flipside of the darkness that has allowed me to escape Bill Miller's clutches is that finding anyone in it is almost impossible. If I happen upon my son, it will be a happy accident.

I go for the dance areas first. People are vacating the total eclipse of the big marquee and flooding into Bacon Court. If I stand by the entrance, Danny may pass me on his way out. He'll be with Julie, but that's tough. I'll insist on having a private word. He can't deny me that.

But he doesn't emerge. I peer around at the giggling, chattering crowd already outside. He isn't part of it. So I grope my way to Locke Court. Here, no one's allowing a little thing like a blackout to spoil their fun. Despite the absence of a sound system, they're all still singing and dancing to 'YMCA'. Unaccompanied. My eyes are now adapted to the gloom and I can just about make out the faces of the dancers.

No Danny.

Then I hear a familiar screech: Bianca the Whore and Lee Watson. I duck and weave through the flailing arms.

'Have you seen Danny?' I ask them.

'He's – with – Stell – a,' sings Bianca in perfect time and without losing his place in the dance.

'Stella? Are you sure?'

'I'm – ve – ry – sure,' he carols.

'Where?'

He gestures vaguely over his shoulder. I fight my way out as a second chorus of 'Young man' bursts out, and then I spot him sitting on the ground in the gateway of the Fellows' Garden.

'Dan?'

He doesn't exactly seem thrilled to see me.

'What was all that about then?'

'All what?'

'You know what.'

'Leave it, Mum.'

'I wish you'd told me what you were planning to do.'

'I did. I told you I'd stick by Julie.'

'Yes, but—'

'I said I'd do the right thing.'

'But that doesn't necessarily mean marriage. Not nowadays. Why did you have to rush into things? I wish you'd given it more time. You and I and Julie and Joan could have got together and worked something out between us.'

'It wasn't any of your business. Or Joan's. It was between me and Julie.'

'And the whole of Billings College.'

'Anyway, it's irrelevant. See you later.'

'Irrelevant?'

'Stop bugging me, Mum.'

'Danny—'

'I said leave me alone. Stop meddling.'

'I can't stand by and watch you flush your life down the toilet.'

'Go away.'

All of a sudden I'm sick of it. In the morning, doubtless I'll return to the attack, but right now I've had it. 'Fine,' I say. 'If that's what you want, fine.' I leave him and go to the bar where I grope around in the dark until I find a bottle of bubbly and drink three glasses in quick succession.

Then the lights come back on, to the accompaniment of a great cheer. The first person I see is April. She's downing shots of tequila like there's no tomorrow.

'What's wrong, April?'

She looks towards me blearily. 'It's bloody Frankie's fault

– as usual. Until she took it upon herself to entertain the troops, Perry was being so nice to me . . .'

'Where is he?'

'Last time I saw him he was dancing. With *her*.'

No need to ask who she means.

'He probably dances with all his students. As a courtesy.'

'Yeah, right.'

'He can't have been with her all evening. Someone said she was dancing with Danny earlier.'

April's voice is weary. 'No, but he might as well have been for all the attention he's paid to me.'

'You looked so happy at dinner.'

'That was before Frankie's début performance. Did you see how he walked out and left me to deal with it? Afterwards I found him hiding away in his rooms, and although he came and danced with me, everything was different. His heart wasn't in it. Then I went to the loo and when I came back he was with *her*. He didn't even notice me. So I left him to it.'

'What happened to Frankie?'

'She did five numbers before they booed her off the stage. Then I collared her and gave her a bollocking for embarrassing her son in front of the whole college.'

'I bet she loved that.'

'She said that Perry had always loved her singing and then she told me to sod off. I haven't seen her since. I wish I never had to see her ever again.'

'I'm no fan of Frankie's, but Perry's a grown man. It's not her fault that he's behaving like a love-struck fool over that girl.'

'So you do agree with me that that's what he's doing? It's not all in my imagination?'

'All I know is that she's trouble. Dan's involved with her as well, you know. I'm not exactly happy about this engagement, but if it breaks up, it shouldn't be because of her.'

'One day she'll go too far.'

'Forget her. Perry's probably looking for you right now. He's probably been looking for ages and couldn't find you in the dark. Why don't we try and find him?'

But April has already gone.

I'm drawn into the milling crowds which, with the return of light and sound, have become even more bacchanalian. The music seems louder, the colours more vivid, the dancing wilder. The three glasses of champagne, added to the rest of the alcohol I've consumed, have taken effect, and I throw myself into the fun with uninhibited frenzy. Live for the moment, Rosa. Let tomorrow take care of itself.

Because the daughters of Zion are haughty and walk with stretch-forthed necks and wanton eyes, walking and mincing and making a tinkling with their feet, therefore the Lord will smite with a scab the head of the daughters of Zion, and the Lord will discover their secret parts.

FRIDAY 24 JUNE

THIRTY-ONE

As the flat grey light of first dawn appears, along with curls of mist creeping up from the river, Billings College resembles the scene of a major disaster area. Couples lie comatose on the grass, cuddling empty champagne bottles as lovingly as the teddy bears of the childhood they've so recently left behind. Girls hobble barefoot through the litter-strewn courts, high heels dangling from nerveless fingers, mascara and lipstick smeared across bleary faces. They cling to their partners' arms in a desperate attempt to stay upright. Some livelier groups of undergraduates are staggering through the Gatehouse on their final adventure of the night – punting down the river to Grantchester. And outside the small marquee, a bedraggled queue of revellers waits for breakfast, noses twitching as the smell of sizzling bacon drifts out into the early-morning air.

The Americans are gone, packed firmly into their limo by the Master at the first intimations of daylight.

'I'd rather they didn't witness the final death-throes,' Hugo had said as he roped me in for a last tour of duty. 'Let's try and sustain the magic. No pumpkins and mice at Billings, eh? Send them off to beddy-byes before the dawn hangovers kick in.'

Now they're safely dispatched to Hugo's satisfaction, I'm wondering if I too can go home to bed. I've come down from my earlier high and decided that staying up all night is the pits. My limbs are aching, my eyelids prickle and burn and I'm teetering on the edge of hallucination. No wonder sleep deprivation's such an effective form of torture. At this moment I'd sell my daughter into slavery for a king-size duvet and a plump pair of pillows.

The Master isn't looking too great, either. In the steely light of morning his round face is haggard and there's a mysterious swelling under his left eye. I remember that he's grieving for his pets. He'll have put it out of his mind for the duration of the Ball, but now the night's nearly over, everything's undoubtedly come flooding back. I don't like the man. This evening I've witnessed him in action. I've seen him pandering to those he believes can do him good and ignoring those he thinks are unimportant. But I still feel sorry for him. From what I can gather, his animals were his family.

'Why don't you go to bed, Hugo? Everything's winding down now.'

'What?' He seems distracted. 'Oh, no. Must see the thing through . . . Must see the thing through. But you've done enough, my dear. Don't let me keep you.'

'I needn't leave quite yet.'

He pats my arm with his dimpled, well-manicured hand. 'You look exhausted. You must go home immediately.'

It's an offer I can't refuse. 'If you're sure . . .'

'Absolutely. And thank you again for all your hard work. You've been splendid. When Bill Miller coughs up the money it will be in no small part due to your efforts.' He gives my arm a coy squeeze. 'The fellow was well and truly bamboozled, wasn't he?'

'Bamboozled?'

'We made a pretty plausible pair, don't you think?'

Me and the Master? Please.

I manage a faint smile and wonder whether to enlighten him about old Bill's bottom-pinching activities. 'Actually, I am feeling pretty knackered. Thanks for inviting me, Hugo—'

At that moment my mobile rings.

'Mum . . .'

'Danny?'

'I need you.'

He sounds so weird. Is he on something? Has getting engaged to Julie succeeded where his teenage years roaming the mean streets of the metropolis failed?

'Rosa? What is it?' Hugo has seen my fear.

'Where are you, Danny?' I can hear breathing – short, jagged breaths. 'Danny, where are you?'

'In the Fellows' Garden.'

'I'm on my way.'

I'm aware as I run that the Master is puffing along behind me, and that people are staring. Some are following.

Danny is up the other end of the garden, on the set of *Othello*, beside Desdemona's marriage bed. He's holding something but I can't make out what it is.

As I come closer to the stage I see that he isn't alone. There's someone in the bed.

My legs have gone on strike. I have to force them up the steps onto the stage.

'Danny?'

Face down on the sheets is a girl. It's Stella.

Danny raises haunted eyes to mine. 'She's dead, Mum.'

'Dead? Don't be silly. Of course she isn't dead. Dead drunk, maybe, but not dead dead.'

But she is undoubtedly very still.

I feel her neck for a pulse. Nothing.

I feel again. I keep my finger there for a long time. Still nothing.

Danny's right. She is dead.

Poor girl. Whatever devious games she was playing, she didn't deserve this. She's so young, scarcely more than a child. Poor, poor girl. How can it be? What's happened here?

Then my stomach gives a sickening lurch and my heart starts pounding. I dismiss what I'm seeing. I'm wrong – I must be wrong. But it's no use.

'Dan . . . her hand.'

It's milky pale with perfect, pearly-pink nails, and it dangles like a drooping lily down towards the ground. On the third finger is a ring. A *diamond engagement ring*.

Everything becomes even more unreal as Danny turns the girl over. Her face is now visible.

Not Stella.

Julie.

Her lips are blue. As blue as the cornflower of her wide staring eyes. Alongside my horror I'm aware of another emotion: bottomless regret. A dreadful acknowledgement of things that will never be.

And then there's an animal howl. I turn. Joan Watkins has come up behind me.

Time stops.

Then she launches herself onto Danny, hitting and pummelling, clawing and scratching.

'Bastard! Murdering black bastard! Fucking savage! I'll kill you! I'll kill you!'

Danny makes no effort to protect himself. Or to deny her accusations.

I finally absorb what it is that he's holding.

A pillow.

Through the roaring in my ears I hear Hugo Mortimer's voice. 'Police. I want to report a murder.'

THIRTY-TWO

They've taken Danny to the police station. Nobody else
Just him.

They think he killed her.

They haven't charged him yet. They say that he's simply
helping them with their enquiries, but it's only a matter o
time. Perry's solicitor is with him but I haven't been allowed
to see him.

They asked me all sorts of questions about him and Juli
– the state of their relationship, the circumstance
surrounding their very public engagement and, crucially
their movements at the Ball.

I had to tell them about seeing Danny crouched in th
gateway of the Fellows' Garden. I knew that if I didn't, i
might make things even worse for him if it subsequentl
came out. I also remembered that in my initial shock I'
babbled something to Hugo Mortimer about my last sightin
of my son.

'What was he doing there? The Fellows' Garden is ou
of bounds to students except during the play.' Hugo hadn'

bothered to curb his accusatory tone. 'This is the last thing the college needs at this particular juncture. Mercifully, the Americans are back at their hotel.'

Thanks for your support, Hugo.

I'll never forget the moments after Joan Watkins was pulled off Danny. People had followed us into the garden to see what was going on. I was glad Danny was so dazed. As I led him backstage, he seemed completely unaware of their avidly curious stares His eyes weren't focusing and his skin felt cold and clammy.

And all of a sudden he was shaking. 'I broke it off with her.'

What?

'I broke it off with Julie.'

'What do you mean? You'd only just proposed.'

'Yes.' He gave a gulping sigh. 'There was no baby, Mum.'

'What?'

'She said she was pregnant so that I'd marry her. Then she couldn't go through with it.'

Poor Julie. Only hours ago I'd been wishing her a million miles away from Danny.

I experienced a sudden huge sense of loss for my unborn grandchild – but the little baby I'd so fervently wished away had never actually existed. How could I feel such regret for a child that never was? Maybe it was sorrow for the dead daughter-in-law I'd never wanted, welcomed or tried to understand.

I couldn't absorb any of this. It was all too much to take.

'How did you find out?'

His voice was heavy with self-condemnation. 'Thanks to my brilliant proposal in front of the entire college, she

decided that I really did love her – baby or no baby. She
thought it was safe to tell me the truth. So she did. And
now she's dead . . .' He looked at me, blank incomprehension in his eyes. 'I thought it was Stella. But it was Julie.'

I stared back at him. My heart started to pound again
'It looks as if she's been suffocated.'

He looked down at the pillow that he was still clutching
'Oh, God.'

The wonder and glory of my twenty precious years a:
Danny's mother flashed before me.

Shortly afterwards, the police took him away.

He was in the chapel, praying for Julie Watkins, wher
Frankie Faraday appeared, wearing something disgusting ir
purple. He felt a little faint. At the tail end of this inter
minable and dreadful night he didn't think he had the
stamina to cope with Frankie.

'God forgives anything, right?' Her voice bounced off the
walls, and reverberated round his skull, producing an instan
headache. 'If someone did summat wrong but was reall
sorry afterwards, would God forgive them?'

'Repentance is a central tenet of Christianity,' he replied
cautiously. 'But I thought you didn't believe in God.' He
swallowed hard, his sense of duty fighting a frantic desire to
barricade himself in the vestry. What did this woman want
What was she trying to say? 'I'm not a Catholic,' he said
'but if there are things you wish to tell me, I would be boun
by confidentiality, just like a priest in the confessional.'

She glared at him. 'I don't have anything to tell you
she snapped. 'Nothing at all.' Then she turned away an
marched out.

What was all that about?

He realised that he was too tired and distressed by the night's events to care. He just wanted to go home and sleep. Trembling with the desire to escape before further interruption, he locked up and walked back to the Gatehouse.

The atmosphere was different from the end of any other Billings May Ball he'd ever known. A post-apocalyptic silence had descended. The place was now deserted except for one policeman guarding the entrance to the Fellows' Garden. Forensic people in white overalls passed him, carrying various cases and bits of equipment. They intensified even further his sense of an alien world. A world destroyed by its own excess. Eyes down, he hurried home, unwilling to further contemplate the abandoned detritus around him.

When he arrived at his room he found Lucas asleep. He was lying across the couch, a hand flung carelessly over his naked torso, as if shielding himself from any unwelcome gaze. As Dominic stared down at him, he was reminded of a painting he'd once seen in the National Gallery – *The Deposition of Christ*. He remembered how the expression of peace on the Saviour's face belied the scarlet wound on the poor injured body being taken down from the cross.

He continued to stare, unable to drag his eyes away. He wished that time would stop and preserve them both in this safe cocoon for ever.

The headache was now a solid band across his forehead.

The boy opened his eyes, and the affection shining out made him want to weep. 'Hi, Unc,' he said. 'Thought I'd crash here. Couldn't face walking back to Bateman Street. You don't mind, do you?'

'Where did you go? You said you'd bring me some supper. You never came. What happened?' The words tumbled ungraciously out. He watched the light fade from Lucas's eyes, but still he couldn't stop. 'You were meant to be helping me.'

When Lucas spoke his voice was full of shame. 'I'm really sorry, Unc. I was with Flora. We had champagne, lots of it. And then I badly wanted to dance. It was the music – it really got to me . . . And then Flora left and this other girl came on to me and—'

'Babylon the great prostitute, seduced you and you fell.' Dominic willed himself to shut up. Suddenly he was sounding like Preacher Man again.

Lucas glared miserably at him. 'It wasn't just that . . .' He hesitated.

'Go on.'

'It wasn't just the music and the dancing.'

'What do you mean?'

'I felt jealous.'

'Jealous?'

'Yes. I suddenly wanted what they all have.'

'They?'

'The students. All that freedom.'

'Freedom?'

'To be what they want to be . . . I decided that for one night I'd pretend I was an undergraduate like them.' He looked at Dominic. 'I'm sorry, Unc. It was daft, I know. I just got carried away.'

Dominic's world shifted. 'I thought you liked working at R&R. You said that's what you wanted.'

'It is, more than anything. But sometimes . . . sometimes

I just wonder what life would have been like if I'd finished school, gone to university.'

Dominic was stricken with guilt. What had he done, keeping his nephew to himself for all these months, taking the boy's declarations about R&R at face value? It had never occurred to him to probe Lucas more closely about what he wanted from life. He'd given no thought at all to the boy's long-term future. He'd just selfishly wallowed in the novel pleasure of unexpectedly having a companion and helper. Someone to care for. Someone to care for him.

Some parent *he'd* turned out to be.

'If that's what you want, you could still do it,' he forced himself to say. 'You could do an access course, apply to university . . .'

'No. Because that *isn't* what I want. I want exactly what I've got – to work with you at R&R. I'm really sorry for leaving you in the lurch.'

The pain in Dominic's head eased momentarily. 'When we've had some sleep, we're going to have a good long talk about your future. But for now, Lucas, it's me who should say sorry. Sorry for my unpardonable rudeness and selfish bad temper. Forgive a foolish and fond uncle.'

'Hey, Unc—'

'Let me get you some breakfast.'

Lucas jumped up. 'I need a piss.' Walking past the window, he came to an abrupt halt. 'What are those police cars doing outside the college?'

'Something terrible's happened. A girl's been found dead.'

'Dead?'

'They think it's murder.'

'You're joking! Who is it?'

'Joan Watkins's daughter.'

'Joan, the admin woman in the office?'

'Yes. It's her daughter, Julie.'

'No!'

'I'm afraid so. She was only nineteen, poor girl.'

'What do they think happened?'

'No one knows. The girl was found on the stage in the Fellows' Garden.'

Lucas sank down into the nearest chair.

'They say she was suffocated.'

'Suffocated?'

'Yes. Lucas, you look terrible. Did you know her?'

'I met her the other day . . . She seemed like a really sweet kid.'

'Yes.'

'Do they know who did it?'

'They're questioning Perry Grimshaw's godson – the boy who's playing Othello.'

'Danny Thorn?'

'Yes.'

'Unc, would you mind if we said a little prayer for her?'

As he knelt down beside his nephew, Dominic felt the headache tighten its grip.

Flora pulled the duvet over her head and tried to blot out the daylight. Blot out her thoughts. Blot out everything. She'd been up all night – why could she not now sleep? She'd never taken drugs but this was what she imagined being on a bad trip to be like: a jumble of sounds and images rioting round her brain – images of the Ball, wild dancing, frenzied music, shrieking merriment. But instead of festive fun, she saw galloping horror. Like the ubiquitous scene in the movies where the hero tries to escape his enemies by running through carnival crowds and someone ends up dead amid the gaudy, garish extravagance.

And then there were the still-images, snapshots burned on her retina: her parents, Stella, Danny, Lucas. And Julie. Above all Julie, cheeks bloodless, eyes wide and staring. Danny turning her over on the big bed. She knew the moment she saw his mother running through Bacon Court. Knew she had to be around to witness the outcome. Standing in the Fellows' Garden, hearing the communal intake of breath. Feeling the breath being sucked from her own body. Feeling the heaviness in her stomach as she looked at Julie's dead face. Turning to leave and coming face to face with Stella.

It's like looking at my own death, Stella had said.

It should be you.

Sit thou silent and get thee into darkness, O daughter of the Chaldeans; for thou shalt no more be called the lady of the kingdoms.

THIRTY-THREE

'Where's our Perry?'

'Haven't a clue.'

'Why not? You're his bloody wife.'

'Please don't shout at me in front of my children.'

'Mummy, *you're* shouting.'

'Shut up, Hector. Go to your room. You too, Cassandra.'

'I hate you. I want my daddy.'

'So do I. I want my daddy. You're a horrid mummy and I hate you too.'

'Upstairs, the pair of you.'

'We hate you!'

'Don't you dare slam that door on your way out! No!'

'It isn't fair to take out your bad temper on the poor babbas.'

'When I want advice from you, Frankie, I'll ask for it.'

'I need to speak to Perry.'

'I haven't seen him since he bailed out on me at the Ball.'

'So where is he?'

'You want him, you find him. And when you do, ask him why he went off with that slut and humiliated his wife in front of the whole college.'

'You don't know what you're talking about.'

'Don't I just.'

'I'll sort it out, don't you worry.'

'What makes you think you have any right to meddle in our business? News-flash, Frankie. Perry's grown up now and he can make his own fuck-ups without your help. You wanted this marriage to fail – you've got your wish. But Perry's done it all by himself. Nothing to do with you.'

'I have to find him before the police do.'

'Police?'

'They want to speak to him.'

'Why should the police want to speak to Perry?'

'They're talking to all the Fellows. About Julie Watkins's death.'

'What?'

'It's standard procedure.'

'Julie's dead?'

'Bugger me, April, where've you been for the last few hours? She was found in the Fellows' Garden. Some bright spark's gone and smothered her.'

'Julie?'

'Yes. They think our Danny had summat to do wi' it since he was standing over her waving a pillow around. They've carted him off to the copshop.'

'Danny?'

'Maybe Perry's in his room at college – what do you think? April, are you listening?'

'Julie?'

'I just said, didn't I? Right, I'm off. Don't give up or him, April. Things aren't always what you think.'

'Aren't they?'

'Perry loves you. Just remember that.'

'Too little too late, Frankie.'

He hadn't had a wink of sleep. How could he, when such a dreadful thing had happened? In his college. In the Fellows' Garden, no less. It was beyond belief. And a Master, he'd had to deal with the fall-out. It had taken hours. He should have been dead on his feet. Instead, so many thoughts bombarded him that he felt he might never sleep again.

If only he'd locked the gate after his little private moment in there when the incident with Tipton had threatened to overwhelm him and he'd needed to escape and tend his wounds for ten minutes. He should have locked it.

Then there was the question of what to do about the Americans. Was it best to tell them about the incident before they saw it for themselves on the local news? Or to hope that they'd leave before finding out? But if they did, nevertheless, find out – which, to be realistic, they surely would at some juncture – what would be their reaction? Would they condemn him as underhand for not saying anything Would they think he and Billings College unworthy of the Miller Foundation's money and support, and go back to Boston, chequebooks firmly closed? Would all his effort have been for nothing?

And then, on top of everything else, Rosa Thorn's son had been arrested for Julie Watkins's murder. To him, seemed very unlikely that the boy would do such a thing

As far as he was concerned, the police had got the wrong man. Danny Thorn was Arts not Sciences, so he hadn't had much contact with the boy, but from the little he knew, he seemed a reasonable sort – in no sense of the word a yob. Let alone a killer. Admittedly, he'd just been doing exactly that, very successfully in his role as Othello, but that was acting. There was a world of difference between playing a murdering Moor and being one.

And Thorn wasn't stupid. If he wanted to kill his girl-friend, he'd hardly have chosen a way that pointed so directly towards himself. Let alone been caught hovering over the body, clutching a pillow.

It didn't make sense. Particularly after the boy's very touching public proposal at the ball, only hours earlier.

Tipton, on the other hand . . .

He knew with utter certainty that Tipton was respon-sible for all the strange things that had happened over the past few days. The man was a psycho – killing Dawkins and the cats demonstrated that beyond doubt. It was lucky he himself wasn't dead – the thing with the nuts had very nearly finished him off. Maybe having tasted blood, so to speak, with the animals, Tipton had finally gone over the edge. Joan Watkins's daughter was a provocative little minx. He'd seen her strutting around college with her short skirts and high heels. She'd probably made some shoddy little assignation to have sex with her fiancé on the set of *Othello*. A Desdemona fantasy, perhaps, with Thorn playing the rapacious Moor. She had, after all, appeared as Stella Grainger's twin last night, and what was all *that* about? Who knows what Tipton might have done if he'd inadver-tently stumbled across her, sprawled invitingly across that big bed on the stage? Maybe for some reason she'd tried to titillate his frigid fancy. And maybe it had all blown up in her face . . .

It sounded like a story from one of the more lurid tabloids. But it was perfectly plausible.

If it could be proved, it would rid him of Tipton once and for all.

I'm expecting to run the gauntlet of a Family Liaison Officer, but instead Joan's door is opened by a man with *Born to Kill* tattooed on his left arm. Julie's eyes, bloodshot and red-rimmed, and set in a billiard-ball skull, glare out at me.

The soldier brother.

'Is it possible to see Joan?'

'Who are you?'

'Rosa Thorn. Danny's mother. You must be Scott.'

For a moment I think his large paw is going to stretch out and snap my neck in half. 'You're having a laugh, incha? You think I'd let anyone connected to 'im come anywhere near my mother?'

'Danny didn't murder anyone.'

'Tell that to the cops. They ain't lookin' for no one else as far as I can see. Now sling yer hook before I do something I'll regret. And you can tell that murdering cunt that I'll swing for him one day. It don't matter how long they put 'im away for, when he comes out I'll be waitin'. You tell 'im, all right?'

Then I hear a faint voice. 'Is it the police, Scott?'

'No, Ma. It ain't nothing.' He starts to shut the door.

I call out as loudly as I can. 'It's Rosa Thorn, Joan. I need to talk. Please.'

'I thought I told you to scarper.' The knotted veins in Scott's massive forearms stand out as he flexes both his fists.

'Let her come up.'

'But, Ma—'

'Please, Scott.'

All Scott wants to do is brain the woman who's spawned the man he thinks is responsible for killing his baby sister. In his place I'd probably feel the same.

'Scott, send her up.'

He shrugs, suddenly helpless, unable to deny his mother anything at this time. 'If you upset her, I'll rip your throat out.'

I wonder if he's done a tour in Iraq yet. I pity any hapless insurgent who has the misfortune to get in his way. He follows me upstairs, inches away, breathing down my neck like some rabid beast.

But I forget all about Scott when I enter the bedroom. It's Julie's. The room of a teenage babe, full of frills and froth, with posters of boy bands on the walls. Every surface is covered in dresses and underwear and shoes – all discarded by an excited girl going off to her first ball with the boy she loves. On her dressing-table, almost hidden in the muddle of cosmetics, tissues and hair appliances, is a framed photo of her and Danny, arms round each other, punting up the Cam. She's laughing and he's kissing her.

On the bed, wrapped in what is clearly Julie's dressing-gown, lies Joan, staring at the ceiling like a corpse in a winding sheet, ramrod straight and dry-eyed.

'He didn't have to settle things that way.'

'Joan—'

'I'd have looked after her and the baby. He needn't have been involved.'

'Please—'

'All he had to do was say. All he had to do was say *I don't love you, Julie, and I don't want this baby.* She would have coped. We all would. He didn't have to kill her. He didn't have to put a pillow over her poor little face and choke the life out of her. What kind of a person does that?'

'Not Danny.'

She doesn't seem to have heard. 'It wasn't just her he murdered. It was my grandchild. I'll never see her children now, will I? I'll never be a granny to her little babies.'

'Joan . . .'

'I hope you can live with yourself. You raised him. I hope you're proud of the job you've done.' She turns finally and looks at me with contempt. 'You never thought she was good enough for your precious son, did you?'

'Please—'

'You thought he could do better. Funny thing is, I knew where you were coming from.'

'Joan—'

'I can say it now. I was jealous. Of your confidence, your easy way with people. Everything about you, really. But no any more. You're not fit to kiss my boots. At least I can hold up my head and be proud of the way I've raised my children We may be nothing special, but we're not criminals. My son' prepared to die for his country. Yours is just a spoiled bra who killed my child because he couldn't face up to his respon sibilities. You should go and hide in a deep hole and neve come out, after what he did. You should thank your luck stars your husband's dead and never had to see this day.'

'Danny didn't kill Julie.'

'And you believe him? At least I knew when my girl was telling the truth.'

Through the deep sorrow I feel for her, the urge to defend my son breaks through. 'Maybe you don't know everything.'

Scott picks up the change in my voice and gives a warning grunt.

'There was no baby. Julie made it up.'

There's a sharp intake of breath and then she's off the bed and slapping me hard across the face.

'You sayin' my sister was a liar?' Scott has my arm in an iron grip.

'You don't have to take my word for it. The post-mortem will tell you.' I try to sound authoritative. This man's grief has made him savage. He could hurt me.

'Post-mortem? Are they going to cut her up? Oh, dear God, no!' Joan is sobbing now.

'Don't, Ma.' The pressure on my arm vanishes as Scott sinks down onto the stairs and covers his face.

In the silence, broken only by the sounds of two people struggling with their sorrow, I battle with the overwhelming desire to leave them alone and not intrude any further. But I must finish what I started.

'I came to tell you that there was no baby, and also because I need you to know that Danny's innocent. He'd never do anything to hurt Julie. He's devastated, Joan.'

She won't even look at me now. But then she picks up a used tissue from the bedside table and scrubs her face so hard I'm surprised the skin doesn't come off.

'She called me three times last night. The first time was to tell me about his proposal. Then later, when she told

401

me it was all off. And then some time after that, she calle
again. She was crying and saying, "He's hurt me, Mum
He's really hurt me." I could hear music in the background
"Lady in Red". I thought she meant he'd hurt her feeling
I said, "Stand up for yourself. Don't let him get to you. Te
him to grow up and be a man." And then she rang off.
thought, I mustn't interfere. I've got to leave them to sor
it out themselves. But I couldn't sleep. I couldn't get he
out of my head. I just had this feeling, see – that thing
weren't right. I sat downstairs for a bit, looking out of th
window, but in the end I couldn't stand it any more. I go
dressed and went up to college. Stanley Gordon let m
through – he could see I was in a right state. I searche
everywhere but I couldn't find her. Then I saw you and S
Hugo. You were running and I knew in my bones that
was something to do with Julie. So I followed you . . . an
there she was. Poor little thing . . . Poor little thing.'

'Danny didn't do it, Joan.'

Scott rises heavily to his feet. 'Best if you go now.'

I couldn't agree more.

As the front door closes behind me I cross over to Jesu
Green and look back at the silent house. What had Juli
ever done to deserve having the life choked out of her?

A thought hits me.

Maybe she hadn't done anything. Maybe she'd bee
mistaken for somebody else.

THIRTY-FOUR

The thought of Stella rubbing up against Lucas on the dance-floor in Locke Court still turned Flora's stomach all these hours later. When she saw them slip away, just before the lights failed, she'd felt such burning fury that she feared she'd self-combust and produce a spectacle to rival the retro light-show on the wall. She started to follow them and settle things once and for all, but then everything was plunged into darkness and by the time she'd fumbled her way through the crowd, they'd disappeared.

Until much later. She'd caught up with them then, or so she thought, but she'd been mistaken.

This morning, she pondered the implications of the events in the Fellows' Garden and decided that they changed nothing.

Stella would probably still be sleeping after her big night out. She never locked her door so it would be easy enough to surprise her. She crept up the stairs and was pleased to see that she'd been right: the door was not locked – in fact,

it was ajar. Then she heard voices inside. One female. On
male. Her heart gave a painful thump.

Lucas. *So much for saving himself for marriage.* He'd slep
with Stella right under her nose. Or to be strictly accurate
right above her head. Flora tried to remember if she'd hear
anything. She thought not. One small mercy at least.

The voices were low, but intense. She had to strain t
hear.

'I thought we were cool.'

'I wish I'd never clapped eyes on you.'

It wasn't Lucas. *It was Dr Grimshaw.*

Flora felt weak with relief. She knew she should leave
but her feet remained rooted to the spot.

'Then why come to my room?'

'To say goodbye.'

'You don't mean that.'

'You've ruined my life.'

'Like how?'

'You've made me do the unthinkable.'

'This thing between you and me was inevitable. It ha
to happen.'

'You don't know what you're talking about.'

'Don't underestimate my feelings, Perry. Just because I'r
young.'

'You don't get it, do you? I have to leave everything I'v
ever loved. And it's all because of you.'

'I'll come too. Then we can be together.'

'Don't come any closer. I can't stand to be anywher
near you.'

'So if you hate me so much, why come to say goodbye.'

'I had to.'

'Why?'

'Because I thought . . .'

'Because you love me.'

Flora tried to see what was happening, but in doing so her sandal fell off and hit the stone floor with a soft thud.

'What was that?'

'Nothing.'

'For your own sake, Stella, stay away from me.'

'Don't go. Please. There are so many things I need to say to you—'

'Leave it. Please.'

He was heading towards the door and Flora. She ran down a few steps and then quickly turned round as if she were coming back up towards him. 'Hi, Dr Grimshaw.'

He looked dreadful. And doubly dreadful at being caught coming out of a student's room. 'Oh. Hello, Flora. Just returning one of Stella's essays. Wanted to make sure she had it before she left for the Long Vac. Did you enjoy the Ball?'

'Very much, or rather I did until . . . I thought Mrs Grimshaw looked lovely.'

'Yes. Yes, she did. Are you off home now May Week's nearly over?'

'I don't know. I was staying till Sunday. We were supposed to do two more nights of *Othello*, but it'll be cancelled after – you know. Isn't it awful?'

'Yes. Yes, it is. So, Flora, if I don't run into you again before you leave, enjoy your summer. Don't let what happened last night spoil things.'

'I can't get it out of my mind. You must feel twice as bad, Danny being your godson. I don't believe he did it.'

'Did what?'

'Especially after proposing in that way. So romantic. He seemed crazy about her.'

'They think *Danny* killed Julie Watkins?'

'Didn't you know?'

'I got rather drunk last night and crashed out in my room. I've only just heard about Julie. Nobody mentioned Danny.'

'They've taken him to the police station. Are you all right, Dr Grimshaw?'

But he was already down the stairs and running through the archway.

Flora returned to her room and reviewed what she'd overheard. Stella had sounded different when she was talking to Perry Grimshaw.

She wasn't playing with him.

She was really keen.

This was a first.

'Anna?'

'Hi, Mum. Thought you'd still be sleeping it off.'

'Something's happened.'

'What?'

'There's been an accident – at the Ball. It's Julie . . .'

'What about her?'

'I'm afraid she's dead.'

There was a shocked silence.

'Anna?'

'How?'

'That's what the police are trying to find out.'

'The police?'

'They have to be involved when there's a sudden death.'

'Oh my God. She once told me she had asthma. I bet in the excitement she forgot to take her inhaler to the Ball. This is terrible. How's Danny?'

'Not good. So I'm staying on here today, if that's OK?'

'I'll catch the next train. I can be with you in a couple of hours.'

'No! You're still in the middle of exams. You need to revise. Dan and I will be home sometime over the weekend and we'll fill you in then, all right?'

'Mum, you sound really odd.'

'It's just been a shock, that's all. Anna, someone's calling me. I have to go now. Don't worry. We'll see you tomorrow, probably. Love to Josh.'

'Mum—'

'Bye, love.'

I can't do it. I can't tell her that her brother's banged up in the cells at Cambridge police station, suspected of murdering his girlfriend. Not until he's in the clear. If the police release him today, then she won't have to go through the gut-wrenching anxiety that's presently tearing me apart.

But for them to release him, they need another suspect.

All morning, the same thought has been running through my mind as I hang around the police station waiting to be allowed to see Danny. All morning the conviction has been growing that it wasn't Julie who was the intended victim.

It was Stella.

Someone mistook Julie for Stella. In the dark, when the lights had failed, it would be an easy thing to do. After all, when I first saw the body, I myself had automatically assumed it was Stella. Same dress. Same hair. Same build. And quite apart from the similarity in appearance, Stella, judging from my short acquaintance with her, was far more likely than poor Julie to have people who didn't wish her well. April, for example.

Immediately I have this thought, I dismiss it. She'd be incapable of doing such a dreadful thing. But I've watched Stella in action, with both Perry and Danny. I've felt pretty alienated myself. If she could have this effect on both me and April, maybe we weren't the only ones.

I need to find out more about her and the people she's come into contact with recently. See who might hate her enough to kill her. She herself is the obvious person to ask but I don't want to alarm her unnecessarily. It's not exactly what you'd want to be told, is it, that the murderer made a mistake and that you were the intended target?

Maybe Hugo Mortimer is the one to give me the lowdown on Stella Grainger. After all, he claims, as Master, to have his finger on the pulse of the college. Rather than hanging around the police station, I'd be far more use to Danny if I could find out something that might point towards the real murderer. Hugo will be my first port of call.

When I arrive at the Master's Lodge I find him striding around in a tizzy.

'Bill Miller's gone up to London today instead of tomorrow.'

'Did he sign on the dotted line?'

'No, he bloody well didn't.'

'I'm sorry, Hugo. I'm sure he'll come through in the end.'

'As I feared, he's got wind of this unfortunate episode with Julie Watkins. I think it's put him right off.'

Unfortunate episode? One way of describing a vicious

murder, I suppose. Hugo clearly sees poor Julie's death only in terms of the damage it might have done to his grand plan.

'It's about Julie that I wanted to talk to you.'

With an effort he tears himself away from the perfidious Americans. 'Is your son still in custody?'

'Yes. But he didn't do it.'

'I know he didn't.'

This is said with such conviction that it startles me. 'You do?'

'The person who did this has been trying his best to sabotage things in this college for quite a while.'

I was right to come to him. Already he's suggesting another suspect. But immediately my flicker of hope is extinguished. I know exactly whose name will emerge from his mouth.

'Dominic Tipton. He's been behind everything that's happened over the past week.'

What a surprise. 'Do you have any proof?'

Hugo scowls. 'Not as such, but he kills animals. It's only a short step from that to killing humans. And he attacked me last night.'

'How do you know it was him who killed your pets?'

His plump face colours up. 'Who the hell else would it be? He'll do whatever it takes to ruin all my plans for the college.'

I can't see Dominic Tipton as a murderer. From what I've heard, he's regarded by many as a saint. Everyone knows the Master's trying to bully him into submission over the Theological Library. Everyone knows he's stressed almost to breaking-point. But a murderer? I don't think so. However, it's pointless trying to dissuade Hugo. He's in the grip of an obsession. All roads lead to poor old Dom.

'You're right,' he's muttering. 'We need proof. No use going to the police without it.'

'Actually, Hugo, I want to run another theory by you. I think Julie was mistaken for Stella Grainger. I believe Stella was the intended victim. Think about it. Julie very successfully copied Stella last night – hair, clothes, everything. I reckon that in the dark somebody killed the wrong girl.'

'Why on earth would Tipton want to kill Stella Grainger?'

Exactly so. Why indeed, Hugo? Give him a break.

I bite my lip and press on. 'What do you know about her?'

Hugo frowned in thought. 'She's hardly one of our first-class minds. Pretty average undergraduate, really. Not much of a team player, either. Doesn't belong to any of the college societies. To my knowledge the BADS production was the first thing she's ever participated in. Must admit I never associated her with Tipton. She doesn't strike me as the God-bothered type. She leaves all that kind of thing to her friend Flora.'

'The girl who played Emilia?'

'That's the one. Joined at the hip, those two. Inseparable. Maybe Flora's the connection to Tipton. Maybe she got him to try and convert Stella. And maybe it all went wrong.'

Dominic again. Hugo's one-track mind is becoming irritating. 'Anything else you know about her?'

'Has half the boys in college running around after her. Can't see what they all go for, personally, but go for her they certainly do. She draws them in and then when they get too close, she spits them out.'

'See what I mean, Hugo? She's a much better bet than Julie.'

'Perhaps you should talk to Flora Mainwaring. She knows more about her than anyone else. And Perry. He's been her supervisor this term. You should speak to him too.'

So the gossip-machine hadn't yet linked Perry's name with Stella's. Something to be thankful for anyway. It was pointless asking Hugo if he knew if Stella had any other people who didn't wish her well. As far as he's concerned, there is only one enemy – and he wears a black suit and a clerical collar. So I ask whereabouts in college Flora and Stella live, and leave him making a call to Claridge's in a last attempt to get Bill Miller back on board.

The headache had become a migraine. It was ages since he'd last had a migraine. It made him feel sick, and the bright lights flashing in his peripheral vision weren't helping either. But there were things to be done, migraine or no migraine. He left Lucas still sleeping on the sofa, crept out and made his way to Bateman Street on his bike. It was difficult to extricate himself from the usual R&R dramas, but he managed. His flock would have to cope without him today. He did what he had to do as quickly as he could, and rode back to Billings. Lucas was still asleep. So deeply asleep, in fact, that for one dreadful moment, Dominic thought he was dead. It filled him with such despair that he cried aloud which, much to his relief, caused Lucas to turn over. Then it was time for him to go out again.

When he finally returned to his rooms, Lucas was gone.

*   *   *

411

Fallen, fallen is Babylon the great. She has become a home for demons and a haunt for every evil spirit. Therefore in one day her plagues will overtake her: death, mourning and famine. Woe, Babylon, city of Power. In one hour your doom has come.

THIRTY-FIVE

I'm in luck. As I dodge around the workmen dismantling the marquee in Bacon Court, I see Flora. Her hair hangs tired and tangled over her shoulders and she's wearing a dirty old T-shirt and torn jeans. There are dark circles under her eyes and her plain, bony face has an unhealthy yellow tinge. A creature of the night, wincing in the brightness of the midday sun, her lanky form strides out across the grass and I have trouble catching up with her.

'Can I have a word?'

She stops abruptly. 'You're Danny's mum, right?'

'Yes.'

'The police are crazy to lock him up. There's no way he could do a thing like that. Especially not since he and Julie sorted things out. That engagement announcement was to die for.' She realises her gaffe. 'I'm sorry – I can't believe I just said that. I can't believe she's dead, either. It's unreal. Totally unreal.'

I explain my mistaken identity theory. At the mention of Stella's name I catch a glimpse of something in her eyes.

'I wondered if you knew anyone who might have it in for her?'

'Everybody loves Stella.'

'I gather you're her best friend?'

Flora's brown eyes meet mine. 'Yes,' she says. 'And I don't know anyone who'd want to harm her.'

'Flora, I want to prove Danny's innocence and to stop anyone else from being hurt. That's all. Anything about Stella that isn't relevant will go in one ear and out the other.'

'Sorry. Can't think of anything.' She stares at two men loading steel poles onto a lorry.

My ever-reliable gut is talking to me. It says that all is not well between Flora and Stella.

'Is that all you wanted? Only I'm in a bit of a hurry.'

I'm about to let her go, but then something makes me say, 'Off to see your boyfriend, are you?'

Where did *that* come from? I don't even know if she has a boyfriend. I didn't see her with anyone at the Ball. But by now I know the area in which Stella is most likely to make enemies.

Men. Boys. Anything in trousers.

If Flora has gone off her best friend, I'd take bets on there being a man involved somewhere. And sure enough, she's blushing. 'Yeah,' she mutters, a large knuckled hand flying up to her face to hide her expression. 'And I'm late already.'

I watch her striding clumsily towards the Gatehouse. She doesn't look like the kind of girl who'd have legions of horny blokes beating a path to her door. So if someone did, and she liked him, she'd want to hold on tight. She wouldn't appreciate anyone muscling in on her territory.

414

I'm pondering this when I catch sight of someone very unlikely emerging from Flora and Stella's staircase.

Frankie.

Heading in the direction of Perry's rooms in Berkeley Court. Has she been to see Stella? If so, no prizes for guessing why. There's only one thing the two of them have in common.

Frankie's not exactly the caring mother, and sabotaging Perry's marriage is her favourite leisure activity. On the face of it, she shouldn't give a damn if he strays from the straight and narrow with Stella.

So why's she looking like she's just started World War Three?

I realise suddenly that Frankie *would* mind about Perry and Stella. She'd mind a hell of a lot.

Not because she wants to save Perry the pain and grief of a broken marriage. Nor because she'd hate the lives of her little grandchildren to be torn apart. No, the reason Frankie wouldn't stand for any hanky-panky is because she couldn't bear her precious image to be tarnished. *My son the Cambridge Professor* – it's something she's always bragging about. She thinks it adds a certain gravitas to her showbiz lifestyle. *My son the disgraced Cambridge Professor, thrown out for fucking his nineteen-year-old student* is something else again. It wouldn't reflect well on her at all. What would the fans think? The fact that Frankie probably has very few fans left is neither here nor there. In her deluded world, the Life and Times of the Fabulous Frankie is the main event for thousands of admirers all over the UK and beyond.

What has she been saying to Stella? There's only one way to find out.

I'm right in assuming that she hasn't been round to admire the view. When I knock on Stella's door, it opens immediately.

'I said get lost.'

It's the first time I've ever seen Stella in the grip of a very strong emotion. Immediately she sees me she tries to suppress it. 'Hi, Rosa.'

She makes no reference to Frankie. Her hand, clutching the door, is trembling. Whatever Frankie said has clearly got under her skin.

'May I come in?'

'Actually, it's a bit chaotic in here. I'm packing for the Long Vac.'

I look over her shoulder into the room, which looks as if it's been burgled. A suitcase is open on the bed, and there are clothes, books and other objects strewn everywhere.

'This won't take a minute. There's something I want to run by you.'

'Oh?' Her tone is guarded. She thinks I'm the second wave of attack, warning her off Perry. In any other circumstances maybe I would be, but for now I need her to listen. It's impossible to soften what I have to say so I come straight out with it.

'I think that you may have been the killer's real target.'

Her face is now expressionless, a gently raised eyebrow the only indication that she's heard.

'The killer might have thought Julie was you last night. If so, they could try again.'

'Oh.'

'Is there anyone who might want to harm you?'

I'm mesmerised by the swirling green of her eyes as she

stares at me long and hard before saying gently, 'The police already have the killer in custody, Rosa.'

It's like a slap in the face.

'Danny didn't kill Julie.' I struggle to keep my cool.

'You know that for certain, do you?'

'Danny couldn't kill anybody.'

She gives an apologetic smile. 'You're his mother. You would say that.'

'Danny's innocent. Which means the real killer's still out there, waiting. Probably for you.'

'Believe me, the police have the right man.'

That's it. If someone does want to choke the life out of her, I'll give them a helping hand. 'You don't know what you're talking about.'

'Yes, I do.' The green eyes are full of compassion. 'You see, I saw him do it. I'm so sorry, Rosa.'

And then she shuts the door in my face, and no amount of hammering and banging on my part will induce her to open it again. Eventually I turn away, and blunder down the stairs.

Danny didn't do it. I know he didn't.

As Flora walked down Trinity Street she caught a glimpse of herself in the window of Heffer's bookshop. She looked like shit. She should have tarted herself up a bit, but she couldn't wait. She'd almost died when Danny's mother had collared her and started on about mistaken identity and whether Stella had any enemies. It would have been good to tell the woman the truth. But all things considered, it was better to keep quiet. No one liked telltales.

The one tale she would tell, was the tale of Stella and

Dr Grimshaw. *And this particular tale was for the ears o* *one person only.*

Her mobile rang and she looked at the caller display. I was Daddy. She didn't pick up. Last night at the Ball he parents had completely ignored her. She knew why: the were ashamed. She didn't come up to scratch. They didn' want their glittering companions to see their dull, ugl daughter. She should have been used to their behaviour b now, but for some reason it felt like the final insult.

So, Daddy, I'll get back to you in my own good time Don't imagine for one moment that I'm at your beck an call any more.

She walked on past Great St Mary's and down Kin Parade, the mobile burning a hole in her pocket. But whe she drew level with Fitzbillies she stopped. Maybe she wa maligning Daddy. Maybe he'd called to apologise, to sa how proud they'd been of her. How beautiful they thoug she'd looked. He'd be very hurt if she didn't respond Leaning against the cake-shop window, she dialle Voicemail.

Mummy says to remind you that we're closing the Londo house for the summer. The staff need a break. If you're at loose end, you could join us in France, I suppose, but I da say you'd prefer to be gadding about with your chums. I' transferred money to your account. It should tide you ov for a couple of months, but let me know if you need mor Cheerio, old thing. Bonnes vacances.

The unique Cambridge mix of shoppers, students an tourists jostled past, but it was as if they inhabited a parall world, separated from her by a transparent but imperm able membrane. She might drift in and out and past then

ut nobody could see her. She tried out a couple of exper-
mental smiles on a group of Japanese tourists, but they all
ooked blankly through her. Ms Invisible – that's who she
vas. Ms Nobody. Her gaze fell on a drain in the gutter.
She felt so small that she thought it might be possible to
lip through the grating, down into the sewers and disap-
ear. Disappear into the Underworld. Cruise the River Styx.
No one would notice.

Fitzbillies' window was full of the most delicious-looking
akes. She walked into the shop, bought two meringues, a
anilla slice and a chocolate éclair, and then ate them sitting
n the steps of the Fitzwilliam Museum.

By the time she'd finished, all was well.

Mummy and Daddy's indifference and Stella's betrayal
ere all part of God's plan.

Which was to give her the incentive to remain in
Cambridge over the Long Vac. To be a full-time volunteer
t R&R. Dom would be delighted. So delighted that he'd
et her stay in the tiny box room upstairs which was presently
store room. She could sleep there, next door to Lucas.
he'd work alongside him, live alongside him, pray along-
de him. All day, every day. He'd see that her devotion to
&R was equal to his own. He'd realise what a perfect team
ley were. Together they would do God's work and by the
utumn their bond would be indelibly cemented. By
Christmas, who knows, they might even be engaged.

Licking the last vestiges of cream from round her mouth,
lora, newly energised and on a massive sugar high, strode
owards Bateman Street.

The place was deserted. It was the heat. The clients of
&R enjoyed the sunshine as much as anyone else. And

the tourist season meant there was plenty of money abou
for those that knew how to find it. No one would be aroun
until supper-time. She peered into Dom's office. Empty.

'Hello?' Lucas called down from his room.

'It's Flora.'

'Hi, Flo. Come up.' His smile was wide and welcomin
'What happened to you last night? I left you dancing an
when I came back you'd gone.'

He didn't desert me, after all. He tried to find me.

When she saw him with Stella he was probably askir
about her. She chose to eradicate from her consciousne
the sight of the two of them locked together. It had bee
dark. Easy to misinterpret things.

'We must have kept on missing each other.' She longe
to touch him. 'Isn't it terrible about Julie?'

He shook his head in bewilderment. 'Unbelievable. Th
guy they've arrested – Danny Thorn – you must know hir
well from doing *Othello*. Did he seem the violent sort? A
you surprised?'

'Yeah, I really am. Although he can be quite moody
nearly bit my head off the other day for no good reasc
. . . But it's a long way from bad temper to murder.'

'Sure.'

'Julie was so happy last night. They'd broken up, yc
know, but yesterday they got back together. Did you he
about his proposal? In front of the whole college?'

'Yeah. And then he goes and kills her.' He looked
Flora and the sympathy in his eyes made her weak wi
love. 'You must feel dreadful. I know you'd become goc
mates, doing the costumes and stuff. You've spent a lot
time with her this week. I'm gutted for you, Flo.'

Flora had an image of Julie furiously mending combat trousers and pouring out the secrets of her heart. She didn't want to think about it. She didn't remotely want to think about herself and Julie. What she'd done to Julie. Not now.

'Can we talk about something else?' she said. 'Something more cheerful?'

His smile was full of understanding. 'OK,' he said. 'But if you ever want to offload—'

Flora cut in. 'Guess what? I've got a piece of very juicy gossip for you.'

Startled at the abrupt change of subject, Lucas laughed. 'Would God approve of this particular bit of juicy gossip?'

'Oh well, if you don't want to know.'

'I'm teasing. Come on, spill.'

'Stella and our English supervisor, Perry Grimshaw.'

Lucas grinned. 'What about them?'

'They're an item.'

'You mean . . . ?'

'Yeah.'

'How do you know?'

'I overheard them.'

'Oh.' The grin remained, Cheshire cat-like, stuck to his face.

'I feel very disloyal saying this – I wouldn't say it to anyone else, but I know I can trust you. Stella tends to string men along.'

'String them along? Why?'

Flora shrugged. 'Different reasons. Sometimes she wants something, sometimes it just – gives her a kick.'

'A kick?'

'Yeah, she can be quite cruel. But with Perry Grimshaw you know what?'

'What?' His voice sliced through her babbling. 'What? Get to the point, Flora.'

'I think she's genuinely in love with Perry. In fact, I know she is. She's crazy about him. I heard her say so.'

Lucas stepped towards her, face now expressionless.

Flora felt a twinge of unease. A stillness had descended on the room and the temperature seemed to have dropped several degrees. She was suddenly freezing, despite the blazing sunshine outside. But still she persevered. It had to be done. Like cauterising a wound. 'It's his wife I feel sorry for. He seemed like such a devoted family man. I thought he was a really nice bloke, the last person to perv on students. But maybe he can't help it. Stella is very beautiful. Maybe it's the authentic grand passion. Judging by the way she was looking at him, she certainly thinks it is.'

'Shut the fuck up!'

'Lucas!'

'Shut your disgusting mouth.'

And then he was on top of her. She could smell the odour of pear drops on his breath.

'Lux! Please! I can't breathe. You're suffocating me . . .'

'Fallen, fallen is Babylon the Great, which made all the nations drink the maddening wine of her adulteries.'

Then suffocation was the last thing she needed to worry about. Suffocation would have been a merciful release.

THIRTY-SIX

I stand in the middle of Bacon Court, and experience the literal meaning of the expression 'I don't know which way to turn'. I move in one direction, then another, then stop, paralysed by indecision. I want to save my son, but I don't know how, short of confessing to the murder myself. Whatever Stella thinks she saw, she's wrong. Danny couldn't kill anybody or anything. I remember him as a small child scrutinising every bit of the pavement as he walked along, in case he accidentally stepped on an insect, and he once cried for two days when Rob had to finish off a pigeon that had crashed against our living-room window and badly injured itself.

Danny's the original gentle giant. Not a killer.

I have to talk to Perry. I need family and he's the nearest thing I have to a brother. Right now, I don't care if he and Stella are doing the beast with two backs, I have to talk through everything that's happened with him. Try and work out what else I can do to help clear my son.

With a bit of luck he might be in college.

When I turn into Berkeley Court I see Frankie. She's peering through Perry's window. Obviously Perry isn't inside, unless he's hiding under the table in an attempt to avoid her. I wouldn't blame him. I try to creep away unnoticed, but I'm too late.

'Rosa! Have you seen our Perry?' Her theatrical voice rings out across the court. Even the gargoyles quake.

'No. I'm looking for him myself. Is he not at home?'

'No, he bloody isn't. There's a letter in his writing, addressed to April, lying on the table in here. We need to open it – find out what he's up to.'

Why? If it's anything to do with Stella, I think I'd rather not know. I've other things to think about. And what's this 'we'? Since when did the Fabulous Frankie and I become Holmes and Watson?

'I don't think that opening Perry's private correspondence is something I want to get involved in.'

'There's a lot at stake here.'

'What are you talking about?'

'Can you pick locks?'

'Frankie!'

At this moment, the Head Porter struts into Berkeley Court, lord of all he surveys. When he sees Frankie, his surly face cracks into a besotted leer.

'Morning, Miss Faraday. How are you after that dreadful business last night?'

Frankie's no slouch when it comes to seizing an opportunity. 'Sick as a parrot, Stanley. That poor young girl, cut off in her prime. I haven't slept a wink.' She sighs tragically and gestures towards the door. 'And now this. It never rains but it pours.'

'What?' Stanley's face is a caricature of concern.

'I left a very important contract in my son's room last night. I'm supposed to send it Special Delivery to my agent, and Dr Grimshaw's gone walkabout.' She gives a little sob. 'I'll lose the job if I don't post it today. A whole six-part TV series. My last chance to revive my career.' Real tears well up in her eyes and trickle down her rouged cheeks.

God knows why Stanley falls for this improbable tale, but he does. He detaches a key from the huge bunch on his belt. 'Have no fear, Stanley's here,' he trumpets. 'Behold, ladies, the master key!' With a great flourish he opens Perry's door.

Frankie plants a kiss in the middle of his purple forehead. 'Stanley, the first song in the first show will be dedicated to you.' She pulls me with her into Perry's room, and grabs the letter from the table. 'Here it is,' she says. 'I just need to read through the fine print before posting it. We'll let ourselves out, Stanley. I won't forget this. I never forget a favour. Bless you, pet.'

Even Stanley can tell he's being dismissed. 'My pleasure, Miss Faraday,' he gushes sycophantically, and executing a small bow, he strides away across the court.

'Right. Let the dog see the rabbit.' Frankie rips open the envelope and takes out the letter. It's a long one and she takes a long time to read it.

'What does it say?' How quickly my scruples have disappeared.

But it has dropped from Frankie's fingers onto the table. Patches of rouge stand out against a face drained of all colour.

'Frankie?'

She shakes her head, unable to speak. Heart thumping, I pick it up.

My Darling,

You will always be my darling, whatever happens.

I should be telling you this face to face, but I can't.

You were right to be suspicious of me. I said you were imagining things, but you weren't. I love you. More than I can possibly say. Nothing will ever change that. But something about Stella drew me in. I wanted to talk to her, hold her, be with her, I struggled to resist the feelings, but I couldn't, however hard I tried.

And I did try. So hard. Until last night, I thought I could beat it.

Over dinner, I was happier than I'd been for ages. You looked wonderful and I felt so close to you. It was like the way things used to be in Sydney before the children were born. A perfect evening. Until Frankie made a spectacle of herself. Normally I don't mind Frankie's messes. She's my mother, I love her. You think I'm blind to her faults, but I'm not. I know exactly what she's like, but last night was a step too far. This time she was trashing the life I've managed to carve out for myself. She showed me up in front of all my students and colleagues. And added to all the trouble that I knew in my heart she was stirring up between us, it was the last straw. I couldn't hack it any more. To my eternal shame I left you to sort it all out, and went and got as drunk as I could as quickly as I could in a bid to forget everything for a few hours. When you found me I saw the pity on your face and I couldn't bear it, so I made sure you left me alone by being as unpleasant as I could. It's all a bit of a blur after that, but at some point I remember joining the cast of Othello for a dance. And then Stella was there. It was me and her, up close and personal. When she asked me to come to the Fellows' Garden, there was no mistaking what she wanted. I told her to go ahead, said I'd catch her up. I knew this was my last chance to cut loose before any real harm was done. I was desperate to find you, but I couldn't. So I had another couple of drinks, and then I thought that if my wife couldn't be bothered to look for me, why should I bother to look for her? Why shouldn't I follow my inclinations for once and have some fun? Other men did. I went to the garden, but Stella wasn't there. I felt dizzy so I lay down on the bed. And then I was dreaming. About how much I loved you. My head was full of you, but then she was there and no matter how hard I tried to push her away, she was there between us and all I could see were those green eyes. I was consumed by a terrible rage; she was destroying everything I held dear. All I wanted was to obliterate that beautiful face – stop it from drawing me in – stop the siren call once and for all. Stop her from ruining our lives. Then suddenly I wasn't drunk any more. There was a shaft of light across the bed and I saw her lying face down beside me. She was very still, but when I touched her I knew straight away that she was dead. And I also knew that it wasn't a dream. It was real. I'd killed her.

No one noticed when I slipped out of the garden. I went back to my room and tried to think, but I must

*have fallen asleep. Next thing I knew, it was morning.
I was still holding out a faint hope that it had all been
a dream. But of course, as you know, it wasn't. I also
discovered it was Julie Watkins I killed, not Stella, and
that poor Danny has been arrested for it.*

*So I have to finish things. I'm so, so sorry, my darling.
By the time you read this it will be all over. Please
forgive me. I swear on our children's lives that I didn't
mean to do it.*

*Kiss my babies for me. I love you all, much more
than I can ever say,*
Perry

'What does he mean – finish things?' Frankie's eyes burn
into mine. 'Has he turned himself in, or . . . ?' She can't
bring herself to say the words.

'I don't know.' I don't want to know either. I should feel
relieved: Danny's off the hook. I *do* feel relieved.

But Perry? My Perry, a murderer? That's almost as
unspeakable as Danny being a murderer. And equally
unlikely. If he hadn't condemned himself out of his own
mouth I'd find it impossible to believe.

'He didn't know what he was doing, Frankie. He thought
it was a dream.'

She nods, eagerly. 'I once read about this woman who
went late-night shopping in Waitrose and was arrested for
nicking a trolleyload of tinned tomatoes. It turned out she
was sleepwalking.'

'Exactly. People do all sorts of things in their sleep. It's
well-documented. I'll phone the police station, see if he's
there.'

But he wasn't. I'm torn between telling the officer about the letter that will prove Danny's innocence even if it does land Perry in it, and finding Perry himself before he does something stupid. I have to make an instant decision. It isn't difficult. Danny isn't in danger down in the cells: Perry might be slitting his wrists right now, this minute.

'We must find him, Frankie.' But Frankie's looking behind me.

Stella stands in the doorway.

The animosity between the two women is palpable.

'Where's Perry?' the girl asks.

Frankie stands up, eyes glittering, a cobra rising from a snake-charmer's basket. 'He's not here,' she says. 'And if he were, you're the last person I'd let anywhere near him. Thanks to you, his life is well and truly buggered.'

'We love each other. There's nothing you can do about it.'

Stella's no longer bothering to hide her feelings. The strength of her will, her determination to take what she wants shines out of her, meeting full on, without flinching, the full force of Frankie's rampant hostility. They're very well matched, these two.

'He doesn't love you.' Frankie brandishes April's letter like a weapon. 'In fact, madam, not only does he not love you, he actually hates you. Detests you. Despises you. You disgust him, just like you disgust me. Last night he tried to kill you. He says so right here in this letter. I wish he'd succeeded. You're the one who should be dead, not Julie Whatsername. You don't deserve to live. You're scum. It's a pity you were ever born.'

A great stillness has enveloped Stella. Her face is milk-pale and impenetrable. 'Where is he?'

'Fuck knows.' Frankie's voice is rising. 'Thanks to you, he's about to do something stupid – if he hasn't already done it.'

'Stupid?'

'He's probably slitting his throat right this minute because he can't live with what you drove him to do.'

Soundlessly, Stella runs from the room.

Frankie follows her out. 'Disgusting depraved slut!' she raves, her voice bouncing off the walls of Berkeley Court. Then she comes back into the room and throws herself down onto Perry's couch. Her fury spurts out of her like pus from a lanced boil. But as she calms down, I see that the rage is giving way to something else: calculation. She's scrutinising me closely, as if trying to predict my reaction to what she is about to say.

'Mind you, even if Perry does go to the police, they might not believe him.'

'What do you mean?'

'They might think he's confessing to protect his godson.'

Excuse me? 'What?'

'Perry's very fond of Danny.'

'Yes—'

'He'd do anything for him. Now Rob's a gonner he thinks of himself as the nearest thing Danny has to a dad.'

'But that doesn't mean—'

'Even as a child he suffered from a ridiculously inflated sense of loyalty.'

Is she saying what I think she's saying? Unbelievable.

'Are you suggesting that Perry's innocent? That he's

written this letter in order to divert suspicion onto himself instead of Danny?'

'You took the words right out of my mouth. I'm glad you agree. He's very unselfish, my Perry, but I can't stand by and let him wreck his life, Rosa. Not even for poor Danny.'

'You cannot be serious.'

Frankie's ignoring me now. 'I'll speak to the police. I'll vouch for what a strain he's been under lately, moving back to the UK and trying to hold everything together with very little help from that Aussie madam. They'll see that the letter's a misguided attempt to save his godson by a man on the edge of a breakdown.'

'Frankie—'

'We needn't show them the letter at all. What's the point? Danny'll be all right. They'll realise that it was a silly accident. They won't do him for murder. It'll be manslaughter – a couple of years, that's all. He's young, Rosa. And strong. Well able to survive a short stretch inside. And he'll fit into prison much better than our Perry.'

'What do you mean?'

'Well, there's a lot like him in there, isn't there?'

'Like what?'

'You know.'

'No, I don't.'

'Not quite English.'

'You mean black?'

She finally realises how completely she's blown it. 'Come on, Rosa. I didn't— There's no need to be such a touchy bugger.'

I take a few deep breaths to steady myself. Then I pick up the letter.

'Frankie, I'm going to pretend I didn't hear any of that. I'm taking this to April, and afterwards I'm going to try and find Perry before he does something stupid.'

Then it comes out: Frankie's bottom line. 'A scandal like this could ruin my career.'

'I'm not listening.' I run all the way to Chesterton Road, trying to put as much distance as I can between me and the Fabulous Frankie.

The bastard was in the chapel, praying. But Hugo didn't care. He went in, all guns blazing.

'The Miller Foundation has turned us down, so my plans for the library will have to be put on indefinite hold. I shan't forget this, Tipton.'

The chaplain stood up and turned slowly towards him, a strange expression on his face. 'So, God did have a plan, after all. Lucas told me I should have more faith in Him.'

'What are you talking about?'

'Believe it or not, Master, in spite of our differences, I'm very sorry. I know how disappointed you must be. It's a harsh thing to bear when all one's dreams go up in smoke.'

'Don't give me that guff. I haven't yet worked out exactly how you're responsible for Julie Watkins's death, but I do know it was you behind all the other things that have happened over the last week.'

Tipton frowned. 'What do you mean?'

'You'd stop at nothing to scupper my plans.'

When Tipton spoke again, his voice was cold. 'Are you accusing me of murdering that girl?'

'If the cap fits. After all, it's not the first time somebody connected to your organisation has met a violent death. I've done my research. Over the past three years, at least two members of R&R have committed suicide, and that's not counting poor Simon Smith last Sunday.'

Tipton regarded him. Hugo had rarely seen a face so bleak. 'If you *had* done your research, you'd know that Emma Blake had an inoperable brain tumour and sadly chose the quick way out, and that Henry Standing had a history of suicide attempts going back several years. His time working with us at R&R had been the longest he'd ever been free of the anguish that plagued him. And as for Simon Smith, if you'd bothered to visit or even phoned the hospital you'd have discovered that he regained consciousness yesterday and has confessed to taking a tab of acid on Sunday evening and being convinced that if he launched himself from his window, he'd be able to fly.'

Hugo felt the situation slipping from his grasp. 'Well, I only have your word for that. The fact is that, ever since the new library became a reality, which it indubitably had with the arrival of the Americans, everything has gone wrong. And I know that you're up to your neck in it.'

'This is nothing more than a witch-hunt. You're obsessed, and it's beginning to show. Maybe the Americans didn't relish trusting their dollars to someone who's showing such clear signs of mental instability.'

'You killed my animals. And what about the other things – the fountain, and the flies, and my contaminated food? Don't try to say you're not responsible.'

A faint smile crossed Tipton's weary face. 'You forgot the power failure last night at the Ball. And the hailstorm.'

'What?' Hugo felt the joy of vindication rising inside him. 'Finally, an admission of guilt.'

'I suggest you consult the Old Testament. Exodus Chapter Seven. God punishes the Pharaoh for not allowing Moses and the Children of Israel to leave Egypt.'

Hugo's childhood had been mired in religious clap-trap. One reason he had no truck with it now. He dimly remembered the story. Rivers of blood and boils and flies. Locusts and dead animals . . . *dead animals*.

'You sick fuck!' he cried. 'You killed Dawkins as part of some re-enactment of the plagues of Egypt?'

Tipton stood, head bowed.

'Answer me, for fuck's sake!'

Finally the man looked up. His dark eyes burned. 'God moves in a mysterious way.'

Hugo left before he did something irrevocable.

THIRTY-SEVEN

His mouth was dry. So dry that he had to fight against the notion that his throat had closed and was stopping the air from reaching his lungs. He'd succeeded in remaining calm whilst Mortimer railed, but now he felt that if someone touched him he'd disintegrate into dust.

He considered himself to be a man of action. He'd been a fisher of men from the beginning, bringing many souls back to God. Where he'd found poverty and despair he'd acted to bring succour – he'd fought against monumental indifference and bureaucracy to set up R&R. But now he felt incapable of even moving, let alone making any decisions. He'd thought that prayer might help, but God was having the day off. He had no answers.

You're on your own, Dominic.

It was all so confusing. So muddling.

No, it wasn't. He was complicating something which was ridiculously simple. *He knew what he had to do. He just didn't want to do it.*

Hardly able to put one foot in front of the other, he left

the chapel and cycled into town. When he arrived at R&F Billy Wizz and a few of the regulars were sitting on th pavement outside the door. They pounced on him with al the aggrieved fury of those, usually regarded as permanentl in the wrong, who, for once in their lives, were right.

'You said "Our door is never closed". That's what yo said. You said there'd always be a place for us. That's wha you said. And what happens? We come back from a har day's beggin' and the fuckin' door's locked.'

'I'm sorry.' He took out his keys and opened up. Th men shambled in behind him.

'Fuck me, the bloody urn ain't even on,' said Billy indig nantly. 'What are we supposed to do for tea then?'

'Try making it yourself.' The words were out before h could stop them. Billy flinched as if he'd been struck Dominic was filled with remorse. 'Sorry, Bill. Bit of a ba day. I'm sure one of the volunteers will be here soon, bu in the meantime, if you could hold the fort – get som water on the boil, I'd be most grateful.' And then, unabl to contain himself any more, he stumbled up the stairs.

'Lucas?' There was no reply and his nephew's door wa shut. Then he heard something inside.

He opened the door. The room was in semi-darkness He could just make out a figure on the bed, curled in foetal position.

'Lucas?' He opened the curtains.

Flora's face was purple and swollen. She held up a han to shield herself from him, revealing a deep slash acros the back. Her jeans were round her ankles, exposing th lower part of her bloody and bruised body. He went to cove her up, but she shrank away from him, terrified.

'Everything all right?' Billy called up the stairs.

He forced himself to respond. 'Look in the cupboard over the sink, Billy – there should be a big tin of biscuits.'

'Right you are, squire.'

Flora was trembling so much that her teeth chattered. He covered her with the sheet and then retreated from the bed and sat down in a chair, as far away from her as he could. 'I'm not going to hurt you, Flora. I'll just sit over here in this chair and when you're ready you can tell me what happened.'

For five or ten minutes it was as if she hadn't heard. Then, just as he was beginning to despair, she sat up, clutching the sheet round herself and retreated to the corner of the bed where it met the wall.

'He's the one.' Her voice was scratchy, barely there at all.

'Who?' As if he didn't know.

'He's the rapist.' She turned her hand over and examined the cuts. 'It's not a Z. It's a bolt of lightning. For Lux. Light. The brightest – and the best, he says.'

Brightest and best of the sons of the morning, Dawn on our darkness and lend us Thine aid.

The words of the carol flooded his mind as an image of his beautiful boy rose up in front of him. His eyes burned in their sockets. He wanted to cry, but no tears came. His body felt as arid and empty as a husk of corn in the desert.

How could Lucas have done this to Flora? How could he have done it to anyone?

'It was all my own fault.'

The desolation in her voice was more than he could bear. 'Of course it wasn't.'

'I told him about Stella and Dr Grimshaw.'

'Told him what?'

'I said that Stella loved Dr Grimshaw. I thought that if he knew she was in love with someone else, he'd stop wanting her and want me instead.' She shivered. 'But then he went mad.'

He felt he'd rather cut out his tongue than ask the final question, but he couldn't evade the truth any more. 'Did he say anything about Julie?'

Flora's voice was scarcely a whisper. 'Yes. He called her a whore . . . He said he'd fixed her.'

A shaft of sunlight suddenly illuminated the room. Dominic looked at the million motes of dust swirling around in it, and wished he were one of them.

'I'm going to call the police now, Flora,' he said.

He wasn't entirely sure that she'd heard him. She'd retreated back into her own world. He made the call and then went downstairs.

'Cuppa?' asked Billy Wizz proudly, standing alongside the steaming urn and doling out tea.

'The police are about to descend,' Dominic said. 'Don't worry – nothing to do with you lot. Point them in the direction of Lucas's room, would you, there's a good chap.'

She hadn't been imagining it. She wasn't just a jealous wife who suspected infidelity lurking around every marital corner. In the middle of coping with the nightmare vision of Perry killing Julie Watkins, one microscopic part of her was conscious of a strange relief. She had been justifiably upset. Her instincts were sound. Perry *had* been cheating on her. The fact that he seemed not to have slept with

438

Stella was irrelevant. He'd wanted to. He'd thought about the bitch, met her, talked intimately to her, let her trespass into April's territory.

'I was right all along,' she said to Rosa, clutching Perry's letter.

'Sod that. We've got to find him. Have you tried his mobile?' Frankie had arrived, hot on Rosa's heels, and was prowling around like a caged beast.

'It's switched off.'

'He never switches it off except when he's lecturing,' April said dreamily.

'What's the frigging matter with her?' April heard Frankie mutter to Rosa. 'Why's she gone all doolally on us? We need her focused.'

'Frankie's right, April. You have to help us find him. You know what he's like. He won't let Danny take the blame for something he's done. He's had plenty of time to go to the police, and since it appears he hasn't, then I'm really scared he might have done something stupid.'

April registered the urgency in Rosa's voice, but it seemed to be coming from far away, and nothing to do with her. Funny how people talked in euphemisms. Why couldn't they come straight out with it, and say that they thought Perry might have killed himself?

He said he still loved her. He said that was why he'd killed Julie. Because he thought that she was Stella. He wanted to get rid of Stella so that she wouldn't come between them any more.

'Mummy, can we have lollies from the freezer?'

April looked at the two hopeful little faces turned up to her. Perry's eyes duplicated in miniature.

439

'OK, possum. Just one each, though.'

'And then can we play on the street like Shane?'

'No. The road's far too busy.'

The little faces pouted in disappointment. She didn't want them to be disappointed. Or hurt. Ever. She broke one of her cardinal rules. 'You can play in the front garden if you like, just this once. But don't go out of the gate – promise?'

'The front garden? Wow!' Hector's eyes shone.

Cassandra hugged her tight. 'I love you, Mummy.' Then she and Hector rushed into the kitchen where they could be heard scrabbling around in the freezer.

So dear. So precious.

Like Perry.

Suddenly the invisible protective shield surrounding her wasn't there any more. The world rushed in and with it unbearable panic. Rosa was right. If Perry hadn't given himself up, then where was he?

'Maybe we should tell the police. Get them to help find him,' said Rosa.

'No!' April found she was shouting. 'No,' she said, trying to regain control over herself. 'I have to speak to him first. Please. It's a small town. I know where he hangs out. I'll find him. Come on, let's go.'

'What about the kids?'

'I'll ask Karen next door to mind them.'

Within minutes they were running across the footbridge onto Jesus Green.

'No sense in taking the car,' she'd said. 'Nowhere to park.'

As they ran down Park Street, Rosa said, 'Pubs first.'

Frankie was already out of breath. 'He's hardly going to top himself in a frigging boozer,' she wheezed.

'Maybe not, but apart from having the biggest conscience in the universe, he's also the biggest coward. If he wants to end it all, he'll need a few pints inside him.'

So they called at the Maypole and the Baron of Beef, back up to the Pickerel and all the way over to the Eagle and many more. A manic tune repeated incessantly in April's brain. *Up and Down the City Road, in and out the Eagle.*

But Perry was nowhere to be found. No one had seen him. No one at all.

Pop goes Perry.

He was standing on Clare Bridge gazing at King's Chapel as if it held all the answers. It was she who had the answers. But he wouldn't listen.

'Go away, Stella.'

'But I love you.'

'You don't know the meaning of the word. Love is April and my children. You were a temporary craziness, but now I'm sane again and I have to deal with the fallout.'

'It's not craziness, you know it's not. Can you honestly tell me that you feel nothing for me?'

The look he gave her was of such dislike that for the first time a scintilla of doubt clouded her certainty.

'It's not *nothing* that I'm feeling.'

'I know—'

'It's pure, unadulterated loathing. I look at your exquisite bloody face and I loathe you for what you've made me do.'

'You don't understand—'

'No, *you* don't understand. I'll spell it out one last time. I don't want anything more to do with you.'

'There are so many things I want to tell you—'

'There's nothing you could say that I'd ever want to hear. Stop pestering. Leave me in peace.'

'Perry, look at me. *Look*. Don't you feel the bond between us?'

'I look at you and I feel sick. I look at you and I want to vomit.'

The vitriol hit her with such force that it was as if he had in reality spewed up all over her. She could smell his hatred. It covered her, dripping off in great gobbets, making her feel contaminated, spoiled.

'Perry?' she said. But he wasn't listening. He was leaning over the parapet looking down into the river. Desolation swept her up, propelling her back down onto the path along the Backs. She looked round at him one last time. 'Perry?'

Then there was a light touch on her back and she found herself wrapped in the arms of an angel.

'*And there appeared a great wonder in heaven, a woman clothed with the sun and the moon under her feet, and upon her head a crown of twelve stars.*'

The desolation melted away. 'Hello, Lucas.'

'Stella, the morning and the evening star,' he said. 'And all the other stars, too. Come with me, Stella.'

THIRTY-EIGHT

It's Frankie who sees him first. Having had no luck in any of the pubs, we're checking the big hotels in case he's booked a room in which to give himself the privacy to overdose or slash his wrists or do whatever dire thing he's planning in order to shuffle off his mortal coil.

We've drawn yet another blank at the University Arms and have trailed disconsolately onto Parker's Piece when Frankie starts bellowing and running. There he is, heading towards the police station on the other side of the green.

'Perry!' Frankie may have been the one to spot him, but it's April who's now off like a jet-propelled rocket. When she reaches him, she flings herself into his arms and the two of them stand locked in a fierce embrace.

'I'm sorry. I'm so sorry,' he's saying as Frankie and I draw level. 'I love you, April. I'm so sorry I've fucked everything up. I didn't mean any of it.'

'I know. I know. It'll be OK. I don't care. I love you. We'll get through this somehow. Just so long as you're alive.

When I thought you'd—' Her voice cracks and she can't go on.

'Thought I'd what?' His eyes widen and he pulls away. He looks from April to me and Frankie. 'You thought I was . . . Oh dear God, no. I've done enough damage to you and the kids. I couldn't do that, too. I just needed some time to sort things out in my head before turning myself in.'

'Sort out what things?'

'Sort out what I'm going to say to Danny, who's locked up like a criminal for something I've done, when he should be with his family, grieving for Julie . . . Sort out why I was running after a girl half my age, when I've already got the best and most beautiful wife in the world.'

April's having trouble speaking. 'And what conclusion have you come to?'

'It's still a complete mystery to me. I've been supervising the bloody girl all term, and never felt a twinge of anything, except chronic impatience at her laziness and stupidity – until this week. I know it sounds like a pathetic excuse, but it's as if, that night she came to dinner, she cast a spell on me or drugged me. Did something that was entirely beyond my conscious control.'

The relief of finding him unharmed makes me brutal. 'Oh, please! Entirely beyond your control? At least take some responsibility. You've done the classic middle-aged man thing – got bored with the status quo and experimented with a younger model. Don't pretend it was black magic.'

'You think I'm making excuses, Rosaleen? I don't blame you. But believe me, that's the way it felt. Anyway, it's over now. I have absolutely no feelings left for Stella Grainger.'

April so wants to believe him. 'But what if it all flares up again, next time you see her?'

'It won't.'

'How do you know?'

'When I sit in my prison cell it won't be her I'm thinking about. It'll be you and the kids. And actually, I *have* seen her, no more than half an hour ago. And I knew straight away that whatever it was, it's categorically gone. For good.'

'You've seen her?'

'She caught up with me earlier. I couldn't even bear to look at her. She made me feel sick. I told her to get lost.'

'Really?'

'Really.'

Perry's words leave a bad taste in my mouth. Whatever game Stella was playing, he's been equally complicit. To demonise her is to deny his own involvement. He's the responsible adult, in a position of trust. She's only nineteen. His student, for God's sake.

At that moment April's phone rings. 'Karen?' Then her face loses all colour. 'We're on our way.' She rings off, and stares at the handset.

'What's happened?'

April looks at Perry. 'It's the kids.' She starts running.

'Are they hurt?'

'They've gone.'

'Gone?' He starts to run after her, then stops.

'Come on.' April's already some distance away.

I follow his agonised gaze: the police station. 'Danny's in there. I have to get him out.'

April is distraught. 'Our children have disappeared,' she shouts back to him. 'I can't do this alone, Perry.'

'You aren't alone. You're with Rosa and Frankie.'

'I need *you*.'

He looks at me.

There's no choice. 'Danny can wait a bit longer,' I say. 'Let's go.'

We run to the cab rank near the bus station, and within seconds we're speeding towards Chesterton Road.

Hector was jubilant. Their plan had worked. Not only had they successfully bullied Karen into letting them play in the front garden, they'd also got her out of the way by begging for some of her mum's homemade biscuits.

'Please please please,' they whined in a tone that they knew from experience usually yielded excellent results. 'Go to your house and get them. Your mummy won't mind. She said we could have some yesterday.'

Karen had given in, as they knew she would. 'You'd best come with me, though,' she'd said. 'I can't leave you out here on your own.'

But they'd set up such a wail at their game being interrupted that she'd finally said, 'I'll only be a minute. Don't you dare leave the garden.'

'No, Karen.'

Once she was out of sight, they put their plan into operation. Earlier in the summer, Mummy had taken them to the Open Air Swimming Pool on Jesus Green. It reminded them of home, of splashing about in the Sydney sunshine, and they'd loved it with a passion. But she'd refused to take them again. She said it was too cold, and too deep for small children who hadn't been swimming for all that long. They thought she was unbelievably mean and vowed that one day they'd nick off by themselves. This afternoon was the perfect opportunity. They knew you had to pay to get in, so they'd taken money from their moneyboxes, and hidden it, with their swimming stuff, under a bush. As soon as Karen disappeared, they grabbed their things, then Hector gave Cassie a piggy back so she could reach the latch on the tall gate, and within seconds they were negotiating the traffic on Chesterton Road. There was lots of it, and it was very fast. Mummy had taught them to look left, right and left again and cross when the road was clear. It was the first time they'd performed this manoeuvre on their own, and it took ages, but eventually there was a gap in the traffic and they skipped across. Giddy with exhilaration, they ran squealing onto the footbridge.

'Suffer the little children to come unto me!'

A giant was blocking their way. He had long tangled hair, and a beard with bits of yukky stuff in it, and although it was boiling hot he was wearing a thick coat tied in the middle with some old string. On his head was a woolly hat full of holes. He was very dirty. Dirtier than any grown-up Hector had ever seen, and in one of his dirty hands he held a long stick. Tied to the stick was a piece of cardboard. There were words on the cardboard, but since Hector couldn't read he didn't know what they were. Not very nice, he suspected. Probably bad swearing words that Mummy wouldn't like.

The other thing about the giant was that he smelled. Like poo and wee and the inside of their kitchen bin.

'Come on, Heccie.' Cassandra tried to move past, but the giant put his free hand on her head.

'Where do you two think you're going?'

'Mind your own bloody business.'

Hector was full of admiration. Cassie was littler than him, but she sounded so brave, even if he could feel her arm trembling against him.

Then he jumped sky high as the giant started shouting. 'Blasphemer!' he roared. 'Seed of Satan!'

Hector wanted to run, but the giant still had hold of Cassie. She burst into frightened sobs. Hector kicked the giant's leg as hard as he could. 'Leave my sister alone!'

'Hey, hey, wassup, Preacher Man?'

It was a new voice. Hector turned round. Someone else was on the bridge. Hector vaguely recognised him. He had a very nice smile and he didn't seem at all scared of the roaring giant.

'Be cool, man,' he was saying. 'Be cool.' Then he stroked the giant like he was a great big doggy until he calmed down. Just watching him made Hector feel calmer too.

'So what gives?'

'Trying to send them home,' mumbled the giant.

'Quite right, too.' Their rescuer turned to Cassie. 'Isn't your daddy Dr Grimshaw?'

Cassie nodded, suddenly shy.

'Does he know you two are wandering around out here without any grown-ups?'

She shook her head.

She looked really guilty, thought Hector. He sprang to her rescue. 'Mummy asked us to go to the shops.' He felt proud of his quick thinking.

'The paint shop. We're going to the paint shop. For some pink paint.' Cassie caught on to what he was doing.

Brilliant! That would fool anyone.

448

The nice man crouched down beside them. 'Oh dear,' he said softly. 'I think that's a great big fat porky. You know what a porky is?'

Cassie went bright red and Hector felt his own cheeks burn. 'A lie,' he whispered.

The nice man wasn't smiling any more. 'That's right. A lie.'

'Behold your sins will find you out.' The giant bent down, his dirty purple face now inches away from Hector. He was frowning in a really scary way.

'You look knackered, Preacher Man. Why don't you go back to R&R for a cuppa,' the nice man said. 'I'll see these two get safely home.'

The giant scowled at Hector and Cassie. 'God is watching you,' he said. 'He sees everything you do. He sees all your sins. And the wages of sin is death.' Then he shuffled over the footbridge onto Jesus Green.

'I'll take you home now,' said the nice man.

'We're not allowed to go with strangers,' Hector said firmly.

'I'm not a stranger. My uncle's a friend of your daddy. His name is Dom. I'm Lucas.'

Hector thought about it. He remembered now – he *had* seen the man before. It was one day when he'd gone to college with Daddy. The man had been talking to the Reverend Tipton.

'Have a sweetie,' the man said, producing a bag from his pocket.

They weren't supposed to take sweeties from strangers, but he was Lucas – he wasn't a stranger. 'Thanks,' said Hector, picking the biggest sweet in the bag.

'Mummy and Daddy are out,' said Cassie.

Hector had an idea. Maybe their plan wasn't ruined after all. 'We badly need to go swimming. Can you take us?'

Lucas thought about it. Then he said, 'We'd have to get your daddy's permission, but I'm sure he'll say yes. What do you say, kids? Should we go up to college and see if he's there? He might even be with my Uncle Dom. Should we go and see?'

Daddy was a soft touch, not like Mummy. He might well say yes. Hector looked at Cassie, who nodded. 'All right,' he said.

Lucas smiled his nice smile. 'Have another sweetie,' he said.

After Flora was taken off to hospital, Dominic had given a statement to the police about Lucas.

Although, when it came down to it, there wasn't much to tell. Lucas's life before last Christmas was an empty page in a closed book as far as he was concerned.

How could he have been so incurious? How could Lucas have done such dreadful things without him having the faintest notion that something was so badly wrong?

When, eventually, he returned to Billings, he wondered if the boy would be waiting for him. And what he'd do if that were the case. Would he have the strength to turn him over to the police?

But his room was empty – too empty, as if the life had been sucked out of it, leaving a two-dimensional shell where even the furniture and objects lacked any kind of substance.

He took out the correspondence he'd kept over the years concerning Lucas's financial affairs. He was still in charge of the boy's money, even though his nephew was over eighteen because it was held in trust until he was twenty-five. Dominic looked up the last payment he'd made before Lucas came back to him. It was to a bank in Phuket. He made a phone call to a Christian Mission in Thailand with whom he'd once had dealings. They put him on to someone else, who put him on to someone else, and within a remarkably short space of time, he knew that Lucas was wanted by the Thai police.

For rape.

Or rather, rapes. There had been several.

So that was why the boy had come to him. What a brilliant plan – to hide away with his uncle, the highly respectable Chaplain of a Cambridge college. He riffled through the rest of the bank correspondence – Indonesia, China, Africa, Mexico – the list of places was extensive. What would he find if he investigated further? He pushed the file away. He couldn't face it.

For the first time in years he'd let his guard down, let someone get close to him. What a gullible fool he'd been.

Then he heard the sound of his door opening.

Only one other person had a key.

For a long time they stared at each other. Then Lucas spoke. 'You know, don't you?'

Dominic could hardly form the words. 'You used me.'

'No.'

'It was all lies.'

'No.'

'I was just your cover story.'

'Unc, let me explain.'

'I don't want to hear. Don't humiliate us both with your deceit.'

'Please listen.'

'I shall never listen to you ever again.'

'I love you, Unc. You mean more to me than any other person on this rotten planet.'

'Stop!'

'It's true I came here to hide away, but . . .'

In spite of himself, Dominic wanted to hear what came after that fateful little word. 'You took me for a fool.'

'It wasn't like that, I swear. At first, OK, you were just someone to hide behind. Good camouflage. But then I started to like it here. I got genuinely attached to all the old boys at the refuge. I'd wake up in the morning looking forward to the stuff I had to do, and looking forward even more to working with you. For the first time since Dad died I felt I had a place where I belonged. With someone who was bothered about me. Someone who respected me, listened to my ideas, talked about future plans that included me. I had a life. And I realised after a while that I'd genuinely started to care about you, that I really wanted to help you, to please you, to be the person you believed me to be. It was like my dad had come back to me. You're so similar to him, you know. It's uncanny sometimes. You look like him, you have the same voice . . . You mean the world to me, Uncle Dom, I swear on his life. And I'm so sorry for hurting you.'

'You completely betrayed my trust. How can I believe anything you say?'

Lucas shook his head, helplessly. 'I don't know.'

For several minutes neither of them spoke.

Then the truth in all its ugliness hit Dominic: it was *he* who had betrayed Lucas, not the other way round. He was the one who'd let an eighteen-year-old boy, still grieving for his beloved father, go off round the world all by himself. How caring was that? If he'd insisted on keeping Lucas here, maybe none of this would have happened. Good old St Dominic – so keen on rescuing every down-and-out in Cambridge that he'd grossly neglected his primary duty of love and care to his dead brother's child.

His shame was limitless.

Lucas finally broke the silence. 'All that plagues stuff – I did that.'

'Yes. I rather thought that was the case.'

'I did it for you.'

Dominic struggled to control the contradictory emotions swimming around in his head. 'Hugo Mortimer nearly died.'

'I thought he'd just develop a rash or something.'

'And his pets?'

'I didn't even know he had any cats. And I only put a tiny sprinkling of poison on the meat. I thought it would just give Dawkins the runs. Nothing more.'

'Those poor creatures died in agony.'

Lucas broke in, eyes blazing. '*I* was in agony! I didn't know what to do for the best. Mortimer was making you ill. You weren't eating or sleeping properly. You'd changed from the cheerful, dynamic person I first knew, to a man at the end of his rope. I couldn't bear it. I watched you getting more and more stressed and it reminded me of Dad before he died. I hated it. I was desperate to stop Mortimer, but I didn't know how. Then one night I was leafing through the Bible, and it suddenly occurred to me that a dose of the Biblical plagues might be just the thing – make him think that the God he claims doesn't exist was punishing him for his stupid plans. Do you see?'

Dominic sighed. 'Yes, I see. I've seen all along . . . I just haven't admitted it. In my own way I completely colluded with you. That's why I feel so responsible.'

'No way, Unc. It was no way your fault.'

'I'm not so sure. At first it made me laugh. The fountain, the flies – all harmless melodrama. The Hand of God courtesy of Cecil B. de Mille . . . wonderful poetic justice But then I let it continue, didn't I? Even when I knew it was getting out of hand. When I heard about Mortimer going into anaphylactic shock, I convinced myself that it was a weird coincidence – a genuine mistake on the part of the kitchen staff and nothing to do with the earlier incidents. Then his animals were killed. My cue to step in. But no. I still pretended ignorance, even to myself.'

'I just wanted to help, Unc.'

Dominic looked into his nephew's eyes and saw that he was speaking the truth. And he remembered the old adage, *Hate the sin. Love the sinner.* Whatever Lucas had done, he still loved the boy. All he wanted to do was to protect him. From the world and, most of all, from himself. But in order to do that, he had to find out about the rest of it. He had to ask all the other unpalatable questions.

There was another one: *For evil to flourish, it needs good men to say nothing.* He couldn't let that happen. Even if the evil was to be found deep in his boy.

And Lucas had only told half the story.

'Do you forgive me, Unc?'

'It's not me who needs your penitence.'

'I won't apologise to *him.*'

Dominic sighed. 'I'm not talking about Mortimer.'

'What do you mean?'

'I accept that you set out to create chaos at the college in a misguided attempt to help me. But I don't understand . . . I *can't* understand the rest.'

'The rest?'

'All those poor girls.'

Lucas's face had been vividly alive in his efforts to explain himself. But now, in an instant, the shutters came down.

Dominic thought he might drown in misery. 'Julie Watkins . . . ?'

The silence in the room was absolute.

Then Lucas shrugged. 'They've arrested Danny Thorn for Julie's murder.'

Dominic took a deep breath. 'But we both know they've got the wrong man, don't we?'

It was the scratch that had alerted him – deep and red across the boy's torso. Like the wound in Christ's torso in the *Deposition* painting. He'd tried to forget it, but once seen, it couldn't be unseen. He cursed the ability of the human brain to make such instantaneous connections that an idea of monstrous ugliness was there, fully formed before he could push it away.

'Someone attacked you last night. Someone with long nails. A girl. Why would any girl do that? Unless you'd tried to harm her . . . The gash on your stomach. I saw it this morning when you were asleep on the couch. It's no ordinary scratch and . . .' He couldn't go on.

'And what?'

'God help me – it made me think about the Cambridge rapist.'

'The rapist?'

'I remembered reading in the paper that one of the victims said the man was muttering religious stuff.'

'What's that to do with me?'

'The attacks started just after Christmas.'

'So?'

'Round about the time you arrived.'

'Oh, man . . .'

'When I finally allowed myself to acknowledge that it was you who'd been responsible for the Biblical plagues . . .'

'Yes?'

'That forced me to contemplate the fact that maybe there was something much worse going on with you.'

'That's quite a leap, Unc. There are loads of people in this town who're into religion. Preacher Man, for instance. He knows half the Bible off by heart.'

'Yes, he does. I heard you only the other week at the refuge, having a Biblical quotation marathon with him. You gave him a good run for his money, Lucas. Billy Wizz ran a book on who'd capitulate first. As I recall, it was Preacher Man.'

Lucas's blue eyes burned into his. 'So all roads led to Lucas, did they, Unc? You thought the unthinkable and decided it made sense. You obviously didn't have much faith in me.'

'Oh Lucas. I so badly wanted to be wrong.'

'How do you know you aren't?'

'I stood there, this morning, looking down at you and telling myself that I must be insane to even contemplate such a terrible thing. But then I saw your shirt. It was lying on the floor. I saw blood on it. When I realised that I couldn't rest until it was destroyed, it told me more clearly

han rational thought ever could, what I truly believed. I
ook it to the boiler room and burned it. Afterwards I went
o R&R, found you a fresh one. Then I made a pact with
myself: if you seemed at all puzzled about me replacing
it for no apparent reason, it would be a sign that I was
wrong.'

'*Cheers, Unc.* That's what I said. *Cheers, Unc.* I remember.'

'As though it were the most normal thing in the world
for me to traipse halfway across Cambridge at dawn to fetch
you clean clothes.'

Lucas's smile was heartbreaking. 'But you love me, Unc.
You'd do anything for me. Like I'd do anything for you.'

'Later that morning,' continued Dominic bleakly, 'I went
to the public library and looked up all the recent back
issues of the *Cambridge Evening News*. I was hoping against
hope that I'd imagined the quote about the rapist and religion, but there it was, in black and white. And then I knew
I was right. And I knew that it was up to me to put a stop
to it all. I went to R&R to find you . . . and found poor
Flora instead.'

'Flora's a fool,' muttered Lucas. 'She should learn to keep
her big mouth shut.'

'And Julie? Was she a fool too?'

Lucas glared at him, intently, as if making up his mind
about something. When he finally spoke, Dominic's blood
ran cold. 'She was the one that got away. I'd spotted her
last Sunday night on Jesus Green, mincing along in her
fuck-me shoes and her tight jeans, with her tits hanging
out. And I knew she needed punishing. But I was interrupted. Then I met her on the first night of *Othello* and
she seemed familiar, but it had been dark on the Green

and I hadn't seen her face, so I wasn't sure. But last night we danced together and I recognised her smell. I have a very strong sense of smell, did you know that, Unc? Anyway, I knew then that she was the one that got away, and no slut gets away from Lux the Light . . . So I fixed the generator and in the confusion I took her to the Fellows' Garden.'

It was the matter-of-fact tone that filled Dominic with horror. No indication, now, that the boy felt he'd done anything wrong.

'You killed her?'

'She tried to phone her mum . . . I had to stop her.'

As if he'd broken a glass, ripped a sleeve on a nail or something equally trivial.

Dominic forced himself to continue. 'And the other girls? Why?'

'To teach them a lesson. They all deserved it – every one of them.'

'But what had they done?'

'What had they *done*?' Lucas was incredulous. 'Haven't you seen them around, Unc? They're all over the place, primping and preening, displaying their bare flesh. Tempting men into sin.'

'No one deserves to be raped, however they choose to dress.'

'But they have to understand the consequences of their actions. They can't be allowed to get away with it. They have to be punished.'

'It's not for you or me to pass sentence on them. We leave that to God, Whose mercy and compassion is infinite.' He knew as he spoke that he might as well have saved his breath, for he could see the light of the fanatic, bright with unreason, burning in his nephew's eyes.

'Don't you read your Bible, Unc? God's with me on this. "*Behold, I am against thee,*" saith the Lord of hosts; "*and I will discover thy skirts upon thy face, and I will shew the nations thy nakedness, and the kingdoms thy shame. And I will cast abominable filth upon thee and make thee vile.*" Nahum, three.'

'But—'

'"*Thou hast played the harlot with many lovers, yet return again to me,*" saith the Lord. "*I find more bitter than death the woman who is a snare, whose heart is a trap and whose hands are chains.*" Isaiah, forty-nine.'

'Lucas—'

'"*Woe to the women who sew magic charms on all their wrists and make veils of various lengths to ensnare people. I will tear off your veils and save my people from your hands and they will no longer fall prey to your power. Then you will know that I am the Lord.*" Ezekiel, thirteen.'

'Stop!'

'"*Come down and sit in the dust, O virgin daughter of Babylon, sit on the ground; there is no throne: for thou shalt no more be called tender and delicate. Thy nakedness shall be uncovered, yea thy shame shall be seen; I will take vengeance and I will not meet thee as a man.*"'

'Be quiet! This is nothing to do with what we believe as Christians. This is selective Old Testament ranting. It's no justification for what you did.'

'"*Come and I will show you the punishment of the great prostitute who sits on many waters.*" Revelations, seventeen. Nothing Old Testament about that.' Lucas's cheeks were flushed and he repeatedly ran his fingers through his blond hair. '"*With her, the kings of the earth committed adultery and the inhabitants of the earth were intoxicated with the wine of her adulteries—*"'

'Hush,' said Dominic. 'Hush now. Enough.' He seized his nephew, took him in his arms and refused to let him go. As Lucas ceased struggling, he started rocking him as if he were a baby. Gradually the manic flow of words slowed to a trickle and finally he felt the boy shudder and be still. After a moment he said, 'All this primitive hellfire stuff, it's an act, isn't it? Part of your plan to convince me you're someone you're not?'

Lucas was silent.

'What I don't understand, though, is that if you're only pretending to be religious, how come you know all these quotations in the first place? Your father wasn't a Christian – it was one of the things that caused us to drift apart – one of the reasons why he didn't bring you to visit when you were a boy. He couldn't forgive me for wasting my life on what he considered to be silly superstition. So I can't imagine that he had anything to do with your extensive knowledge of the Bible.'

When he finally spoke, the boy's voice was harsh. 'A hundred hotel bedrooms scattered across the globe. And the Gideon Bible in the drawer of every bedside table. Hours spent waiting for Dad to come back from work . . . or from visiting his whores.'

'Nicholas visited prostitutes?'

'It was for my sake. He didn't want to replace my mum with a proper girlfriend.'

'Oh, Lucas . . .'

'I used to worry that one day he'd do what Mum did and not come back at all.'

'My poor boy.'

'I found lots of passages in the Bible that seemed written just for me and so I used to learn them off by heart and recite them out loud to take my mind off things while I waited for Dad.' He looked at Dominic. 'Through His Holy Bible God spoke to me daily in those bedrooms. He was my friend. My only friend. He still is. My belief is real. The Bible says it all. I don't need any parson or priest to teach me His word. God tells me very clearly what I have to do.'

'And what's that?'

'He says I have to stop them. Stop all the harlots.'

'Harlots?'

'Yes, harlots. Like my mother.'

'Your mother?'

Then Lucas was crying. Dry, gasping sobs, torn out of him in spite of all his efforts to remain in control. Dominic continued to hold him close and waited for the storm to cease.

'She preferred other men to her own husband. Can you believe that, Unc? She's still out there somewhere, wallowing in filth, the promiscuous, whoring cunt.'

So that was what it was all about.

Dominic was filled with unutterable sorrow. Wasn't that what it was always about? A helpless child's impotent pain becomes an adult's uncontrollable rage. How many evils in the world, how many wars, revolutions, massacres and murders, could be traced back in one way or another to the trauma of a neglected, abused or abandoned child?

'Oh Lucas, why didn't you tell me any of this?'

'You couldn't have changed anything. *Cursed be the day wherein I was born*, Unc. *Let not the day wherein my mother bore me be blessed.*'

'*Wherefore came I out of the womb to see labour and sorrow, that my days should be consumed with shame?* Are your days consumed with shame, my poor boy?'

Lucas tried to pull away, but Dominic held on to him.

'If you are truly sorry, God will forgive you.'

'My mother must have cursed the day I was born. Otherwise she'd have stayed with me, don't you think? Dad too. He jumped off that bridge, you know. They said it was an accident, but it wasn't. He finally realised that she was never coming back and he couldn't live without her any more. You see, I wasn't enough to keep him tethered to life.'

'My poor, poor boy.'

'When I saw you getting more and more stressed, I thought the same thing was going to happen. I thought I'd lose you too, and I couldn't bear it.'

'Lucas, you do know that what you've done is very wrong?'

In his arms the boy suddenly became still.

'You do know that it's not for you to play God?'

Lucas looked at him. Dominic flinched at the misery in his eyes.

'Pray with me. Ask God for forgiveness. Repentance is the first step towards redemption. You know that. We preach it every day at R&R. *Forgive us our trespasses as we forgive them that trespass against us . . .*'

But some sea-change had taken place in the boy. He wasn't paying attention any more. Instead, he pushed

Dominic away and, jumping up, paced across the small room to peer through the window. Then he opened the door and checked the corridor. 'I need you to do something for me, Unc. One last thing.'

'Lucas . . .'

'Call Dr Grimshaw. It's about his kids.'

Dominic's stomach lurched. Suddenly he was in a different ball-game. 'Why?' He struggled to sound calm and non-accusatory.

'It's for her. She wants to see Grimshaw.'

'Who does?'

'She has issues, as they say. With him.' The boy spat out the words.

'Who are you talking about?'

'Babylon the Great. The mother of prostitutes and of the abominations of the earth.'

'Lucas, you're making no sense.'

'Jezebel, Delilah, Judith, Eve, Lilith, whoever. She thinks she's running the show, but she doesn't know what you and I know, Unc. She doesn't know about Lux, who turns darkness into light. She doesn't know that I now see her for what she really is.'

Trying to control the awful sick feeling inside him, Dominic realised his time alone with his nephew had to come to an end. He urgently needed to call the police. Surreptitiously, he put his hand in his pocket and located his mobile. If he could press 999, maybe they'd be able to trace the call. Meanwhile he'd keep talking in the hope that he could divert Lucas and prevent him from seeing what he was trying to do.

'Who are you talking about? Flora? If so, whatever she

wants with Perry and his children will have to wait till she's out of hospital. You really hurt her, Lucas.'

The boy shrugged.

'But why? She isn't in the least like these other girls you describe.'

'That's what I thought. I thought she was different and special.'

'She is. She's a lovely girl. I did hope the two of you would make a go of it . . . But just because you found you couldn't love her, you didn't have to do such dreadful things.'

'She's a spiteful little troublemaker with the mind of a whore. She deserved everything she got.'

'Nobody deserves that – nobody. But what's her interest in Perry's children?'

Lucas didn't answer. Dominic was trying desperately to locate the nine button on his phone, but his fingers were sweating and slipping around. It was impossible.

'What are you doing, Unc?'

'Nothing.'

'Show me.'

Reluctantly, he produced the mobile.

'Call Grimshaw,' Lucas said. 'Tell him his children are here, and then give that to me.' Lucas looked at him, eyes full of sorrow and reproach. 'You want me to trust you, Unc?' he said. 'Well, I trust you just as much as you trust me.'

Dominic made the call.

THIRTY-NINE

Back at Perry's we find a frantic Karen.

April is distraught. 'Why were they in the front garden, anyway? You know we don't allow it.'

'They said you'd let them play out there this morning and I knew they weren't fibbing because I saw them myself when I went to the shops for my mum. I'm sorry. I'm sorry. It's all my fault.'

'Yes, it bloody is, you stupid little—' Frankie spits.

Perry cuts in. 'Mum, this isn't helping. We have to get the police.'

But then the phone rings.

When we reach Billings, we see people gathered round the Gatehouse. Staring up at Stella and the two small forms on either side of her.

They stand on the parapet of the walkway, between Raphael and Gabriel.

I had never realised quite how high the Gatehouse is.

And the parapet is right at the very top. I'm dizzy just lookin up at it.

The children, tiny and fragile, cling onto Stella's hand The smallest puff of wind could blow them off the wal When they see us, they wave.

'Stella says she'll teach us how to fly,' shouts Hector. He so far away I can hardly hear him.

Cassandra sounds less cheerful. 'I didn't think huma beans could fly, but Stella says they can if they think ver hard about it.'

Beside me, April moans.

Perry's voice is dry as an autumn leaf. 'Quite right, Cassie he calls. 'Humans can't fly. We leave that to the birds. Ge down now. You might fall.'

Cassandra's face registers triumph and relief in equa measure. 'I told you she was wrong, Heccie,' she said, he voice floating down to us on the summer air. 'I want m mummy now.' She tries to clamber back onto the walkway but then her little body flops like a rag doll as she's jerke to her feet.

'You can't go, Cassie. Hector will think you're a coward won't you, Hec?'

Hector giggles nervously. 'Are you sure I can't fly, Daddy?

'Hector. Get down.'

The little boy tries to pull away from Stella. Then hi smile freezes and even from this distance I can see th panic in his eyes. 'Daddy,' he calls. 'She won't let go.'

April moans again.

'We know you're angry with Perry,' I call up to Stella 'but don't take it out on the kids.'

'Go away.'

'Please, Stella.' April's voice is scarcely more than a whisper.

'They're going to fly with me. Aren't you?' Stella jerks her hands again and the children scream. April screams too.

'Shut it, for Christ's sake,' Stella screams back.

'She can't help it, you evil cow. They're her babbies,' yells Frankie.

'And you'd know all about that, wouldn't you?' Stella shouts down at her.

'I'll do anything you want. Just let my children go.' Perry is desperate. 'What *do* you want, Stella?'

'Ask *her*.' Stella's eyes are still fixed on Frankie.

'Why don't you lot sling your hook,' Frankie snaps to the small crowd. 'The less of an audience the mad bitch has for her antics, the better.'

'I thought you liked an audience, Frankie. The bigger the better. I thought an audience was the only thing that ever really mattered to you.' Each one of Stella's words is deadly. 'Overture and beginners, please. It's showtime.'

Perry grabs Frankie. 'What's she on about, Mum?'

'How should I know? She's bonkers, isn't she? You just concentrate on getting them kiddies down. That's all that matters.' But her eyes flick from side to side like a feral animal.

Meanwhile, the voice continues. 'Showtime, kiddy-winkles. Are you sitting comfortably? Silly me – of course you aren't. You're not sitting at all. You're standing up here with me, inches away from oblivion.'

The words bombard us mercilessly. 'Once upon a time, a promiscuous old slapper with one brain cell discovers that the indigestion she's been suffering from isn't indigestion,

and the middle-aged spread she can't control isn't middl
aged spread. She's pregnant, and it's far too late for an abo
tion. Remember, Frankie?'

For a moment, it seems as if Stella is going to fling herse
down, bringing the children with her. Then she pulls bac
There's a sharp intake of breath from the crowd. Now th
words are vomited into the air like rapid machine-gun fir
each burst lethal.

'She can't tell anyone – it might damage her career, an
that would never do. She doesn't even tell her son, who
away at university. He'd be disgusted if he knew what hi
old mum got up to between the sheets. So she takes herse
off to a private nursing home and gives birth. "It's a dea
little girl," the nurses cry. But that cuts no ice with the ol
slapper, who immediately puts her up for adoption and goe
off without a backward glance to do a summer season i
Bournemouth. The dear little girl never quite fits in wit
her adopted family so when she turns eighteen she trace
her mother. The old slapper doesn't want to know an
sends her packing with a flea in her ear, but not withou
letting it slip that there's a half-brother – an academic at th
University of Sydney in Australia. The dear little girl doe
some research and discovers that this brother is soon to tak
up a post in the English Department at Billings College
Cambridge. She hatches a brilliant plan. She applies to h
college to read English. To her great joy she's awarded
place, and when he finally arrives she's already there waitin
And what's more, she's wangled him as her supervisor.'

A groan issues from deep inside Perry.

'She decides she won't tell him who she is straight awa
in case he rejects her just like the old slapper did. There

ime enough and she's very patient. She'll make him like
ier so much that when she finally reveals she's his little sister,
ie'll be truly thrilled. She sees what a nice bloke he is, what
i great wife and children he has. What a great life he has.
The more she sees, the more she likes. She really does. She's
blissfully happy and spends hours devising various scenarios
n which she reveals the truth, and in all of them he joyfully
welcomes her into his life as his precious little sister. It's
wonderful. This brother is the best thing that's ever happened
o her. Thinking about him, watching him, attending his
ectures, having weekly supervisions and the odd chat in the
iCR – it takes over her life. But then she realises that some-
hing even more momentous has happened.'

'I want to wee.' Hector's bottom lip trembles.

'Don't interrupt. Aunty Stella's talking,' Stella snaps.

Even from so far below we can see the tears of terror
spilling down Hector's fat little cheeks.

'She no longer wants to tell him that she's his sister.'

'For pity's sake,' Frankie implores her.

'When did *you* ever show *me* any pity?'

'I can explain—'

'She no longer wants to tell him that she's his sister.' Her
voice is now directed at Perry. 'We all know why, don't we?'

'Oh, God,' April whispers.

Perry's face is grey.

'We fell in love.' The words batter our ears. 'You fell in
ove with me, Perry. You fell in love with your own sister.'

He sinks down in the road, arms over his head, as if
shielding himself from her attack.

'No.' April's voice is a whisper on the wind. 'Frankie, tell
ne it isn't true. It can't be.'

But it's clear that it is. What I see in Frankie's eyes make me shudder. Or rather, it's what I don't see that's so frightening: a total absence of love or compassion for he discarded daughter.

'It's very common, to fall in love with a sister or brother you've never known. I've read a lot about it. Genetic affinity. Can you hear me, Perry? Genetic affinity. With siblings who've been raised separately, the usual barriers to intimacy don't operate—'

Perry leaps to his feet. 'Shut your foul mouth,' he roars, causing the children's by now uncontrollable sobbing to shoot up another octave.

'But there's still this powerful blood bond,' Stella persists. 'A call of like to like, that can trigger a deep physical attraction.'

Perry turns to April. 'I didn't sleep with her. You must believe me.' He shudders.

But April's eyes are fixed on Hector and Cassandra 'Whatever you feel about him now, however much you hate him, please don't harm my children,' she calls pitifully 'They're only little. It isn't their fault, any of this.'

'Yes, it is.'

'Why?'

'Because he loves them.'

'Of course he does. They're his flesh and blood. They're your blood too.'

'And he doesn't love me.' Her voice is inexorable, an as cold as the grey stone archangel next to her. 'He doesn't love me at all. Not one tiny bit. Why should they have his love and not me?'

'Please . . . They've done nothing to you.'

'I adore Perry. I'd die for him. You have no idea how strong that feeling is. More powerful than your insipid affection, that's for sure. But I can't have him, can I? I can't have the one person in all the world that I truly want. That hurts. Really badly. You can't imagine how much it hurts. And it's him doing this to me – making me feel so bad. So I want him to hurt too. I want him to know what it feels like to lose the thing he loves the most.'

April steps forward. 'Take me instead. Perry loves me just as much as he loves his children. Let my babies go. I'll come up there and do whatever you want. Just let my babies go.'

'Too late.'

Stella's moved to the front edge of the wall. Hector and Cassandra jerk along with her like two little marionettes. Then, just as I am convinced that they must all plummet to their deaths, there's another sound. It comes from behind her on the walkway. Startled, she drops the children's hands.

It's Dominic Tipton and his nephew. As Stella lets go of the children, the two men leap forward and snatch them to safety.

I'm weak with relief.

April rushes into college to find her son and daughter, but Perry stands as if petrified. His eyes are glazed, his skin clammy, and two hectic spots of colour have appeared on his pale cheeks.

Lucas climbs onto the parapet alongside Stella. Robbed of her little companions, she seems disorientated and sways perilously forward. The crowd gasps.

Lucas pulls her back from the edge. 'I said I'd come back to you, after I'd seen my uncle, didn't I?'

She nods.

'I promised I'd tell you a secret.'

She nods again.

'Here you go, then.' He leans towards her, as if bestowing a treasured confidence. 'It wasn't Danny Thorn who killed Julie Watkins. It was me. I'm beyond the pale now, Babylon. Beyond God's forgiveness.'

Stella stares at him. She seems stunned. 'No,' she says.

Beside me, Perry makes an inarticulate noise.

'I didn't mean to,' continues Lucas. 'All I wanted to do was punish her like all the other sluts. Show her that there were consequences to her actions. Teach her a lesson. I didn't even realise she was dead until my uncle told me later. It must have been when she was trying to phone her mum. I put my hand over her mouth to keep her quiet, you see. I must have held it there for too long. But I didn't mean to. And now I'm a killer . . .'

He's holding her tight now. 'Before that, while I was doing what I had to do to her, Babylon, I blurred my eyes and imagined it was you. But I knew it wasn't, not really. It didn't matter, though. I knew your turn would come later.' He kisses the top of her head. 'Because of how I once felt about you, I've done what you asked. I brought you the children and I brought you your brother. But now it's time for us both to face up to things.'

Stella doesn't take her eyes off him.

'I am Lux, God's Light-Bearer. I punish filthy sluts who tempt men into sin. I punished Flora and I punished Julie, and now I'm going to punish you, the biggest whore of all.' He sighs. 'Until yesterday, I thought you were perfect. Inside and out. But now . . .'

'Now?'

'Now I have to punish you, Babylon, even though it breaks my heart.'

To my astonishment, a smile is slowly creeping across Stella's face.

'You've squandered the beauty God gave you, Babylon. You've opened your legs and wallowed in filth.'

But Stella, for some bizarre reason, seems to find this funny.

'Why are you laughing? Have you no shame?'

'You're so wrong,' she says. 'You think you know everything, Lux the Light, but you're so, so wrong.'

'Don't mess with me.'

'I'm probably the only woman in Billings College to whom that little rant of yours doesn't apply.'

'What do you mean?'

'I'm still a virgin.'

Lucas shakes his head sorrowfully. 'You're a lying whore, like all the others.'

'It's true.'

'You're no virgin, Babylon.'

'But I am. I've been waiting, you see. Saving myself for Perry.' The laughter dies away as she looks forlornly down at Perry. 'But he didn't want me. He never came.' Then she turns back to Lucas. 'It's too late now for anything except the truth, Lucas. No point in any more lies. I really am a virgin, and you didn't kill Julie.'

Beside me, there's a jerk of shock from Perry.

'You didn't kill her,' Stella goes on. 'You couldn't have done.'

'Why not?'

'Because I did it, all by myself. With no help from anyone.'

Perry's hand gropes for mine. It's shaking.

Lucas looks from Stella to Perry. Eventually, as if making up his mind about something, he nods. *'Thou hast stolen my heart, my sister, my spouse; thou hast ravished my heart with one of thine eyes, with one chain of thy neck. I see it all now, Babylon.'*

Perry groans again.

'Perry said he'd meet me in the Fellows' Garden,' Stella is saying. 'And I knew that we were going to be together. That the empty space inside me would finally be filled. One flesh at last. I went up onto the stage and there he was, but he wasn't waiting for me. He was fast asleep beside Julie Watkins, with his arm flung across her breast. Stupid Julie Watkins. Thieving little slag. She'd stolen my hair, my clothes, and now Perry. I could forgive her the other things, but not him. Then she opened her eyes and said "Thank God you've come". After stealing Perry away from me she had the nerve to say that. So I took the pillow, I put it over her face, and I held it there. She struggled for ages. I thought she'd never stop. And all the time Perry was moaning in his sleep. After she stopped moving, I left. I couldn't stand the noise he was making. It sounded like Death.'

Perry makes another inarticulate sound. It's drowned out by the howl of sirens. The police have finally arrived.

An officious PC bustles across to us. 'Move along, please.'

'No,' says Perry. He gestures towards Stella. 'She's – my sister.'

'All right, sir, you can stay for now. But you must stand

further back. What about you two?' He looks at me and Frankie.

'We're family.'

Frankie grunts.

Another officer has produced an unnecessary loudhailer. 'Step down from the wall,' he intones to the precariously balanced figures. 'Step down from the wall.'

Stella and Lucas give no sign that they've heard. They seem to be engrossed in some form of silent communication.

Dominic Tipton appears beside us. The pain on his face is unbearable as he stares up at the young couple, whose ethereal beauty seems eerily untarnished by the dreadful things they've both done.

'Come down, Lucas,' he calls. 'Don't leave me. You helped to save the children. That proves you aren't beyond redemption. Come down. Please. God will forgive you. *Though your sins be as scarlet they shall be as white as snow.*'

But Lucas is shaking his head. 'It's too late, Unc.'

All animation seems to drain out of Dominic. His gaunt face is the colour of old parchment. 'Lucifer, the Light-Bearer. Once most favoured of all God's Archangels,' he whispers. 'May your brothers guide you back to God, my dearest boy.'

And for one moment, looking at the sun glinting on Michael, Raphael and Gabriel, I think I see their great feathered wings move protectively around Stella and Lucas.

Then Stella calls out, 'Perry? It's your forgiveness I need, not God's. Say you love me.'

But Perry says nothing.

'I'm your sister. You must love me a little bit.' Her eyes are filled with yearning.

Perry looks back, unsmiling.

'Say it,' I whisper.

But he doesn't respond. I can't even tell if he's heard me.

'*Perry*. Tell her you love her.'

Finally, he speaks. 'Come down, Stella. Then we'll talk.'

'You can't say it, can you?' Her voice catches in a sob.

Lucas strokes her face. 'Hey, Babylon. It doesn't matter now, does it?'

She finally takes her eyes off Perry, brushes away her tears and stares up at Lucas. 'No,' she whispers. 'You're right. It's far too late for all that.'

Lucas takes her hand. *'The light of the wicked shall be put out, and the spark of his fire shall not shine.'* His words drop with perfect clarity, like pebbles into a still pond. *'My breath is corrupt, my days are extinct. The graves are ready for me.'*

He smiles at Stella and she smiles back at him.

Together they step out into space.

Seconds later they lie, broken and twisted, on the pavement.

Beside me I dimly hear Dominic Tipton speaking. *'How are you fallen from Heaven, O Lucifer, son of the morning,'* he says. *'How are you cut down to the ground?'*

SATURDAY 25 JUNE

FORTY

He hadn't slept. Thoughts of Lucas jostled through his brain all night long in a neverending requiem: Lucas and himself poring over expansion plans for R&R, Lucas tenderly bathing Preacher Man's blistered feet in a bowl of warm water, Lucas and Flora flicking foam over each other as they administer nit shampoo to a line of old men, their laughter echoing round the shabby washroom at R&R, Lucas pottering about the college chapel, lighting candles, arranging hymn books. Lucas serving breakfast at R&R with his usual grace and good-humour.

Lucas with his gentle teasing, the light of Dominic's life.

The light that was now extinguished.

The grief was a physical pain, which he could not imagine ever leaving him. Something he would drag around wherever he went, a permanent disability. Something that would stand between himself and the rest of the world forever. Something that had deprived him of the light and left him in permanent darkness.

He returned repeatedly to his own part in the trail of mayhem and destruction. Why had he not acknowledged to himself what was happening? What clues had he missed? Why had he not loved the boy when it mattered most, after his father's death? Why had he let Lucas slip away when he should have kept him close? He knew that for the rest of his life he would blame himself. There was even a moment when the thought of carrying this heavy burden around forever became too much, and he contemplated following Lucas down into the pit.

But that was not his way, and by morning, in spite of feeling crippled by grief, he was clear about what he had to do.

Soon after breakfast he went to the Master's Lodge. The housekeeper showed him into the sitting room. The Master was staring out of the window, beside his chair an empty dog-basket.

'Terrible business, Tipton. A black day for the college.' He seemed to realise that this was, even by his standards, insensitive. 'And for you, of course. I'm very sorry for your loss. Even if your nephew was . . .'

'The police will have told you that Lucas was responsible for raping those women. What they won't have said, because they don't know, is that it was he who killed Dawkins and perpetrated all the other mischief that has afflicted Billings over the past week. So on his behalf, I too must apologise, Hugo. In his defence, he told me he didn't mean to kill the animals, just give them a stomach upset. Likewise with the nuts.'

The Master's eyes glittered. He nodded brusquely but didn't speak.

'The other reason I came to see you was to hand in my letter of resignation.'

He'd thought Mortimer would be overjoyed. Instead, the man merely said, 'Oh.'

'I shall always blame myself for what has happened. I failed Lucas when he most needed me, and as a result great damage has been done to you and many others. I wish to make reparation in some way, but not here. I can't stay here. There are too many bad memories for me here now, and your plans for this college sadden me too much. I thought I'd fight you to the finish, but after yesterday I don't have the strength or the will.'

The Master stirred in his seat. 'There's really no need for this.' The words were dragged out of him. 'There seems to be a general feeling in the Senior Common Room that we should both put aside our differences and pull together for the sake of the college. As I've already told you, the plans for the new library are now on hold, and . . .' He momentarily closed his eyes as if willing himself to continue.

'All the same, I have to go.'

The Master tried and failed to hide his relief. 'In that case, there's nothing more to be said.'

'I'll be leaving as soon as I've organised something to keep R&R up and running.'

'I see.'

'So I'll say goodbye, Hugo.'

When he returned to his room, Flora was waiting for him.

Dom seemed surprised to see her up and about. Truth be told, she would have preferred to lick her wounds in the unreal atmosphere of hospital for a few more days, isolated from the world outside. But they needed the bed so they'd

discharged her with an appointment to see a rape coun
sellor and a recommendation that she had somebody t
look after her when she got home.

Like who?

Not her parents. She hadn't let the hospital contact them
She couldn't face it. *Flora messes up again* – that's wha
they'd say. Today they were off to France. They wouldn'
be best pleased if her affairs caused them any delay. Flor
couldn't imagine confiding in either of them, anyway. Fo
a start they'd say that she'd brought it upon herself. That'
what they always said whenever anything unpleasan
happened to her.

In this case, they'd be right: she had brought it upor
herself. Her actions this week had been despicable. Thi
morning when she'd woken up, it felt like a bad dream
She couldn't believe the things she'd done – sawing througl
the stairs on the stage – what was that all about? And the
itching-powder episode . . . And the other little manipula
tions and lies – to Julie, about Julie . . . She must have beer
suffering from some midsummer madness. All in all, the
rape was a very fitting punishment: she'd wanted Lucas and
she'd gone out of her way to get him.

And she'd succeeded.

Lucas had indeed given himself to her.

Be careful what you wish for . . .

As she stood in Dom's room, the cosy room where she'c
spent hours with him and Lucas, going over plans for R&R
or arguing about the big questions, and how Christianit
helped formulate the answers, she couldn't believe it had
all ended.

She felt utterly alone and bereft. In one night she'd beer

obbed of everything that had ever meant anything to her. Her parents would never be what she wanted them to be; her best friend was a conniving deceitful killer; and the man she'd loved so obsessively was a rapist. Stella and Lucas were both dead, and in the manner of their death they'd excluded her right to the last. They were dead. So she couldn't even face them with what they'd done and demand answers. Stella and Lucas . . . dead. She repeated the words over and over in her head, but they lacked any kind of reality.

What was real was her own wretched self. She caught sight of her face, even uglier than usual, reflected in Dom's window. What was it about her that had attracted such deception and duplicity? It must be an ingrained corruption that called like to like. That must be why nobody halfway decent cared about her.

Suddenly she was overtaken by sobs. They gushed out of her like a burst water main. She stood in the middle of Dom's room and she howled.

Face rigid with alarm, Dom hovered around her. 'Flora, Flora. My dear . . . Please. It's all right. It will be all right, you'll see. We'll get through somehow. Please don't cry. I can't bear to see you so distressed. Come, come, sit down, sit down, please.' Patting her awkwardly, he led her over to the sofa, his thin face ravaged with concern.

Then something extraordinary happened. As she looked into his dark, grief-clouded eyes, the tectonic plates of her reality shifted and a thought struck her with great force: she wasn't alone or uncared for. Dom cared. In fact, looking back over the past year, she realised he was the only person who had ever really cared about what happened to her,

the only one who had properly listened, the only one wh
had consistently made her feel good about herself. Th
only one who had brought real colour and comfort to he
life, and given her a sense of her own value. Even no
in the middle of his own despair, he was striving to comfo
her.

The realisation stopped her tears and made her babbl
'May I stay at R&R over the Long Vac? I could help yo
run the place. You'll be short-handed now all the studer
volunteers are going home, particularly now that Lucas—

His face fell.

She was horrified. She'd got it all wrong. He didn't war
her either. She had to get out before she made a fool c
herself again. She jumped up and groped her way toward
the door.

'Flora?'

'Just remembered something I have to do.' She clutche
at the door-knob.

'Don't go.' His hand, with its long, sensitive fingers, wa
suddenly gripping hers. Then he pulled it away as if he'
been scalded. 'You're very welcome to stay at R&R over th
summer,' he said, 'but I won't be around. I've resigned a
Chaplain of Billings. I'm going away.'

She hadn't thought there were any more bits of her lif
left to disintegrate. Her desolation deepened. It swirle
round her in icy blasts. She wanted desperately to ask wh
but it was none of her business. Why should he share hi
plans with her? She was only a student volunteer. Nothin
special. He certainly didn't have to give her an account c
his doings.

'I'm going abroad.'

'Oh.' She didn't have the strength to hide her misery.

He picked up a pile of papers. 'This is a record of all the countries Lucas visited before he came here. I've reason to think that he's done what . . . what he did to you . . . in many of these places. I can't undo the damage, but I can try to make reparation. I'm going to find all the women he hurt and use his money to help them.'

'What about R&R?'

'R&R can function without me. The Salvation Army will take over, I dare say. I'm sure they'll be very grateful for your support.'

Flora realised something: she didn't want to help run R&R if he wasn't there with her. She looked at him. Pain, grief and exhaustion were etched over his fine-boned features. For the first time she saw him as a man and not a priest and she was struck by an urge so strong that it made her tremble, to rip off that cloak of loneliness in which he was always wrapped.

'Let me come with you.'

'What?'

'I can help. Some of these women will still be very traumatised. They won't trust you because you're a man. I can bridge the gap. Not just because I'm female but because I was also one of his victims.'

He stared at her, transfixed.

'Let me come with you,' she repeated.

Slowly he nodded, his dark eyes glimmering with something that looked like hope.

April and Perry faced Frankie over the kitchen table. April had forgiven Karen sufficiently to allow her to take Hector

485

and Cassandra onto Jesus Green. There were things bette
talked about when the children were out of the way.

She was running on empty. Bringing her children home
yesterday, and making sense of things for them, while a
the same time assimilating the intricate horrors of Stella'
life and death, and trying to help Perry come to terms with
what had happened and his part in it, had left her numb

In the immediate aftermath, her primary concern had
been the children. What did you say to a couple of four
year olds who'd been through what they had?

But she had always believed in being straight with her
children. The truth was usually the best option. Or rather,
the bare bones of the truth.

For small children, new to the world, every fresh experience is accepted at face value, because they have nothing
with which to compare it. Hector and Cassandra appeared
remarkably matter-of-fact about their experiences, approaching things from their own unique perspective. They
didn't seem overly concerned with their abduction and
adventure on the parapet. Their preoccupations were exclusively familial.

'Why did Stella say she was our aunty?'

'Because she's Daddy's sister.'

Cassandra nodded, thoughtfully. 'So she and Daddy are
like me and Heccie?'

'Yes.'

'Why did you never say she was our aunty?'

'Daddy didn't know until yesterday.'

'Why not?'

'She was adopted.'

'What's adopted?'

'Another mummy and daddy brought her up.'

'Why?'

'Because when she was a baby, her real mummy couldn't look after her.'

Hector frowned. 'If she's Daddy's sister, does that mean Granny's her real mummy?'

'Yes.'

'So why couldn't Granny look after her?'

April looks at Perry. 'We don't know.'

'Will she come and live with us?'

Perry sat, white-faced and silent. April took a deep breath. 'I'm afraid she had an accident. After Reverend Tipton lifted you down from the wall, she slipped and fell.'

'Splat,' said Hector.

'What?'

'Splat. Like in the cartoons when people fall off cliffs and things. Splat.'

'Will the hospital make her better?'

'No, Cassie. She was too sick . . . I'm afraid she died.'

They regarded her with solemn eyes.

'It was very high up,' said Hector eventually.

'She was a naughty girl to take us up there,' said Cassandra. 'We might have fallen too. And hurt ourselves.'

There was a short silence while they both assimilated what they'd been told.

Then Hector spoke again. 'When we see her we'll tell her she's very, very naughty,' he said.

'Yes, we will,' agreed Cassandra. 'I'm going to give her a smack.'

April signalled to Perry for help. But he didn't respond. She forged on. 'I told you, darling, she's dead. That means you won't be able to see her again. Ever. Do you remember when you found Goldie floating on top of the fish tank, and I said he was dead, and we buried him in the garden?'

'Will we bury Aunty Stella in the garden?'

'No.'

'Good,' said Cassandra. 'I liked Goldie, but I didn't like her. She was pooey. I'm hungry. When's supper?'

'Can we have chocolate mousse for pudding?' said Hector.

'You can have anything you want,' she said, banishing an unwanted image of their little bodies lying lifeless beneath the Gatehouse.

Later that night, she and Perry were woken by two small forms creeping into their room. 'Can we sleep in your bed?' whispered Cassandra.

And now, this morning, with them out of the way it was time to tackle Frankie, who had remained closeted in her room since returning home yesterday.

Perry had been only too happy to leave her undisturbed. 'I don't know whether I can face her after what she's done,' he'd said to April.

'She's your mother,' said April, surprising herself. 'You can't let it fester. You have to sort it out.'

'She was Stella's mother too,' he'd replied.

But soon after the kids and Karen had left, they'd caught Frankie trying to sneak out of the door with her suitcases.

'Where are you going?' said Perry.

'I thought I'd bugger off – give you a chance to calm down.' Her grief for her dead daughter clearly hadn't interfered with her interest in her own appearance. She looked band-box fresh as she stood in the hall, furtively eyeing the front door and freedom.

'You don't leave this house until you tell me everything.'
He bundled her into the kitchen.

'What's to tell?' Frankie muttered defensively. 'I had a
baby. Couldn't keep her. She grew up, turned into a nutter,
made it her mission in life to destroy us, and now she's dead.
End of story. Good riddance to bad rubbish, I say.'

April felt nauseous. She groped for Perry's hand.

His voice was tight with the effort to remain in control
of his emotions. 'Why did you never tell me about her?'

'Look, pet, it all happened a long time ago. She had her
life. We had ours. I thought it best not to stir things up.'

'But when you first found out you were pregnant, didn't
you think I deserved to be told?'

'You were a sanctimonious little gobshite back then. I
knew if I said I was having a baby you'd want me to keep
it, and there was no way that was happening. My career
was going through a very sticky patch. A bloody baby would
have finished it off.'

'You gave away my sister just so you could pursue your
shoddy career?'

'Flaming 'ell, Perry, you haven't changed – you're still a
sanctimonious little gobshite! My shoddy career put bread
on the table, so don't you dare sit in your frigging ivory
tower and sneer. It was murder bringing up one child on
my own, let alone two. You haven't the first idea.' She jerked
her head at April. 'You've got Walzing Matilda here to wipe
your kids' snotty noses. I had no one, so don't you preach
at me.'

'But you didn't bring me up. You left all that to Rosa's
parents.'

'And I couldn't have lumbered *them* with another baby,

could I? They'd only just got shot of you.' She stands up. 'I've had enough of this third degree. I'm off.'

'No chance.' Perry glares at her until she sits down again. 'Why didn't you tell me about Stella when she finally traced you? Didn't it occur to you that I might have been thrilled to find that I had a sister?'

April watched Frankie and knew from experience that she was trying on different tales to find the one that best fitted.

'I didn't tell you because I didn't like her,' Frankie said eventually.

'She was your daughter!' Perry exploded.

'I could see she were a bloody troublemaker.'

It takes one to know one, thought April.

'I didn't want her coming anywhere near you and your lovely little family,' Frankie said virtuously. 'And,' she continued in triumph, 'I were right, weren't I?'

April couldn't stay silent any longer. 'But you knew she was a student at Billings—'

'No, I didn't – not until I saw that play. It gave me a proper turn, I can tell you, when she walked out on t'stage. If you remember, I made an excuse in the interval and buggered off.'

'And didn't it occur to you at that point, that it was time to come clean?'

'I was in shock. I didn't know what to do.'

Perry's hand, clutching April's under the table, was shaking. 'And when you realised that I had – I had feelings for her?'

'I couldn't cope, all right? Your own sister. It was disgusting.'

April wanted to hit her. 'But he didn't know she was his sister!' she found herself shouting. 'Because the one person, apart from Stella, who could have told him, chose to stay silent.'

'The day after the play I collared her and handed over shit-loads of money. She promised she'd bugger off, but she didn't, did she, the lying little toe-rag.'

'Why didn't you tell me?' Perry repeated, breathing hard, his face a mixture of misery and rage.

'Because it made me sick. And besides, what was the point? I thought if she went away it would all fizzle out and that you'd forget her.' She made a great show of looking at her watch. 'Is that the time? I'd best love you and leave you. I've a train to catch. Things to see. People to do.'

'She was your child. Don't you have *any* feelings for her?' Perry looked at his mother as if for the first time.

'She wasn't my child. I gave birth to her, but that's as far as it goes. And now I'm going to do my level-best to forget all about her. I suggest you do the same. Least said, soonest mended. I'm off. If the police need me, they've got my mobile number.'

April had never seen Perry look at his mother in that way before: a combination of incredulity and disgust. 'You really don't give a shit, do you?'

'She's not my problem. Never was.'

'You hard-hearted old bitch!'

'Not so much of the old,' Frankie said shirtily.

She hasn't realised, thought April. She doesn't know she's finally blown it.

'I spent my childhood,' said Perry, 'scrabbling about

for your love. I cherished every careless little scrap of affection from you, in spite of all the evidence that the only person you loved was yourself. Well, hallelujah, I've finally seen the light. Get out of my house and don't come back.'

'I'll pretend I didn't hear all that, pet. You're tired and emotional. You don't know what you're saying.'

'I know exactly what I'm saying. I don't want to see you ever again.'

Frankie looked from him to April. The penny was finally dropping. 'This is your doing, lady. I don't know what lying filth you've been whispering into his lug-hole, but don't think it'll work because it won't. Nothing and no one ever comes between me and my lad.'

Perry cut in. 'Do not, I repeat, do not speak to my wife in that way. Unlike you, I do know how to love. And I love April. More than you'll ever know. And I'm ashamed of myself for not protecting her more thoroughly from your shabby little manipulations.'

Frankie rose to her feet and this time Perry made no move to stop her. Her small black eyes had narrowed to tiny slits. 'You mardy little shite,' she snarled. 'You were a pain in the arse, right from being a babby. You used to make me sick with all your clinging and snivelling. I couldn't wait to get shot of you. And nothing's changed. Well, I've had it up to here. As far as I'm concerned, your psycho sister's not the only one who's dead to me.' Then she turned on her heel and left the kitchen. Within seconds the front door slammed.

April put her arm around Perry's rigid body. 'She didn't mean that,' she said. 'She'll be back.'

'I hope not.'

'She's your mother,' said April for the second time that morning.

They clung together for a long time. When Perry finally pulled away he said, 'I need to go to Stella's room.'

April's stomach turned. 'Why?'

'I want to look at her things.'

'Why?' she said again.

'I need to get some idea of who she really was – what kind of a sister she might have been. To try and see her as a sister and not as something else. Will you come with me?'

April had spent long hours last night after the children were settled, talking to Perry about his feelings for Stella. Feelings that had ambushed him so suddenly and nearly destroyed everything they had together. The powerful call of blood to blood that he'd mistaken for something else. She was trying to come to terms with it and to help him do the same. It was early days, of course. It would take a long time for the wounds to finally heal. If ever. She recognised that she had one thing in common with Frankie: essentially she wanted to forget Stella Grainger. But unlike Frankie, she loved Perry more than life itself and couldn't bear to see his pain. If going to Stella's room would help him, then that's what they would do. 'Let's go,' she said. 'Before Karen brings the kids home.'

But when they arrived at Stella's room, someone was there before them. A man and a woman of indeterminate age and appearance, standing, bewildered, in the centre of the room. The woman's eyes were swollen with weeping. In her hands she held a photograph.

'Can I help you?' The man sounded defensive.

April realised who they were: Stella's parents. The ones who wiped away her tears, bandaged her cut knees, listened to her childish hopes and dreams. Beside her she could feel Perry trembling. He too had worked out who this sad pair must be.

'I'm Dr Grimshaw, Stella's English supervisor,' he said. 'I'm very sorry for your loss.'

The man smiled sadly. 'We lost our Stella a long time ago,' he said. 'To be honest, we never really had her, did we, love?'

The woman handed Perry the photograph: Stella and Flora, sitting on the grass in Bacon Court, arms wrapped round each other, giggling. 'She was very beautiful, though, wasn't she?'

'Yes,' said Perry. 'She was.' He scribbled his address on a piece of paper and handed it to the man. 'When you've finished here, perhaps you'd come and have coffee with us. There are some things we need to talk about.'

FORTY-ONE

He now understood how easy it was for prisoners to become institutionalised. He'd spent less than twenty-four hours in police custody, yet even so his newly experienced freedom still felt conditional and he kept finding himself waiting to be told what to do and where to go. He was supposed to be packing, but instead he kept drifting across to the window and looking out over Locke Court. It was as if he was expecting someone, but he didn't know who it could possibly be. The only two people he wanted to see were both dead. Mum said that Stella had tried to frame him for Julie's murder. He'd really like to be able to ask her why she'd done that – why she hated him enough to try and ruin his life. But now he'd never know.

And Julie? He couldn't believe that Julie didn't exist any more. It wasn't possible. He felt that at any moment there would be a knock on his door and she'd be standing there, asking him to be nice to her, to love her again. But he couldn't. That was his crime. He kept rerunning the events of the Ball, as if in some strange way the repetition of his thoughts could bring about a different outcome. He saw himself going into the Fellows' Garden for a bit of peace and quiet, to think about Julie's deception undisturbed and get it into some kind of perspective. He saw himself climbing the wooden steps and crossing the stage to where the girl with the cropped blonde hair lay face down. He'd thought it was Stella. Why had it never occurred to him that it might be Julie? He'd wondered what she'd do if he woke her up. Would she wind her arms round his neck, and pull him down beside her? Why not? He was free now. Julie was history. After what she'd done he owed her nothing. There was no reason now why he shouldn't be with Stella. He'd seen the pillow lying on the ground and picked it up, meaning to place it under her head, but when he'd touched her pale back he'd known immediately. No one was that still.

And later, when he turned her over, it was Julie.

His poor little Julie. Who was so desperate to regain his love that she'd even tried to become Stella in the vain hope that that might do the trick.

Later, in the police, cell, he'd wanted to die. If he hadn't abandoned her last night, she'd still be alive. It was his fault. He might just as well have killed her himself with his own bare hands.

However, today, after a long talk with his mother, he'd got things back into some kind of proportion. Whatever else, he was not Julie's killer. He accepted that now. But even so, an old pop song endlessly repeated in his mind: *If only I could turn back time* . . .

And then there was Stella, the beautiful enigma. The girl he thought he was falling for in a big way.

Perry's sister. Julie's killer. And, like Julie herself, now very dead.

All that green and gold beauty gone forever.

He couldn't get his mind around what she'd done and how he felt about her. In fact, he'd stopped even trying. He knew the only way to survive the next few days without falling apart, was to bury all thoughts of her until he was stronger and more able to deal with it all.

Rosa was throwing clothes into a suitcase. 'Earth to Danny Boy! Let's do this as quickly as we can. I told Anna we'd be home by mid-afternoon.'

Home. With Mum and Anna and Josh. Jamming with Dwaine and Delroy. Being normal. No more Cambridge. He couldn't wait to be gone. He emptied his desk drawers wholesale into a bin bag. No time for sorting out. He'd do that at home.

There was a knock on his door. When he saw who was standing there, his heart twisted painfully in his chest.

Joan Watkins.

'Can I come in?'

'We're in a bit of a rush, Joan,' said Rosa, in protective mode. 'We're packing up and going back to London today.'

'It's cool, Mum. Come in, Joan.'

Joan's face was blotchy and swollen. 'I guessed you'd be off as soon as you could. I just wanted to say sorry.'

'Sorry? You've nothing to be sorry for.'

'Sorry that Julie lied to you about the baby.'

He didn't want this. He didn't want to think about Julie and the baby that never was.

Joan ploughed on. 'She wasn't a dishonest person. You know that.'

'Yes.'

'She did what she did because she loved you, Danny She wanted you back. That's why she told such a silly lie.

'Yes,' he repeated dully. That Julie loved him was the one thing he did know. If ever someone had loved not wisely but too well, it was her.

'Will you come to the funeral?'

He nodded, too choked to speak.

'Do you have our number in London?' His mum was trying to be brisk.

'Yes.'

'Give us a call when you know the details. We'll be there. I am so sorry, Joan.'

He finally found his voice. 'Me too. And I'm sorry I couldn't love Julie as she deserved to be loved. She was a fantastic person. I can't believe she's dead. She was my first love, Joan. I'll never forget her.'

This time it was Joan who couldn't speak. Danny hugged her pitifully thin body. 'I'm sorry,' he whispered again.

After she'd gone they finished packing and loaded everything into the car which Rosa had parked outside the college.

'Time to be on our way,' she said, looking up at the Billings Archangels. 'Be good, guys. See you in the autumn.'

Cambridge floats above the fens in its own crystal bubble. A bubble from which I'm more than happy to be escaping. As we head back to London on the Trumpington Road I feel as if I'm breathing properly for the first time in days.

'Let's burn rubber,' I say, but my son is looking sombre. 'Are you OK, Dan?'

'I'm taking a year out.'

This is not what I expected to hear.

'But your degree—'

'What about it?'

'You can't just abandon it. A degree from Cambridge University isn't something to relinquish lightly. Your dad would have a fit if he could hear you.'

'Calm down, Mum. No need to blow a gasket. I didn't say I was going to abandon it. But with everything that's happened they'll be only too happy to let me defer for a year. The Dean said as much to me earlier today. It won't be a problem, honest.'

'But what will you do?'

'Travel. See the world. Get away from this place. It'll be cool, Mum, trust me.'

'Wouldn't it be better to just buckle down, do your third year, get your degree and then travel?'

'Pull over. Please.'

I find a convenient spot to stop the car.

He turns to face me. 'Going back isn't an option. I have to put some time and distance between me and Cambridge.'

'Isn't that called running away from your problems?'

'Call it what you like, it won't change my decision. Josh said recently that he wants to visit Trinidad – see his old mates. I'll go with him, I think, and then take off from here – South America first, and then we'll see.'

'You won't be able to forget what happened that easily. You can't leave your head behind.'

'I know that. I'm not stupid. But one of the reasons I got so involved with Julie in the first place was fear. Fear of the big wide world. Dad dying started it off, I think. I wanted to create a nice safe haven where nothing could harm me. What happened this week makes me realise that the world out there waiting to crash in however much I try to ignor it. So I'm going to confront it head on and see what happens

He's serious. He will do this. With or without my blessing I have to let him go.

I take his beloved face between my hands. 'Then Go West Young Man,' I say. 'And don't forget to send a postcard.'

Thorn

Vena Cork

In the city's open spaces, there is time to kill . . .

A tragedy has changed Rosa Thorn's life for ever. Now she has to start again with a new job, a new school for her children and some empty space in her life. But strange things start to happen . . .

When a growing sense of unease turns into sudden violence, Rosa fears for her safety and even more so for the wellbeing of her children. For her daughter is the subject of someone's demented infatuation. But like a diseased town fox, the real threat stalks the shadows, in the night-black recesses of the under-growth, not just of the city, but of the human mind . . .

Vena Cork's astonishing, thrilling debut novel is as shocking as it is unputdownable – a brilliant, menacing, psychological thriller that takes you to the edge of darkness.

'One of those rare and energetic books you can't put down yet don't want to end' *The Times*

'An outstanding debut' *Time Out*

978 0 7553 2394 4

headline

The Art of Dying

Vena Cork

At an exhibition of her late husband's paintings, Rosa Thorn is shocked by the wild antics of certain artists. Is the art world a place where the normal rules of behaviour don't apply?

When she realises she's being followed, her fear escalates. There is someone out there determined to invade her life. Then one of the artists is found dead. The police conclude it is suicide, but Rosa discovers inconsistencies in the evidence.

And when she delves more deeply into this world where appearances are seductive but don't match reality, she will need every ounce of her wit and intelligence to come out of it alive . . .

Praise for Vena Cork:

'This gripping, edgy novel is good, believe me. She hooks her reader from the start' Colin Dexter

'A compelling, dark-hued psychological thriller that eerily captures some of London's more sinister undercurrents and sense of menace' *Guardian*

'One of those rare and energetic books you can't put down yet don't want to end' *The Times*

978 0 7553 2397 5

<u>headline</u>

Now you can buy any of these other bestselling
Headline books from your bookshop
or *direct from the publisher*.

FREE P&P AND UK DELIVERY
(Overseas and Ireland £3.50 per book)

The Cat Who Had 60 Whiskers	Lillian Jackson Braun	£6.99
Stripped	Brian Freeman	£6.99
Red River	Lalita Tademy	£7.99
Dead and Buried	Quintin Jardine	£6.99
Smoked	Patrick Quinlan	£6.99
Copper Kiss	Tom Neale	£6.99
The Death Ship of Dartmouth	Michael Jecks	£6.99
Jacquot and the Master	Martin O'Brien	£6.99
A Passion for Killing	Barbara Nadel	£7.99
Guardians of the Key	Clio Gray	£6.99

TO ORDER SIMPLY CALL THIS NUMBER

01235 400 414

or visit our website: www.madaboutbooks.com

Prices and availability subject to change without notice.